International bestselling author

PENNY JORDAN

presents

The Sheikh's Bride

*Two exotic, exciting, fantastic
tales of seduction and passion
in the desert heat*

D1435028

Coming soon:

featuring

**The Arabian Mistress
by Lynne Graham**

**The Sheikh's Wife
by Jane Porter**

The Sheikh's Bride

Containing

**The Sheikh's Virgin Bride
& One Night with the Sheikh**

PENNY JORDAN

*M&B™ and M&B™ with the Rose Device
are trademarks of the publisher.
Harlequin Mills & Boon Limited, Eton House,
18-24 Paradise Road,
Richmond, Surrey TW9 1SR*

THE SHEIKH'S BRIDE © Harlequin Books S.A. 2006

The Sheikh's Virgin Bride and *One Night with the Sheikh* were
first published in Great Britain by Harlequin Mills & Boon
Limited in separate, single volumes.

The Sheikh's Virgin Bride © Penny Jordan 2003
One Night with the Sheikh © Penny Jordan 2003

*ISBN 13: 978 0 263 85092 5
IISBN 10: 0 263 85092 7*

109-0906

*Printed and bound in Spain
by Litografía Rosés S.A., Barcelona*

THE SHEIKH'S VIRGIN BRIDE
by
Penny Jordan

Penny Jordan has been writing for more than twenty years and has an outstanding record: over 150 novels published including the phenomenally successful A PERFECT FAMILY, TO LOVE, HONOUR & BETRAY, THE PERFECT SINNER and POWER PLAY which hit *The Sunday Times* and *New York Times* bestseller lists. Penny Jordan was born in Preston, Lancashire, and now lives in rural Cheshire.

Penny Jordan has a fabulous new novel available in October 2006. Look for *Master of Pleasure* in Mills & Boon Modern Romance™.

CHAPTER ONE

'DID you check out the sexy windsurfer attendant like I told you?'

'Yeah! He was everything you said and more—much, much more. He's coming up to my room later. Mind you, he did say that he'd have to be careful. Apparently he's already on a warning from this Sheikh Rashid—the guy who co-owns the hotel—for fraternising with guests.'

'And you did more than just "fraternise", right?'

'Yeah, much, much more.'

From her seat under the protective sun umbrella of the rooftop bar of the Marina Restaurant where she had just finished lunch, the conversation of the two women standing next to her chair was plainly audible to Petra. Still discussing the sexual attributes of the Zuran resort complex's windsurfing instructor, they started to move away. Realising that one of them had dropped her wrap, Petra picked it up, interrupting their discussion to return it and earning herself a brief thank you from its owner.

As they walked away, still engrossed in their conversation, Petra grinned appreciatively to herself, murmuring wholeheartedly beneath her breath, 'Thank *you!*'

Although they didn't realise it, thanks to them she had just been given access to the very thing she had been looking for for the last two days!

As soon as they were out of sight she got up, collecting her own wrap, although unlike them she had chosen to eat her lunch wearing a silky pair of wide-legged casual trousers over her tankini top, instead of merely her swimwear.

Shading her eyes from the glare of the sun, she summoned the waiter who had served her her meal.

'Excuse me,' she asked him, 'can you tell me where the windsurfers are?'

Half an hour later Petra was lying on a sun lounger, carefully positioned by the attentive beach attendant who had asked her where she wanted to sit so that she had a direct and uninterrupted view of the stunning man-made bay which was home to the resort's pleasure craft, and an equally direct and uninterrupted view of the windsurfing instructor she had overheard discussed so enthusiastically over lunch!

She could certainly appreciate just why her fellow guests had waxed so lyrical about him!

Petra was used to seeing good-looking muscular men; she had attended an American university and, since the death of her parents in an accident when she was seventeen, she had travelled extensively both in Europe and Australia with her godfather, the senior British diplomat who had been her parents' closest friend. She'd become, therefore, quite familiar with the sexy beach bum super-stud macho type of man who thought he was heaven's gift to the female sex.

And this man certainly filled all the physical specifications for the type! And then some!

He could easily earn a living modelling designer underwear, Petra acknowledged as her own rush of sensual heat caught her discomfortingly off guard.

But as she watched him Petra was unwillingly forced to admit he had something else; something extra.

He was gathering up some discarded boards, and even the regulation smart hotel shorts had the effect of heightening his sexuality rather than discreetly concealing it.

Across the distance that separated them Petra could some-how sense his maleness, and almost feel the testosterone-laden aura that surrounded him. The movement of his body as he worked reminded Petra of the coiled suppleness of a hunting panther—every movement, every breath a perfect harmony of honed strength and focus, not one single jot of energy wasted or superfluous.

She could see the way the sunlight highlighted the mus-cle structure of his arm as he held the windsurfer, the breeze tousling the thick darkness of his hair. From beneath their designer sunglasses she suspected that every woman on the beach must be watching him, and perhaps holding their breath as they did so, as she herself was doing. He had a mesmerising presence about him that was wholly and shockingly sexual, a rawness that Petra acknowledged was compelling, challenging, and very, very dangerously excit-ing! Oh, yes! He was exactly what she needed! The more she watched him, the more she was sure of it!

Compulsively she watched him from the safety of the distance that separated them.

Over an hour later, on her way back to her luxurious hotel suite, Petra was busily making plans. As she crossed the busy *souq* area of the complex, Petra paused to watch in admiration as a craftsman skilfully hammered a piece of metal into shape.

It was no wonder that this particular complex had re-ceived such worldwide acclaim. From the seductive appeal of its Moorish design, with its fragrant enclosed gardens, to its palatial extravaganza of expensive boutiques and the traditional flavour of its recreated *souq*, the complex breathed magic and romance and most of all wealth.

Petra still could not get her head round the fact that in all there were over twenty different restaurants situated around the complex, serving food from virtually every part of the world, but right now food was the last thing on her mind.

From her hotel bedroom Petra could just about see the beach. The sexy macho windsurfer had disappeared midway through the afternoon, climbing aboard one of the gleaming and very obviously fast boats moored at the adjoining marina, and Petra's last sight of him had been of the sunshine gleaming on the thick darkness of his hair and the golden bronze of his tanned skin.

He was back now, though, even though the beach itself was deserted as the sun started to dip towards the horizon. Methodically he was collecting the abandoned windsurfers, and the other small pleasure craft the complex made available to its guests.

This was the perfect opportunity for her to do what she had been wanting to do ever since she had overheard the two women discussing him!

Before her courage could desert her she picked up her jacket and headed for her suite door.

Down on the beach it was almost dusk, the cool chill in the air reminding Petra that, despite the fact that the daytime temperature was in the high twenties, in this part of the world it was still winter.

For a second she thought she was too late, that the beach bum had gone, and her heart plummeted sharply with disappointment—her gaze searching the darkening beach.

As she stood looking out across the pretty marina Petra was so lost in her own thoughts that the sudden darkness of a shadow thrown across the fading light shocked her.

Spinning round, she sucked in her stomach on a shocked breath as she realised that the object of her thoughts was standing in front of her, and so close to her that a single step forward would bring them body to body.

Instinctively Petra wanted to step back, but the stubborn pride that her father had once insisted she had inherited directly from her grandfather refused to let her move.

Lifting her head, she took a deep breath, then exhaled it unsteadily as she realised that she had not lifted her head enough, and that right now instead of making contact with his eyes her gaze was resting helplessly on the curve of his mouth.

What was it they said about men with a full bottom lip? That they were very sensual, very tactile…men who knew all the secret nuances of pleasures the touch of those male lips could have on a woman?

Petra felt faintly dizzy. She hadn't realised he was so tall. What nationality was he? Italian? Greek? His hair was very dark and very thick, and his skin—as she had had every opportunity to observe earlier in the day—was a deep, warm golden brown. He was fully dressed now, in a white tee shirt, jeans and trainers, and somehow—despite his casual clothes—he was disconcertingly much more formidable and authoritative-looking than she had expected.

It was almost fully dark; tiny decorative lights were springing up all around them, illuminating the marina and its environs. Petra could see the searing flash of his eyes as his glance encompassed her. First almost dismissively, and then appraisingly, his body stiffening as though suddenly alerted to something about her that had caught his interest, awakened his hunting instinct, changing the uninterest she could have sworn she had initially seen in his eyes to a narrowed intense concentration that pinned her into wary immobility.

If she turned and ran now he would enjoy it—enjoy pursuing her, tormenting her, she decided nervily. He was that kind of man!

Despite the fact that she was wearing a perfectly respectable pair of jeans and a shirt, she suddenly felt as though he could see right through them to the flesh beneath her clothes, that already he knew every curve of her, every hidden secret and vulnerability. She was not used to experiencing such feelings and they threw her a little off guard.

'If you've come looking for one-to-one lessons, I'm afraid you've left it too late.'

The open cynicism in his voice was something she had not been prepared for, and both it and the look he was giving her burned her skin. Petra suspected she could hear a hundred generations of male contempt for a certain type of female wantonness.

'Actually, I don't need lessons,' she told him, immediately rallying her pride. She had learned to windsurf as a young teenager, and although he wasn't to know it she'd reached competition standard.

'No? Then what do you need?' his soft insultingly knowing response shocked through her.

Petra could understand how those women had been so excited by him! He possessed a sexual aura, a sexual magnetism that dizzied her senses. His air of control and self-assurance hinted tauntingly at the fact that he considered he had the power to overwhelm and dominate her if he chose to do so, that he knew precisely the effect he had on her sex! This was a man whose very existence spelled a very distinct kind of predatory male dangerousness in any language. Which was exactly why he was so perfect for what she wanted, she reminded herself as she tussled with an unfamiliar and ignominious urge to turn and run whilst she still had the option to do so.

Irritated by her own weakness, she refused to give in to it. In her time she had faced down a wide array of men for a wide variety of reasons, and there was no way she was going to be out-faced by this one! Even if it was the first time she had ever been made so overwhelmingly aware of a man's sexuality that she could barely breathe the air that surrounded them because it was so charged with raw rogue testosterone.

Ignoring what she was feeling, Petra took a deep breath and told him firmly, 'I have a proposition to put to you.'

In the silence that followed her statement he must have moved slightly, she recognised, because suddenly she could see his full face—and what she could see made the breath seize in her lungs. She had known this afternoon that he had the kind of powerful male allure that could neither be imitated nor acquired, but now she realised that he also had the kind of facial features that would have made a Greek god weep with envy.

The only thing she couldn't see was the colour of his eyes. But surely with such colouring they had to be brown. Brown! Inwardly Petra allowed herself to relax a little. Brown-eyed men had never appealed to her. Secretly she had always hankered for a man with the cool magnetism of pure silver-grey-coloured eyes, having fallen in love with the hero of a book she had read as a young teenager whose eyes had been that colour.

'A proposition?' The cynical uninterest in his voice made her face burn a little. 'I'm a man,' he told her bluntly. 'And I don't go to bed with women who proposition me. I like to hunt my own prey, not be hunted by it. Of course if you're really desperate I could give you directions to a place where you might have more luck.'

As she felt her fingers curling into small, angry fists, Petra had to resist the instinctive temptation to react to his insult in the most basic female way possible. Satisfactory though it might initially be, slapping his face was hardly going to be conducive to concluding her plan successfully, she reminded herself wryly. At least his attitude confirmed her assumption that he was a sexual predator—not the kind of man a potential husband would want consorting with the woman he wanted to make his wife. In short this man was ideal for her purpose.

'It isn't that kind of proposition,' she denied firmly.

'No…? So what kind is it, then?' he challenged her.

'The kind that pays well and isn't illegal,' Petra replied promptly, crossing her fingers and hoping inwardly that her comment would have piqued his interest.

He had moved again, and now Petra realised that it was her turn to have her features revealed to him in the increasing illumination of the decorative lights.

She wasn't a vain person, but she knew that she was generally considered to be attractive. But if this man found her so, he certainly wasn't showing it, she acknowledged as she was subjected to a cool visual inspection that made her itch to step back into the protective shadows, her arms wrapped protectively around her body.

'Sounds fascinating,' he mocked her laconically. 'What do I have to do?'

Petra allowed herself to begin to relax. 'Pursue me and seduce me—very publicly,' she told him.

Just for a second she had the satisfaction of seeing that she had surprised him. His eyes widened fractionally before he controlled the movement.

'Seduce you?' he repeated. And now it was Petra's turn to be surprised, and unpleasantly so, as she marked the sharp curtness in a male voice that had abruptly become disconcertingly chilly.

'Not for real,' she told him quickly, before he could say

anything more. 'What I want is for you to pretend to seduce me.'

'Pretend? Why?' he demanded baldly. 'Do you already
have a lover you wish to make jealous? Is that it?' he
guessed insultingly.

Petra glared at him.

'No, I do not. I want to pay you to ensure that I lose
my...my reputation.'

For one unguarded moment Petra saw his face and wondered exactly what the sudden frown creasing his forehead
and the complete stillness of his body meant.

'Am I allowed to ask why you want to lose it?' he asked
her.

'You can ask,' Petra told him. 'But I don't intend to tell
you.'

'No? Well, in that case, I don't intend to help you.'

He was already turning away from her and Petra started
to panic.

'I'm prepared to pay you five thousand pounds,' she
called out to him.

'Ten thousand and then we might...just might have a
deal,' he told her softly as he stopped and turned to look
at her.

Ten thousand pounds. Petra felt sick. Her parents had
left her a very generous trust fund, but until she turned
twenty-five, there was no way she could raise such a large
sum without the approval of her trustees—one of whom
was her godfather, who was after all part of the reason why
she needed to do this in the first place.

Her body slumped in defeat.

He was still walking away from her, and had almost
reached the end of the beach. In another few seconds he
would be gone.

Swallowing against the bitter taste of her own failure,
she turned away herself.

CHAPTER TWO

REFUSING to give in to the temptation of watching him disappear, Petra fixed her gaze on the sea.

Most people, on first seeing her, assumed that Petra carried either Spanish or Italian blood in her veins. Her skin had a soft creamy warmth and her dark brown hair was thick and lustrous, her bone structure elegant and delicately patrician. Only her brilliant green eyes and the narrow straightness of her small nose, combined with her passionate nature, gave away the fact that she possessed Celtic genes, inherited through her American father's Irish ancestry. Very few people guessed that her colouring came from an exotic blending of those genes with her mother's Bedouin blood.

She could feel the evening breeze lifting her hair, its coolness raising tiny goosebumps on her skin, but they were nothing to the rash of sensation that flooded atavistically through her body as she suddenly felt the pressure of a male hand on the nape of her neck.

'Five thousand, then—and the reason,' a now familiar silken voice whispered in her ear.

He had come back! Petra didn't know whether to be elated or horrified!

'No haggling!' the silken voice warned her. 'Five thousand and the reason, or no deal.'

Petra's throat had gone dry. She didn't want to tell him, but what option did she have? And besides, what harm could it really do?

'Very well.'

What was it that was making her voice sound so tremulous? Surely not the fact that his hand was still on her nape?

'You're trembling,' he told her, so accurately tracking and trapping her own thoughts that his intuitiveness shocked her. 'Why? Are you afraid? Excited?'

As he drawled the soft words with deliberate slowness, almost whispering into her ear, his thumb stroked against the side of her throat, trapping the pulse fluttering there.

Stalwartly Petra wrenched herself free and told him resolutely. 'Neither! I'm just cold.'

She could see the taunting cruelty in the mocking curve of his smile.

'Of course,' he agreed. 'So, you want me to publicly pursue and seduce you?'

He questioned her as though he had suddenly grown bored with tormenting her, like a domestic cat suddenly tiring of the prey it had caught as a plaything rather than for food. But this man was no domesticated fireside pet! No, everything he did had a raw, untamed danger about it, a warning of power mockingly leashed.

'Why? Tell me!'

Petra took a deep breath.

'It's a long and complicated story,' she warned him.

'Tell me!' he repeated.

Briefly Petra closed her eyes, trying to marshal her thoughts into logical order, and then opened them again, beginning quietly, 'My father was an American diplomat. He met my mother here in Zuran when he was posted here. They fell in love but her father did not approve. He had other plans for her. He believes that it is a daughter's duty to allow herself to be used as a pawn in her family's empire-building.' As she spoke Petra could hear the anger and the bitterness in her own voice, just as she could feel it surging inside her—a mixture of a long-standing old pain on behalf of her mother and a much newer, bitter anger for herself.

'My grandfather refused to have anything to do with my mother after she ran away with my father. And he forbade his family—my mother's brothers and their wives—from having anything to do with her either. But she told me all about him. How cruel he had been!' Petra's eyes flashed.

'My parents were wonderfully, blissfully happy, but they were killed in an accident when I was seventeen. I went to live in England with my godfather who, like my father, is a diplomat. That's how they met—when my godfather was with the British Embassy in Zuran. Everything was fine. I finished university and then I travelled with my godfather, I worked for an aid agency in the field, and I was…am planning to take my Master's. But then…

'A short time ago, my uncle came to London and made contact with my godfather. He told him that my grandfather wanted to see me. That he wanted me to come to Zuran. I didn't want to have anything to do with him. I knew how much he had hurt my mother. She never stopped hoping that he would forgive her, that he would answer her letters, accept an olive branch, but he never did. Not even when she and my father were killed. He never even acknowledged her death. No one from my family here came to the funeral. He would not allow them to do so!'

Tears of rage and pain momentarily filled Petra's eyes, but determinedly she blinked them away.

'My godfather begged me to reconsider. He said it was what my parents would have wanted—for the family to be reconciled. He told me that my grandfather was one of the major shareholders in this holiday complex and he had suggested that both I and my godfather come and stay here, get to know one another. I wanted to refuse, but…' She stopped and shook her head. 'I felt for my mother's sake that I had to come. But if I'd known then the real reason why I was being brought out here—!'

'The real reason?' There was a brusqueness in the male voice that rasped roughly against her sensitive emotions.

'Yes, the real reason,' she reiterated bitterly.

'The day we arrived my uncle came here to the hotel with his wife, and his son—my cousin Saud. He's only fifteen, and... They said that my grandfather wasn't well enough to come, that he had a serious heart condition, and that his doctor had said that he needed bed rest and no excitement. I believed them. But then, when we were on our own together, Saud accidentally let the cat out of the bag. He had no idea, you see, that I didn't know what was really going on!'

Petra shook her head as she heard her voice starting to tremble. 'Far from merely wanting to meet me, to put right the wrong he had done to my parents, what my grandfather actually wants is to marry me off to one of his business partners! And, unbelievably, my godfather actually thinks it's a good idea.

'Although at first he tried to pretend that I had got it wrong and misunderstood Saud, in fact my godfather thinks it's so much of a good idea that right now he's incommunicado in the far east—on official diplomatic business, of course—and he's taken my passport with him! ''Just meet the chap, Petra, old thing.'' ' She mimicked her godfather's cut-glass upper class British voice savagely. ' ' 'No harm in doing that, eh? Who knows? You might find you actually rather like him. Look at British nobility. All from arranged marriages, and with pretty good results generally speaking. All that love tosh. Doesn't always work y'know. Like to like, that's what I always say—and from what your uncle has to say—it seems like this Sheikh Rashid and you have lots in common. Similar cultural heritage. Bound to go down well with the Foreign Office. And the Prime Minister…awfully keen on that sort of thing, y'know. I've heard it on the grapevine that the White House is one hundred per cent behind the idea.'''

'Your grandfather wants you to marry a man who is a fellow countryman of his, and a business colleague, as a PR exercise for diplomatic purposes? Is that what you're telling me?' He cut across Petra's angry outburst incisively.

Petra could hear the cynical disbelief in his voice and didn't really blame him for his reaction.

'Well, my godfather would like me to think that's the only motivation for my grandfather's behaviour, but of course he isn't anything like so high-minded or altruistic,' she told him scathingly.

'From what I've managed to find out from Saud, my grandfather wants me to marry this man because as well as being a fellow shareholder in this complex he is also very well connected—is in fact related to the Zuran Royal Family, no less! My mother was originally supposed to marry a second cousin of the Family before she met and fell in love with my father. Her father—my grandfather—considered it to be a very prestigious match, and one that would bring him a lot of benefits. I suppose in his eyes it is only fitting that since he couldn't marry my mother off to suit his own ends I should now take her place as a…a victim to his greed and ambition!'

'Does your mixed heritage disturb you?' His unexpected question threw Petra a little.

'Disturb me?' She tensed, anger and pride ignited inside her. 'No! Why should it?' she challenged him. 'I am proud to be the product of my parents' love for one another, and proud to be myself as well.'

'You misunderstand me. The disturbance I refer to is that

caused by the volatile mixing of the coldness of the north with the heat of the desert; Anglo Saxon blood mixed with Bedouin, the hunger for roots and the compulsion that drives the nomad and everything that those two polar opposites encompass. Do you never feel torn, pulled in two different ways by two different cultures? A part of both of them and at the same time alien to them?'

His words so accurately summed up the feelings that had bedevilled Petra for as long as she had been able to recognise them that they stunned her into silence. How could he possibly know that she felt like that? The tiny hairs on her skin lifted as though she were in the presence of a force she could not fully understand—a strength and insight so much more developed than her own that she felt in awe of it.

'I am what I am,' she told him firmly as she fought to ignore the way he was making her feel.

'And what is that?'

Anger darkened her eyes.

'I am a modern, independent woman who will not be manipulated or used to serve the ends of a machiavellian old man.'

She could see the shrug he gave.

'If you do not want to marry the husband your grandfather has chosen for you then why do you simply not tell him so?'

'It isn't that easy,' Petra was forced to admit. 'Of course I told my godfather that there was totally and absolutely no way I was going to agree to even meet this man. Never mind marry him. That was when he announced that he had to leave for the far east and that he was taking my passport with him. To give me time to get to know my grandfather and to rediscover my cultural heritage, was how he put it, but of course I know what he's really hoping for. He's hoping that by leaving me here, at my grandfather's mercy, he will be able to pressure me into doing what he wants. My godfather retires next year, and no doubt he's hoping that the government will reward him for his work—including arranging a high-profile marriage to Sheikh Rashid— with a Peerage in the New Year's honours list. And what makes it even worse is that, from what my cousin Saud has told me, it seems the whole family believe I should be thrilled to think that this…this…man is prepared to consider marrying me,' Petra concluded bitterly.

'Like normally marries like in such circumstances,' the cool, almost bored voice pointed out. 'I understand what you are saying about your grandfather's motivations, but what about those of your proposed husband? Why should this…?'

'Sheikh Rashid,' Petra supplied for him grimly. 'The same Sheikh Rashid who, from what I hear, does not approve of your…behaviour with his female guests!'

The quick, hard look he gave her caused Petra to say immediately, 'I heard two women discussing you earlier on—' She stopped. 'As to why the Sheikh should want to marry me…' Petra took a deep breath. 'You might well ask. But apparently he and I have something in common— we are both of mixed parentage, only in his case I believe that it was his father who provided his Zuran heritage and not his mother. More importantly, The Zuran Royal Family consider the marriage to be a good idea. My godfather says that it will cause great offence if he refuses a marriage they have given their seal of approval, and great offence to mine if he refuses me. However, whilst I know enough about Zuran culture to know that for either of us to refuse the other once negotiations have commenced is considered to be an unforgivable insult, I know too that if he were to have reason to believe that morally I am not fit to be his wife he could honourably refuse to accept me.'

'There's an awful lot of supposition going on here,' came the wry comment.

But when Petra shot him a fulminatingly angry look, and demanded, 'Are you trying to say that it's all in my imagination? Then there's no point in us wasting any more of one another's time!'

He gave her a small semi-placatory look and offered conciliatingly, 'So! I understand the motivation, but why choose me?'

Petra gave a small cynical shrug.

'Like I said, I heard a couple of female guests discussing you earlier, and from what they were saying it was obvious that…'

When she stopped speaking, he prompted her softly, 'That what?'

'That you have a reputation for enjoying the favours of the women who stay here. So much so, in fact,' she added, tilting her chin defiantly, 'that you have already been reprimanded for your behaviour by…by Sheikh Rashid, and are in danger of losing your job!' Petra gave a small shudder. 'I don't know how those women can cheapen themselves! I might not want an arranged marriage, but there is no way I would ever prejudice my own personal moral beliefs by indulging in a meaningless sexual fling a…a cheap sexual thrill!' Through the darkness Petra was suddenly acutely conscious of his gaze fixing intently on her.

'I see… So you don't want an arranged marriage and you don't want cheap sexual thrills. So what do you want?'

'Nothing!' As he turned his head Petra saw the mocking way he raised his eyebrows and defended herself immediately. 'What I mean is I don't want anything until I meet a man who…'

'Who matches up to your very high standards?' he suggested tauntingly.

Crossly Petra shook her head.

'Please don't put words into my mouth. What I was going to say was until I meet a man I can love and respect and…and want to…to commit myself to emotionally, mentally, cerebrally, sexually—every which way there is. That is the kind of relationship my parents shared,' she told him passionately. 'And that is the kind of relationship I want for myself and one day want to encourage my own children to aspire to.'

'A tall order, especially in this day and age,' came the blunt response.

'Perhaps, but one I think it worth waiting to fulfil,' Petra told him firmly.

'Aren't you afraid that if you finally meet this paragon he might be deterred by the fact that your reputation—?'

'No.' Petra interrupted him swiftly. 'Because if he loves me he will accept me and know and understand my values. And besides…' She stopped, her face burning as she realised just how close she had come to telling him that the fact that she had so far not met such a man and was still a virgin would tell its own story to the man who eventually claimed her love. 'Why are you asking me all these questions?' she demanded sharply instead.

'No reason,' he replied laconically.

Through the darkness Petra could sense him evaluating her.

'So,' he announced at last. 'You are offering to pay me five thousand pounds to pursue and seduce you and publicly ruin your reputation.'

'To pretend to,' Petra corrected him immediately.

'What's wrong?' he taunted her. 'Having second thoughts?'

'Certainly not!' Petra denied indignantly, and then gasped in shock as he closed the distance between them and took her in his arms, demanding shakily, 'What are you doing?'

He smelled of clean night air and warm male skin, of the dangerous heat of the desert and the cool mystery of the night, and her whole body quivered in helpless reaction to his maleness. The slow descent of his head blocked out the light and the glitter of his eyes mesmerised her into unmoving stillness.

'We have made a pact! A bargain!' she felt him murmuring against her lips.

'And now we must seal it. In the desert in times gone by such things were sealed in blood. Shall I prick your skin and release the life blood from your veins, to mingle it with my own, or will this suffice?'

Before Petra could protest his mouth was on her own, crushing the breath from her lungs. Oh yes, she had been right, she recognised weakly. He was as swift and as deadly as the panther she had mentally likened him to earlier...

A tiny frantic moan bubbled in her throat as she felt her body's helpless response to the mastery of his kiss. She had been right to fear the passionate expertise indicated by that full bottom lip. There was a slight roughness about his face that chafed slightly against her own soft skin, and she had to fight to control the instinctive movement of her hand towards his face to touch that distinctive maleness. As he released her lips it seemed for some inexplicable shaming reason that they were determined to cling to his. Panic flooded over her, and before she could stop herself she bit fiercely into his lip in defiant pride.

The shock of the taste of his blood on her tongue held her immobile.

As she tensed herself for his retaliation she felt his hand wrapping round the slenderness of her throat.

'So…you prefer to seal our bargain in blood after all? There is more of the desert in you than I had realised.'

And then before she could move his mouth was on hers again, crushing it with the pressure of a kind of kiss that was totally outside anything she had ever experienced. She could taste his blood, feel the rough velvet of his tongue, hear the frenzy of a desert storm in her own heartbeat and the relentless, unforgiving burn of its sun in the touch of his hand against her throat.

And then abruptly he had released her, and as he raised his head for a brief moment Petra saw his face fully illuminated for the first time.

His eyes were open and shock reeled through her as she discovered that they were not, after all, as she had imagined dark brown, but a pure, clear, cool, steely silver-grey.

'We have the whole morning at our disposal, Petra. I thought you might like to go shopping. There is an exclusive shopping centre nearby, which has some wonderful designer shops, and…'

With a tremendous effort Petra tried to concentrate on what her aunt was saying to her.

She had telephoned Petra the previous evening to suggest that she show her something of the city and its shops. Whatever she thought about her grandfather's behaviour, Petra could not help but like her aunt by marriage—even if she had been the one to speak to Petra self-consciously the very day her godfather had left.

'Your grandfather knows how disappointed you must be that his doctor's orders mean that he is unable to see you just yet, Petra, and so he has arranged for a…a family friend who…who has a major financial interest in it, to give

you a guided tour of the hotel complex and to show something of our country. You will like Rashid. He is a very
charming and very well-educated man.'

Petra had had to bite on her tongue to prevent herself
from bursting out angrily that she knew exactly who and
what Rashid was—thanks to Saud's innocent revelations!

She had been awake for what felt like virtually the whole
of the night, reliving over and over again those moments
on the beach and wondering how she could ever have been
stupid enough to allow them to happen, and had then fallen
into a deep sleep which had left her feeling heavy-eyed.

The combination of that and the nervous edginess that
was making her start at every tiny sound had exhausted
her, and shopping was the last thing she felt like doing.
Besides, what if *he* should try to get in touch with her?
Would he do that, or would he expect her to seek him out
on the beach and perhaps throw herself at him in the same
shameless way she had heard that the other women had
done? The thought made her stomach tense nauseously. No,
their arrangement was that he was the one who had to pursue her, she reminded herself. Pursue and seduce her, a tiny
inner voice whispered dangerously to her...

Seduce her. A fierce shudder ran through her, causing
her aunt to ask in concern if she was cold.

'Cold? In nearly thirty degrees of heat?' Petra laughed.
Her aunt might protest that in Zuran it was winter, but to
Petra it felt blissfully warm.

'Your grandfather hopes to be well enough to see you
very soon,' her aunt continued. 'He is very much looking
forward to that, Petra. He keeps asking if you look anything
like your mother...'

Petra tried not to be affected by her aunt's gentle words.
'If he really wanted to know he could have found out a

long time ago—when my mother was still alive,' she pointed out, remaining unforgiving.

It was so tempting to tell her aunt that she knew the real reason she was here in Zuran, but she had no wish to get her young cousin into trouble.

'What do you think of the hotel complex?' her aunt was asking her, tactfully changing the subject.

Petra toyed with the idea of fibbing but her conscience refused to allow her to do so.

'It's…it's breathtaking,' she admitted. 'I haven't explored all of it yet, of course. After all it's almost like a small town. But what I have seen…'

She particularly liked the traditional design of the interconnecting hotel and villa complexes, with their private courtyards filled with sweetly scented plants and fruit trees, and the musical sound of fountains which had reminded Petra immediately of both the Moorish style of Southern Spain's architecture and images her mother had shown her as a child of Arabian palaces.

'When Rashid shows you round you must tell him that. Although unfortunately it may be several days before he is able to do so. He sent word to your grandfather this morning that he has been called away on business on behalf of The Royal Family… Another project he is working on in the desert.'

'He works?' Petra made no attempt to conceal her disbelief. From what Saud had told her, her prospective suitor sounded far too wealthy and well-connected to do something so mundane.

'Oh, yes,' her aunt assured her. 'As well as having a large financial interest in this complex he also designed it. He is a very highly qualified architect and greatly in demand. He trained in England. It was his mother's wish that he should go to school there, and after her death his father honoured that wish.'

An architect! Petra frowned, but she had no intention of showing any interest in a man she had already decided to despise.

'It sounds as though he is a very busy man,' she told her aunt. 'There really is no need for him to give up his time to show me round the complex. I am perfectly capable of exploring it on my own.'

'No. You must not do that,' her aunt protested once they were on their own again.

'No? Then perhaps Saud could accompany me?' Petra could not resist teasing her.

'No…no! It is best that Rashid should show you. After all, he is the one who designed the complex and he will be able to answer any questions you might have.'

'And his wife?' Petra questioned innocently. 'Will she not mind him spending his precious free time with me?'

'Oh, he is not married,' her aunt assured her immediately. 'You will like him, Petra,' she assured her enthusiastically. 'You have much in common with one another, and—' She broke off as her mobile phone started to ring.

Her aunt reached beneath her robes to retrieve her phone. But as Petra listened to her speaking quickly in Arabic, she saw her aunt's face crease in anxiety. 'What is it?' she demanded as soon as the call was over. 'Is it my grandfather? Is he—'

Furious with herself for her unguarded reaction, and for her concern, Petra stopped speaking and bit her lip.

'That was your uncle,' her aunt told her. 'Your grandfather has suffered a relapse. He knows that he has been ordered to rest but he will not do so! I must go home, Petra. I am sorry.'

Just for a moment Petra was tempted to plead to be allowed to go with her—to be allowed to see her grandfather, the closest person to her in blood she had—but quickly she stifled her weakening and unwanted emotions. Her grandfather meant nothing to her. How could he when she so obviously meant nothing to him? She must not forget the past and his plans for her. No, she was certainly not going to be the one to beg to see him. Her mother had begged and pleaded and had suffered the pain of being ignored and rejected. There was no way that she, Petra, was going to allow her grandfather to do the same to her!

After a taxi had dropped her off outside the hotel, Petra made her way into the lobby. With the rest of the day to herself there were any number of things Petra knew she could do.

The complex had its own *souq*, filled with craftspeople making and selling all manner of deliciously irresistible and traditional things, or she could leave the hotel and enjoy a gondola ride through the man-made canals that bisected the complex, or walk in the tranquillity of its gardens. And of course she could simply chill out if she so wished, either by one of the several stunningly designed pools, including a state-of-the-art 'horizon pool', or even on one of the private beaches that belonged to the complex.

The pools and beaches were reached via a man-made 'cave' below the lobby floor of the hotel, where it was possible to either walk or be taken in one of the resort's beach buggies.

Once there, as Petra had already discovered, a helpful employee would carry her towel to the lounger of her choice, and position both it and her beach umbrella for her before summoning a waiter in case she wanted to order a drink.

Nothing that a guest might need, no matter how small—

or how large—had been left to chance in the planning of the complex or the training of its staff. Petra had travelled all over the world, both with her parents, her godfather, and on her own, and she had already decided that she had never visited anywhere where a holidaymaker's needs were catered for so comprehensively and enthusiastically as they were here.

But of course she was not here on holiday—even if her closest girlfriends at home had insisted on dragging her round some of London's top stores before she had left, to equip her with a suitably elegant wardrobe for her trip.

Baring in mind her own innate modesty, and the country she was travelling to, Petra had eschewed the more *outré* samples of resort wear her enthusiastic friends had pointed out to her—although from what she had seen of her fellow holidaymakers' choice she could have chosen the briefest and most minimal bikini and still have felt comparatively over-dressed compared with some of them.

Instead she had opted for cool, elegant linens and discreet tankini beach sets, plus several evening outfits including an impossible to resist designer trouser suit in a wonderfully heavy cream matt silk satin fabric, which the salesgirl and her friends had tried in vain to convince her she should wear with simply the one-button jacket fastened over her otherwise naked top half.

'You've got the figure for it,' the salesgirl had urged her, and her friends had wickedly agreed. But Petra had refused to give in, and so a simple cream silk vest with just a hint of a pretty gold thread running through it had been added to her purchases.

A rueful smile quirked her mouth as she remembered the more outrageous of her two friends attempts to persuade her to buy a trendy outfit they had seen in a London department store: a fringed and tasselled torso-baring top, with a pair of matching lower than hip level silky pants which had revealed her belly button, claiming mock innocently that it would be perfect for her to wear in a country that celebrated the art of belly dancing.

Petra had known when she was being wound up. Her smile deepened as she instinctively touched her smooth flat stomach with her fingertips. Hidden beneath her clothes was the discreet little diamond navel stud she had bought herself just before she'd left home to replace the one she had been wearing whilst her recently pierced flesh had healed up.

No one, not even her friends, knew of the uncharacteristic flash of reckless defiance which had led to her having her navel pierced the very day after her godfather had finally ground down her opposition and persuaded her to come to Zuran.

Secretly Petra had to acknowledge that there was something dangerously decadent and wanton about the way the tiny diamond she had bought for herself flashed whenever it caught the light, but of course no one was ever likely to see it, or to know of her rebellious emotional reaction at having to give in to her grandfather's desire for her to visit his country.

Thinking of her grandfather made Petra frown. Just how serious was his heart condition? She had assumed from her uncle's original calm, almost casual reference to it that it was not a particular cause for concern.

Was he as ill as her aunt seemed to believe? Or was it simply a ploy, a means of manipulating her and putting pressure on her? Petra was fiercely determined that she would not give one inch to the despot who had caused her mother so much pain, and she was convinced that he was playing the kind of cat and mouse game that her mother had often told her he was an expert at, using his supposed poor health as a means of keeping her in dark about his real plans for her. Naturally such behaviour on his part had put her on her mettle and alerted her most defensive and hostile reactions. But what if she had been wrong? What if her grandfather was genuinely very ill?

Although it would have been impossible for her not to be emotionally touched by the warmth of her aunt and uncle's reception of her, and their concern that she might be disappointed at being deprived of what they seemed to assume was a much longed for meeting with her grandfather, Petra's antipathy towards her grandfather had been intensified by his emotional manipulation and had caused her to harden her heart even more against him.

She had every right to both mistrust and dislike him, she reassured herself. So why was she feeling somehow abandoned and rejected—excluded from the anxious family circle which had gathered protectively around him? Why did she feel this sense of anxiety and urgency to know what was going on? Why did she feel this sense of pain and loss?

Her uncle or her aunt would ring her at the hotel if they thought it was necessary; she knew that. But that wasn't like being there, being part of what was happening, being totally accepted.

A family walked past her in the foyer, on their way to the piano lounge, its three generations talking happily together. A deep sense of anguish welled up dangerously inside Petra. Grimly she tried to suppress what she was feeling. She had always been too vulnerable to her emotions. Her Celtic inheritance was responsible for that! Against her will she discovered that she was remembering how she had felt as a child, knowing that she was different, sensing her mother's pain and helpless to do anything to alleviate it, envious of other children she knew who talked easily and confidently about their adoring grandparents.

She was letting her feelings undermine her common sense, she warned herself. Her grandfather had only brought her here for one reason and it had nothing to do with adoring her! To him she was merely a suddenly valuable pawn in the intricate game he so enjoyed playing with other people's lives, using them to advance his own lust for power.

But if he was ill…seriously ill…if…something should happen before she had the chance to meet him….

Swallowing against the sharp lump in her throat, Petra headed for the lift. She would go upstairs to her room and decide how she was going to spend the rest of the day.

The suite her family had booked her in to was elegantly luxurious and large enough to house a whole family. Not only did it have a huge bathroom, complete with the largest shower Petra had even seen, as well as a sunken whirlpool bath, it also had a separate wardrobe-filled dressing room, and a bedroom with the most enormous bed she had even slept in, as well as a private terrace overlooking one of the complex's enclosed gardens.

Letting herself into the suite, Petra walked over to the dressing table and put down her bag. As she did so she glanced into the mirror and then froze as in it she saw the reflection of the bed—and more importantly the man lounging on it: her would-be seducer and partner in crime! His hands were clasped behind his head as he watched her, his body covered in nothing more than the towel he had wrapped around his hips. Tiny drops of moisture still glinting on his skin testified to the fact that he must have only recently stepped out of the shower—her shower, Petra reminded herself, unable to stop her eyes widening in betraying shock as she turned round and stared at him in disbelief.

Her suite, like the others on the same floor, and like the palatial owners suite above them, could only be reached by a private lift for which one needed a separate security card!

But for a man like this one anything and everything was possible, Petra suspected.

Like someone in a trance, she watched as he swung his feet to the floor and stood up.

If that towel he had wrapped so precariously around his body should slip...

Nervously she wetted her suddenly dry lips with the tip of her tongue. His own mouth, she suddenly realised on a flush of dangerous raw heat, bore a small fresh scar. Mesmerised, she tried to drag her gaze away from it...from him...

Had someone turned off the air-conditioning? she wondered dizzily. The room suddenly seemed far too warm...

He was walking towards her now, and in another few seconds... Automatically she backed away.

CHAPTER THREE

As though it was someone else who was actually speaking, Petra heard her own voice, thick and openly panicky, demanding, 'What are you doing in here?'

She could have sworn that her nervousness was amusing him. There was quite definitely a distinct glint in his eyes as he replied easily, 'Waiting for you, of course.'

'In here and…and like that?' Petra couldn't stop the indignation from wobbling her voice. 'What if someone else had been with me…my aunt…?'

Carelessly he gave a small shrug.

'Then you would have achieved your purpose, wouldn't you? Besides, we needed to talk, and I needed to shower, so it made sense for me to deal with both those needs together.'

He looked so totally at home in her suite that she felt as though she was the interloper, Petra acknowledged, and she wasn't even going to begin to ask just how he had managed to gain access to it.

'You could have showered in your own accommodation,' she told him primly. 'And as for us talking—I had planned to come down to the beach later.'

'Later would have been too late,' he told her. 'This is my afternoon off. And as for my own accommodation—' he gave her a wry look '—do you honestly suppose that the hotel staff are housed as luxuriously as its guests?'

Petra's throat had gone dry—not, she quickly assured herself, because of that sudden and unwanted mental image she had just had of him standing beneath the warm spray

34

of the shower…his naked body gleaming taut and bronze-gold as he soaped the sculptured perfection of the six-pack stomach that was so clearly revealed by the brevity of the towel that did little more than offer the merest sop to modesty—hers and quite obviously not his, Petra reflected indignantly as he strolled round the room, patently unconcerned that the towel might slip!

'How…how did you manage to find me? I didn't tell you my name and you didn't give me yours.'

'It wasn't hard. Your grandfather is very well known.'

Petra's eyes widened. 'You know him?'

The dark eyebrows rose mockingly.

'Would a mere itinerant worker be allowed to "know" a millionaire?'

'And your name is?' Petra pressed him.

Was she imagining it, or had he frowned and hesitated rather longer than was necessary?

'It's Blaize,' he told her briefly.

'Blaize?' Petra looked at him.

'Something wrong?' he challenged her.

Petra shook her head.

'No, it—it's just that I had assumed that you must be Southern European—Italian, or…or Spanish or Greek. But your name…'

'My mother was Cornish,' he told her almost brusquely.

'Cornish?' Petra repeated, bemused.

'Yes,' he confirmed, boredom beginning to enter his voice as he informed her, 'According to my mother, her ancestors belonged to a band of wreckers!'

Wreckers. Well, that no doubt accounted for his colouring, and for that sharp air of danger and recklessness about him, Petra reasoned, remembering that Cornish wreckers were supposed to have pillaged galleons from the defeated Spanish Armada, taking from them not just gold but the high-born Spanish women who were sailing on them with their husbands as well.

Blaize. It suited him somehow. Blaize.

'So now that we've got the civilities out of the way, perhaps we can turn our attention to some practicalities. This plan of yours—'

'I don't want to discuss it now,' Petra interrupted him. 'Please get dressed and leave…'

She was beginning to feel increasingly uncomfortable, increasingly agitated and aware of the effect his virtual nudity was having on her!

'What's wrong?' he questioned her sharply. 'Have you changed your mind? Has your family perhaps managed to persuade you to consider this man they have chosen for you after all? After all, there are worse things to be endured than marriage to a very wealthy man…'

'Not so far as I am concerned,' Petra told him sharply. 'I can't imagine anything worse than…than a loveless marriage,' she told him passionately.

'Have you ever been in love?' he questioned her, answering his own question as he said softly, 'No, of course you haven't. Otherwise…'

There was a glint in his eyes that was making Petra's heart beat far too fast. She was still in shock from discovering him in her room and, even worse, her senses were still reacting to the totally relaxed and arrogant male way in which he was now lounging against the wall, arms folded across his chest, tightening the muscles in them in a way that for some reason refused to allow her to withdraw her fascinated female gaze from them.

'Whether or not I have ever been in love has nothing whatsoever to do with our…our business arrangement,' Petra reproved him sternly.

'When are you supposed to be being introduced to Rashid?'

Petra frowned. 'I...I don't know! You see at the moment I'm not even supposed to know what my grandfather has planned. My aunt has dropped several discreet hints about Rashid, pretending that he is just a kind family friend who has offered to...to show me round the complex, but...'

When Blaize's eyebrows rose, Petra explained defensively, 'It seems that he doesn't merely have a large financial interest in it, but that he helped design it as well. According to my aunt, he's a trained architect.'

Petra wondered uncomfortably if Blaize could hear the slight breathlessness in her voice. If so she hoped he would assume it was because she was impressed by her would-be suitor's academic qualifications rather than by the sight of Blaize's own muscles!

'When is he to show you around?'

Petra shrugged her shoulders.

'I don't know. According to my aunt, Rashid the Sheikh has been called away on business.'

'And you are no doubt hoping that by the time he returns enough damage will have been done to your reputation to have him questioning your suitability to be his wife? Well, if that is to be achieved we should not waste any time,' Blaize told her, without waiting for her response. 'Tonight everyone who is anyone on the Zuran social scene will be out and about, looking to see and be seen, and the current in place for that is a restaurant here on this complex called The Venue. It has a Michelin-starred chef and boasts a separate music room where diners can dance. I think that you and I should make our first public appearance there tonight. Dress is formal, and there is a strict admissions policy, but as a guest of the hotel and a woman that won't be a problem for you!'

'It sounds expensive,' Petra told him doubtfully.

'It is,' he agreed. 'But surely that isn't a problem? You did tell me that you are staying here at your family's request, and as their guest, and since the cost of dining in the restaurant can be debited to your room—'

'No! I couldn't possibly do that,' Petra denied immediately, unable to conceal either her distaste or her shock. But far from being contrite, Blaize merely looked amused.

'Why ever not? You have to eat, don't you?'

'I have to eat, yes,' Petra acknowledged. 'But I can't possibly expect my family to pay for...'

As she paused, struggling to find the right words to express her feelings, Blaize shrugged and told her bluntly, 'Either you were serious about this plan of yours or it was just a childish impulse that you're now regretting. In which case, you're wasting my time as well as your own—'

'I *am* serious,' Petra interrupted him quickly.

'Very well, then. We eat late here, so I shall meet you downstairs in the foyer at nine-thirty—unless of course you want me to come up to your room to collect you a little earlier, which would give us time to...'

'No,' Petra said firmly, her face burning as she saw the amused look he was giving her.

'How very much the epitome of a nervous virgin you look and sound right now! Are you one?'

Her face burning even hotter, Petra told him fiercely, 'You have no right to ask me that kind of question.'

Laughing softly, Blaize shook his head. 'Who would have thought it? Now you *have* surprised me! A nervous virgin who wants to be considered openly sexually available. You really don't want this marriage, do you?'

'I've just told you I am not prepared to discuss my...my personal private life with you...'

'Even though you expect me to publicly convince others

that I am very much a part of that personal private life…very, very much a part of it?' he said softly.

There was a look in his eyes that was making Petra's insides quiver with tension and indignation. How dared he make fun of her? It occurred to her that somehow or other he had managed to turn their relationship around so that he was the one who was in control of what was happening rather than her. A presentiment shiver brushed over her skin, warning her that she might be in danger of getting herself involved in a situation that she ultimately could not control. But before she could analyse her fears properly the doorbell to her suite suddenly rang, the shrilling sound activating her inner alarm system and throwing her body into immediate anxiety.

'It's okay,' Blaize informed her easily. 'That will be Room Service. I ordered something to eat.'

'*You* ordered…' Petra stared at him, and then looked frantically towards the suite door as the bell rang again. 'You can't—' she began, and then stopped, pink-cheeked, as she realised Blaize was laughing softly at her.

'You know,' he said, 'I think that this is going to be fun. Have you any idea how tempting it is to really shock you, little Miss Prim?'

Still laughing, he leaned forward and cupped her face with his hand, brushing her unsuspecting mouth with his own before releasing her and disappearing into the bathroom just before the suite door opened and the meal he had ordered was brought in.

'Panic over?'

Automatically Petra looked towards Blaize as he emerged from the bathroom, still wearing merely the towel, with an electric razor in one hand whilst he smoothed the skin of his newly shaved jaw with the other. Then she quickly looked away as her heart did a triple-flip before losing its balance and slamming heavily into her chest wall.

What on earth was the matter with her? So he was having a shave. So what?

So what? The voice of moral female indignation inside her retorted angrily; what he was doing was an act of deliberate male intimacy…shaving in her suite…in her bathroom…

'Mmm. I could get used to this,' he told her appreciatively as he studied the well-laden trolley. 'Pour me a cup of coffee, would you?' he called out to her as he turned back towards the bathroom. 'Black and strong, no sugar.'

Pour him a coffee! Who on earth did he think he was?

'Oh, by the way,' he told her, pausing as he reached the bathroom door. 'I've already booked us a table at The Venue for tonight, and told them to bill it to your room. We were lucky. They were virtually fully booked. Are you sure you don't feel like short-circuiting things? I could move in here and…'

'No!'

Petra's denial was an explosive sound of outrage and panic, but far from shaming him it just seemed to add to her tormentor's amusement.

Relaxing against the open doorway, he told her wickedly, 'You know, I think I could really enjoy making this seduction the real thing, if you want me to.'

'No.' This time her denial was even more vehement, her eyes huge and storm-lashed as she added in a strangled voice, 'Never.'

'Ah, yes! I forgot that you're saving yourself for the man of your dreams! Well, take care he doesn't turn into a nightmare… Is that my coffee?' he added easily, coming to rescue the cup that she was in danger of overfilling.

Furious with herself for her automatic response to his original request, Petra snatched the cup back from him.

'No, it isn't' she denied. 'It's mine. You can pour your own.'

Unperturbed, he shrugged and reached for the coffee pot, leaving Petra to digest her hollow victory along with the bitterly strong coffee she had claimed.

Broodingly she watched as Blaize tucked into the meal he had ordered with obvious relish. This wasn't what she had envisaged when she had initially approached him. What she had had in mind was an open and obvious flirtation on the beach, perhaps a couple of very public outings and maybe a meal together thrown in.

'Come and sit down and have something to eat. I ordered enough for both of us,' Blaize told her.

'So I see,' Petra agreed waspishly.

There was no way she could let her family pay for whatever Blaize had added to her bill. Thankfully she had come away with plenty of traveller's cheques and her credit cards, and her godfather—no doubt motivated by guilt—had pressed a very generous sum of money on her before he had left for the far east.

'I'm a working man,' Blaize told her cheerfully.

'I'm glad you reminded me,' Petra replied. 'And, talking of your work, shouldn't you…?'

'Don't worry,' he assured her. 'I had some leave owing to me, so I've arranged to take some time off. That way I can be free to do whatever you want me to do. If our Rashid is prepared to take you sight unseen, so to speak, then I dare say he's going to be pretty hard to shift. So you and I are going to have to make sure that we're convincing. Are you sure you don't want me to move in here?' he pressed, looking wistfully at her large bed.

'Perfectly sure,' Petra told him through gritted teeth.

'And just as soon as you've finished I would be grateful if you would get dressed and leave.'

'Leave? So soon? I thought we could spend some time getting to know one another a little better.'

To Petra's chagrin she knew that her expression had betrayed her even before he started to laugh.

'You're going to have to do much better than this if you expect to convince anyone that you've ever done anything more than exchange chaste kisses with a man—never mind that you and I are lovers,' he warned her when he had stopped laughing.

'The whole purpose of my paying you is that your reputation is dire enough to do the convincing for both of us!' Petra reminded him flintily.

'You look very hot and uncomfortable,' Blaize responded, ignoring both her comment and her ire. 'I can recommend the shower. In fact, if you like—'

'No! Don't you dare…' Petra stopped him, hot-cheeked.

'Dare what?' he asked her mock innocently. 'I was only going to say that I could alter the height of the shower head for you if you wanted me to.'

Petra gave him a fulminating look.

'Thank you, but I'm perfectly capable of doing that for myself,' she told him.

She bitterly regretted having let slip to him the fact that she was still a virgin. He obviously thought it hugely entertaining and would no doubt continue to goad and tease her about it. Unless she found a way of stopping him!

Petra tensed as the telephone in her suite started to ring. Before answering it she glanced at her reflection in the mirror. She had almost finished getting ready and she was wearing her new cream trouser suit. Warily she picked up the receiver, only to discover that her caller was her aunt.

'I meant to ring you earlier,' she apologised. 'Are you all right? I feel so guilty about leaving you on your own.'

As she assured her that she was fine, Petra waited for her aunt to make a firm arrangement for her to visit her family and finally meet her grandfather. But instead of issuing any invitation there was a small awkward silence from her aunt, and then an unconvincing and rushed explanation that certain family obligations meant it would not be possible for them to spend any time with her on the following day.

'At least your grandfather is feeling a little better. Although the doctor says that he must still rest. He is longing to see you, Petra, and—'

If anything her aunt's voice sounded even more unconvincing, Petra reflected bitterly.

Well she certainly wasn't going to turn herself into a liar by saying that she was longing to see *him*. She had no idea what he was hoping to achieve by what he was doing, unless it was to make her feel so isolated and alone that she practically fell into her proposed suitor's arms out of gratitude to him for rescuing her from her solitude.

'It is such a pity that my own family, my sisters and their children, are out of the country right now,' her aunt was continuing. 'But as soon as Rashid gets back—'

'You mustn't worry about me, Aunt,' Petra interrupted her. 'I am perfectly capable of entertaining myself. As a matter of fact...' Petra paused, wondering how much she ought to say.

But her aunt obviously wasn't listening properly because she cut across what Petra was saying, telling her, 'There are several escorted trips from the resort that you might enjoy taking, Petra, whilst you wait for Rashid to return. The gold *souq,* for one. Oh, I must go. I can hear your grandfather calling for me.'

There was barely time for Petra to wish her goodbye before her aunt had rung off.

As she turned towards the mirror to apply her lipstick Petra discovered that her hand was shaking slightly.

Because she was angry, she told herself—*not* because she was nervous at all at the thought of spending the evening with Blaize. She was angry because she knew instinctively that her aunt was not being entirely honest with her.

Mentally she tried to picture her grandfather, using the vivid verbal images her mother had drawn for her, and those she had gained herself from studying the robed men she had seen moving with imperious arrogance through the hotel. He would be bearded, of course, his profile hawk-like and his expression harsh, perhaps even vengeful as he confronted her, the child of the marriage he had fought against so bitterly and so unsuccessfully.

It was impossible for Petra to get her head round the mindset of a father who had turned from being protective and loving to one who refused so much as to hear his once beloved daughter's name spoken, simply because she had chosen to marry the man she loved.

In the mirror her own reflection confronted her. At home in England she was often conscious of looking out of place, her colouring and the delicacy of her fine-boned body giving her an almost exotic beauty, but here in her mother's country, conversely, she felt very Celtic.

Her mother! What would *she* think of the course of action Petra was taking? What would she think of Blaize?

Snatching up her purse, Petra refused to allow herself to pursue such potentially unsettling thoughts.

The lobby of the hotel was the busiest Petra had seen it since her arrival. A large group of designer-clad women and their male escorts were standing by the entrance to the piano lounge and Petra's eyes widened as she saw the jewellery the women were wearing.

Her own outfit was provoking a few assessing and appreciative female glances, as well as some much more openly male admiring ones, but Petra was unaware of them as she looked round anxiously for Blaize.

'There you are. I was just about to come up and collect you.'

Whirling round, Petra rounded her eyes as she stared at Blaize. He was dressed formally in clothes she immediately recognised as being the very best in Italian tailoring, and which she knew must have cost a small fortune. No wonder more than one of the diamond-decked women were studying him with such open sexual interest!

On the wages he must earn there was no way he could possibly afford such clothes, Petra decided, which must mean...

She didn't like the unpleasant cold feeling invading her stomach, or the lowering realisation that she was probably far from being the first woman to pay Blaize for his 'services'—although of course the services she was paying him for were no doubt very different from those normally expected by his benefactresses.

'What's wrong? You look as though you've just swallowed something extremely unpleasant.'

His intuitiveness triggered a sharp spiral of warning.

'I was just wondering what's going to be on the menu tonight,' she replied smoothly.

He might have caught her off guard this afternoon, but tonight was going to be different. This time she was going to make it plain to him that *she* was the one in charge of events and not him!

'These days Zuran is renowned for the variety and standard of its restaurants, as you are about to discover.'

As he spoke he was guiding her across the foyer, one hand protectively beneath her elbow. Petra would have liked to pull away, to put some distance between them, but the crush of people in the lobby made it impossible, and besides, she firmly reminded herself, the whole point of being with him was that she was *seen* to be with him!

However, instead of heading for the exit, as she had expected him to do, Petra discovered that he was guiding her in the direction of the large glass doors that opened out into one of the formal garden courtyards, beyond which lay the largest of the network of canals which criss-crossed the complex.

'I thought we were going out to dinner,' she said, hanging back a little as two uniformed men held open the doors for them.

'We are,' Blaize told her, giving her a quizzical look as he ushered her outside. 'What's wrong?' he teased her. 'Did you think I was taking you out into the courtyard so that I could indulge in a little private tuition before we faced our public?'

He laughed softly, the hand which had been beneath her elbow suddenly grasping her upper arm and holding her so close to his own body that she could feel the laughter vibrating as they walked out into the heavy satin warmth of the indigo-dark night.

'In a garden? Where anyone might see us. Oh, no… If *that* was my intention I would have taken you somewhere far, far more private…'

'Like your official accommodation, you mean?' Petra challenged him bitingly, determined not to let him think that she was in the least bit affected by what he was saying.

'You remind me of a little cat, all sharp claws and defensive temper. Take care that you don't tempt me to teach you how to purr with pleasure and use those claws only in the heat of passion...'

'We aren't in public, yet,' was all Petra could think of to say in retaliation and she mentally blessed the darkness for concealing her hectically flushed face. 'So you can save the practised seduction scenario until we are!'

They had almost crossed the garden now, and the canal lay in front of them. As they reached it Blaize raised his hand to summon one of the gondoliers waiting several yards away.

'This isn't the quickest way to reach the restaurant, but I think it is certainly the most...relaxing,' he informed her in a soft murmur as the gondola was brought to a halt in front of them.

As Blaize helped her into the gondola Petra wondered helplessly if anything could possibly be more romantic— or more hackneyed!

Clever lighting had transformed the daytime appearance of the resort into a place of magic and mystery, designed to appeal to the senses. Strawberry-scented vapour floated over their heads in a pale pink cloud, and in the distance Petra could see and hear fireworks. As they passed the *souq,* a fire-eater performed for a watching group of teenagers whilst a 'merchant' loaded his wares onto a waiting camel train, causing Petra's heart to give a small unsteady thump.

The one thing she wanted to do whilst she was in Zuran was take a trip into the desert. Her aunt might speak enthusiastically about shopping malls and the fabulous gold and diamond *souq,* but it was the desert that called most strongly to Petra in a siren song that whispered to her that to know it was her heritage.

Deep in her own private thoughts, she jumped when Blaize touched her arm. The gondola swung into an ornately decorated private landing from which a red carpet led towards a building so unmistakably Parisian in concept that Petra could only stare at it in bemusement.

Several other people were already standing in front of the entrance to the restaurant, and as she felt Blaize's hands on her body when he helped her from the gondola Petra immediately tensed in rejection of the sexual intimacy, instinctively uncomfortable about other people witnessing it.

'Don't do that!' she protested when Blaize bent his head and allowed his breath to graze intimately against her skin as he brushed her hair from her face. 'The women who paid for your clothes might have enjoyed being pawed in public, but I don't.'

The minute she had finished speaking Petra knew that she had gone too far. It was there in the sudden stiffening of his body and the glacial glitter in his eyes.

It was useless to try to explain that her own panic at her body's helpless reaction to him had motivated her rash words—and besides, her pride would not allow her to do so. So Petra tensed and bent her head beneath the savage lash of his softly spoken retaliation.

'For your information no woman has ever…ever…paid for my clothes. And as for your comment about "pawing"—be thankful that your innocence protects you from the consequences of such a comment—for now!'

In silence, but with her head held high, Petra turned towards the red carpet. Not for anything was she going to admit—even to herself—how much she longed for the protective warmth of Blaize's hand beneath her elbow as she watched the other diners entering the restaurant, the men in their robes and their women couturier-clad and holding themselves with a proud elegance Petra secretly envied.

'More wine?' Blaize asked as their waiter hovered solicitously, holding the wine bottle. Immediately Petra shook

her head and covered her still half-full glass with her hand.
The meal they had just been served had been outstandingly
good—with every mouthful Petra had been reminded of her
first grown-up meal in Paris, a birthday treat from her parents. Everything from the decor and the whole ambience
of the place, right down to the subtle perfume of the candles
on the tables, replicated the chicest of Parisian restaurants,
and Petra knew she would not have been surprised to hear
French itself being spoken.

'Coffee, then?' Blaize was asking as he signalled her
refusal to the hovering waiter.

Nodding her head, Petra warned herself that if she was
not careful she might be in danger of falling for her own
fiction, so well was Blaize playing the part of attentive and
adoring lover. But then, of course, no doubt he had had
plenty of practice, she reminded herself grimly.

Petra dreaded to think about the impact the cost of the
meal was going to make on her credit card, but there was
no way she could feel comfortable allowing it to be debited
to her suite.

As she waited for the waiter to bring her coffee she was
suddenly aware of being studied by the occupants of a
nearby table—a group of three couples.

The arrival of the waiter with her coffee momentarily
distracted her, but as she glanced away from them Petra
could have sworn that Blaize gave the tiniest warning shake
of his head when one of the men started to get up, as though
he was about to come over to their table.

As soon as the waiter had gone, Petra demanded, 'Who
is that…?'

'Who do you mean?' Blaize questioned her, frowning
slightly.

'The man you just looked at,' Petra said. 'He was about to come over, but you—'

'I didn't look at anyone,' Blaize denied.

'Yes, you did,' Petra insisted. 'I saw you…'

'You're imagining things,' Blaize told her. 'Which man do you mean? Point him out to me.'

Irately Petra did so, but when Blaize looked deliberately in his direction the man Petra had pointed out looked pointedly through them before averting his gaze.

Giving her an ironic look, Blaize shrugged his shoulders meaningfully whilst Petra's face burned. She had obviously been wrong after all, but she wasn't going to give Blaize the satisfaction of admitting it!

'When you have finished your coffee perhaps you would like to dance,' Blaize suggested. 'After all, we are supposed to be lovers, despite that virginal look of yours…'

Petra's mouth compressed and she put down her coffee cup with a small clatter.

'That's it!' she told him forcefully. 'From now on every time you so much as mention my…my…the word "virgin" I shall fine you five pounds, and deduct the money from your fee! I am paying you to help me escape from a marriage I don't want. Not to…to keep on bringing up something which has nothing whatsoever to do with our business arrangement!'

'No? I beg to differ,' Blaize informed her softly. 'I am supposed to create the impression that I am seducing you,' he reminded her. 'Who is going to believe that if you insist on looking like a—'

'Five pounds,' Petra warned him.

'Like a woman who does not know what it is to experience a man's passion,' Blaize finished silkily.

She had finished her coffee and Blaize had summoned the waiter to ask for the bill.

Immediately Petra reached for her bag to remove her credit card.

'What are you doing?' Blaize demanded curtly, when he saw what she was doing.

'I can't let my family pay for this. It would be… immoral…' Petra told him.

'Immoral… To allow them to pay for a meal? But not apparently immoral to allow them to believe that you are sleeping with me…a man you picked up on the beach…'

'My body is mine to do with as I wish,' Petra hissed furiously to him as the waiter arrived with the bill. She already had her credit card in her hand, but to her disbelief before she could place it on the saucer Blaize had picked up the bill.

'I shall deal with this,' he told her coolly, 'You may reimburse me later.'

Turning to the discreetly waiting waiter, he murmured something to him that Petra couldn't catch, handing the man the bill which he immediately walked away with.

Several minutes later, as they made their way to the separate music room, Petra felt as though everyone else in the restaurant was watching them. She was being over-sensitive, of course. She knew that. No doubt it was only the female diners who were watching Blaize, she told herself wryly.

The music room and its dance floor were very dimly lit, and as she heard the provocative strains of the sensual music that was being played, watched the way the dancers already on the floor were moving, she automatically pulled back. This wasn't dancing. It was…it was sex on the dance floor—and there was no way *she* was going to allow Blaize to hold *her* like that. No way she dared allow him to hold her like that.

Why not? It wasn't, after all, as though he was her type,

she reminded herself robustly, and she knew that no matter how outwardly sensual and romantic he might appear he felt nothing whatsoever for her. They were here for a purpose, and the sooner it was achieved the sooner she would be free to return home.

Squaring her shoulders, she allowed Blaize to guide her towards the dance floor.

Seconds later, held in his arms, her face pressed into his shoulder whilst his hand smoothed its way down her back, coming to rest well below her waist, Petra acknowledged that she had perhaps been over-confident about her ability to control her body's physical reaction to him.

He was a practised seducer, she told herself in her own defence. A man who had perfected his seduction technique on an unending stream of women…

'Relax… We're supposed to be lovers, remember…'

'I am relaxed,' Petra told him through gritted teeth.

'No, you aren't!' he corrected her. 'You're petrified that I'm going to do something like this to you…'

As he finished speaking he slid his hand into the hair at the nape of her neck, gently tugging her head so that his lips could graze along her throat and then nibble tormentingly against her ear. Just the feel of his breath made her whole body quiver in shocked delight as his thumb tracked the betraying pulse beating increasingly fast at the base of her throat.

'Have you any idea how very, very much I want you…?'

The throaty words he whispered against her mouth caused Petra's eyes to widen—until she remembered that he was simply acting…playing the part she was paying him to play.

'Shall I take you back to your room and show you how much? Remove the clothes from your delectable sexy body and stroke and kiss every inch of it before—'

Petra gasped as he reached for her hand and told her rawly, 'Feel what you're doing to me...'

She tried to pull free but it was too late. He was already placing her hand against his body, and she could feel the heavy thud of his heart against her palm.

'Come closer to me,' he said, drawing her deeper into his embrace, and then whispering, 'Closer than that! So close that I can pretend I have you naked in my arms, your silky skin next to mine...'

Petra knew that the heat filling her could not be blamed on the lack of air in the room, but stubbornly she refused to acknowledge what was really causing both it and the shivery, achy, tight pangs of longing that were running riot inside her body, inciting a rebellion she was terrified she might not be able to control.

Somehow she managed to put enough distance between them, to raise her head and tell him huskily, 'I want to leave.'

'So soon? It's only just gone midnight?'

Petra could feel her panic increasing. If he kept her here on the dance floor, holding her the way he was, for very much longer— It was all very well for her brain to know that he was simply acting, but her body seemed to be finding it almost impossible to differentiate between fact and fiction. It was responding to him as though...as though... she...actually wanted him!

'It's been a long day, and my aunt will probably be telephoning me early in the morning to update me on my grandfather's condition!'

'I thought you weren't interested in his health.'

'I'm not,' Petra denied immediately. 'It's just...'

Blaize had released her now, and was standing in front of her searching her face with far too sharp a gaze. Instinctively Petra wanted to hide herself—and her feelings—from him—to protect herself from something, some-one she was rapidly coming to realise might potentially offer a far more serious threat to her future happiness than she felt comfortable acknowledging.

Why was he affecting her like this? After all, he wasn't the first male she had danced intimately closely with, or been kissed by; he was not even the first male who had caused her to want him! She might not as yet have had a lover, but she knew what it was to feel desire, to feel emo-tionally drawn to someone. She had gone through all the normal early teenage crushes on a variety of male icons, from popstars to football heroes, and she had even fancied herself in love a couple of times. But this was the first time she had been so powerfully and intimately aroused that she felt in fear of not being able to control those feelings!

'It's just what?' Blaize prompted her, breaking into her anxious thoughts.

'I don't want to talk about it,' Petra replied, stubbornly shaking her head.

'Very well, then. If you're sure you want to leave, and you're not just making an excuse to escape from my arms because you're afraid that you might enjoy being there too much...'

Petra glared at him, outwardly angry but inwardly hor-rified by his insouciant comment. He was probably just testing her...teasing her, she reassured herself. After all, he couldn't possible know what she was feeling...could he?

'Oh, I could never do that,' she told him firmly, giving him a carefully manufactured smile as she added sweetly, 'After all, I've never liked crowds!'

She had expected her put-down to silence him, but in-stead he simply demanded softly, 'Meaning?'

'Meaning that the space within your arms is crowded

with the women who have already been there,' Petra answered him forthrightly.

However, instead of being abashed, Blaize simply shrugged and told her carelessly, 'I am thirty-four years old. Naturally there have been…relationships…'

It was on the tip of Petra's tongue to tell him that it wasn't his 'relationships' she was referring to, but the other women whom she suspected had paraded in and out of his life—and his arms—in an unending and highly impermanent line. But instead she simply shook her head and started to walk away from him.

He caught up with her by the door, just as the doorman and his uniformed attendants sprang into action—almost as though they were royalty, Petra thought as she stepped onto the red carpet which led from the restaurant door to the pathway and the car park and canal.

'I think I'd rather be driven back,' Petra announced hurriedly. There was no way, in her present vulnerable mood, that she wanted to share the intimacy of a moonlit gondola ride back to her hotel with Blaize!

She had half expected him to talk her out of her decision, but instead he simply raised his hand to summon one of the waiting buggies.

Their silent return to the hotel was somehow more unnerving for Petra than even those moments on the dance floor. She couldn't understand how it was that a man in Blaize's position, who behaved as he did and who was after all being paid by her, could somehow manage to be so convincingly autocratic and superior!

Once inside the hotel, as he pressed the bell for the lift for her, Blaize told her firmly, 'The more obviously we are seen in public together, the better. So tomorrow I suggest that we make arrangements to that end. There are several organised trips we could take together.'

'Organised trips?' Petra interrupted him, frowning. 'But surely it won't be enough for you to simply be seen with me by my fellow visitors? We need to be seen together by people who are known to Rashid.'

'Zuran is a small place. I am sure that our... friendship...will soon come to his ears,' Blaize replied as the lift arrived.

He stepped into it with her and pressed the button for her floor.

'You don't need to come up with me,' Petra protested immediately, but the doors had already closed and the lift was in motion.

'What is it you are so afraid of?' Blaize mocked her when the lift had stopped. 'That I might kiss you, or that I might not?'

'Neither!' Petra denied forcefully.

'Liar!' Blaize taunted her softly. 'You are a woman, after all, and of course you want—'

'What I want,' Petra interrupted him angrily outside her suite door, 'is for you to remember that I am paying you to act as my lover in public, and that is all!'

As she spoke she was fumbling in her bag for her key card, thankfully finding it and swiping it.

Blaize's hand was on the door handle and Petra held her breath as he pushed the door open. What would she do if he insisted on coming into her room? If he insisted on doing even more than that? Her heart suddenly seemed to have developed an over-fast and erratic heartbeat, and instinctively Petra put her hand on her chest, as if she was trying to steady it.

As he held open the door for her Blaize switched on the suite lights. Petra's mouth felt dry, her body boneless and soft, the blood running hotly through her veins. She closed her eyes and then opened them again as she heard the small but distinctive click of the suite door closing.

Whirling round, she opened her mouth to tell Blaize that she wanted him to leave, and then closed it again as she stared at the empty space between her own body and the closed door where she had expected him to be.

Blaize had gone. He had not come into her suite! He had simply closed the door and left. Which was exactly what she had wanted…wasn't it?

CHAPTER FOUR

PETRA had finished her breakfast and the waiter had cleared away the room service trolley, leaving her with a fresh pot of coffee and the newspaper she had ordered.

She had eaten her breakfast outside on her private patio, in the pleasurable warmth of the early morning sunshine, and by rights she ought to be feeling contently relaxed.

But she wasn't!

Her mobile phone started to ring and she picked it up.

'Petra?'

The unexpected sound of her godfather's voice banished her mood of introspection.

He was ringing from a satellite connection, he told her, and would not be able to stay on the line very long.

'How are you getting on with your grandfather?' he asked.

'I'm not,' Petra responded wryly. 'I haven't even seen him yet. He hasn't been well enough, apparently.'

'Petra—I can't hear you!' She heard her godfather interrupting her, his own voice so faint that she could barely hear it. 'The line's breaking up. I'm going to have to go. I'll be out of contact for the next couple of weeks. Government business...'

A series of sharp crackles distorted his voice so much that Petra couldn't make out what he was saying, although she thought he was telling her that he loved her. Before she could make any response the line had gone dead.

Miserably she stared at the now blank screen. There would be no point in her trying to ring back; she had no idea exactly where her godfather was and she didn't have a number.

It was a pity that she hadn't been able to beg him to send her her passport before the line had broken up! Now her only means of escape from her unwanted marriage was quite definitely via Blaize.

As a tiny shower of tingling excitement skittered dangerously down her spine Petra warned herself that she was being foolish—and gullible! Why had she allowed Blaize to manoeuvre her into agreeing to last night's expensive meal, when surely her purpose could have been just as easily if not even better achieved via a short interlude on the beach with him?

She glanced at her mobile. Perhaps out of good manners she ought to at least telephone to enquire after her grandfather's health. A little nervously Petra dialled the number of the family villa.

An unfamiliar male voice answered, throwing Petra into confusion. Hesitantly she asked for her aunt, and was asked for her own name. Several seconds later Petra breathed out in relief as she heard her aunt's voice.

A little uncomfortably, asked after her grandfather.

'He has had a good night,' her aunt told her. 'But he is still very weak. He insisted on going to morning prayers, although he was not supposed to do so. Unfortunately he had instructed his manservant to drive him there before I realised what was going on. I am so glad that you have rung, Petra. It will mean such a lot to him to know of your concern.'

The genuine warmth and approval in her voice was making Petra feel even more uncomfortable, and rather guilty as well, even though she tried to reassure herself that she had nothing to feel guilty about.

'You are being wonderfully patient,' her aunt continued.

'I promise you it won't be long now before you will be able to see him. I had intended to telephone you myself, to ask if you would like to go round the spice *souq* tomorrow morning, and then perhaps we could have lunch together?'

'I…that sounds very nice,' Petra accepted lamely. Feeling even more uncomfortable and guilty, she quickly ended the call.

She needed to see Blaize, she decided firmly, to make sure that he realised she was the one in charge of things and not him. He had said that he would make contact with her, but she was being driven by a sense of anxious urgency.

She wanted…needed to see Blaize now!

Half an hour later she stood on the beach, trying to cope with the frustration of explaining to the anxious to please lifeguard and the young man who was now in charge of the windsurfers what she wanted. But they didn't seem to recognise Blaize from her description, Petra slowly forced herself to count to ten.

It wasn't their fault that they didn't know Blaize! The fault lay with her, not with them, for not making sure that she was able to get in touch with him. Thanking the two young men for their attempts to help her, she made her way back to her hotel.

It was lunchtime but she wasn't really hungry; the emptiness inside her could not be satisfied with food! She had been infuriated by the way Blaize had tormented her about her virginity, and disturbed by her own physical reaction to him. Of course there was no way she had really wanted him to kiss her last night, but just supposing that he had.

Quickly Petra pressed the lift button, hoping that no one had noticed her flushed face or the fierce shudder that had gripped her body.

What on earth was the matter with her? Petra derided

herself scornfully as the lift carried her smoothly and effortlessly upwards. She might be a virgin but that did not mean she was sexually repressed or unaware—so naïve and vulnerable that all it took to arouse her was one look from a predatory experienced male!

But if Blaize *had* kissed her... If he had then she would have had the common sense to reject him and send him packing, she assured herself firmly. Theirs was a business relationship and that was the way she intended it to stay!

The lift had stopped. She got out and made her way to her suite, holding her breath as she opened the door. But this time there was no virtually naked man reclining on her bed. Much to her relief! Or so she told herself.

Half an hour later she was still trying to decide what she was going to do with the rest of her day. A little restlessly she paced her terrace. She wasn't really in the mood for the beach. The guidebook she had found suggested several walks through the city which took in various points of interest. Quickly she went to find it, picking it up and flicking through it.

There was one walk which took in the older parts of the town, including a tour of the home of a former ruler. It had now been turned into a museum documenting the social, cultural, educational and religious history of the area.

Firmly Petra told herself that it would do her good to have something other than her grandfather and the problems he was causing her to occupy her mind. After changing into a pair of white linen trousers and pulling on a loose long-sleeved cotton top, Petra left her suite.

Outside the afternoon sunshine was strong enough to have her reaching for her sunglasses whilst she waited for the concierge staff to summon her a taxi. Out of the corner of her eye she saw an immaculate shiny black stretch limousine pulling up a few yards away from her.

Curiously she watched as a flurry of anxious attendants hurried to open doors and several very important-looking robed men got out of the vehicle. Watching them discreetly, Petra suddenly stiffened, and then relaxed, shaking her head ruefully. Just for a second she had actually thought that in profile one of the robed men looked like Blaize! How ridiculous! Of course it couldn't possibly be him! It wasn't only her preoccupation with her grandfather she needed to clear out of her thoughts, she told herself grimly as she headed for her waiting taxi.

She had spent so much time inside the museum that outside it was going dark, Petra realised as she drew a deep breath of evening air into her lungs, her head full of everything she had just seen.

It wasn't just Zuran's history and past she had just experienced, it was also part of her own—which of course was why the contents of the museum had so absorbed her. Inside the museum, for the first time she had actually felt a sense of awareness and recognition of her Bedouin roots, and with that the first tentative, uncurling delicate tendrils of belonging. For the first time in her life she was actually recognising and acknowledging that she needed to know more about this country—not just for her mother's sake but for her own.

There was a faint scent on the wind that caused her to lift her head and look towards the desert. There on the wind was the scent of her past, her destiny, and instinctively her senses recognised it. She was part of a proud race of people who had roamed this land when Cleopatra had been Queen, when Marco Polo had made his epic journey along the silk road.

Without thinking about what she was doing Petra

reached down and scooped up a small handful of sand, letting it trickle slowly through her fingers. Her country...

Her eyes blurred with tears. Fiercely she blinked them away.

A group of people hurried past her, accidentally jostling her, and the mood was broken. It was almost dark and she was hungry. She hailed a cruising taxi and gave him the address of her hotel.

Hesitantly, Petra scanned the hotel foyer. She had booked herself a table for dinner at the complex's Italian restaurant, but now, standing in the foyer and realising that she was the only woman there on her own, she was beginning to have second thoughts. But Zuran was an extremely cosmopolitan and safe country, she reminded herself stoutly, and the complex was geared to the needs of the visitor— even a solitary female such as herself.

Tonight she had dressed a little less dramatically, in a simple black linen dress that buttoned down the front. Its neat square neckline showed off the delicate bones at the base of her throat and the proud arch of her neck, just as the plain gold bangle she was wearing on her wrist revealed the fragility of its bone structure. The bangle had originally belonged to her mother, and Petra touched it now, seeking its comforting reassurance.

She wasn't used to dining in public alone but she refused to eat a solitary meal in her suite!

The clerk at the hotel's guest relations desk assured her that she didn't have very far to walk to the Italian restaurant—which, he explained, was situated in its own private courtyard and could be reached on foot or by gondola.

Taking a gondola was too dangerous, Petra decided. It might remind her of last night and Blaize! She started to frown. All day she had been on edge, expecting Blaize to get in touch with her, but he had not done so. Because he had found someone more profitable to spend his time with, both financially and sexually? She had already seen that there was no shortage of admiring women eager for his company.

Pausing in mid-step, Petra firmly reassured herself that the funny little ache she was experiencing had nothing at all to do with any jealousy. Her? Jealous of Blaize's other women? How ridiculous!

The clerk had been right when he had told her that the restaurant wasn't very far away. Petra turned a corner and found herself in the courtyard he had mentioned to her.

The middle of the courtyard was filled with fountains and pools, the jets of water from them making intricate patterns suddenly broken by an unexpected powerful surge that sent one of the jets soaring into the air, much to the delight of a group of watching children who screamed and clapped their hands in excitement.

Smiling indulgently, Petra made her own way towards the restaurant.

Given her previous evening's experience, with the 'Parisian' Michelin-starred restaurant, she supposed she should have expected that the Italian trattoria would be equally authentic, and it certainly was—right down to the strolling musician and the appreciative genuinely Italian waiters, who ushered her to a table and handed her a menu.

Half an hour later, when Petra had just started to relax and feel comfortable as she sipped her wine and enjoyed the seafood starter she had ordered, the restaurant door opened and a group of brashly noisy young men burst in.

Petra could tell from the reactions of the restaurant staff that they were not entirely at ease with the loud-voiced demands of the new arrivals. To Petra, familiar with the behaviour of a certain type of European male, it was obvious that the men had been drinking. Their attitude towards the staff was bordering on the aggressive, and although none of them looked particularly intimidating they were in a pack, and like all pack animals they possessed a certain aura of volatility and danger.

They were speaking in English, demanding that they were given a table large enough to accommodate them all and refusing to listen when the *maître d'* tried to tell them that the restaurant was fully booked.

'Don't give us that, mate,' one of them objected. 'We can see for ourselves that you've got plenty of empty tables.'

Discreetly Petra affected not to notice what was going on when the waiter removed her empty plate and returned with her main course. But as she thanked him for her meal, she suddenly heard one of the men saying, 'Hey, look at that over there—the brunette sitting on her own. We'll have that table there, mate,' he continued, pointing to the empty one next to where Petra was seated.

She tensed warily. She could tell that the *maître d* was trying to persuade them to leave, but it was obvious that they had no intention of doing so. She tried not to betray her discomfort as they surged round her, sitting at three of the tables close to her own so that she was almost surrounded by them.

They were ordering more drinks whilst making crudely off-colour comments about their sexual proclivities and deliberately staring at her, trying to force her to return their eye contact.

Petra wasn't exactly frightened. She lived in London, after all, and considered herself to be relatively streetwise. But in London she would never have been eating on her own, or been in a situation which would have made her so vulnerable.

She was uncomfortably aware of the diners at the two other tables, young couples with children, getting up and leaving, whilst the raucous behaviour of the men around her became even more unpleasant.

Although she hadn't finished her meal, Petra recognised that it was impossible for her to stay. The newcomers were making no attempt to order a meal and instead were becoming even more disorderly. A bread roll flew past her head, quickly followed by another as two men on tables either side of her began to hurl them at one another.

'First to get one down her dress gets a free round!' one of the men sang out.

Petra had had enough.

As calmly as she could she stood up, but to her horror, instead of allowing her to walk past them, the men immediately surrounded her, making openly sexually suggestive comments both to her and about her to one another that made Petra's throat and face burn with disgust and anger.

She could see that the restaurant manager was on the telephone, and the *maître d'* was doing his best to assist her, begging the men to step back otherwise he would have to ask them to leave.

'Going to pick one of us, are you, sweetheart?' the most obnoxious of the gang smirked at Petra. 'Or shall we choose for you? Which one is going to be first, lads?' he demanded, turning to his friends.

The *maître d'* intervened, protesting, 'Please, gentlemen, I must ask you to leave—'

'We aren't going anywhere, mate,' Petra's tormentor told him drunkenly.

'Oh, but I think you are...'

The coolly incisive sound of Blaize's voice cut through

the loud-mouthed vulgarities like tempered steel slicing into flaccid flesh, his appearance shocking Petra even more than it obviously did the gang.

Instinctively she turned towards him, her expression betraying both her disbelief and her fear.

'In fact, I think I can safely say that not only are you going to leave the restaurant, you are going to leave the country as well.'

One of the gang started to laugh.

'Come off it, mate. You can't make us do anything! There's only one of you and a dozen or us, and besides…we're here for the races, see.'

'The restaurant manager has already summoned the police,' Blaize informed them coolly. 'There is a law in this country against men harassing women, and in Zuran laws are reinforced.'

Petra could hear sounds of new arrivals outside the restaurant, and it was obvious so could the gang.

Suddenly they began to look a lot less sure of themselves. Blaize was holding out his hand to her. Shakily Petra pushed her way past the men and went to his side, just as the restaurant door opened and several stern-looking uniformed police officers came in.

'Come on,' Blaize instructed Petra, taking hold of her arm. 'Let's get out of here…'

Petra was only too glad to do so. And only too glad of the protection of his firm grasp on her arm as he ushered her back to her hotel.

She could see the grim look on his face, and the way that his mouth had compressed, somehow making him look very austere and stern.

Once they were inside the hotel, Petra thought she saw him give a small curt nod in the direction of the guest relations desk and the clerk seated there, but as he bustled her towards the lift she decided that she must have imagined it.

As the lift moved upward, Petra expelled a small shaky sigh of relief.

'You don't know how pleased I was to see you—' she began, but Blaize stopped her, his expression forbiddingly grim.

'What the hell where you doing?' he demanded furiously. 'Why didn't you leave? Surely you must have realised...'

The unexpected harshness of his attack coupled with its unfairness shocked her into silence.

The lift stopped and they both got out. Her legs, Petra discovered, were trembling and she felt slightly sick.

Outside her suite, she tried to open her bag to find her key card, but her fingers were shaking so much she dropped it. As she bent down to retrieve it Blaize beat her to it, picking up her bag and opening it. Absently Petra noticed how tiny it looked in his hands. He had well-groomed nails, immaculately clean, and his fingers were long and lean. The fleshy pad just below his thumb mesmerised her, and she couldn't stop staring at it.

Distantly a part of her recognised that she was probably in shock, but that knowledge was too far away and vague for her to really comprehend it. Instead she simply accepted it gratefully as a rational explanation for the tremors that were now beginning to visibly shake her body, and the tight, aching pain that was locking her throat and preventing her from defending herself.

'Do you realise what could have happened if the manager hadn't...?'

'I tried to leave,' Petra told him, suddenly managing to speak. 'But they wouldn't let me.'

They were in the suite and the door was closed. Her

shock suddenly accelerated out of the distance and rico-
cheted towards her. Tears flooded her eyes and her body
shook violently.

'Petra!'

Now the anger she could hear in Blaize's voice sounded
different.

'Petra!'

As he repeated her name he made a sound, somewhere
between a groan and a growl and then suddenly he was
holding her in his arms.

Valiantly Petra forced back her tears. She could feel
Blaize's hand stroking her hair. Tilting back her head, she
looked up at him, and kept on looking, drowning in the
molten mercury glow of his eyes as her lips parted and her
head fell aback against his supporting arm.

'Petra…'

As he lowered his head she could feel the warmth of his
breath tantalising the quivering readiness of her lips. She
had wanted this…him…from the moment she had walked
into her room the previous day and seen him lying on her
bed, she acknowledged dizzily, as she breathed in and felt
the hard pressure of his mouth against her own.

Passion! It was just a word! How could it possibly convey all that she was feeling, all she was experiencing—
every nuance of sensation and emotion that burned and
ached through her as his mouth moved over her own, taking
her deeper and deeper into a world of dark velvet forbidden
pleasure?

There was nothing to warn her when the protective inner
barriers she had erected against him came tumbling down—
no flash of insight, no mental alarm call, no frantic conscience voice. Nothing to impede the delirious intoxication
of her senses running wild, her body clamouring for the
freedom to express its longings!

She could feel his lips moving against her mouth and then her ear as he spoke to her warningly. 'You're in shock, Petra, and this isn't—'

Frantically Petra blotted out what he was trying to say, closing her ears to it and then closing his mouth as she placed her hand against his jaw, moved her mouth back to his, her lips eagerly showing him what she wanted.

She felt him stiffen, heard his indrawn breath and held her own, suddenly sharply aware of his hesitation. But as she leaned against him, her body still trembling, but no longer out of any fear other than that he might leave her, she looked into his eyes and saw the fierce, predatory look of male hunger glittering there, and felt a sweetly powerful sense of female triumph.

She kissed him slowly, and then waited, whilst her glance slid longingly from his eyes to his mouth. Like someone in a dream she reached up and traced its shape with the tip of her finger, and caught her own bottom lip between her teeth as she felt—and saw—the shudder that rocked him.

'This isn't a good idea.' She heard him groan as he lifted her hand from his mouth and pressed a fiercely sensual kiss in its palm. Now his glance was on her face—and not just her face, she recognised as her heart gave a series of heavy, excited thuds when it dropped to her body.

'Why not?' she whispered dangerously back to him.

'Because,' he told her thickly, 'if I touch you now…here…like this…'

Petra quivered violently as his hand barely brushed against her breast and then returned to cup it gently, whilst even more tantalisingly his thumb rubbed slowly across her taut nipple.

'Then,' Blaize was continuing huskily, 'I shall need to touch you again and again, and then I will have to…'

Her flesh was melting like ice cream covered in the sensuality and irresistibility of pure hot chocolate, Petra decided, and what Blaize was doing to her was making her long to have his hands…his body against her own body. Her naked body…

The small sound of longing she made was smothered by the heat of his kiss. The sound of their mutually charged breathing filled the room, and then, disconcertingly, Petra heard the mood-destroying clatter of the fax machine. Automatically she tensed, just as Blaize released her and then stepped back from her.

'That should not have happened,' she heard him saying tersely as he turned his back to her. 'It isn't part of our deal.'

Not part of their deal! Chagrin, discomfort, shame and angry humiliation—Petra felt them all in an icy shock wave that brought her back to reality.

Stiffly she headed for the fax machine, more to give herself something to do than because she was anxious to read its message. When she eventually managed to get her gaze to bring it into focus properly, through the turbulence of her thoughts, it turned out to be merely a flyer from a local tour company, highlighting one of their special offers.

As she focused on the wavering print, willing herself not to turn round and look at Blaize, she heard the door to her suite quietly open and then close again.

Even though she continued to focus on her fax message Petra knew just from the feel of the air around her that Blaize had left.

Some time…one day, maybe…she would be glad that this had happened, she told herself fiercely. She would be glad that they had been interrupted and that he had left her! One day. But not now!

CHAPTER FIVE

MISERABLY Petra pushed her uneaten breakfast away and focused determinedly on the brilliantly sunlit scene beyond the windows of the hotel's breakfast room.

She had decided to eat here this morning rather than on her own in her room, primarily because she had hoped that the busyness of having other people around her would take her mind off the events of the previous evening—and Blaize.

Blaize! Every time she thought about him—which was far, far too often for her own peace of mind, she was swamped by opposing feelings of longing and angry self-contempt, plus a sense of bewilderment and disbelief that she could have ever got herself in such a situation. How could she possibly want him?

Petra frowned as she glanced from the informal breakfast dining area into the hotel foyer, which this morning seemed to be filled with far more uniformed and slightly on edge-looking members of staff than she could remember seeing there before.

The waiter had come to clear away her virtually untouched breakfast, and to spend time before going to meet her aunt Petra walked over to study the board outside a small private office, advertising the trips organised by the hotel. One in particular caught her eye, and she read the details of it a second and then a third time.

An escorted drive into the desert, plus an overnight stay at an exclusive oasis resort where it was possible to experience the wonder and majesty of the desert at first hand!

The desert... Quickly, before she could change her mind, Petra went into the office, emerging ten minutes later having made herself a booking. A full night away from Blaize should surely give her time to assess the damage her physical reaction to him was having on her moral beliefs and get herself back in balance again—give her some 'time out'.

As she walked towards the foyer a subtle voice whispered inside her head that there was an even more reckless and dangerous way of stopping a conflagration in its tracks: namely fighting fire with fire. But by using what? Her own sexual need to destroy itself? As in not just giving in to it but actively encouraging it, fanning it into an inferno that would turn and destroy itself?

There was just enough time for her to go to her suite and tidy up before meeting her aunt. Petra smiled at the nervous-looking group of uniformed staff hovering close to the private lift that went to the penthouse suite.

'Everyone looks very busy today,' she commented.

One of the uniformed men rolled his eyes and explained in a semi-hushed whisper. 'There is a meeting upstairs of the hotel owners.'

The hotel owners. Petra's heart did a nervous little shimmy. Did that mean that Rashid had returned? And if he had how long would it be before he sought her out?

'Mmm...it smells heavenly,' Petra acknowledged with a smile as she sniffed the golden nugget of frankincense her aunt was holding out to her. They were in the spice market, where her aunt had haggled determinedly and very professionally for some spices before picking up the frankincense and offering it to Petra to smell. A little wonderingly now, Petra studied the nugget in her hand.

There was something really awesome about standing

here in the new millennium handling something which had been familiar to people from civilisations so ancient it was barely possible to comprehend the time that separated them. There was something about this land that did that to a person, Petra recognised as she handed the nugget back to the robed vendor, nodding her head in agreement as her aunt suggested a cooling glass of pressed fruit juice.

'I have some good news for you.'

Petra saw that her aunt was beaming, as she handed Petra her drink.

'Your grandfather is feeling much better and he has asked me to invite you to visit him this afternoon.'

Petra almost spilled her drink. Was it merely a coincidence that her grandfather should invite her to visit him at the same time as Sheikh Rashid had returned to Zuran? Her body stiffened defensively.

'I'm sorry, but I'm afraid that won't be possible. I…I have other plans.' Petra was proud of the way she managed to keep her voice so calm and cool, even though she was unable to either meet her aunt's eyes or prevent herself from turning her glass round and round in her hands.

She could sense from the quality of silence that her response was not the one her aunt had been expecting, and immediately she felt guilty and uncomfortable. The last thing she wanted to do was upset or offend her aunt, who had been unstintingly kind to her—but she knew just what her grandfather's real plans for her were, Petra firmly reminded herself.

Her aunt was smiling, but Petra could see that her smile was a little strained.

'Your grandfather will be disappointed, Petra,' her aunt told her quietly. 'He has been looking forward to meeting you, but of course if you are busy…'

'I…I have arranged to take a trip into the desert tomorrow,' Petra heard herself explaining, almost defensively, 'and there are things I need to do beforehand...'

A little gravely her aunt inclined her head in acknowledgement of Petra's explanation.

Her aunt insisted on accompanying Petra back to her hotel, but once there refused Petra's suggestion of a cup of coffee.

Her aunt was on the verge of stepping into the taxi the concierge had summoned for her when, on some instinct she couldn't begin to understand, Petra suddenly hurried after her, telling her huskily, 'I've changed my mind. I...I will come and see my grandfather...'

Petra sank her teeth into her bottom lip, mortified by her own weakness as her aunt beamed her approval and gave her a warm hug.

'I know this cannot be easy for you, Petra, but I promise you your grandfather is not an ogre. He has your best interests at heart.'

A tiny little trickle of warning ran down Petra's spine as she absorbed her aunt's unwittingly ominous words. But it was too late for her to recall her change of mind now.

'Your grandfather rests after lunch, but I shall arrange for a car to collect you and bring you to the villa to see him. The driver will pick you up here at four thirty, if that is convenient?'

There was nothing Petra could do other than nod her head.

She had been half expecting that Blaize would try to make contact with her—after all she had as yet still not paid him anything for his services—but there were no messages waiting for her, and no Blaize either!

Petra tried to tell herself that the lurching sensation inside her chest was simply because she was anxious to discuss the day's developments with him—on a purely business basis, of course—and to determine what course of action should follow. It was only natural, surely, that she should feel both anxiety and a sense of urgency now that Sheikh Rashid had returned. And as for last night—well, what was a kiss, after all? If she had blown both it and her reaction to it a little out of proportion, only she knew it! She wasn't so naïve as to deceive herself that kissing her had meant anything special to Blaize.

So why hadn't he been in touch with her? And why hadn't she insisted on him furnishing her with a means of getting in touch with him?

It was gone two o'clock, but despite the fact that she had not been able to eat her breakfast she did not feel hungry. Her stomach was churning in apprehensive anticipation of her coming meeting with her grandfather, and her tension was turned up an unpleasant few notches by the added anxiety of Rashid's return and the lack of contact from Blaize.

It was time for her to get changed, ready for her meeting with her grandfather. Petra hesitated as she surveyed the contents of her wardrobe. The linen dress and jacket would be a good choice, modest but smart, or perhaps the cool chambray…or… Her hand trembled slightly as she removed a plain dark trouser suit from the cupboard. Simply cut in, a matt black fabric it was an outfit that would always be very special to her. It was the suit her mother had bought her just weeks before her death—a good luck present to Petra for her pre-university interviews.

Instead of wearing it for her interviews, Petra had actually worn it for her parents' funeral. But whenever she touched the soft fabric it wasn't that bleak, shocking day she remembered, but the teasing love in her mother's eyes as she had marched her into the boutique and told her that she was going to buy her a present—the happiness and pride in her smile as she'd insisted that Petra parade in front of her in virtually every suit in the shop before she had finally decreed that this particular one was the right one.

This suit held her very last physical memory of her mother's touch and her mother's love, and sometimes Petra would almost swear she could even smell her mother's scent on it—not the rich Eastern perfume that had always been so much a part of her, but *her* scent, her essence.

Sharp tears pricked Petra's eyes. Her mother might not be here with her now, but in wearing this suit Petra somehow felt that she was taking a part of her at least with her— that they were both together, confronting the man who had caused her so much pain.

The suit still fitted, and in fact if anything was perhaps slightly loose on her, Petra acknowledged as she studied her reflection in the mirror.

It was almost half past four. Time to go down to the foyer.

Her business-like appearance attracted several discreet looks as she made her way to the exit. Once again a red carpet was very much in evidence, leading to where several huge shiny black limousines were waiting, flags flying.

Petra studied them with discreet curiosity as she waited for her own transport to arrive, but her interest in the limousines and their potential occupants was forgotten as a sleek saloon car pulled up in front of her and her cousin Saud got out of the front passenger seat, grinning from ear to ear as he hurried towards her.

As she hugged him, Petra was vaguely aware of a sudden stir amongst the limousine chauffeurs, and the emergence of a group of immaculately robed men from the private entrance. But it was Saud who stopped to gaze at the group, grabbing hold of her arm as he told her in an excited voice, 'There's Rashid—with his great-uncle.'

'What? Where?' Her heartbeat had gone into overdrive, but as Petra craned her neck to look in the direction Saud was pointing the last of the robed men was already getting into the waiting limousine.

'Have you met him yet?' Saud demanded as the cars pulled away 'He's cool, isn't he…?'

Petra suppressed her grim look. It was becoming plain to her that her young cousin hero-worshipped her proposed suitor.

'No, I haven't,' she answered him, getting into the waiting car. But as they drove away from the hotel a sudden thought struck her. 'So, was Rashid wearing robes?'

'Yes that's right,' Saud confirmed.

'Despite his Western upbringing?'

Saud looked baffled. 'Yes,' he agreed, then smiled. 'Oh, I see! Rashid's father and his uncle—who is a member of our Royal Family—were very, very close. Rashid's great-uncle has acted as a…a sponsor to Rashid since his parents' death—they were killed when their plane crashed in the desert. I do not remember, since I was not even born then and Rashid himself was only young, but I have heard my father and my grandfather talk of it. Rashid was away in England at the time, at school, but his great-uncle welcomed him into his own family as though Rashid were his son. It is a great honour to our family that his great-uncle favours Rashid's marriage to you. It is just as well that you are a modest woman though, cousin, because Rashid does not approve of the behaviour of some of the tourists who come here to Zuran,' Saud told her.

'Oh, doesn't he?' She demanded with dangerous softness. 'And what about his own behaviour? Is that—'

'Rashid is a very moral man—everyone who knows him knows that. He has very strong values. Zara, my friend and second cousin, says that she feels embarrassed for her own sex when she sees the way that women pursue him. He is very rich, you know, and when they come to the hotel complex and see him they try to attract his attention. But he is not interested in them. Zara says that this is because...' He paused with a self-conscious look in Petra's direction, but she was too infuriated by his naïve revelations to pay much attention.

'Rashid is a very proud man and he would never permit himself or anyone connected with him to do anything to damage the name of his family,' Saud continued solemnly.

At any other time Saud's youthful fervour and seriousness would have brought an amused and tender smile to Petra's lips, but right now his innocent declaration had really got her back up and reinforced her fast-growing animosity to this as yet unmet man, who had patronisingly deigned to consider her as a potential wife.

Well, he was going to discover in no uncertain terms, and hopefully very soon, that she was exactly the type of woman he most despised!

In fact, Petra reflected grimly, the more she heard about Sheikh Rashid the more she knew that there was no way she could ever want to marry him!

They had reached the family villa now, and Petra held her breath a little as they drove through the almost fortress-like entrance into the courtyard that lay beyond it.

Her grandfather insisted on remaining in what had been the family's original home when Zuran had been a trading port and the family rich merchants—although, as her aunt had explained to her, in recent years Petra's uncle had persuaded him to add a large modern extension to the villa. In this older part, though, traditional wind towers still decorated the roofline.

The family no longer adopted the traditional custom of separate living quarters for women, as Petra's mother had told her had been the case when she was a girl, but her aunt quickly explained to Petra, once she had been ushered inside to a cool, elegantly furnished salon, that her grandfather still preferred to keep his own private quarters.

'Kahrun, his manservant, will take you to him,' her aunt informed her. 'He has been very ill, Petra,' she continued hesitantly, 'and I would ask that you…make allowances for…for his ways, even though they are not your own. He loved your mother very much, and her death…' She paused and shook her head whilst Petra forced herself to bite back on her instinctive fierce need to question what her aunt was saying.

A maid arrived with a welcome drink of strong fragrant coffee. Her mother had never lost her love of the drink, and just to smell it reminded Petra so much of her.

Several minutes later, when Petra had refused a second cup, a soft-footed servant arrived and bowed to her, before indicating that she was to follow him.

Her heart thudding but her head held high, Petra did so. They seemed to traverse a maze of corridors before he finally paused outside a heavily carved pair of wooden doors.

The room beyond them was cool and shadowy, its narrow windows overlooking an enclosed garden from which Petra could hear the sound of water so beloved by desert people. The air inside the room smelled of spices—the frankincense she had breathed in this morning, and sandalwood, bringing back to her vivid memories of the small box in which her mother had kept her most precious memories of her lost home and family.

As her emotions momentarily blurred her vision it was impossible for Petra to fully make out the features of the man reclining on the divan several feet away from her.

She could hear him, though, as he commanded, 'Come closer to me so that I may see you. My doctor has forbidden me to overtire myself and so I must lie on this wretched divan on pain of incurring his displeasure.'

Petra heard the small snort of derisive laughter that accompanied the complaint as she blinked away her emotional reaction.

Her mother had described her father in terms that had conjured up for Petra a mental vision of a man who was cruelly strong and stubborn—a man who had overwhelmed and overpowered her mother emotionally—and now that her vision was clearing she had expected to see all those things reflected in him now. But the man in front of her looked unexpectedly frail. One long-fingered hand lay on top of the richly embroidered coverlet, and Petra could see in his profile the pride her mother had described to her so often. But in the dark eyes whose scrutiny seemed to search her face with avid hunger she could see nothing of the rejection and anger that had hurt her mother so badly.

'I don't look very much like my mother,' Petra told him coolly.

'You do not need to look like her. You are of her, and that is enough. Child of my child! Blood of my blood! I have waited a very long time for you to come here to me, Petra. Sometimes I have feared that you would not come in time, and that I would never know you with my outer senses. Although I have always known you with my heart. You are wrong,' he added abruptly, his voice suddenly stronger. 'You are very like my Mija. She was the child of my heart—my youngest child. Her mother was my third wife.'

Angrily Petra looked away.

'You do not approve. No, do not deny it—I can see it in your eyes. How they flash and burn with your emotions! In that too you are like your mother.'

Petra couldn't trust herself to speak.

It had shocked her, though, to realise how frail he looked. She had known that he would be old—he had been in his forties when her mother had been born—but somehow she had convinced herself that he would still be the strong, fierce man her mother had remembered from her own childhood. Not this obviously elderly white-bearded person whose dark eyes seemed to hold a mixture of compassion and understanding that unsettled her.

Somehow the curt words she had intended to speak to him, the demands she had planned to make to know just why he had wanted to see her, the cynicism and contempt she had planned to let him see, refused to be summoned.

Instead…instead…

As she lifted her hand the gold bangle caught the light. Immediately her grandfather stiffened.

'You are wearing Mija's bracelet,' he whispered. 'It was my last gift to her… I have a photograph of her here, wearing it.'

To Petra's astonishment he reached out and picked up a heavy photograph album which Petra hadn't previously noticed, beckoning her to come closer so that she could see what he wanted to show her.

As his frail fingers lifted the pages Petra felt her heart turn over. Every photograph in the book was of her mother, and some of them…

She could feel her eyes starting to burn with tears as she recognised one of them. It was a photograph of herself as a very new baby with her mother. Her father had had exactly the same picture on his desk, in the room which had been his office when he'd worked at home!

Immediately she put out her hand to stop him from turning any more of the pages, unable to stop herself from demanding in a shaky voice, 'That photograph—how…?'

'Your father sent it to me,' he told her. 'He sent me many photographs of you, Petra, and many letters, too.'

'My father!' This was news to Petra, and it took her several minutes to absorb it properly. It was hard enough to accept that her father could have done such a thing, but what was even harder was knowing that he had kept his actions a secret from her. And from her mother? Petra felt cold. Surely not? What could have motivated him when he had known how badly her mother had been hurt by her father's actions?

As her glance met that of her grandfather Petra knew that he could see what she was thinking.

A little awkwardly he beckoned her to move closer to him. When she hesitated, he told her, 'There is a box, over there. I would like you to bring it to me.'

The box in question was sitting on an intricately carved table, its surface smooth and warm to Petra's touch. She could tell just by looking at it that it was very old.

'This belonged to my own grandfather,' her grandfather said as she took it to him.

'He was a merchant and this box went everywhere with him. He said that it had originally been made for one of the sultans of the great Ottoman Empire.' He gave a small smile. 'He was a great story-teller, and many times as a small child I would neglect my lessons to sit at his feet and listen to his tales. Whether they were true or not!'

As he was speaking he was reaching for a heavy bunch of keys, searching through them until he found the one he was looking for.

His fingers, obviously stiffened by old age, struggled to insert the key in the tiny lock and then turn it, but once he had done so and pushed back the lid Petra was aware of the mingled scents of sandalwood and age that rose from its interior.

She couldn't see what was inside the box, but waited patiently as her grandfather sighed and muttered to himself, obviously sifting through its contents until he had finally found what he wanted.

'Read this,' he commanded her brusquely, handing her a worn airmail envelope.

'It is your father's letter to me, telling me of your birth.'

Hesitantly Petra took the envelope from him. She wasn't sure she was ready to read what her father might have written. All her life she had looked up to him as a man of strong sturdy morals and infinite compassion, a man of the highest probity and honour. If she should read something that damaged that belief...

'Read,' her grandfather was urging her impatiently.

Taking a deep breath, Petra did so.

The letter was addressed to her grandfather with true diplomatic formality, using his titles.

'To he who is the father of my beloved wife Mija,

I have the felicitation of informing you that I am now the proud father of the most beautiful baby daughter. I had thought when Mija came into my life that there could be no place in it to love another human being, so great and all-encompassing is my love for her, but I was wrong. I write to you now as one father to another to tell you of the most wonderful, precious gift we have received in Petra's birth, and to tell you also that we now share common ground—we are both fathers—we have both been granted the unique privilege of being gifted with daughters.

And it is as a father that I write to you begging you to reconsider your decision regarding the exclusion of Mija from your family—for your own sake and not ours. I have made a solemn vow that I shall surround Mija with all the love she will ever need. We have each other and our beautiful daughter and our lives will be filled with love and joy. But what of you? You have turned away your own daughter and denied yourself her love and that of the grandchild she has given you.

I beg you to think of this and to put aside your pride. I know how much it would mean to Mija to have word from you, especially at this time.

Whatever your decision, I have made a vow to my daughter that I shall ensure that you, her grandfather, and the rest of the family are kept informed of her life.

The letter bore her father's formal signature at its end, but Petra could barely focus on it as the paper trembled in her hand and her eyes stung with tears. It shamed her that she could have doubted her father for so much as a single heartbeat.

As he took the letter from her, returning it to its envelope and replacing it carefully in the box before relocking it, her grandfather said gruffly, 'Your father was a good man, even though he was not the man I would have chosen for my Mija.'

'My father was a wonderful, wonderful, very special man,' Petra corrected him proudly.

Had her mother known what her father had done? If so she had never spoken of it to her, but then neither had her father! Suddenly, despite her private knowledge of her grandfather's secret purpose in wanting her here in Zuran, she was glad that she had come!

'He understood my feelings as a father,' her grandfather acknowledged.

Petra had to close her eyes to conceal the intensity of the emotions that rushed over her.

'You say that now! You claim to have loved my mother.

But you never made any attempt to contact her—to…'
Petra refused to say the word 'forgive', because so far as
she was concerned her mother was the one who had the
right to extend that largesse, not her grandfather! 'You must
have known how much it would have meant to her to hear
from you!'

Impossible for her to hold back her feelings—or her
pain—any longer. Petra knew that her grandfather must be
able to hear it in her voice just as she could herself.

'When she left you told her that you would never permit
her name to be spoken in your hearing ever again. You said
that she was dead to you and to her family, and you forbade
them to have anything to do with her. You let her die—'

Petra heard herself sobbing like a lost child. 'You let her
die believing that you had stopped loving her! How could
you do that?'

As Petra fought for self-control she could see the pain
shadowing her grandfather's eyes, and suddenly it seemed
as though he shrunk a little, and looked even older and
more fragile than he had done when she had first walked
into the room.

'There is nothing I can say that will ease your pain. No
words I can offer you will lighten either your burden—or
my own,' she heard him saying sombrely. 'It is still too
soon. Perhaps in time… But at my age time is no longer
either a friend or an ally. I am sorry that we have not been
able to make you properly welcome here in your mother's
home, Petra, but now that that old fool my doctor has
ceased his unnecessary fussing I shall give instructions that
a room is to be prepared for you. We have much to discuss
together, you and I.'

Like his desire to see her married to the man of his
choice? Petra wondered suspiciously, abruptly back on her
guard; he might look frail and sorrowful now, but she

couldn't forget the cunning and deceit which history had already proved him capable of.

And once she was living here beneath his roof she would virtually be a prisoner. With no passport she had no means of leaving the country! Which meant it was imperative that she persisted with her plan to have Rashid refuse to consider her as a wife.

Even if that meant seeing Blaize again and the risk that could entail?

Unable to give herself a truly rational answer, Petra diverted her own thoughts by telling her grandfather, in a cool voice she intended would make him fully aware of her determination to retain her independence, 'I have made arrangements for an overnight trip into the desert tomorrow, so—'

'The desert!' To her surprise, his eyes lit up with pleasure and approval. 'It is good that you wish to see the land that is so much a part of your heritage. I wish that it was possible for me to go with you! But you shall tell me all about it! I shall inform your hotel that Kahrun will be collecting you to bring you here once you return.'

He was beginning to look tired, but instinctively Petra sensed that his pride would not allow him to admit any weakness. Whatever else she had been lied to about, Petra could see now that so far as his health was concerned he had genuinely been ill. It was there in the greyish tinge to his skin, the vulnerability of his frail frame. An unexpected—and unwanted—emotion filled her: a sense of kinship and closeness, an awareness of the blood tie they shared that she simply had not been prepared for and which it seemed she had no weapons to fight against. He was her grandfather, the man who had given life to the mother she had loved so much, a potential bridge via which she could recapture and relive some of her most precious memories.

Swallowing against the lump in her throat, Petra got up, and as her grandfather reached out his hands to her, Petra placed hers in them.

'Beloved child of my beloved child,' he whispered brokenly to her, and then the door opened and Kahrun, his manservant, arrived to escort her back to the hotel.

It was only when she was finally being driven back to her hotel by Kahrun that Petra mentally questioned just why she had not challenged her grandfather with her knowledge of his plans for her. Had the emotions he had displayed been genuine and as overwhelming as they had seemed? Or had he simply been manipulating the situation and her for his own ends? Surely she wasn't foolish enough to be influenced by her own unwilling acknowledgement of his frailty, a long-ago letter from her father, and a few emotional words?

But there was more to the situation than that! A lot more! In his presence, in the home which had once been her mother's, Petra had abruptly been forced to recognise and acknowledge a deep subterranean pool of previously hidden emotions.

Her parents' deaths had forced her to grow up very quickly, to become mature whilst she was still very young, and in many ways had forced her to become her own parent. Her godfather, kind though he was, was a bachelor, a man dedicated to his career, who had had no real idea of the emotional needs of a seventeen-year-old girl. Had she been a different person, Petra knew, she might quite easily have gone off the rails. Her godfather's lifestyle meant that she had been allowed a considerable amount of unsupervised freedom, and she had been called upon to make decisions about her life and her future that should more properly have been made by someone far more adult. The result of this had been that she'd had to 'police' her own behaviour, and to take responsibility for herself, emotionally and morally.

Now, today, in her grandfather's room, she had suddenly realised just what a heavy burden those responsibilities had been, and how much she had yearned to have someone of her own to carry them for her—to counsel and guide her, to protect her, to love her! How much, in fact, she had needed the family which had been denied to her! And how much a small, weak part of her still did...

That was where her real danger lay, she recognised. It lay in her wanting the approval and acceptance of her 'family' so much that she could fall into the trap of allowing herself to exchange her freedom and independence for them!

The weight of her own thoughts was beginning to make her head ache.

CHAPTER SIX

GRIMLY Petra blinked the slight grittiness from her eyes as she studied her reflection in her bedroom mirror. She had barely slept, and when she had she had been tormented by confusing dark-edged dreams in which she was being pursued by a white-robed persecutor, his features hidden from her. In her nightmare she had called out to Blaize to rescue her, but although she could see him he had not been paying any heed to her pleas, had instead been engrossed with the scantily clad bevy of women surrounding him.

Only once had he actually turned to look at her, and then he had shaken his head and told her cruelly, 'Go away, little virgin. I do not want you.'

And now, even though the night was over, Petra felt as though its dark shadow still hung over her. There was hardly any time left for her to convince Rashid that she was not a suitable bride, and once again Blaize had made no attempt to get in touch with her.

Lethargically she moved away from the mirror. She had already packed an overnight bag, as instructed by the fax she had received from the tour operator, and she was dressed in what she hoped would be a suitable outfit of short-sleeved tee shirt and a pair of khaki combat-style pants with sturdy and hopefully sand-proof trainers. She had, as instructed, a long-sleeved top to cover her arms from the heat and the sand, a hat, a pair of sunglasses and a large bottle of water. But the sense of adventure and intrigue with which she had originally booked the trip had gone, leaving in its place a lacklustre feeling of emptiness.

Because she hadn't heard from Blaize? A man she had known less than a week? A man who quite patently cynically used his sexuality to fund a lifestyle that was in direct opposition to everything that Petra herself believed in! She couldn't possibly really be trying to tell herself that she was emotionally attracted to him? That in such a short space of time he had become so necessary to her that a mere twenty-four hours without him had left her feeling that her whole life was empty and worthless?

Now she was afraid, Petra admitted shakily, and with good reason! What she was thinking truly was cause for the horrified chills running down her spine! There was no way she could allow herself to be in love with Blaize.

Be in love? Since when had love entered the equation? she tried to mock herself.

Only two days ago she had been finding it hard to admit that she just might find him sexually attractive. Two days before that she had barely known that he existed. Yet here she was, trying to talk herself into believing she loved him! No, not trying to talk herself into it, trying to talk herself *out* of it, Petra corrected herself swiftly.

Her telephone rang. Quickly she picked up the receiver. It was the front desk informing her that her transport had arrived.

Picking up her overnight bag, Petra told herself sternly that a little breathing space would do her good. What a pity she was living in the modern century, though, and not a previous one where it might have been possible for a traveller attached to a camel train to pass through a country's borders without the necessity of producing a passport…

A group of newly arrived holidaymakers were filling the foyer, and the concierge staff had no time to do anything more than point Petra in the direction of the waiting vehicle she could see outside, a logo painted on its side.

Even with her sunglasses the sunlight was so strong that she was momentarily blinded as she headed for the four-wheel drive vehicle, and it was whilst she was still trying to accustom her eyes to the brilliance that she felt strong hands relieve her of her overnight bag, and then grasp her waist to help her into the front passenger seat of the vehicle.

She heard the slam of the passenger door, and then the closing rear door. As her driver climbed into the driving seat she turned her head to look at him, her eyes widening in shock as she realised just who her driver was!

'Blaize!' she exclaimed weakly. 'What are you doing here?'

Petra tried to drag her gaze away from him as she gulped in air. Her chest had gone so tight it hurt, and she could feel the heat surging through her body as it reacted with telltale swiftness to his presence.

'You booked a trip into the desert,' he told her laconically as he set the vehicle in motion and drove off.

'Yes… But…'

'But what?' he challenged her with an almost bored shrug. 'I thought it made more sense for me to take you. The desert can be a very seductive place, so I've been told, and your intended isn't going to like knowing that his bride-to-be has spent the night in the desert with another man. How did you get on with your grandfather? Is all forgiven?' he asked her flippantly.

'My mother is the one who is owed forgiveness,' Petra told him quietly. 'And she died believing that he had stopped loving her.'

There was a small silence before Blaize responded in a voice that sounded unfamiliarly serious.

'Then I imagine that your grandfather will find it extremely difficult to forgive himself.'

'His feelings are of no concern to me!' Petra told Blaize

angrily, and then stopped speaking as an inner voice told her that she was not being entirely truthful. 'I thought that he was pretending to be ill,' she heard herself telling Blaize.

'And was he?' he asked.

'No,' Petra acknowledged. 'But that still does not mean he has the right to do what he is trying to do to me—use me for his own selfish ends.'

'Perhaps he thinks this marriage will be beneficial for you,' Blaize suggested. 'His generation still believe that a woman needs a protector, a husband, and it would keep you here, close to your mother's family, and provide for you financially.'

'What?' Petra stared at him in disbelief. 'How can you say that after what I have told you? My feelings…my needs…are the last thing he is thinking about.'

'You mean *you* believe they are! If you were to leave Zuran now, what would you do…where would you go?'

Petra glared at him. Why was he suddenly trying to play the devil's advocate? For amusement?

'I would go home…to the UK. I'm twenty-three, and although I have a good degree I would like to get my Master's. There's so much social inequality in the world that needs addressing—working in the field for the aid agency showed me that. I would like to do something to help other people.'

'As a rich man's wife you could do far more than as a mere fieldworker.'

'I've already told you—I could never marry a man I did not love and respect. And from what Saud has told me it sounds as though I would be expected to treat Rashid as though he's a minor god! Saud hero-worships him, and can't wait for me to marry him so that he can officially claim Rashid as a relative. And of course he isn't the only one! From the sound of it, my whole family are delirious with joy at the prospect of this marriage. All I seem to hear is ''Rashid this'' and ''Rashid that''…'

'Your cousin seems to be a positive wealth of information about the man.'

There was a certain dryness in Blaize's voice that made Petra frown a little. 'Saud is young and impressionable. Like I said, he obviously hero-worships Rashid, and thinks he can do no wrong.'

'A young person sometimes benefits from a role model and mentor.'

'Oh, I agree. But if a man who quite plainly divides women into two separate groups—good and bad, moral and immoral—whilst no doubt maintaining for himself the right to live exactly as he chooses, is not, in my opinion, a good role model—'

'If you look to your left now, you might just catch a glimpse of the royal horses being exercised,' Blaize interrupted her calmly.

Stopped in mid-tirade, Petra was tempted to continue with her diatribe—but then she saw the horses and their jockeys, and the sheer thrill of seeing so much power and beauty kept her silent as she inwardly paid homage to the spectacle they created.

'You are still totally opposed to this marriage, then, I take it?' Blaize asked her several minutes later.

'Of course. How could I not be? I can't marry a man I don't love.'

'You might find you could come to love him after the marriage.'

Petra gave him a scornful look.

'Never,' she denied vehemently. 'And anyway even if I did, I somehow doubt that the Sheikh is likely to return my feelings. No, all our marriage would mean to him would be the successful conclusion to a diplomatic arrangement.

I've got to make him change his mind and refuse to even countenance the idea.'

'Have you thought that he may feel the same way about this situation as you do yourself? Have you thought of contacting him and perhaps discussing things with him?'

Petra gave him a withering look.

'Unlike me, he has had the chance to refuse to become involved! After all, without his tacit acceptance the whole situation could simply not exist. Anyway, why are you suddenly so keen to promote him? Don't you want to earn five thousand pounds any more?' she demanded.

Or was it perhaps that he wanted her out of his life because he had sensed how she felt about him? A man like him would quite definitely not want the complications of having a woman fall in love with him!

Fall in love? But she hadn't done that, had she? Petra closed her eyes in helpless self-anger. Hadn't she got enough unwanted emotional pain to carry through life as excess baggage already, without deliberately inviting more?

'Hang on tight. We'll be leaving the highway soon and going into true desert terrain,' Blaize warned her, without taking his eyes off the road.

Petra gasped and clung to her seat as they veered off the road and crested the first of a series of sand dunes, following what to her was a barely discernible track—although Blaize did not seem to be having any trouble in finding and following it.

Within minutes it seemed to Petra the road had vanished and the landscape had become a vast expanse of sand dunes, stretching from horizon to horizon. A little anxiously she swivelled round in her seat, craning her neck to look in the direction they had just come.

'How...how do you know the way?' she asked Blaize a little uncertainly.

'I can tell the direction we are travelling by the position of the sun,' he said with a small dismissive shrug, and then added derisively, 'And besides, these all-terrain vehicles are equipped with navigation systems and a compass. Essential in this type of country. A bad sandstorm can not only reduce visibility to nought, it can also wipe out existing trails. See that over there?' he commanded, pointing in the direction of where a bird was hovering motionless, a mere dot in the hot blue emptiness of the sky.

'What is it?' Petra asked him.

'A hunting falcon,' he told her, reaching into the compartment between them. As he did so his fingertips inadvertently brushed against her knee and immediately her body reacted, pouring a lava hot molten tide of sharp longing through her. Petra could feel her whole body tightening in wanton hunger for him. If she turned to him now, covered his hand with her own, his mouth with her own; if she reached out and touched him as she wanted him to touch her… But it was too late. He had already moved away and was producing a pair of binoculars, which he offered to her. Binoculars! When what she wanted him to offer her was…was himself!

'Take a closer look,' he instructed her. 'It will probably be a trained bird. A number of Zuran's richest inhabitants maintain their own falconries, where birds are reared and trained. It's an ancient craft which is still practised here.'

As Petra watched the bird suddenly turned and wheeled and was quickly out of sight, as though responding to some unseen summons.

'They often have displays of falconry at the desert village where we'll be spending the night,' Blaize informed her. 'Most people find the birds too fearsome to approach, but in actual fact the camels are probably more dangerous.'

'So my mother told me,' Petra replied.

She was finding it a little disconcerting that Blaize, the beach bum, should so suddenly and unexpectedly prove to be so knowledgeable about the local culture and history. Not wanting to be outdone, she was quick to remind him that she was, after all, a part of that culture, even if this was the first time she was experiencing it firsthand.

There was quite definitely a stirring awesomeness about the desert, but Petra was finding it difficult to give her exclusive attention to her surroundings because of the effect that Blaize himself was having on her.

But that did not mean that she had fallen in love with him, she reassured herself fiercely. Just because her heart was beating with an unfamiliar speed, and she dared not look properly at him because when she did she wanted to keep on looking...and do much, much more than just merely look, she admitted breathlessly. But that did not mean...anything. In fact it meant nothing—nothing at all other than that she was physically aware of him.

Aware of him and responsive to him... And surely, if she was truly honest with herself, not just physically...

'You look flushed,' she heard Blaize telling her brusquely. 'You must make sure that you drink plenty of water. The desert is the last place to get dehydrated.'

Perhaps she ought to be glad that he believed her heightened colour was caused by the sun's heat rather than guessing that it was caused by the unwanted sensuality of her own desire for him, Petra reflected inwardly.

She had believed that her mother's reminiscences of her own childhood trips into the desert had prepared her for what she might expect, but Petra still found that she was holding her breath and then expelling it in a sharp sound of excitement as they crested yet another sand dune. There before them, shimmering beneath the sun's heat like a mirage, lay the oasis and the encampment which had been recreated to give tourists like herself a taste of what desert living had been all about in the days when Nomad tribes had still roamed the desert, travelling from one oasis to another.

Several other four-wheel drive vehicles were already parked close to one another and Blaize pulled up next to them.

'Wait here,' Blaize told her. 'I'll go and find out which tent has been assigned to us.'

To *them*? Petra's stomach muscles were quivering with the effort of controlling her emotions when Blaize returned several minutes later and she walked into what was more properly a pavilion than a mere tent, at the farthest edge of the encampment. She discovered that it was divided inside into three completely separate sections, which comprised a living room area, complete with rich, patterned oriental carpets and silk-covered divans, as well as two separated bedrooms. The shower block, Blaize informed her, was more mundanely housed on its own, and provided up-to-the-minute facilities.

Petra was only half listening to him. She had unfastened the doorway leading to one of the bedrooms and was staring in disbelieving delight at its interior.

Unlike her very modern bedroom at the hotel, this really was straight out of an Arabian Nights fantasy.

The interior 'walls' of the pavilion were hung with a rich mixture of embroidered silks in shimmering oriental colours, embellished with gold thread which caught the light from the lamps placed on low, heavily carved chests dotted around the surprisingly spacious room.

The bed itself, whilst only slightly raised off the rug-covered floor, like the walls was covered in beautiful silk throws, and from the ceiling there hung sheer muslin voiles, currently tied back, which Petra suspected would cover the whole bed when untied. The effect was one of unsurpassable opulence and sensuality, and Petra was half afraid to even blink, just in case she discovered that the entire room was merely a mirage.

'Something wrong?' she heard Blaize asking from behind her.

Immediately Petra shook her head.

'No. It's…it's wonderful…'

'Arabian Nights meets MGM,' Blaize pronounced briefly and almost sardonically as he glanced past her into the room.

'It's beautiful.' Petra defended her new temporary home.

'Officially, it's the honeymoon suite,' Blaize informed her drily, adding, 'But don't worry—just in case they don't get any honeymooners—or if they do but they fall out— they keep the other room kitted out as a second bedroom.'

The honeymoon suite! Why had they been given that? Or had Blaize perhaps asked for it deliberately, to reinforce the idea that they were lovers?

'If you want to have a camel ride, now's the time,' Blaize was continuing, patently oblivious to the sensuality and allure of the silk-hung bedroom and the temptation that was affecting Petra so forcibly.

'More coffee?'

Smiling, Petra shook her head, covering her cup with her hand in the traditional gesture that meant that she had had enough.

It was nearly eleven o'clock in the evening, and the dishes had been cleared away following their evening meal, ready for the entertainment to begin.

Petra could feel the excited expectation emanating from the gathered onlookers as the musicians changed beat and out of one of the tents a stunningly beautiful woman shimmied, dressed in a traditional dancing costume, jewels sparkling on her fingers and of course in her navel as she swayed provocatively to the sound of the music. Her body undulated sensuously, her dark eyes flashing smoky temptation above her veil as she rolled her hips, her whole body, and most especially the bare, smooth, taut brown expanse of her belly in rhythmic time to the music.

To one side of her a group of tourists were passing a hubble-bubble pipe between one another, the girls giggling softly as they breathed in the sweet taste of the strawberry-flavoured smoke. Its effect was supposed to be mildly euphoric, and Petra hesitated a little when it was passed on to her.

'If you don't try it you have to pay a forfeit and get up and dance with our belly dancer,' the tour guide with the large party who had just passed her the pipe teased Petra.

Rather than appear standoffish, Petra took a quick breath, relaxing as she smelled the innocuous scent of the strawberries and then offering the pipe to Blaize, only to realise that he had got up and walked away. He was talking to the falconer, who was still holding one of his now hooded birds, the gold tooling on the leather gloves, gleaming in the firelight.

As she handed the pipe back to the waiting tour guide, Petra realised that she wasn't the only woman there looking at Blaize. The belly dancer was focusing her gaze and her openly inviting body movements on him, ignoring the rest of them and turning to face him, moving closer and closer to him.

And as for Blaize...! A sensation of sheer white-hot jealousy knifed through Petra as she saw the way he was watching the dancer and smiling at her.

Petra had believed that she knew pain, but now, shockingly, she realised that all she had experienced was one of its many dimensions. Right now, watching Blaize look at another woman when she ached, yearned, needed to have him look only at her, unlocked for her the door to an agonising new world of pain!

Thoughts, longings, needs hitherto denied and forbidden broke loose from the control she had imposed on them, one after the other, until she was exposed to an entire avalanche of them. They buried for ever any possibility of her denying what her feelings for Blaize really were!

Frantically she struggled to make sense of what was happening. In the eerie pristine silence that followed the inner explosion, her thought processes were frozen.

How was it possible for her to love Blaize? Petra felt as though she had suddenly become one of those small figures in a child's snowstorm ball, who had just had her whole world and all her perceptions of what was in it turned vigorously upside down. But say she had got it wrong. Say she did not really love Blaize. Mentally she tried to imagine how she would feel if she were never to see him again.

The intensity of her pain made her catch her breath. Was this how her mother had felt about her father? It must have been. But things had been different for her mother, Petra had to remind herself. Her mother had known that her love was returned…shared… That she was loved as much as she herself loved.

The music was reaching a crescendo, and Petra shivered as she felt and saw the raw sensuality of the dancer's movements, her passionate determination to make Blaize notice her, choose her. Blaize himself had turned round and was watching her. The girl danced faster and faster, and then as the music exploded in climactic triumph she flung herself bodily as Blaize's feet.

Petra could tell from the reaction of the guides and the

robed men watching that this was not the normal finale to the dance. Instinctively she knew that the girl did not normally offer herself with such sexual blatancy to one of the male onlookers the way she just had done to Blaize, and immediately her own jealousy burned to a white heat.

She wanted to run to the girl and push her away—to tell her that Blaize belonged to her. But of course he did not!

The audience were good-humouredly throwing money onto the floor for the dancer, as they had been encouraged to do, but the dancer remained prostrate in front of Blaize, not acknowledging their generosity. It was left to one of the male fire-eaters who had been entertaining them earlier to pick it up.

As Petra watched Blaize watching the girl she wondered what he was thinking. He said something to one of the men he had been speaking with, who inclined his head as though in deference to Blaize before going over to the girl and bending towards her.

What was the man saying to her? Petra wondered jealously. What message had Blaize given the man to give her? Had he told her that he would see her later? The girl was getting up. She looked at Blaize, a proud, challenging flash of dark eyes, before walking slowly away, her hips swaying provocatively as she did so, her spine straight.

How could any man resist such an invitation? Petra wondered bleakly. Why would a man like Blaize even try to do so? And why, oh, why did a woman like her have to fall in love with him?

The evening was drawing to a close. People were finishing off their drinks and retiring to their pavilions.

Petra looked towards Blaize, who was still talking to the falconer and some other men. The dancer had disappeared, and Blaize was showing no signs of coming over to her or even looking at her.

Tiredly Petra got up and made her own way to their pavilion, collecting her things and then heading for the shower block. Too much was happening to her too quickly. Since arriving in this country she had been forced to confront aspects of herself and her feelings that it was very hard for her to accept.

Suddenly, standing beneath the warm spray of the shower, she longed achingly to be able to turn back the clock and return to a time when she had known nothing of the complexities that meeting her grandfather would bring. A time when she would have laughed out loud in disbelief if anyone had suggested that she would fall in love with a man like Blaize.

The camp was settling down to sleep when she made her way back to her pavilion. The soft glow of the lamps added to the air of mystery and enticement of its interior.

Someone had placed a dish of dates on one of the low carved tables in the sitting area, and silk cushions were placed invitingly on the floor in front of it, but Petra had no stomach for the sweetness of the dates—no stomach for anything, really, she admitted, now that her heart was soured by the anguish of her unreturnable love for Blaize. After all, even if he were by some impossible means to return her feelings, how could there be any future for them?

It wasn't a matter of money. That didn't come into it. Blaize could have had nothing and she would have loved him proudly and joyously. But how could she feel anything other than disquiet and distress at loving a man who used himself in the way that Blaize did? It was that which hurt her more than anything else! Even more than thinking about him with another woman? The belly dancer for instance?

Petra curled her hands into small fists. Where was he now? He was not in his room. The fabric covering the entrance to it was tied back so that she could see that the space beyond was empty.

Unlike hers, the 'walls' of his room were hung with darker, heavier fabric, which if anything was even more richly embroidered in gold than her own. Opulent fur-mimicking throws were heaped on the bed. There was a beautiful rug on the floor and a dish of sweet almond cakes on the table in front of the divan, along with a pot of richly fragrant coffee.

It was a setting fit for an Arabian prince, Petra reflected admiringly. And a retreat to which that same prince could bring the dancing girl of his choice, a dangerous inner voice taunted her.

Quickly Petra suppressed it. Blaize was no prince, Arabian or otherwise, and as for the dancing girl...

But where was he? Virtually the whole camp seemed to have settled down to sleep, and yet there was no sign of him.

Restlessly Petra paced the small pavillioned sitting area, tensing as the opening flap was abruptly pushed back and Blaize came in. He was stripped to the waist, a towel round his shoulders, his hair damp, and as he came in he brought with him the scent of the night and the desert—and of himself.

Petra felt her insides turn softly, compliantly liquid, longing pulsing through her as she gazed helplessly at his body.

She hadn't truly appreciated its magnificence the first time she had seen it, hadn't been able to sense its male capacity for sensuality and female pleasure, but now she could.

Abruptly her eyes narrowed, her gaze focusing on the angry claw-marks on his arm, which were still oozing blood slightly. Immediately the earth rocked beneath her feet and she was savaged by her own jealousy.

He had been with the dancer, and she had clawed her mark of possession on him!

Her mark of passion!

Before she could even recognise what she was doing, never mind stop herself, Petra had clenched her hands into small fists and advanced on him, demanding furiously, 'Where have you been? As if I didn't know! Was she good? Better than the rich tourists who pay you for your favours?'

'What...?'

Like lightning the changing expressions chased one another across his face, frowning disbelief followed by a warning, taut concentration. In its place followed an even more dangerous flash of sheeting anger and his mouth compressed and a tiny nerve pulsed in his jaw.

But Petra was in no mood to heed warning signs, and her eyes glittered with a fury every bit feral as his as she stated sarcastically, 'Silly me! I thought the whole purpose of us being here together was to convince the outside world that *we* are lovers! But obviously I was wrong and it's not! No—what's obviously far more important to you than honouring the arrangement we made is enjoying the...the sexual favours of an...an oversexed belly dancer. But then of course the two of you have something in common, don't you? You both sell your sexual favours for money and—'

Petra gave a small squeak as she was suddenly lifted off her feet. Her arms were in a vice-like grip as Blaize held her so that their eyes were on the same level.

'You should check your facts before you start throwing insults like that around,' he told her, biting the words into small barbed insults, his mouth barely moving as he hurled them lividly at her. 'If you were a man— But you aren't, are you?' he demanded, his voice suddenly changing to a soft sneer as he added, 'You aren't even much of a woman...just an over-excited, over-heated virgin, aching with curiosity to know what it's all about. No, don't deny it. It's written all over you—all over every single one of those big-eyed looks you keep on giving me when you think I don't notice. You're just desperate to find out what sex is, aren't you? Well, I'm sorry to disappoint you, but you just don't have what it takes to encourage me to let you find out!'

Every single word he had uttered had found its mark, and Petra felt as though she was slowly dying from the pain of the wounds he had inflicted. But there was no way she was going to let him see that—no way she was going to stop fighting...

'You mean that I haven't offered you enough money?' she taunted him recklessly.

'Enough money?' To Petra's disbelief, he threw back his head and laughed harshly.

'Despite what you so obviously think, it isn't money that turns me on, Petra, that makes me want a woman, ache for her so I can't rest until I possess her in every way there is. Until I wake up with her beside me in the morning, knowing that her body still wears my touch, inside and out, that she is so much a part of me that she still smells of me. But you don't know anything about that, do you? You know nothing about a man's desire...the compulsion that drives him to want a woman. Shall I show you? Is that what you want?'

Petra knew that she ought to deny what he was saying...refuse what he was offering her. But all she could do was let her gaze cling helplessly to his, her body motionless in his arms as he lowered his head towards hers!

As his lips touched hers she made a tiny almost mute sound at the back of her throat. Now she knew what it was like to be driven by a need, a thirst so all-consuming that it burned the soul as well as the body—to crave something, someone, to the point where the pain of that craving was an eternal torment. No Nomad lost in the desert could crave water with anything like the same intensity as she craved Blaize right now!

She moaned as he kissed her, wrapping her arms as tightly around him as she could, savouring the hot, deep thrust of his tongue and pressing close to him.

She could feel the anger pulsing through his body, but she was beyond caring which emotion drove him just so long as he never, ever lifted his mouth from her own.

And then, before she could stop him, he was wresting his mouth from hers, telling her savagely, 'Why the hell am I doing this? I must be going crazy! The last thing I need—or want—right now is—' He had stopped speaking to shake his head, but Petra could guess what he was thinking! What he had been about to say!

The last thing he needed—or wanted—was her!

Driven by the pain of his abrupt rejection of her, held deep in the grip of a primitive urge, an emotional, immediate reaction to his cruel taunting words she couldn't control, Petra lashed out at him, her hand raised.

And when, more by accident than anything, her hand hit the side of his jaw his own shock was mirrored by the expression in her eyes as they rounded and darkened. She shuddered convulsively, as though he had been the one to hit her.

She felt him release her and her feet hit the ground. She knew she must have moved, because suddenly she was in her own bedroom, lying curled up in the centre of the lavish bed whilst her whole body trembled with shock and pain, but she had no awareness of having got there—no awareness of anything since that awful moment when she had felt as well as heard the crack of her open palm against his skin.

How could she have done such a thing? She was totally opposed to all forms of violence. It disgusted her to the point where she felt physically sick that she had acted in such a way, but her dry aching eyes refused to provide her with the comfort of cleansing tears to wash away her guilt.

CHAPTER SEVEN

PAINFULLY Petra stared into the emptiness surrounding her. It was barely twenty minutes or so since Blaize had left her, but to Petra each one of those minutes had felt like an hour as she fought to come to terms with the shock of her own uncharacteristic behaviour. She was being tormented—not just by her unwanted love for Blaize, but by her guilt at the way she had behaved as well.

No matter how righteous her cause or how much provocation she believed she had been made to suffer, she still could not excuse or forgive herself for what she had done. To have been so driven by her own demons that she had resorted to physical violence! A shudder of self-loathing and moral outrage gripped her body.

According to the code by which she had been brought up by her parents, she owed Blaize an apology. Never mind that his own behaviour was open to question—his behaviour was something she was not responsible for. Her own was a different matter.

Apologise to him? After what he had said? After what he had done? After the way he had inflamed her senses, her body, until she had ached so feverishly for him that her longing overwhelmed everything else and then rejected her! Never, never. Never, not even on pain of torture, Petra swore dramatically to herself.

But five minutes later, with her conscience digging into her painfully, refusing to be ignored no matter how tightly she cocooned herself in her righteous indignation and tried to smother its nagging little voice, Petra finally gave in. If she waited too much longer she would be disturbing Blaize in the middle of his night's sleep!

Nervously, she reached for her robe and took a deep breath.

In the outer room the oil lamps had burned low, casting soft long shadows against the darkness.

Surely her apology could wait until morning? a craven little voice urged her. Blaize might well already be asleep. But Petra refused to allow herself to listen to it. She had done something wrong and now she must make amends!

Taking a deep breath, Petra lifted back the entrance fabric to Blaize's bedroom. In the few seconds it took her eyes to adjust to the darkness she could hear the noisy, anxious slam of her own heart against her ribs, and instinctively she placed one hand against it, as though trying to silence it.

The full moon outside lifted the darkness just enough for her to be able to make out Blaize's sleeping form beneath the bedcovers. He was lying on his side, with his face towards her, but turned into the pillow so that she could not tell whether he was awake or not. Tentatively she whispered his name, but there was no response. Was he asleep?

If she left now he would never even know she had been here. Longingly she looked back towards the exit, but the stubborn pride her father had always teased her about, that she had inherited from her grandfather, refused to allow her to make a craven escape without first checking that he was actually sleeping.

Head held high, she walked over to the bed. Like her own it was easily wide enough for two people. Uncertainly she looked at Blaize. Was he asleep? He certainly wasn't moving. Quietly she crept a little closer, automatically balancing one knee on the bed as she did so in order to get a closer look at him.

Tentatively she whispered his name. If he didn't respond

and was asleep then she could return to her own bed with a clear conscience and save her apology until the morning, knowing that she had at least tried to deliver it!

He hadn't uttered a sound. Exhaling softly in relief, Petra started to back away—and then froze as with shocking speed he reached out and gripped her wrist, demanding tauntingly, 'Sleepwalking Petra?'

His fingers burned against her skin, and as though he had guessed his thumb probed the uncoordinated thud of her pulse as though he was monitoring her reaction to him.

'Your blood is racing through your body like a gazelle fleeing from the hunter.'

'You…you startled me. I thought you were asleep!'

She winced a little as he released her, gritting a soft expletive under his breath. Moving with the swift stealth of a panther, throwing back the bedclothes, he reached out to relight the oil lamp on the table beside the bed, taunting her softly, 'If you thought I was asleep then what exactly are you doing here?'

Far from being asleep, he sounded dangerously alert, Petra recognised.

As she gave a small nervous shudder his expression changed abruptly. Frowningly he questioned her, 'What is it? What's wrong? Don't you feel well? The desert air can sometimes…'

'I'm fine,' Petra assured him quickly. 'It isn't…' Catching her bottom lip between her teeth, she struggled to drag her distracted…besotted gaze away from his naked torso. Like her, he obviously did not favour pyjamas. But unlike her, she suspected, from the brief glimpse she had just had of one lean muscular hip and the telltale dark shadowing of hair running down over his taut flat stomach, Blaize did not even adopt the modesty of wearing briefs to sleep in!

'Fine?' he repeated. 'Then what…?'

He looked fully awake now. And fully alert too, Petra recognised with a sinking, almost queasy sensation gripping her stomach. Thinking about delivering a short but noble speech of apology in the privacy of her own bed was one thing: actually doing it whilst she was poised semi-crouched on the edge of Blaize's bed, with her mind more on the fact that he was undoubtedly naked beneath the silky throw than on what she was supposed to be doing, was very much another! And if she wasn't careful…if she wasn't very, very careful indeed…she might just be in grave danger of totally ignoring what she had come here to do…

The scratches on Blaize's upper arm caught her attention. They had stopped bleeding but they still looked raw, and even slightly inflamed.

As she dragged her gaze away it met Blaize's, and was held there trapped…hypnotised…

'For your information, they were *not* caused by Shara…the dancer,' he told her quietly. 'The falconer had a new young bird he was training and it became over-excited. I offered to help him.' He gave a small shrug. 'As I told him, once she matures she will make an enviably loyal bird. She resented being handled by someone who was not her master and she let me know it.'

'A falcon scratched you?' Petra breathed, her face flooding with guilty colour. Now she owed him not one but two apologies.

Helplessly she looked back to his arm, and then, unable to stop herself, she leaned forward and gently caressed the broken skin with her lips, tenderly kissing the line of each scratch.

As she kissed the last one she felt Blaize's body quiver. Sombrely she turned her head and looked into his eyes.

'I came to apologise,' she told him quietly. 'I should not have...have done what I did.'

There was a small tense pause through which she could feel her own emotions pulsing, as though they possessed a life force of their own, whilst she waited for him to speak, and once again she found that she was having to wet her dry lips.

His thickly groaned, 'Don't do that, Petra!' followed by an even thicker, 'Why...why did you have to come in here?' drove the colour from her face, redefining the delicacy of her bone structure and highlighting her fragility. She started to move away, her eyes widening as Blaize followed her, grasping hold of her wrists and holding them against his bare chest as he looked deep into her eyes, before his gaze dropped, heavy-lidded with sensuality, to her mouth.

In the thick, taut silence that enveloped them while Blaize lit the lamp next to the bed Petra made the interesting scientific discovery that it was possible to find that one could not breathe even with open airways, parted lips, and an ample supply of oxygen!

'You know that you shouldn't really be here, don't you, my little virgin?'

His little virgin? Petra's heart jumped like a hooked fish throwing itself against her ribcage.

'I...'

I can go, Petra had been about to say. But speech had suddenly become impossible because Blaize was kissing her...kissing her with a mind-drugging, slow, sweet simplicity that was nothing more than the merest touch of his lips against hers, over and over again, and then again, until all she wanted to do was live off their touch, to feel it for ever.

Somehow she was now kneeling upright on the bed, and

so too was Blaize, so that they were body to body. His naked body next to her very scantily clad one!

Petra could feel the heavy, fierce thud of his heart beneath her hands as he held them against his chest.

He was kissing the tip of her nose, her closed eyelids, with tiny butterfly kisses that brushed the taut planes of her cheekbones whilst the hands pinning her own set them free, lifted to cup her face, to push the hair back from it so that his lips and then his tongue could investigate the delicate and oh, so sensually sensitive whorls of her ears.

Petra heard herself whimpering, an unfamiliar distant sound that was a needy plea for even more of the pleasure he was inflicting on her. Blindly she turned her head, seeking the warmth of his mouth.

His hands shaped her throat, holding it, his thumb measuring the frantic leaping pulse at its base. Her small curled fists still lay against his chest, the rasp of his body hair against her skin disturbingly sexual.

His hands were on her shoulders, beneath her wrap, stroking her skin, sliding the fabric away.

In the soft light of the lamp he had lit Petra could see their reflection in a mirror. Her skin looked milky pale against the warm tan of his, her breasts surely swollen, its taut peak surely a deeper, hotter colour as it pressed against him, flushed and pulsing with the desire that ached right through her.

If he were to touch her there now, cup her breast, roll his fingertip around her nipple… Her whole body stiffened in response to her own thoughts and it was as though somehow he had read her mind and felt her desires. His hand cupped her breast and his mouth returned to hers, his lips brushing over it with tantalising and then tormenting delicacy, making her lips part with hungry longing and her body press into his.

Wantonly she ran her tongue-tip over his lips, until he captured it and drew it between his teeth, caressing it with his own before his tongue slid deeper and deeper into the moist sweetness of her mouth.

As she moaned her pleasure deep in her throat, Petra felt him jerk away from her.

'Petra, no!' he told her thickly. 'This isn't—'

Not wanting to hear what he was obviously going to say, Petra put her fingertips to his lips, silencing him, kissing his face wildly, with fierce, impassioned little kisses as she breathed in his ear, 'Yes… Yes, it is!'

Removing her fingers, she pressed her mouth to his, her body to his, rubbing herself sensuously against him. Virgin she might be, but that did not mean she didn't understand what passion was…what wanting him was!

As she slid her hands over his body, helpless to stop herself, she felt him tense and then shudder. His skin felt like hot oiled satin, and Petra knew she could never, ever get enough of the feel of it beneath her hands. She kissed his throat, lingering over the place where his Adam's apple pressed hard against his skin, stroking it with her tongue, nibbling at his skin, taunting him with her desire and daring him to refuse to share it.

When he didn't move she curled her fingers in the soft thick hair on his body, tugging wantonly on it and flicking her tongue against the tiny peak of his flat male nipple.

'Petra, you are a virgin,' she heard him protesting rawly. 'I can't…'

As she abandoned her torment of his throat, and her lips moved down along the line of hair toward his stomach, she could almost hear him grinding his teeth. Her tongue rimmed his flat belly button, her love for him filling her with a sensual bravado that normally would have shocked her. She had never dreamed that the first time she made love she would be the one taking the initiative, making moves so bold and provocative that they shocked her almost as much as they excited her.

'I don't want—' she heard Blaize groan thickly.

But her fingertips were already exploring the taut strength of his arousal, lending her the confidence to whisper daringly, 'Oh, yes, you do,' before returning to her task of laving the maleness of his flat belly with her inquisitive tongue.

There was a muscle pulsing there that fascinated and compelled her. Wickedly she traced it with lingering appreciation, so raptly lost in the pleasure of what she was doing that it caught her completely off guard when Blaize suddenly took hold of her, depositing her on the bed and holding her there whilst he looked down at her, his gaze skimming her face and then her body, her breasts, her narrow waist. She saw him frown and looked down at her own flesh, realising that he was staring at the tiny diamond glinting in her belly.

'Who gave you that?' she heard him demanding fiercely.

For a few seconds Petra was bemused, and her fingertip touched the diamond in confusion.

'Who was he, Petra?' she heard Blaize reiterating savagely—so savagely, in fact, that she was unable to prevent the entirely female thrill of excited pleasure rippling through her. He was jealous! She could tell. For a heartbeat she fantasised about pretending that he had a rival, that another man had looked at her body and laid claim to it, put his badge of possession on it. But her natural honesty reasserted itself.

'I bought it myself—for myself!' she told him truthfully. 'I heard a couple of girls discussing me at a party, saying that I was the type of person who was too pure and naïve to wear anything like this, and so...' She gave a small dismissive shrug.

'This is a gift that only a man would give a woman,' Blaize was insisting, his eyes smokily charcoal, hot with male possession and desire.

'Not these days,' Petra contradicted him wryly.

'Then where else have you adorned yourself?' Blaize was demanding softly, and his hand moved lower down her body, his head bent over her.

Now it was his turn to torment her, to kiss her with surely far more expertise and deliberate enticement and sensuality than she had done him as he traced a line of kisses from her breastbone right down to her quivering belly.

As she had done to him he rimmed her navel with tiny kisses, and then the tip of his tongue, but then, before Petra could stop him, he tugged delicately on the diamond whilst his hand covered her sex, his thumb slowly probing an entrance between its tightly furled outer covering in a way that made her heart turn over inside her chest whilst the whole of her body turned molten and fluid with arousal.

'Nowhere else,' she heard herself whisper, but even as she said them she knew that the words were not needed, that Blaize had discovered for himself that her body possessed no other form of adornment!

Withdrawing slightly, he looked down at her whilst she quivered from head to foot—but not with apprehension or regret.

'I want you,' she told him huskily. 'I want you now, Blaize.'

But as she reached for him he shook his head.

'Wait!' he told her, reaching out to open a small cupboard beside the bed.

'I just hope that whoever planned this as a lovers' retreat did some proper forward planning,' Petra heard him mutter.

Bewildered, she waited, trying to peer past his shoulder, and then when she did see what he had been searching for her face coloured self-consciously.

Until now all 'safe sex' had meant to her was an expression that applied to other people!

But of course Blaize was more experienced, far more worldly than she was herself, and shakily she admitted that she was thankful that he was being so conscientious!

She even felt a tiny little thrill of excitement, knowing what he was doing, what it was leading up to! And when he was ready and he turned back to her, wrapping her in his arms and kissing her slowly and thoroughly before caressing her body, she shivered in passionate urgency.

She had thought that she knew what wanting him, aching for him felt like! But she had been wrong!

Enshrined in the street lore of her girlhood, the received wisdom of a hundred magazine articles and books, she had carried a certain protective wisdom that 'first times were not good times'—but she had been wrong about that too!

She hadn't known just how proactive her own role would be, how proactive she would want it to be as she reached and touched, stretched and invited, as she shuddered in the exquisite indescribable sensation of having him slowly enter her, slowly fill her…

But she knew now.

She hadn't known either how easily she would find the words she could hear echoing the pace of his deepening thrusts, which told him all that she was feeling and wanting.

But she knew that now too.

Every breath he took as he filled and completed her—against her skin, in her ear, in the thud of his heartbeat against her own, deep inside her body, where it radiated out in golden waves—was the breath of life itself.

And then, just as she thought she had accustomed herself

totally to the feel of him, he changed the pace, increasing its intensity, deepening it, letting her feel the strength of its power, letting her see that her body was ready for such intimacy.

And it was!

Mindlessly Petra clung to him, lifting herself against him so that he could go deeper, fuller, stronger, so that the intimacy they were sharing was so intense, so sweetly, savagely unbearable that it had to shatter, hurling them both through paroxysm after paroxysm of pleasure and into the beautiful golden peace that lay beyond it.

'Mmm.' Sleepily, Petra drew a small heart on the smooth skin of Blaize's bare shoulder with her fingertip. He was asleep and she could see the dark fans his eyelashes made against the warmth of his tanned skin in the soft light of the lamp. She had been asleep herself until a couple of minutes ago, but it seemed that her body didn't want to waste a moment of the time it could have with Blaize in sleep when she could be awake, watching him, touching him…loving him.

There—she had acknowledged her love! Admitted it! Accepted it?

She closed her eyes, testing the words inside her head. I love him. I love Blaize.

Yes, it was true. She could tell that from the way her whole being responded to the inner vibration of the words. She loved him! She loved Blaize.

She moved closer to him, bending her head to replace her fingertip with her lips, slowly retracing her heart with tiny whisper-light kisses.

His skin felt so warm, his body so excitingly different from her own and yet now so wonderfully, preciously familiar.

From now until the very end of her life she would remember tonight. Until the day she died she would be able to close her eyes and recreate his image inside her head. Her hands would never forget what it had felt like to touch him; her lips would never forget the taste of his, the heat of his mouth, the way he had kissed her.

Her eyes soft and dark with her own emotions, Petra traced the shape of his arm and then the length of his back, the curve of his buttock.

'Two can play at this game.'

Petra gasped as Blaize's hand suddenly slid over her, down to her waist and then up again to cup her breast, whilst his voice echoed in her ear.

'You wouldn't be trying to take advantage of a sleeping man, would you?' he teased her.

'I just wanted to see if you felt as good as I remembered,' Petra told him honestly.

She felt him move, tensing a little, as though her words had somehow touched a raw nerve, or were something he didn't really want to hear. But she decided that she must be wrong when he demanded, 'And do I?'

As he spoke his thumb was deliberately teasing the unexpectedly taut and excited peak of her breast.

The shock of discovering how easily and quickly he could make her feel so hungry for him distracted her. Her hands were already curling, weaving rhythmically against his skin as her body started to pulse and ache.

Eagerly she kissed his throat and then his mouth, making a soft, taut sound of need deep in her throat as she pulled his head down towards her breast.

The sensation of his lips covering her nipple, caressing it, drawing it deeper into his mouth, made her dig her fingers into the hard muscles of his back. Already she was imagining the feel of him inside her, aching for it and for him, so much that she reached out and ran her fingertips down his body, touching him with a knowing intimacy that would have shocked her twenty-four hours ago.

Against her breast he made a sound she couldn't decipher, smothered by the urgency of her compelling need as she arched against him and gloried in the swelling hardness of the male flesh beneath her touch.

Blaize had released her breast and rolled onto his back. She felt his hands on her waist. To lift her away? Swiftly she bent her head towards his body, her lips touching the hard shaft of flesh that compelled her, that she knew would complete her!

'Petra…Petra…'

Her name was a raw, tormented sound of broken male control that filled her with sweetly savage pleasure.

His hands were still on her waist, but this time as he lifted her it was not away from him but towards him.

As he positioned her Petra shuddered, her eyes huge and dark with the realisation of how quickly and wantonly her body had adjusted to its newly dominant role.

Slickly they moved together, deeper, stronger, faster, whilst she stared into the mask of agonised pleasure that was Blaize's face, his need openly revealed to her as he cried out and his body jerked in fierce spasms just as the pleasure exploded inside her.

She was trembling so much that she couldn't move, couldn't do anything other than lie against him whilst he wrapped his arms around her and rocked her.

'That shouldn't have happened,' she heard him telling her in a voice that was raw with emotions she didn't have the energy to analyse as a fog of exhaustion enveloped her.

'That should *not* have happened,' he repeated.

'Yuck, camel's milk! How totally disgusting!'

Petra forced herself to try and smile as the girl next to

her, sharing the communal breakfast they had been served at the tourist village, turned towards her, waiting for her to respond to her friendly comment.

Ordinarily Petra knew that she would have enjoyed joining in the good-natured atmosphere of the alfresco breakfast they had been served. But when she had woken up this morning she had woken up alone and in her own bed!

Blaize must have carried her there whilst she was asleep. Why hadn't he wanted her to stay with him? Why hadn't he wanted to keep her with him?

Now last night's euphoria had disappeared, leaving her feeling frighteningly hollow and cold inside.

What she needed right now more than anything else was Blaize's presence, Blaize's reassurance—and most of all Blaize's love!

CHAPTER EIGHT

'THANKS for the lift...'

Petra watched as the young tour guide reiterated his grateful thanks to Blaize, before jumping down out of the Land Rover.

They had all been on the point of departing from the oasis when the tour guide's Jeep had refused to start.

Places had been found for his passengers in other vehicles, but unfortunately there had not been enough room for him, so Blaize had offered to give him a lift back to the complex.

Of course his presence had made it impossible for Petra and Blaize to discuss anything personal, but Petra suspected that she minded this far more than Blaize did.

The truth was that he was probably relieved she couldn't say anything about last night, Petra acknowledged unhappily.

After all, if he had felt anything for her—even a mere small percentage of the love she knew she had for him—then he would have told her so last night, instead of returning her to her own bed and then treating her this morning as though...as though she meant nothing to him!

She might mean nothing to him, but he meant everything to her!

Still, at least one good thing had come out of last night, she tried to tell herself with a brave attempt at cynical courage.

Rashid certainly wasn't going to want to marry her now. Not once he knew she had spent the night with another man! Given herself to another man! A man, moreover, who didn't love or want her!

Determinedly Petra tried not to give in to her own despair.

That wasn't true, she argued mentally with herself. Blaize had wanted her!

Her or just a woman…any woman?

Her pain was so intense that she didn't dare to even look at Blaize, just in case he might read her feelings in her eyes and feel even more contempt for her than he no doubt already did. All she meant to him was a meal ticket and a few hours of casual and no doubt quickly forgettable sex! She had known what he was all along, she reminded herself, so why had she been so stupid? So reckless with herself and her love? What had she been thinking? That with her he would be different? That her love would make it different? Why, why, why had she closed her eyes so deliberately to reality? Why had she ignored everything she knew about him and the way he lived his life?

Because her love for him had given her no choice, Petra recognised bleakly. Because, against her love, common sense and logic had no real weapons at all!

Acidly painful tears burned the back of Petra's throat. They were outside her hotel now, and without giving Blaize the opportunity to say anything she opened the door of the Land Rover and got out.

As she walked away she thought she heard Blaize calling her name, but she refused to stop.

It might be too late to stop herself from loving Blaize, but it was not too late for her to salvage her pride and her self-respect!

If she had meant anything to him…anything at all…he would have told her so last night.

*　　*　　*

An hour later, having exhausted every rational and several very irrational combinations of reasons and excuses for Blaize's behaviour, and still had to return to the unwanted, unbearable truth that he had simply been using her and, having done so now, no longer wanted her, Petra heard someone knocking on the door to her suite.

Immediately, despite everything she had just told herself, her heart leapt, whilst relief and joy poured through her. It was Blaize! It had to be! She had got it all wrong! There was a rational explanation for the distance he had put between them, and he had now come to explain everything to her—to apologise for hurting her and to tell her how much he wanted her, how much he loved her.

Her whole face illuminated with happiness and love, Petra ran to open the door.

Only it wasn't Blaize who was standing outside; it was her cousin Saud. In the shock of her disappointment Petra could only stand and stare at him uncomprehendingly.

'Are you packed yet?' she heard him asking her.

'Packed?'

'I told my mother she should have rung ahead to check that you were ready!'

Ready! Guiltily Petra realised that today was the day she was due to move in to the family villa. She had been so wrapped up in her love for Blaize and what had happened between them that she had totally overlooked the plans that had been made.

'I…I'm running a bit late, Saud,' she told him. After all, it was technically the truth. 'I'm sorry…'

'That's okay,' Saud assured her easily. 'I'm not in any rush. Did you enjoy your trip into the dessert with Rashid? I saw him driving you there,' he added casually.

Petra stared at him, her body completely immobile, like

that of someone caught up in the dark power of a sorcerer's spell.

'Rashid?' she questioned. Her lips were having trouble framing his name, and her heart had started to beat with heavy-doom laden thuds that rocked her whole body. 'You saw me with Rashid?'

'Yes, in one of the safari company's Land Rovers,' Saud confirmed.

'But I wasn't with—' Petra began to protest, and then stopped as Saud continued with a wide grin.

'My mother's already planning the wedding. She thinks…'

'Rashid,' Petra mouthed, forcing her lips to accommodate themselves to his name, whilst her body shook with the enormity of what Saud had said. 'But…'

But what? she asked herself numbly. But she had not been with Rashid. She had been with Blaize! Blaize who was not Rashid…who could not be Rashid…

'I suppose Rashid is working upstairs in the Presidential Suite now, is he?' Saud was chattering on happily. 'Has he taken you to see his new villa yet? The one he has just had built out by the private oasis he bought?' Saud was asking her excitedly. 'Did he show you his horses? And his falcons? I'd love a falcon of my own, but Dad says it's out of the question—especially if I'm to go to university in America.'

'Saud, I'm not…I'm not packed yet. Could you come back a little later, say in an hour?' she asked him jerkily, interrupting his enthusiastic and excited conversation.

'Sure!'

Petra stared blankly at the door Saud had closed behind him.

Saud had said that he had seen her with Rashid. But the

man she had been with was Blaize. Which meant either that Saud had been mistaken or…

There was a vile sickening sensation clawing coldly at the pit of her stomach, a suspicion inside her head that wouldn't go away.

The Presidential Suite. That was on the top floor. White-faced, but determined, Petra opened the door of her suite and headed for the lift.

What she was thinking couldn't be true, it just couldn't! Saud had to be mistaken, but she had to find out, she had to know…to be sure!

Only one lift went all the way to the Presidential Suite, and when she got out of it Petra was trembling violently—although whether from shock, fear or fury, she didn't really know.

Blaize could not be Rashid. It was totally implausible that he might be, totally impossible! But somehow the re-assurances she was trying to give herself had a disconcertingly hollow and empty sound to them.

In the private hallway to the suite, a thick, lushly rich carpet muffled her footsteps—but not her racing heartbeat. Nervously Petra stared at the closed door in front of her.

What was she doing here? Blaize was a beach bum, a chancer, an adventurer who lived on his wits and other people's money, a man with no moral beliefs, who made his own rules—and then broke them. Rashid, in contrast, from what she had heard about him, was a seriously successful businessman, a man ruthlessly focused on his own goals, a man prepared to marry a woman he did not know for his own advancement and benefit.

They could not be one and the same person. It was unthinkable that they might be. Unthinkable, unsustainable, unendurable! Of course it was! Saud had simply made a mistake.

Feeling slightly calmer, Petra pressed the doorbell and waited.

The door swung inwards, and a male voice demanded curtly, 'Yes?'

The voice was the same, but the businesslike crispness certainly wasn't!

Her throat muscles virtually paralysed with shock and disbelief, Petra stared up into Blaize's face. Only he wasn't Blaize. He was… He was…

Ignoring the bare arm that Blaize had placed across the half-open doorway, Petra pushed her way past him and into the suite.

She had obviously disturbed Blaize, or rather Rashid, as she now knew him to be in mid-shower, to judge from the rivulets of moisture still running over his skin down to the towel he had draped round his hips.

'How could you?' she demanded chokily. 'How dare you? Why did you do it? Why…? Let go of me,' she spat as he suddenly took hold of her arm, her face white with shock and fury. 'Let go of me,' she repeated, as Blaize—Rashid, she corrected herself bitterly—virtually dragged her into the elegant sitting room.

If she had either shocked or shamed him, he certainly wasn't showing it.

'Not until you've calmed down and you're ready to listen to reason,' Rashid told her calmly. 'Come and sit down and I'll get you a cool drink. You look as though you need one.'

A cool drink! Petra tried to pull free of him and found that she could not.

'What I need,' she told him through gritted teeth, 'is an explanation of…of what is going on…of why you pretended to be someone you quite obviously are not…'

'I was going to tell you,' Rashid interrupted her curtly. 'But—'

'Liar!' Petra cut across him. 'You're lying to me. Just like you've lied to me all along! Let go of me,' she demanded fiercely. 'I can't bear having you touch me. I—'

'That wasn't what you said last night,' Rashid reminded her grimly.

Petra shuddered, unable to stop herself from reacting—not just to his words, but also to her own feelings, her memories…

'In fact, last night, as I recall, you seemed to find my touch a good deal more than merely bearable! Remember?'

When Petra refused to answer Rashid goaded her.

'Shall I help you to do so?'

As Petra gave a sharp gasp of shock he drew her closer to him. Petra tensed as she felt the dampness of his skin through her thin top. Her mind knew how gravely, how devastatingly, how unforgivably he had behaved towards her, but her body seemed only to know that he was its lover, its love.

'If I were to kiss you now,' he began softly, the words whispering tormentingly against her tightly closed lips, 'then…'

He stopped speaking and lifted his head as the suite door suddenly opened and a tall grey-bearded man strode in, his bearing immediately marking him out as a person of eminence and rank.

'Rashid, our new American project—how long do you think—' he began, and then stopped as he took in the scene in front of him, its apparent intimacy.

Eyes as sharp and dark as a falcon's made Petra feel as though she was as pinioned beneath their gaze as she was by Rashid's grip.

'Highness, please allow me to present to you Miss Petra Cabbot.'

Highness!

Petra gulped, sensing the cool air of regal disapproval emanating from the newcomer as he looked from Rashid to Petra and then back to Rashid again before saying quietly, 'I see!'

He left a brief but telling pause before asking Petra politely, 'Your godfather is well, I trust, Miss Cabbot? He and I were at Eton together.'

'He's—he's in the Far East,' Petra managed to croak, wondering if she dared add that he was there with her passport—which right now she needed very much.

'Indeed.' The princely head was inclined towards her. 'He is a very shrewd statesman, as was your father. Statesmen of world-class stature with far-seeing eyes are very much needed in these turbulent times.'

Her face burning, Petra moved out of earshot of the two men whilst the Prince spoke with Rashid.

Despite the Prince's politeness, Petra was uncomfortably aware of his evident, if unexpressed disapproval of her presence unchaperoned in Rashid's suite.

The moment the Prince had left, Petra made to leave herself. But immediately Rashid shook his head, closing the door firmly and standing in front of it as he said grimly, 'You do realise what this means, don't you? What will have to happen now that the Prince has seen you here alone with me?'

'You were the one who introduced me to him,' Petra reminded him defensively, ignoring his question.

'Because I had no other option,' Rashid told her savagely. 'If I had chosen not to introduce you it would have been a tacit admission that it was because honourably I could not do so…because you were my whore! There is nothing else for it now. You will have to marry me! Nothing less can save your reputation or that of your family!'

Petra stared at him in shocked disbelief.

'What?' she croaked. 'We can't!'

'We can and we are,' Rashid assured her grimly. 'In fact, we don't have any other option—thanks to you!'

'Thanks to me?' Petra glared at him. 'Thanks to me? What does that mean? I wasn't the one...'

'It means that since His Highness found you here in my apartment unchaperoned, I now have no other option than to marry you. It was obvious what he thought.'

'What...? That's...that's ridiculous,' Petra protested. 'Why didn't you just tell him the truth?'

'Which truth?' Rashid demanded scornfully. 'The truth that says last night you gave yourself to me? Last night...'

'Stop it...stop it.' Petra demanded in anguish, before accusing him recklessly, 'You've done all this deliberately, haven't you? Just so that you can get your own way and force me to marry you—for the financial benefit you'll get out of it! Just as a matter of interest, what is marriage to me worth to you, Rashid?' Her temper was burning white-hot. 'A good deal more than the traditional camels, I am sure! One hotel...two...an office block and perhaps a dozen or more villas thrown in? And why stop there? I know that the Royal Family's hotel interests extend all over the world, and—'

'You're overreacting.' Rashid cut across her increasingly emotional words curtly. 'If you would just allow me to explain—'

'Explain what?' Petra demanded bitterly. 'Explain that you deliberately lied to me and...and plotted and planned to...to use me for...for your own ends?'

'Me—use *you*. I wasn't the one who came into your

room,' Rashid reminded her icily. 'Into your bed! If anything, if anyone is to blame for the situation we now find ourselves in, Petra, it is you and your wretched virginal curiosity! And, contrary to what your juvenile imagination has decided, it is for that reason that I have no option other than to do the honourable thing and marry you.'

'Because I was a virgin! That's crazy!'

'No. You are crazy if you honestly believe there can be any other outcome to what happened. We have to marry now. Apart from any other consideration there is the fact that you could have a child.'

Petra stared at him.

'But…but that isn't possible,' she started to stammer. 'You…you…took precautions…'

She tensed as she heard him draw an exaggeratedly deep breath.

'Indeed I did—the first time!' he told her derisively. 'The second time I did not, and the second time I…'

'You planned all this, didn't you?' Petra repeated furiously, panicked by both the situation and Rashid's grim anger. 'You deliberately lied to me and—'

'Do you really think I like or want this any more than you do? And as for planning it! You obviously haven't listened properly to me, Petra. As I've just told you, I wasn't the one who crawled into your bed! Nor was I the one who begged—'

With a small chagrined moan Petra forced back the shocked emotional tears that were already stinging her eyes.

'How many more times do I have to tell you that for me not to marry you now would not just relegate you to the status of a…a plaything, it would humiliate your grandfather and his whole family?' Rashid said bitingly. 'Quite apart from the fact that you were alone in here with me in an intimate situation—do you really think the fact that we spent the night together last night went unnoticed? Has it really not occurred to you yet that this morning you so obviously looked...'

'No! I won't listen to any more,' she protested.

Every word he said was like a knife in her heart. She could hardly take in what was happening. What he had said. She had enough to do trying to come to terms with the fact that the man she had thought of as Blaize was in actual fact someone quite different, without having to cope with this additional shock!

'None of this need have happened if you had just been honest with me that evening down on the beach,' she threw at him wildly. 'If you had told me then.'

'When you first approached me I had no idea who you were. I had just returned from a business trip to discover that the idiotic young man who looked after the wind-surfers, who I had already had to warn on more than one occasion about his familiarity with the female guests, had been discovered by one of our guests in bed with his wife. Naturally I had had to sack him, and I had gone down to the beach simply to walk and think.'

'You were putting away the windsurfers,' Petra accused him bitterly.

Rashid gave a small shrug.

'An automatic habit. I worked on a Californian beach as a student, and just seeing them lying untidily there...'

'You could have told me who you were! Stopped me...' Petra persisted. 'You may think that you have been very clever, tricking me like this, but I won't marry you, Rashid.'

'You don't have any other choice,' he told her starkly. 'Neither of us do! Not now! I cannot—'

'You cannot what?' Petra demanded, refusing to allow him to finish speaking. 'You cannot afford to offend the

Royal Family? Well…well, tough! No way am I going to marry you just to…to save your precious reputation—'

She stopped in mid-sentence as Rashid cut across her, his voice sharply cynical. '*My* reputation? Haven't you listened to anything I have just said? It is your own you should be thinking about! Your own and that of your family. Because what I cannot do, Petra, unless I marry you, is protect you from the gossip that is now bound to occur. And not just about you! I have far too much respect for your grandfather to want to publicly humiliate him by having it known that I have not offered you marriage.'

'Fine! Your conscience is clear, Rashid! You have offered me marriage. And I am refusing to accept!'

'Despite the fact that you could be carrying my child?'

For a moment they looked at one another. Petra could feel herself weakening, remembering… But then she made herself face reality. He had lied to her, totally and without compunction, tricked and deceived her, and she could never overlook that, not if she wanted to retain her own self-respect, what little there was left of it!

Determinedly she told him, 'It could also be that I am not carrying your child! I won't marry you, Rashid,' she reinforced.

'Unfortunately, I am tied up with business meetings which cannot be cancelled or delayed until the day after tomorrow. But rest assured, Petra, on that day I shall be calling on your grandfather to formally request your hand in marriage.'

So intense was her sense of fury and frustration that Petra simply couldn't speak. Giving Rashid a savagely bitter look, she headed for the door.

To her relief he allowed her to pass through it without making any attempt to stop her or to say anything else.

Calling on her grandfather to request her hand in marriage. She had never heard of anything so archaic! Well, she would soon make it plain to him that his proposal was neither wanted nor acceptable!

CHAPTER NINE

'AUNT SORAYA,' Petra exclaimed warmly as she saw her aunt approaching her. 'I thought you were going out to spend the day with your friend.'

Her aunt had already told Petra with some excitement that she had been invited to visit an old schoolfriend whose daughter had just become betrothed to an extremely wealthy and highly placed prince.

To Petra's concern her aunt immediately looked not merely flustered but also acutely distressed, with large tears filling her soft brown eyes.

Taking hold of her hands in her own, Petra begged her, 'Aunt, what is it? What's wrong? Please tell me—has something happened to your friend or her daughter?'

Emotionally her aunt shook her head.

'Please,' Petra urged her. 'Tell me what's wrong?'

She had, she realised, become closer to her aunt than she had imagined she would, and the older woman's air of vulnerability made her feel very protective of her.

'Petra. I did not wish to tell you this,' her aunt was saying unhappily. 'The last thing I want to do is to hurt or anger you.'

Hurt or anger her?

Petra began to frown as a cold finger of icy intuition pressed warningly against her spine.

'I was to have seen my friend and her daughter today,' her aunt admitted, 'But she has telephoned to say that the visit must be cancelled. It is nothing personal against you, Petra. At least not intentionally! My friend understands that

you did not mean to… Well, she knows you have had a
European upbringing. It is just that she has her daughter to
protect, and the family of her husband-to-be are…are very
traditional in their outlook…'

She was beginning to stumble slightly over her explanation in very obvious embarrassment, but Petra had already guessed what was coming.

Even so it was still a shock to have her aunt confirm her
fears.

'There has been gossip about you, Petra! I know, of
course, that there will be a perfectly acceptable reason
for…for…everything…but my friend has heard that you
are known to have been alone with Rashid, and that you
and he—'

She broke off, blinking away her tears and pressing her
hand to her mouth as though she could hardly bring herself
to say any more.

'I cannot believe that Rashid would knowingly behave
in such a way, that he would expose you to…that he should
not behave honourably and…'

'Offer to marry me?' Petra suggested grimly. 'Well, as
a matter of fact, Aunt, that is exactly what he has done.
Although I…'

'He has!' Suddenly her aunt's face was wreathed in a
relieved smile. Reaching out, she hugged Petra warmly,
patently oblivious to the cynicism Petra had been intending
to convey in her voice. 'Oh, Petra I am so happy… So
overjoyed for you…for you both. He will make you a wonderful husband. Your grandfather will be so very very
pleased.'

'No, Aunt, you don't understand,' Petra tried to protest,
suddenly beginning to panic as she realised the interpretation her aunt had put on her admission. It was one thing
for her to tell her aunt for the sake of her own pride and

her aunt's comfort that Rashid had offered to marry her, but she had never intended that her aunt should assume she was pleased or, more importantly, that she actually intended to accept.

However, having made her own interpretation of Petra's words her aunt proved stubbornly hard to change!

Rashid had proposed! Of course it was impossible that Petra might have refused, and every attempt Petra made to tell her that she had done just that was greeted with amused laugher and comments about Petra's 'teasing' until Petra herself fell silent in despairing exasperation.

'I should have trusted Rashid, of course,' her aunt was saying. 'Although it was very thoughtless of you both to put your reputation at so much risk, Petra. Your mother would have hated knowing that people were beginning to talk about you the way they were,' she reproved her gently.

Her mother! Petra's heart suddenly ached. Her mother would have hated knowing that her daughter's name was being bandied about in a scurrilous way, that was true, but she would not have condemned her for what had happened. Petra knew that as well.

'So, you and Rashid are betrothed,' her aunt was saying happily. 'We are going to be so busy, Petra. Oh, my, dear,' she said, giving Petra another hug. 'I had not meant to tell you this, but now that you have put my mind at ease with the news of your betrothal I feel that I can. Had Rashid not offered you marriage, it would have done our family a very great deal of harm, and lowered our standing in the community to such an extent that my own husband's business would have been badly affected—as would your cousin's chances of making a good marriage. And as for your grandfather… I do not exaggerate, Petra, when I tell you that I think the shame might have killed him.'

Killed him!

Petra stood frozen within her aunt's warm embrace, feeling as though she had suddenly walked into a trap which had sprung so tightly around her that she would never be able to escape. And it made no difference at all that she had unwittingly and foolishly been the one to spring that trap herself!

There was no way out for her now. For the sake of her family she had no alternative other than to marry Rashid!

'Oh, Petra! You look so beautiful,' her aunt whispered emotionally. 'A perfect bride.'

They were standing together in Petra's bedroom at the family villa, waiting for Petra's grandfather to escort her to the civil marriage ceremony that would make her Rashid's wife.

After the civil ceremony there was to be a lavish banquet held in their honour in the specially decorated banqueting suite of the hotel.

Petra's aunt had spent virtually the whole of the last three days there overseeing everything, along with some of Rashid's female relatives, but despite her exhortations Petra had not been able to bring herself to go and view the scene of her own legal entrapment.

There was no point, she knew, in trying to tell her aunt that she did not want to marry Rashid. The older woman had a ridiculously high opinion of him and would, Petra knew, simply not be able to accept that Petra herself hated and despised him.

Rashid knew it, though—she had made sure of that the day he had come to formally ask her grandfather for her hand in marriage.

Unable to refuse him outright as she had wished, for the sake of her aunt and her family, she had had to content herself with a bitterly contemptuous and hostile glare at him when her grandfather had summoned her to receive his proposal.

'I am pleased to see that you have had the good sense to realise there is no alternative to this—for either of us,' he had managed to tell her grimly, gritting the words to her so quietly that no one else could hear them.

And, as though that hadn't been bad enough, she had then had to endure the miserable, humiliating parody of being forced to pretend that she wanted to accept his proposal!

However, she had managed to avert her face when he had leaned towards her to kiss her, so that his mouth had merely grazed her cheek instead of touching her lips.

Beneath his breath he had taunted her, 'How very modest! A traditional shrinking bride! However, I already know just how passionate you can be beneath that assumed cold exterior!'

And now there was no escape for her.

Her attendants—a swarm of pretty chattering girls from her aunt's extended family and Rashid's—had already left for the hotel in their stunning butterfly-hued outfits, and soon Petra herself would be leaving with her grandfather. She tensed as her bedroom door opened and her grandfather came in.

Giving her veil a final twitch, her aunt left them on their own.

As he came towards her Petra could see that her grandfather's eyes were shining with emotion. 'You are so like your mother,' he whispered. 'Every day I see more and more of her in you. I have something I would like you to wear today,' he told her abruptly, producing a leather jewellery box and removing from it a diamond necklace of such delicate workmanship that Petra couldn't help giving a small murmur of appreciation.

'This is for you,' she heard her grandfather telling her. 'It would mean a great deal to me if you would wear it today, Petra.'

Now Petra could understand her aunt's insistence on choosing a fabric for her wedding gown which was sewn with tiny crystals. Originally, when the silk merchant had come to the house with a selection of fabrics, Petra had wondered bitterly just what kind of fabric would best suit a sacrificial offering. It had been her aunt who had fallen on the heavy matt cream fabric with its scattering of tiny beads with an exclamation of triumph.

Petra could feel her grandfather's hands shaking as he fastened the necklace for her. It fitted her so perfectly that it might have been made for her.

'It was your mother's,' he said. 'It was my last gift to her. She left it behind. She would have been so proud of you today, Petra. Both your parents would, and with good reason.'

Proud of her? For allowing herself to be tricked into a soulless, loveless marriage?

Panic suddenly filled her. She couldn't marry Rashid. She wouldn't! She turned to her grandfather, but before she could speak her aunt came back into the room.

'It is time for you to leave,' she told them both.

As her grandfather walked towards the stairs Petra made to follow him, but her aunt suddenly stopped her. 'You are not wearing Rashid's gift,' she chided her.

Petra stared at her.

'The perfume he sent you, which he had specially blended for you,' her aunt reminded her, clicking her tongue as she hurried over to the table and picked up the heavy crystal bottle.

'No...I don't want to wear it...' Petra started to say, but her aunt wasn't listening to her.

Petra froze as the warm, sensual scent surrounded her in a fragrant cloud.

'It is perfect for you,' her aunt was saying. 'It has the youthfulness of innocence and the maturity of womanliness. Rashid has chosen well. And your mother's necklace is perfect on you, Petra. Your grandfather has never stopped missing her or loving her, you know.'

As her throat threatened to close up with tears, Petra demanded huskily, 'If he loved her so much then why didn't he at least come to the funeral? Even if he could not have been there he could have sent a message… something…anything…'

All the pain she had felt on that dreadful day, when she had stood at her parents' graveside surrounded by their friends and her father's family and yet feeling dreadfully alone, was in her voice.

She heard her aunt sigh.

'Petra, he would have been there. But there was his heart attack—and then when your godfather wrote that he did not think it a good idea that you should come here to us, that you had your own life and friends, he was too proud to…to risk a second rejection.'

Petra stared at her. She had known that her grandfather had made a very belated and seemingly—to her—very reluctant offer to give her a home, following her parents' death, but she had had no idea that he had been prevented from attending their funeral by a heart attack.

'A heart attack?' she faltered. 'I…'

'It was his second,' her aunt informed her, and then suddenly looked acutely uncomfortable, as though she had said something she should not have said.

'His second?' Petra had known nothing of this. 'Then…when…when did he have his first?' she demanded with a small frown.

Her aunt was becoming increasingly agitated.

'Petra, I should not have spoken of this. Your grandfather never wanted... He swore us all to secrecy when it happened because he didn't want your mother to feel...'

'My mother?'

She gave her aunt a determined look.

'I am not leaving this room until you tell me everything,' she informed her sturdily.

'Petra, you will be late. The car is waiting, and your grandfather...'

'Not one single step,' Petra warned her.

'Oh, dear. I should never... Very well, then. I suppose it can do no harm for you to know now...after all, it was your mother your grandfather wanted to protect. He loved her so much, you see, Petra... He loved his sons, of course, but he had that love for her that a father will often have for his girl-child. According to my husband he spoiled her outrageously, but then I suppose that is an older brother speaking. When she left like that, your grandfather was beside himself...with anger...and with despair. He had planned so much for her...

'Your uncle—my husband—found him slumped across his desk, holding your mother's photograph. The doctor did not think he would survive. He was ill for a very, very long time. Oh...I should not have told you—not today,' her aunt said remorsefully as she saw how pale Petra had gone.

'All those wasted years,' Petra whispered. 'When they could have been together—when we could all have been together as a family!'

'He missed her dreadfully.'

'But my father wrote, sent photographs...'

Her aunt sighed.

'You have to understand, Petra. Your grandfather is a very proud man. He couldn't bear to accept an olive branch extended by your father. He wanted…needed to know that your mother still wanted him in her life, that she still loved him.'

'She believed that he would never forgive her,' Petra told her chokily, shaking her head.

'When the news came that your parents were dead, your grandfather…' Her aunt paused and shook her head. 'It was a terrible, terrible time for him, Petra. He couldn't believe it. Wouldn't accept that she was gone, that he had lost her. When he had his second heart attack we honestly believed that it was in part because he simply no longer wanted to live. But mercifully he recovered. It was his greatest wish then that you might come to us, but your godfather— wisely, perhaps, in the circumstances, thought it best for you that you remained in an environment that was familiar to you. But your grandfather never gave up hoping, and when he knew that your uncle was to meet your godfather he begged him to try to persuade you to come here. I can't tell you how happy you are making him today, Petra. I wish you every happiness, my dearest girl, for you most certainly deserve it.'

As her aunt leaned forward to embrace her Petra felt her eyes burn with emotional tears.

In a daze she made her way out to the waiting car and her grandfather. Suddenly she was seeing him with new eyes. Loving, compassionate eyes. As she sat beside him she reached out and touched his hand. Immediately he clasped hers.

'You may kiss the bride!'

Petra felt her whole body clench against the pain of what was happening. Unable to move, she felt the coldness thrown by Rashid's shadow as he bent towards her.

She waited until the last possible second to turn her head

away, so that his dutiful kiss would only brush her cheek and not her lips. But to her shock, as though he had known what she would do, as she moved so did he, lifting his hand so that to their audience it looked at though he were cupping the side of her face in the most tender gesture of a lover, unable to stop himself from imbuing even this, a formal public rite, with the possessive adoration of a man deeply in love.

Only she knew that what he was actually doing was preventing her from turning away from him, that he was reinforcing to her his right, his legally given right as her husband, to demand her physical acceptance of him.

His mouth touched hers, and she trembled visibly with the force of her anger. She had believed in him, trusted him, loved him, but all the time he had been deceiving her, lying to her. How could she ever trust her own judgement again?

She would have to be constantly on her guard against it! And against him?

He moved, the smallest gesture that brought his nose against hers in the merest little touch, as though he wanted to offer her comfort and reassurance. Another lie…another deceit…and yet for an instant, caught up in the intensity of the moment, she had almost swayed yearningly towards him, wanting it to be real!

Suddenly Petra felt desperately afraid. She had thought in her ignorance that it would be enough simply for her to know what Rashid was to stop herself from continuing to love him, but now, shockingly, she wasn't so sure!

She hated him for what he had done; she knew that! So why did he still have the power to move her physically, to make her want him?

What was she thinking? Was she going crazy? She did

not want him. Not one tiny little bit! Fiercely she pushed against him. To her relief he released her immediately.

The ceremony was over. They were man and wife!

'I never knew that Rashid's middle name was Blaize.' That was her cousin Saud, flushed and excited, openly proud of his new relationship with his hero.

'Petra, my dear, your father would have been so proud had he been here today.'

Numbly Petra smiled automatically at the American Ambassador.

'Petra, you look so breathtakingly beautiful,' his wife, an elegant Texan with a slow drawl said with a warm smile. 'Doesn't she Rashid?' she demanded, causing Petra to stiffen, the tiny hairs on the back of her neck lifting as Rashid turned to look at her.

'She is my heart's desire,' Rashid responded quietly, without taking his gaze off her.

'Petra, take him away and hide him before I turn green, you lucky girl,' the Ambassador's wife teased.

'I am the one who is lucky,' Rashid corrected her.

'He certainly is,' Petra chimed in brittly. 'Today he isn't just gaining a wife, are you, Rashid? He's gaining the opportunity to design a new multi-million-pound-complex, and—'

'I'm certainly going to need some good commissions if I'm to keep you in the style your grandfather is accustoming you to.' Rashid cut across her outburst in a light drawl that masked the icy, glittering look of warning only she could see. 'At least if that necklace you're wearing is anything to go by.'

'Yes, it's gorgeous,' another of the guests enthused.

Petra tensed as she felt Rashid's hand beneath her elbow.

'I don't know why you're so determined to play the adoring husband,' she told him bitterly.

'No, I don't suppose you do,' he agreed.

'Why didn't you tell me that your second name was Blaize?'

He gave a small dismissive shrug.

'Does is it matter? Rashid or Blaize—I am still the same man, Petra. The man who—'

'The man who lied to me and trapped me,' Petra snapped at him. 'Yes, you are.'

Out of the corner of her eye she could see his mouth compress.

'We're married now, Petra, and—'

'For better, for worse… Don't remind me. We both know which it will be, don't we?'

'Look, it doesn't have to be like this, Petra. After all, we both already know that we have something in common, some shared ground…'

'And what ground would that be? The ground you're hoping to design another billion-pound complex on? Money! Is that all you can think about?'

Petra tensed as she felt his grip move from her elbow to her upper arm and tighten almost painfully on it as he bent his head and whispered with menacing silkiness in her ear, 'I would have thought that I had already proved to you that it is not. But if you wish me to show you again…'

Petra jerked away from him as though she had been scalded.

'If you ever, ever try to force me to…to accept you as my husband physically, then—'

'Force you?'

For a minute he looked as though she had somehow shocked him, but then his expression changed, hardening.

'Now you are being ridiculous,' he told her curtly. 'There

has never been any question of my doing any such thing. Even though…'

'Even though what?' Petra challenged him bitterly. 'Even though legally it is your right?'

She was almost beside herself with misery and anguish mixed to a toxic consistency by an over-active imagination and the fear that she was not as indifferent to him as she wanted to be.

Now that the ceremony was over she was face to face with the knowledge that tonight she would be his wife—his bride. He was a sensually passionate man; she already knew that! If he chose to consummate their marriage would she have the strength to reject and deny him?

'Rashid, your uncle has been looking for you…'

Petra released her breath in a sigh of relief as he moved away from her.

Several hours later, blank-eyed with exhaustion and misery, Petra stared bitterly in front of her, wishing she was anywhere but where she was and anyone but who she was—or rather who she was now.

Her godfather had not been able to join them. No doubt he would save his celebrations until after the New Year and the announcement of his peerage, Petra reflected savagely.

Her marriage to Rashid had been trumpeted in the press as the romance of the year, but of course she knew better! She hated Rashid more than she had ever thought it possible for her to hate anyone, she decided wearily, and she knew she would never, ever forgive him for what he had done to her.

Finally the celebrations were drawing to a close. Finally her attendants were coming to carry her away to the suite that had been set aside for her to change out of her wedding dress and into her 'going-away' clothes.

'Where is Rashid taking you on honeymoon? Do you know?' one of the girls, a married niece of her aunt, asked Petra before shushing the knowing giggles of some of the younger bridesmaids.

Petra was tempted to reply that she neither knew nor cared, but good manners prevented her from doing so.

'I don't really know,' she replied instead.

'It's a secret. Oh, how romantic,' another of the girls exclaimed enviously.

Yet another chimed in, more practically, 'But how did you know what clothes to pack if you don't know where you are going?'

'She's going on honeymoon, silly,' another one submitted. 'So clothes won't—'

'Stop it, all of you,' the oldest and most sensible of her attendants instructed. 'You are supposed to be helping Petra, not gossiping like schoolgirls. You must not worry. A man as experienced as Rashid will know exactly what to do!' she soothed Petra. 'I can remember how nervous I was on my wedding night. I had no idea what to expect, and I was terrified that my husband would not know what I needed, but I should have had more trust in him…or rather in my mother.' She grinned. 'She had ensured that I had all the right clothes—although I suspect if it had been left to Sayeed I might not.'

Clothes! She was talking about clothes! Petra didn't know whether to laugh or cry!

At last it was over and she was ready, dressed in the simple cream trouser suit she had bought in the exclusive shopping centre nearby. The plain diamond ear studs which had been her mother's, and which she had worn since her death, had been removed from her ears and replaced by the much larger pair which had been part of Rashid's wedding present to her. She felt like ripping them out and destroying them, but of course that wasn't possible, with her attendants exclaiming excitedly over the clarity and perfection of the stones, obviously chosen to complement the diamonds in her platinum engagement and wedding rings.

She had been misted with a fresh cloud of Rashid's perfume, and handed the minute scraps of silk and lace that her aunt was pleased to call underwear—Petra still couldn't believe that such minute scraps of fabric could cost so very, very much. Her manicure and pedicure had been checked by her eagle-eyed chief attendant, who seemed to believe that it would be a lifelong reflection on her if Petra was not handed over into the hands of her new husband looking anything less than immaculate. Now she was apparently ready to be handed into the care of her husband like a sweetmeat to be unwrapped and enjoyed—or discarded as he saw fit!

'Come—it is time. Rashid is waiting,' her chief attendant announced importantly.

As Petra looked towards the closed door to the suite the busy giggles fluttering around her died away.

'Be happy,' the chief attendant told her as she kissed her.

'May your life be full of the laughter of your children and the love of your husband,' the second whispered, as all the girls queued up to offer her their good wishes for her future and exchange shy embraces with her.

'May the nights of your marriage be filled with pleasure,' the boldest-eyed and most daring told her.

The noise from outside her suite was becoming deafening.

'If we do not open the door soon Rashid might break it down,' someone giggled, and there was an instant flurry of excited and delighted female panic as the door was pulled open and Petra was prodded and pushed through it.

The assembled wedding guests standing outside cheered

exuberantly when they saw her, but Petra barely noticed their enthusiasm. Across the small space that separated them her bitter gaze clashed with Rashid's.

Like her, he was dressed in Western-style clothes. Designers the world over would have paid a fortune to have Rashid wearing their logo, Petra decided with clinical detachment, refusing to allow her heartbeat to react to the casual togetherness of his appearance. Place him in any city in the world and he would immediately be recognised as a man of style and class, a man of wealth and knowledge. Wealthy, educated people like Rashid shared a common bond, no matter what their place of birth, Petra acknowledged distantly.

Silently he extended his hand towards her.

The crowd started to cheer. Briefly Petra hesitated, her glance going betrayingly to the windows, as though seeking freedom, but someone gave her a firm little push and her fingertips touched Rashid's hand and were swiftly enclosed by it.

With almost biblical immediacy, the crowd parted to allow them to pass through. The huge double doors to the private garden of the banqueting suite were flung open, and as they stepped out into the softness of the night perfectly timed fireworks exploded, sending sprays of brilliantly coloured stars showering earthwards.

At the same time they were deluged with handfuls of scented rose petals, and the air was filled with a pink-tinged cloud of strawberry scented *shisha* smoke. Doves swooped and flew, and a cloud of shimmering butterflies appeared as if by magic—music played, people laughed and called out good wishes to them, and Rashid drew her relentlessly towards the exit to the garden.

As he touched her arm and held her for one last second to face their audience, he whispered wryly in her ear, 'Your aunt wanted me to whisk you away on an Arab steed, complete with traditional Arabic trappings, but I managed to dissuade her.'

Caught off guard by the note of humour underlining his words, Petra turned automatically to look at him. 'You mean like a prince from an Arabian fairytale? Complete with medieval accoutrements including your falcon?'

'I suspect she would have wanted to pass on the falcon— for the sake of the doves—and I certainly would not have wanted to expose my prize birds to this fairground.'

As she looked at him Petra felt her heart suddenly miss not one beat but two.

As though a veil had abruptly lifted, giving her a clear view of something she had previously only perceived in a shadowy distorted fashion, she recognised an unwanted, unpalatable, unbearably painful truth!

In believing that logic, reality, anger and moral right were enough to destroy her unwanted love for Rashid she had deceived herself even more thoroughly and cruelly than Rashid himself could ever have done.

Had she married Rashid because secretly deep down inside she still wanted him? Still loved him? Petra was filled with self-contempt and loathing, her fiery pride hating the very idea!

She had believed that her most dangerous enemy lay outside the armed citadel of her heart, in the shape of Rashid himself, but she had been wrong. Her worst enemy lay within herself, within her own heart, in the form of her love for him.

But Rashid must never ever know that. She must forever be on her guard to protect herself and her emotions. She and they must become a fortress which Rashid must never be allowed to penetrate!

*   *   *

'Welcome to your new home!'

For the first time since they had left the hotel Rashid broke the silence between them. They had driven into the courtyard of the villa several seconds earlier, its creamy toned wall, warmed to gold by the discreet nightscape lighting. Her whole body rigid with the effort of maintaining the guard she was clinging to so desperately, Petra had discovered that her throat had locked so tensely that she couldn't even speak!

Once inside the villa she felt no more relaxed—quite the opposite.

'It's late, and it has been a very long day,' she heard Rashid saying calmly. 'I suggest that we both get a good night's sleep before you begin another round of hostilities. I have arranged for you to have your own suite of rooms. Not exactly the traditional way to conduct a wedding night, perhaps, but then it is not as though it would be our first time together.' Her gave a small dismissive shrug whilst Petra struggled to assimilate a feeling which was not entirely composed of relief! 'This has been a stressful time for you, and you need a little breathing space, I suspect, to accustom yourself to what is to be. Despite your comments earlier, I can assure you that there is no way I intend to…to force the issue between us, Petra!'

Petra stared at him. He sounded so controlled, so calm, so…so laid-back and casual almost. And as for his comment about arranging for her to have her own rooms—that was not at all what she had been expecting!

From the moment he had proposed formally to her this night had been at the back of Petra's mind. This moment when they would be alone as husband and wife. Fiercely she had told herself that no matter what kind of pressure he put on her to break down her resolve she would not allow him to touch her!

And yet now he was the one telling her that he did not want her!

A distinctly unpleasant mix of emotions filled her. Shock, disbelief, chagrin…and…

Disappointment? Most certainly not! Relief—that was what she felt. Yes, she was perhaps just a touch disappointed that he had stolen her thunder by not allowing her the satisfaction of being the one to tell him that she didn't want him. But at the end of the day what really mattered was that she was going to be free to sleep on her own…without him. Sleeping in her own bed and not his…just as though they were not married at all. And that was just what she wanted. Exactly what she wanted!

At last she was on her own. Which was just what she wanted. So why couldn't she go to sleep? Why was she lying here feeling so…lost and abandoned? So unwanted…and unloved and so hurt?

What was it that she longed for so much? Rashid? Blaize?

No! What she ached for, so much that it hurt, Petra acknowledged tormentedly as she burrowed into the emptiness of her huge bed, was to be able to trust the man she loved. Because without such trust, without being able to be open and honest with one another, how could two people possibly claim to share love?

CHAPTER TEN

A LITTLE apprehensively, Petra surveyed the other women crowding into the exclusive enclosure.

It was the start of the horse racing season and Petra suspected that by now, after over a month of marriage, she ought to be familiar with the high-octane and very glamorous nature of the social events to which her position as Rashid's wife gave her an entrée.

In the short time they had been married they had already had the tennis championships, and a celebrity golf tournament, in addition to a whole host of business events sponsored by the Royal Family in which Rashid, as one of their most favoured architects and a business partner, had played a high-profile role.

And now, within a few days, it would be the most prestigious event of the Zuran social calendar—the Zuran Cup, the world's most glamorous horse race.

Horses, trainers, jockeys, owners and their elegant wives had been pouring into Zuran all month—the whole city was in a state of excited expectancy over the race and its eventual winner.

Rashid was entering his own horse, an American-bred and Irish-trained three-year-old stabled at his training yard close to the racecourse. Along with a mere handful of other specially favoured owners, Rashid was permitted to use the actual racecourse itself for training purposes.

Petra and Rashid were due to entertain a group of businessmen and diplomats and their partners from America and Europe, and for the duration of Race Week they would be staying at the hotel complex with their guests.

Unlike some of the other wives, Petra had not found it necessary to fly to Paris or Milan to order a series of one-off couture outfits for the event—although she had taken her aunt's advice and been to see a visiting top milliner to ensure that her hat for the occasion was 'special' enough for her position as the wife of an owner of one of the competing horses.

At the breathtakingly stunning villa he had designed and had built, in its equally breathtaking setting of his private oasis, they had entertained a variety of prominent politicians, sportsmen and women and businessmen from all over the world, including the UK, and never once on any of those occasions had Rashid faltered in enacting his own chosen role of devoted husband.

But in private things were very different. Rashid kept to his own suite of rooms in the villa, as she did hers, and when they were not entertaining or being entertained Petra hardly saw him.

He was either working, visiting various projects he was involved in virtually all over the world or, when he was at home, he would be down in the stables where he kept the racehorses he had in training, discussing their progress with his racing manager.

Of course Petra had commitments of her own. She had been invited to join the Zuran Ladies Club, headed by Her Highness—the club's remit being to provide a common ground for the exchange of ideas between women belonging to different nationalities and cultures. She had gone to women's lunches and fund-raising events, and an embryo friendship was developing between her and her most senior wedding attendant—a relative of her aunt by marriage. But these were the outer layers of her married life.

The inner ones were very different and very painful.

Common sense told her that the discovery she had not conceived Rashid's child should have been greeted with relief. Instead she had spent the night silently weeping with anguished disappointment. His child would at least have been something of him she would have been allowed to publicly love.

And that was the private pain which was slowly destroying her.

Outwardly, in the eyes of other people, she must seem as though she had everything anyone could possibly want, Petra reflected as she checked her appearance in her bedroom mirror.

Rashid, who was currently away on business and was not due to return for another two days, had kept his promise not to touch her. Indeed, he quite obviously found it a very easy promise to keep; his relaxed calm politeness whenever they were together made her grit her teeth together against the fury of physical and emotional confusion she herself was enduring.

How was it possible for her to want him so much when he quite obviously did not want her? She lay in bed at night aching for him. Longing for him, thinking about him—fantasising about him, if she was honest—and then in the morning was filled with such a sense of self-revulsion and despair at her own lack of self-control that she despised herself even more than she did him.

He treated her as distantly as though she were merely a visiting house guest—an outsider to his world and life to whom he was obliged to be polite. She had absolutely no idea what he might be thinking or feeling about their marriage, or about her, and that further intensified her sense of loneliness and frustration. It was not natural to live in the way they were doing, and her body, her mind, her heart, her spirit rebelled against it.

She wanted to share her life and herself fully with the man she loved, but how could she do that when that man was Rashid, a man who did not love her in return? A man she could not trust!

She paused in the process of packing her clothes for their Race Week stay in the hotel complex, a tiny, fine tremble of sensation electrifying her at the thought of seeing Rashid. Angrily she dismissed it. She reminded herself firmly instead that she was due to visit the racecourse stables to discuss with Rashid's trainer what arrangements needed to be made with regard to guests visiting the stables to view the horses.

Already, although they were still in March, the temperature had climbed well into the high thirties, and Petra dressed accordingly, in cotton jeans and a long sleeved tee shirt, plus a hat to protect her head from the sun.

The young man Rashid had appointed as her driver smiled happily at her as he opened the car door for her.

Petra had timed her visit to coincide with the end of the morning exercise session, and when she walked into the yard it was bustling with activity as the newly exercised horses were returned to their stables.

Rashid's manager and trainer were standing together on the far side of the stable yard talking to one another as Petra walked in. Several other groups of people were in the stable yard, including two small dark-haired children.

Smiling at them, Petra started to make her way towards Rashid's manager and trainer, but as she did so she saw one of the children suddenly dart across the yard, right into the path of the highly strung, nervously sweating young horse being led across the yard by his handler.

As the horse reared up Petra reacted instinctively, making a grab for the child and snatching him from beneath the horse's hooves.

She could hear the uproar going on all around her; the shrill squeal of fear from the horse and the even shriller scream of panic from the child, the groom's anxious voice, the voices of the onlookers, and then the breath was driven out of her lungs as the world exploded in an agonising red mist of searing pain followed by a terrifying sensation of whirling darkness as she hit the ground.

Blearily Petra opened her eyes.

'Ah, good, you've finally come round properly.'

A uniformed nurse smiled at her. Weakly Petra began to move, and then winced as she felt the pain in her shoulder.

'Don't worry, it isn't serious. Just a very nasty bruise, that's all,' the nurse comforted her cheerfully. 'You were lucky, though, and the little boy you rescued was even luckier.'

The child! Petra sat up anxiously and then gasped as pain ripped through her shoulder.

'Are you sure he's okay?' she pressed the nurse.

'He's fine—in fact I think his father is in a worse state of shock than he was. They are related to the Royal Family, you know. Cousins, I think. The father couldn't sing your praises highly enough. He is convinced that if you hadn't acted so promptly the horse might have killed his son.'

'It wasn't the horse's fault!' Petra protested. 'The yard was busy, and he was obviously nervous... Ouch!' She winced as the nurse readjusted the strapping holding the protective pad in place against her skin.

'Don't worry, I'm just checking to see if you've stopped bleeding.'

'Bleeding?' Petra frowned.

'The horse's shoe caught your shoulderblade, and as well

as inflicting a wonderful-looking bruise it's also broken the skin. It looks fine now, though.'

'Good—in that case, I can get dressed and go home,' Petra said.

'Not until the doctor has given you the all-clear,' the nurse warned her.

Half an hour later Petra was sitting fully dressed on the side of her bed, frowning mutinously at the young doctor confronting her.

'Look, I can't stay in overnight,' she told him firmly. 'We're less than a week away from Race Week, and I've got a hundred things I have to do. You've said yourself that you're ninety-nine per cent sure that I don't have concussion, and—'

'I would still prefer you to stay in overnight, just to be on the safe side,' the doctor was telling her insistently.

Petra shook her head.

'There really isn't any need. I promise you I feel fine.'

'We should at least alert your husband to what has happened,' the doctor persisted.

Rashid. Petra tensed. Right now he was in London, overseeing some problem with the alterations to the hotel which the Royal Family had just acquired to add to their portfolio of hotel properties. He wasn't due back for another two days, and she could just imagine how he was going to feel if he was dragged back on account of a wife who emotionally meant nothing whatsoever to him at all!

Determinedly she set about convincing the young doctor that there was no reason why Rashid should be unnecessarily alarmed about a mere minor accident, when he would be home within a couple of days anyway, and to Petra's relief he seemed to accept her argument.

When it came to allowing her to go home, though, he

was harder to persuade, but in the end he gave in and said that provided she was not going to be left on her own, and that there was someone there to keep an eye on her, he would agree to discharge her.

Assuring him that there was, Petra held her breath whilst he checked her bruised shoulder, and then wrote her a prescription for some painkillers, before finally agreeing to her discharge.

An hour later she was on her way home, gritting her teeth against the unexpectedly intense pain in her shoulder as she was driven slowly and carefully back to the villa by her very protective and anxious young driver.

Once there, she was fussed over by Rashid's staff to an extent that made her grit her teeth a little and insist that they stop treating her as though she was a fragile piece of china.

Within an hour of her return she had received so many concerned telephone calls that she was refusing to take any more, and the largest reception room of the villa was filled with floral tributes—including an enormous display from the Royal Family, thanking her for rescuing one of their family.

Ignoring the dull, nagging ache which even the strong painkillers she had been given at the hospital had not totally suppressed, Petra went into the room she used as her office and started to go through the sample menus submitted to her by the hotel's senior chef.

Their guests would be dining in one of the hotel's private dining rooms, and Petra worked into the evening, meticulously checking the profiles she had been given of their guests against the chef's suggested menus, stopping only to eat the light meal which Rashid's housekeeper brought her and to reassure her that she was feeling completely fine apart from having an aching shoulder. At midnight Petra decided that she had had enough and tidied away her papers before making her way to her suite.

The live-in staff had their own quarters, separate from the main villa. Quite what the housekeeper thought of a newly married couple who slept apart Petra had no idea, but the housekeeper had confided to her that Rashid had had her suite of rooms completely redecorated prior to their marriage, even though the villa was brand-new and the rooms had previously been unoccupied.

The villa embraced the best of both Eastern and Western cultures, and had a clean, almost minimalistic look that reminded her of certain exclusive West Coast American homes belonging to friends of her parents, where modern simplicity was broken up and softened by the intriguing addition of single antique pieces. In the case of Rashid's villa, there was an underlying sense of traditional Moorish décor which really appealed to Petra's senses. Even the colours he had chosen were sympathetic to the eye and the landscape: pale sands, soft terracottas, a delicate watery blue-green here and there to break up the neutral natural colours.

Stunning sculptures and pieces of artwork made subtle statements about Rashid's wealth and taste, fabrics made to delight the touch as well as the eye softened any starkness—and yet the villa felt alien and unwelcoming to Petra.

Despite its elegance and comfort, something essential was missing from it. It was a house empty of love, with no sense of being a home, of having a heart! To Petra, acutely sensitive about such things, it lacked that aura of being a place where people who loved one another lived.

She winced a little as she removed the bandage from her back and shoulder, but when she peered over her shoulder to study her reflection in the mirror in her bathroom she was relieved to see that, despite the livid bruising swelling her skin, the raw scrape on her flesh looked clean and had stopped bleeding. As she stood beneath the warm spray of a shower that was large enough for two people to share with comfort she winced a little with pain. She would have some discomfort for some days to come, the doctor had warned her.

It was the horse she felt most sorry for, Petra decided ruefully a little later as she discarded her wrap and slid naked into her bed. The poor animal had been nervous enough before the incident.

Her bed felt deliciously cool. It had been made up with clean, immaculate linen sheets that day. Forlornly Petra turned onto her side. The bed was huge, making her feel acutely conscious of the fact that, despite her marriage, she was still living the life of a partnerless woman. A woman whose husband did not want her, did not desire her, did not love her. Whilst she…

Whilst she had not gone one single night since her marriage without longing for Rashid to be here with her, without giving in to the hopeless, helpless temptation to recreate those hours she had spent in his arms at the oasis. Tiredly Petra closed her eyes against the slow fall of threatening tears.

Abruptly Petra opened her eyes, wincing as she tried to move her painfully stiff shoulder.

'Petra, are you all right?'

She gave a small gasp of shock as she stared into the darkness to where Rashid was sitting beside the bed.

'Rashid!'

Immediately she struggled to sit up, ignoring the dull nagging ache from her shoulder as she clutched the bed-clothes to her body, her heart thudding furiously.

'You weren't supposed to be coming back yet! What are you doing here?'

'What do you think I'm doing here?' he answered her grimly. 'I received a message to say that you had been involved in an accident and that there were grave concerns that you could be suffering from concussion. Naturally I caught the first flight back that I could.'

'You didn't need to do that.' Petra protested. 'I'm perfectly all right…apart from a stiff shoulder,' she added ruefully.

Whilst she had been speaking Rashid had switched on the lamp at the side of her bed.

Petra sucked in her breath as she saw him properly for the first time. She had never seen him looking so formidably severe, harsh lines etched from his nose to his mouth, his expression wintry and bleak.

'I'm sorry that you had to come back—' she began.

'What on earth were you thinking about?' Rashid overrode her apology. 'Is marriage to me really so unbearable that you prefer to throw yourself under the hooves of a horse and be trampled to death?'

Petra stared at him, stunned by the bleak bitterness in his voice.

'It wasn't like that,' she protested. 'There was a child…I simply acted instinctively, as anyone would have done.'

His frown deepened.

'I hadn't heard about a child, only that there had nearly been a terrible tragedy and that you had insisted on leaving the hospital even though there was concern that you might not be well enough to do so.'

'I have a bruised shoulder, that is all.' Petra told, him making light of her injury. The truth was that she was far more interested in discovering why the thought of her being injured had brought him all the way home from London than in discussing her very minor bruises with him.

'When I spoke to the hospital the doctor said that he was concerned there was a risk that you might experience concussion.'

'You came back because of that?' Petra was openly incredulous.

'He warned you that you should not be on your own,' Rashid told her grimly.

'He admitted that the risk was minimal and that he was virtually one hundred per cent sure that I would be okay. And anyway I'm not on my own—the staff—' Petra began.

'Are not here to keep a proper watch over you,' Rashid interrupted her. 'But I am.'

As he spoke he moved, and Petra saw how tired he looked.

'Rashid, I'm fine,' she told him. 'Look, why don't you go to bed and—'

'I'm staying right here,' he told her flatly.

Petra sighed. 'I promise you, there is no need. If I hadn't felt completely well I would not have come back to the villa.'

'That's fine. But, like I just said, until I'm convinced that you're okay I'm staying here,' Rashid reiterated.

Petra sighed again, hunching her uninjured shoulder defensively as she told him tiredly, 'Have it your own way, Rashid, but honestly there's no need for you to stay.'

As he reached out to switch off the light Rashid instructed her flatly, 'Go back to sleep.'

Quietly Petra moved her head. She could hear Rashid breathing, but she couldn't see him sitting in the chair beside her bed. And then, as she looked across the bed, she saw him.

He was lying on his back on the bed beside her fast asleep.

The moon was up and full, casting a soft silvery light through the gauzy curtains of her room. Propping herself up on one elbow, she studied Rashid's sleeping form. Watching him sleep and seeing him so vulnerable sent a huge wave of tenderness aching through her.

At some stage he had unfastened the shirt he had been wearing and the white fabric was a pale blur against the darkness of his skin. There was evidence of his long day in the dark shadow bearding his jaw, and her muscles tensed a little in female response to such evidence of his maleness. Before she could stop herself she was reaching out to touch his jaw experimentally with her fingertips, and she felt her tenderness give way to sharply spiked desire.

As her fingers started to tremble she snatched them away, curling them into a fist and imprisoning them with her other hand. But, although she had managed to stop herself from touching him, she couldn't stop herself from looking at him, her love-hungry gaze fastening greedily on his mouth, his throat, the exposed flesh of his torso.

Now it wasn't just her fingers that were trembling, it was her whole body! She could feel the hot urgency of her own desire seeping into every nerve-ending—seeping, flowing, flooding through her until it swamped her completely.

Rashid! Tormentedly she mouthed his name, and then jumped back as he stirred in his sleep, his eyes starting to open.

By the time he had fully opened them she had retreated to her own side of the bed and was lying defensively still as she tried to feign sleep.

'Petra?' She heard the anxiety in his sleep-thickened voice as he leaned towards her. His hand touched her throat, checking her pulse, monitoring its frantic race.

'Petra, wake up,' he was commanding her.

'Rashid, it's all right—I do not have concussion,' she told him briefly, guessing what he was thinking, turning her head to look at him and trying to shrug off his hand as she did so.

But suddenly he had gone completely still, his hand lying against her throat with heavy immobility. His gaze was fixed on her breasts, naked and exposed by her inadvertent negligence in failing to pull the covers up over her body.

She knew immediately and instinctively that he wanted her, and she knew just as instinctively that he would keep to the promise he had made her on the day of their wedding not to force himself on her.

All she needed to do was to reach for her covers and turn away from him. If that was what she wanted...

And if it wasn't? Hardly daring to acknowledge what was going through her mind, Petra held his gaze. She could feel the longing and need curling through her, gaining force and power, filling her until her whole body felt like a highly tuned instrument of desire, openly aching for his touch. She could feel her breasts swell and lift, her nipples tighten and ache, her belly sink in slightly against the desire flooding her sex.

Lifting her hand, she curled her fingers around his forearm, slowly caressing it, her eyes wide open as she gazed up into his.

She could feel the open tremor of his body at her touch, see the way he was fighting to draw extra air into his lungs. What was he thinking? Feeling? A fierce surge of excitement and power filled her as she read the answer in the hot gleam of his eyes and the immediate response of his body!

'Hold me, Rashid,' she commanded him boldly, shuddering violently as he did so, tightening his arms around her so that they were body to body, so that she could feel the heavy, exciting thud of his heart.

'Love me!' she whispered passionately against his hot skin, knowing that he could not hear the betraying words, only feel the warmth of her breath.

She heard—and felt—the low growl of sound he made deep in his throat! Frustration? Longing?

Her body responded to it immediately, her lips parting eagerly for the savage sweet pleasure of his kiss.

Instantly she was plunged into a spiral of aching need, a swift descent into the thick velvet heat of her own most primitive longings. Her hand pressed to the back of Rashid's head, she urged him to increase the pressure of his mouth against her own, until all rational thought was suspended beneath its bruisingly passionate heat.

Petra knew that she should have been horrified by and contemptuous of her own behaviour, that she should have totally resisted her own desire. But instead she could feel her heart turning over inside her chest and then slamming heavily into her ribs as shockingly elemental and savage emotions exploded into life inside her. She had wanted this so much, she recognised dizzily. She had wanted, needed him so much!

'Petra,' Rashid groaned against her mouth. 'This isn't...'

He moved, his hand accidentally brushing against her breast, and Petra froze. In the darkness she could feel his gaze searching the distance between them, penetrating the moon-silvered darkness and then fixing unerringly on the betraying peak of her nipple, where it pouted with deliberate invitation so dangerously close to his stilled hand.

'Petra?' This time when he said her name it held a different note, a male huskiness and timbre that her sensitive female ears interpreted as an open acknowledgement of his desire for her.

She could feel the power that his desire for her gave her. She was all Eve, a wanton temptress, holding her breath whilst she willed him to reach out to her, for her, already knowing the pleasure he would give her.

Very slowly his hand moved back towards her breast. Petra exhaled shakily, and then closed her eyes as he stroked her skin with the lightest of touches—so light that it was little more than a breath, and yet so sensual that her whole breast seemed to swell and yearn towards him.

'Petra.'

This time her name was muffled beneath the slow, lingering kisses he was threading around the base of her throat like a necklace. A necklace that reached down between her breasts and was then strung from the upper curve of one breast to the other.

At some stage Petra had started to tremble. Tiny little inner secret tremors at first, but by the time Rashid was cupping one breast in his hand, laving the delighted pink-flushed crest of the other with his tongue, they had turned into galvanic shudders of uncontrollable mute delight. And then not so mute, when Petra was forced to bite down hard on her bottom lip to prevent herself from crying out aloud.

When Rashid saw what she was doing he lifted his mouth from her nipple to watch her, and then slid his finger into her mouth, freeing her bottom lip whilst he told her thickly, 'Taste me instead, Petra!'

Her whole body reacted to his words, swept with a molten need that burned openly in her eyes.

'Yes! *Yes!*' he told her savagely, even though she had said nothing, spoken no question. But Petra knew that he had heard the silent hungry longing of her body, seen her need for him in her eyes.

'Yes,' he repeated more softly. 'Whatever… However…

Every which way you want, Petra. Every way, until you beg me to end our mutual torment.'

As he was speaking he was kissing her. Tiny slow kisses that were a torment in themselves as his hands shaped her body, effortlessly drawing from it everything that it ached so wantonly to give him and everything that she herself did not.

Her need, herself, her life. Her love…

She cried out in shocked denial under the touch of his tongue against her sex, and then cried out again in a low, guttural woman's cry of acknowledgement of the pleasure he was showing her. But when he moaned in response, and placed her hand on his body, her reaction caused him to lift his head and demand rawly, 'Did you think you are the only one to have pleasure in what I'm doing, in the feel of you, the heat of you, the taste of you? I've hungered for you like this Petra, for this intimacy with you…this possession of you.'

As he stopped speaking he turned his head and kissed the inside of her thigh. Petra trembled and then moaned as he kissed her again, more intimately. Her longing for his physical possession of her overwhelmed every other emotion she felt surging through her in an unstoppable, undammable torrent.

Petra didn't know if she had actually reached for Rashid or if he had simply known how she felt, how she ached…how she loved and needed. But suddenly he was there, where she most wanted him to be. Where she most needed him to be. Filling her with surge after powerful surge of exquisite sensation and unparallelled ecstasy.

She wanted it to never end. And yet she knew she would die if she did not reach the summit, the frantic crescendo of her completion. She thought she already knew the sensation, the pleasure, the fulfilment, but when the spasms began and she felt the hot sweet thickness of Rashid's own release within her she knew that all she had known had been a pale remembered shadow of real pleasure.

CHAPTER ELEVEN

'PETRA, are you sure you are all right?'

'Grandfather, I am fine,' Petra fibbed as she turned away from him to prevent him from seeing her tears.

He had arrived unexpectedly that morning, just after Rashid had left to visit the stables, anxious to find out how Petra was for himself.

'No, you aren't,' he insisted, coming up to her and turning her towards him. 'You are crying. What's wrong?' he asked sternly.

Petra bit her lip. She still felt seared, scorched, shamed by her memories of the previous night! And there was no point in her trying to mentally blame Rashid! She had been the one to instigate things…even if he had carried them…and her…to a point…place…she had never imagined existed!

She was furious with herself for her weakness, unable to accept her own behaviour. How could she have been so weak-willed as to give in to temptation? Why couldn't she make herself stop loving him? Especially when she knew there was no future for them; when she knew she couldn't trust him.

He didn't love her. He might have returned early from his business trip. He might have made love with her last night…he might even have stayed with her until she had fallen asleep. But he had never made any attempt to talk to her, to tell her…

To tell her what? That he loved her? But she already

knew that he did not, didn't she? She already knew that he had been forced to marry her!

They were trapped in a marriage which could only cause them both misery. And now, thanks to her behaviour last night, there could be additional complications. What if this time she *had* conceived his baby?

'You are not happy,' her grandfather was persisting. 'You are too thin…too pale. This was not what I expected when you and Rashid married. You are so obviously suited to one another in so many ways.' He started to frown.

Petra stared at him. Suited to one another! How could he think that?

'In your eyes, perhaps,' she told him unhappily. 'But no…! We should never have married. Rashid feels nothing for me. He doesn't love me and…I—'

'Petra, what nonsense is this?' her grandfather demanded immediately. 'Of course Rashid loves you! That has never been in any doubt! It is quite obvious how he feels about you from the way he talks about you, from the way he has behaved towards you.'

'No!' Petra stopped him in disbelief 'You're wrong! How can you say that he loves me? The only reason Rashid married me is because he…he had to!'

'Had to?' To Petra's consternation her grandfather actually laughed. 'What on earth gave you that idea? It was most certainly not the case at all!'

He gave her a wry look. 'It is, of course, true that the pair of you would logically be expected to marry, having spent so much time together unchaperoned, but I can assure you that there was no obligation for Rashid to marry you other than his own desire to do so! And I can also tell you that that desire sprang entirely from his love for you!'

Her grandfather shook his head. 'And, besides, Rashid would never have allowed himself to be involved in such a potentially compromising situation if he had not been passionately in love with you!'

Her grandfather spoke with such conviction that Petra was dumbfounded.

'There is only one reason Rashid married you, Petra,' he repeated. 'And that is quite simply that he loves you.'

'If that is true then why has he never told me so himself?' Petra asked emotionally, reluctant to allow herself to trust what she was hearing.

'Have you told him of your love for him?' her grandfather challenged her gently.

Biting her lip, Petra had to confess that she had not.

'But you do love him?' her grandfather persisted.

Petra could not bring herself to reply. She could see that her grandfather was frowning.

'If I have misjudged your feelings, Petra, then you must say so,' she heard him telling her with gentle firmness. 'Much as I like and respect Rashid, you are my granddaughter. If you have discovered that you do not love him, if you are in any way unhappy, then you can come home with me now and I shall speak to Rashid if you wish.'

Petra's eyes darkened with emotion.

'I feel so confused. There is so much I...I believed...I thought...' She stopped and took a deep breath. 'I thought that Rashid married me because of the financial benefits our marriage would bring him,' she confessed, blurting out her despair.

'The financial benefits?' Her grandfather looked bemused. 'Petra—' he began, but Petra stopped him, rushing on fiercely.

'Saud told me everything, Grandfather. You mustn't be cross with him. He didn't realise that I didn't know there was a...a plan to have me marry Rashid—whether I wanted to or not! Saud hero-worships him so much that he thought

I would be pleased…thrilled. I know all about…everything.
Even my godfather seemed to think it was a good idea. So
much so that he abandoned me here without my passport
so that I couldn't leave…'

'Petra, Petra. My dear child. Please! You are distressing
yourself so unnecessarily!'

Petra fell silent as she heard the pain in her grandfather's
voice. 'Come and sit down here beside me,' he commanded
her gently.

A little reluctantly she did so.

'You are right in thinking there was a suggestion that
you and Rashid should meet one another, and that it was
felt that…that you had a great deal in common—but you
must understand that a suggestion was all it was, made
more in jest than anything else. Saud obviously eaves-
dropped on that conversation and leapt to incorrect as-
sumptions…' He frowned. 'You may be sure that I shall
have some strong words to say to him about his behaviour
and his actions in passing on his totally unfounded as-
sumptions to you. As you say, he greatly admires Rashid…
But I can assure you that Rashid immediately insisted that
what was being suggested was totally out of the question.
Rashid has far too much pride, too much of the same spirit
I can see so clearly in you, to ever allow anyone else to
make that kind of decision for him,' he told her ruefully.

'As for your godfather.' He gave a small rueful shrug.
'He is a statesman and a diplomat—who knows what such
men think? Intrigue is their bread and meat. If it does not
exist then they create it!'

Petra had to acknowledge that there was some truth in
his assessment of her godfather, even if his description of
him leaned towards the slightly over-cynical.

Shaking his head, he continued, 'After losing Mija there
was no way I would ever want to repeat the mistake I made

with her. There was only one reason I wanted you to come to Zuran, Petra, and that is because you are my grandchild and because I longed so much to see you!'

'Grandfather, I know that you and Rashid are in business together,' Petra persisted. 'And that he is dependent on the patronage of the Royal Family! I know that there were diplomatic reasons…'

Petra stared at her grandfather as he started to laugh.

'Why are you laughing?' she demanded, offended.

'Petra, Rashid is a millionaire many times over in his own right, from the inheritance left to him by his father. We do have business interests in common, yes—and indeed the Royal Family are great admirers of his work—but Rashid is dependent on no one's patronage!'

Shaking his head, he added huskily, 'Petra, I did your mother a terrible wrong, but the price I paid is one I shall pay to the end of my days. There is never a sunrise when I do not think of your mother, nor a sunset when I do not mourn her loss.'

Petra blinked, her eyes wet with fresh tears. Instinctively she knew that her grandfather was telling the truth.

'Are you still feeling unhappy? Do you want to come home with me now?' he asked her. 'I shall speak with Rashid for you, if you wish. The decision is yours, but it seems to me that it would be a pity if two such well-matched people should lose one another through a simple matter of pride, and lack of communication and trust.'

Her grandfather made it all sound so easy!

'No… No, I do not wish you to speak to Rashid,' she answered him.

'I…I…can do that myself…'

The smile he was giving her made her colour self-consciously.

'It isn't for me to interfere, but you are my granddaughter,' he told her gently. 'It seems to me that you and Rashid are very well suited. You are both strong-minded, you are both proud, you share a spirit of independence; these are all good things, but sometimes such virtues can lead to a little too much self-sufficiency—claimed not because that is what a person necessarily wants but because they believe it is what they have to have in order to protect themselves. I think that both you and Rashid are perhaps afraid to admit your great love for one another because you fear the other will think you weak and in need.'

His intuitive reading of her most private and hidden feelings astonished Petra.

Part of the reason she had fought so hard to resist her love for Rashid *had* been because she feared its intensity. Could it be true, as her grandfather had implied, that Rashid felt exactly the same?

She was, she recognised, still trying to come to terms with the fact that she had made such an error of judgement in assuming why he had married her. But he had made no attempt to defend himself to her, had he? Out of pride? Or because he didn't really care what she thought? And he had deceived her about who he really was!

'Sometimes in life we are tested where we are most vulnerable. There are many ways of being strong, many reasons for being proud,' her grandfather was continuing gently. 'Only you can decide whether or not your love for Rashid is worth fighting for, Petra—whether it means enough to you for you to take the risk of reaching out to him, openly and honestly. Rashid has already taken that risk by marrying you. It is his way of saying how much he wants to be with you. Remember he has married you in free will and of his own choice. Perhaps it is now time for you to take your risk!'

Silently Petra absorbed his words. He had given her an

insight into the workings of Rashid's mind and heart that she had not previously contemplated, and the possibilities springing to life from that insight were giving her an entrancing, an intoxicating, an impossible to resist picture of what they could share together.

'I have additionally been instructed to give this to you,' her grandfather continued, changing the subject. He handed her a beautifully decorated piece of rolled parchment and a flat oblong package.

Petra frowned. 'What is it?'

'Open it and see,' he said with a smile.

Hesitantly Petra did so, her glance skimming the letter written on the parchment and then studying it more slowly a second time, before she turned to the package and quickly unfastened it.

'It's a letter from the father of the little boy—the one at the stables,' she told her grandfather. 'He has written to thank me and he has…' Her voice tailed away and she gave a small gasp as she studied the contents of the package.

'It's ownership papers for a…a horse…a yearling…'

'Bred out of the Royal stables,' her grandfather supplied for her. 'They are very grateful to you for what you did, Petra. You saved the life of a very precious child…and at no small risk to your own.'

'But a horse!' Petra was overwhelmed.

'Not just a horse,' her grandfather corrected her with a smile. 'But a yearling whose breeding means that he may one day earn you, his owner, the Zuran Cup!'

From the balcony of the Presidential Suite Petra could see down to the beach. Race Week and all its excitement and busyness was over. She and Rashid had said goodbye to their last guests and in the morning they were due to leave the hotel for the villa.

Rashid's horse had come in a very respectable fourth, and Petra's grandfather had teased him that he might soon find himself in the position of having his wife's horse competing with his own.

There had been no opportunity for them to be on their own together since the night Rashid had made love to her at the villa, or for Petra to raise the subject she was desperately anxious to talk to him about.

According to her grandfather, Rashid loved her!

On a sudden impulse Petra left the suite and hurried towards the lift.

It was already almost dusk, the sun loungers around the pool empty, the beach deserted apart from one lone figure collecting the discarded windsurfers.

For a second his unexpected appearance checked Petra, and then she took a deep breath. She had initially intended to come down here merely to think, but perhaps fate had decided to take a hand in events.

The sand muffled her footsteps, but even so something must have alerted Rashid to her presence because he turned round to watch her in silence.

His formal clothes had been discarded and he was wearing a tee shirt and a pair of jeans.

Trying to control her nervousness, Petra walked up to him. His silence unnerved her, and she moistened her lips with the tip of her tongue, her face flushing as his gaze trapped the small betraying movement.

'I…I…have a proposition I want to put to you,' she told him, superstitiously crossing her fingers behind her back as she spoke.

How was he going to react? Was he going to walk away? Was he going to ignore her? Was he going to listen to her? Petra knew which she wanted him to do!

'A proposition?'

Well, at least he was responding to her, even if she could hear a grim note of cynicism in his voice.

'What kind of proposition?'

'I have a problem and I think you could be the very person to help me,' she said.

It was a relief that it was now fully dusk and he couldn't see her face—although she suspected that he must be able to hear the anxiety and uncertainty in her voice. If she had felt nervous the first time she had propositioned him then she felt a hundred—no, a thousand times more so now. Then all that had been at stake had been her freedom; now it was her whole life…her love…everything!

'I need you to help me find out if the man I love loves me. Until today I believed that he didn't, but now it seems I might have been wrong.'

'The man you love?' he questioned, and there was a new note in his voice that sent Petra's pulses racing.

'Yes. I love him so much that I'm almost afraid to admit just how much—even to myself, never mind to him—and I thought…'

'Yes?'

He had moved so swiftly and silently, and she had been so engrossed in her own anxiety, that his sudden proximity to her caught her off-guard.

'I thought you might be able to show me a way to show him just how I feel…' she said huskily.

'Oh, you did, did you? What inducement exactly were you planning to offer me in return for my co-operation?'

There was a distinct huskiness in his voice now, and Petra allowed herself to relax just a little.

'Oh…' She pretended to consider. 'I was rather thinking in terms of…er…payment in kind…'

'Uh-huh…'

Uh-huh. Was that going to be his only response? Nothing

more? Nothing more positive? More encouraging? Fresh uncertainty gripped her.

'If you aren't interested—' she began.

'Did I say that?' He was standing even closer to her now.

'No,' she admitted. 'But…'

'If you really wanted to prove to him that you do love him, I think a good place to start would be right here,' she heard him murmur. 'Right here, in his arms, like this…'

His arms were closing round her, holding her tight. Relief melted the tension from her bones.

'Like this?'

Was that thrilled little squeak really her voice?

'Uh-huh. And then you might show him that you liked being here by putting your arms around his neck, looking up in his eyes and…'

'Like this, you mean?' Petra whispered.

'Sort of… You're on the right track—but it would be even better if you did this!' Rashid told her, showing her what he meant as he brushed her lips with his own.

'Mmm… But what if I want to kiss him properly?' Petra asked him.

'Well, then I think you should go right ahead,' Rashid replied. 'But I ought to warn you that if you do that, he could very well want to…'

Sometimes actions could speak far more informatively than words, Petra decided dizzily as she daringly silenced Rashid's soft-voiced instructions with the loving pressure of her mouth against his.

It was a long, long time before either of them wanted to speak again, but when they had finally managed to stop kissing one another Rashid told her masterfully, 'I think our negotiations might be better conducted somewhere more…private.'

'Oh?' Petra gave him a mischievous look. 'Have you anywhere specific in mind? Only I am staying at the hotel.'

'What I have in mind,' Rashid responded softly, with an erotic undertone to his voice that made her heart dance in excited anticipation, 'is a very large bed, in a room that is preferably soundproofed so that no one can hear your cries of pleasure other than me...'

Since he was threading each word on a necklace of kisses round her throat, in between teasing her lips with the briefest of sensual contacts with his mouth, Petra was not really able to focus on too many specifics—although the words 'bed' and 'pleasure' did manage to penetrate her dizzying mist of euphoria.

As he kissed his way up the side of her neck and nibbled on her earlobe she demanded huskily, 'So it is true, then—you do love me?'

So abruptly that it shocked her, Rashid released her. For a moment Petra went icy cold with fear, but then she saw the expression in his eyes.

'I fell in love with you here on this beach, the evening you propositioned me,' Rashid told her quietly. 'Up until then you had just been a name I had heard mentioned in connection with your grandfather—someone who shared a similar parental background to my own, yes, but there are many, many offspring of mixed marriages living here.' He gave a small dismissive shrug. 'And then you accosted me here, and told me your wild tale of believing you were about to be forced into marriage to a man I admit even I was beginning to despise after I had listened to your description of him! And I thought that Saud liked me!' he commented drolly.

Petra had the grace to give him an abashed look.

'My grandfather told me that I'd got it all wrong, and that Saud had misunderstood what he had overheard!'

'A passing comment, between business partners, that was never intended to be taken seriously. Knowing how concerned your family was about your grandfather's health, and the effect your visit might have on it, I volunteered to show you something of the complex. But never for one moment did I intend to do so with a view to seeing if you might be a suitable wife!'

'Did you really fall in love with me that night?' Petra couldn't resist asking him.

'When I asked you what kind of man you wanted, and you told me…' He paused and looked away from her, before looking back again. 'I am a very wealthy man, Petra, and naturally I have been pursued by the kind of woman who sees a man only in terms of the financial benefits she can gain from him. When you spoke so passionately of your feelings and your beliefs, your hopes and desires for the way you wanted your life and your love to be, they so closely mirrored my own that I knew I could not let you walk away from me. And then I kissed you.'

'And you knew then?'

Petra knew that her voice was trembling, and that Rashid would be able to hear quite clearly the joy and incredulity in it, but now she felt no need to hide her feelings or to feel ashamed of them.

'Yes,' Rashid acknowledged simply.

'I knew then, and I was determined to court you…and woo you…but unfortunately I hadn't reckoned on your stubborn determination not to fall in love with the man you believed me to be. I was beginning to panic. I was afraid that I might lose you. And then you found out who I was and I thought I *had* lost you. I wasn't going to allow that to happen. Not when I knew just how good things could be for us.'

Petra gave him a wry look. 'So you had made up your mind that I loved you, had you?'

'Quite simply I could not bear to think of how my life would be if you didn't!'

His admission dissolved any potential suspicion of arrogance or lack of respect for her feelings so immediately that Petra could only look softly at him.

'And,' Rashid continued huskily, 'I hoped—especially after the way you had given yourself to me with such wonderful passion and completeness—that you loved me. But I knew that time was running out for me, that as Rashid I could not continue to be "away on business" for much longer. And then came the desert.'

'When you couldn't take your eyes off the belly dancer!' Petra reminded him challengingly.

'I know her—after all, she is an employee of the hotel complex and she knew who I was! I was afraid that she might inadvertently give me away! But then you came to me…to my bed…and I knew I had to take a chance and find some way of keeping you permanently in my life. When you came to the hotel suite, to confront me, I seized on the opportunity it gave me to insist that we marry out of desperation.'

'But you said nothing, Rashid… You were so cold—so indifferent…'

'I felt guilty,' he admitted. 'I had railroaded you into marriage to get what I wanted…and I knew that I shouldn't have done that.'

'There are lots of things you shouldn't have done,' Petra mock reproved him. 'Including giving me a separate suite of rooms and tormenting me by letting me think that you didn't care.'

'But now you know that I do care,' Rashid whispered softly. 'You are the oasis of my life, Petra, the cool enriching gift of water to my parched desert. You and you alone have the power to make my heart bloom and flower.'

Misty-eyed, Petra listened to him.

'I want to go home, Rashid,' she told him shakily.

'Home!' He didn't try to hide either the starkness in his voice or the tormented, anguished pain in his eyes. 'You want to leave me! Perhaps I deserve it, after what I have done, but I cannot bear to let you go, Petra. Please, just give me a chance to show you, prove to you, how much I want to make you happy, to give you love. If you are not happy here in Zuran then we can live somewhere else— anywhere else that you choose—so long as you let me live there with you!'

Immediately Petra realised that he had misunderstood her, but his reaction was all the proof she could have asked for of just how much he did love her.

'I meant I want to go home with you, to our home,' she corrected his misunderstanding. 'To our home, our room, our bed...home to you, Rashid. You are my home, and wherever you are that is where my home is,' she told him with quiet sincerity.

As he wrapped her in his arms and proceeded to kiss her with fierce passion Petra could feel the fine tremble of his body.

'You know that I shall never, ever let you go now, don't you?' Rashid whispered to her. 'You are mine, Petra. My wife, my love, my life, my heart!'

ONE NIGHT WITH
THE SHEIKH
by
Penny Jordan

PROLOGUE

'YOU won't forget your mummy whilst I'm away working, will you, my precious baby girl?'

Mariella watched sympathetically as her younger half-sister Tanya's eyes filled with tears as she handed her precious four-month-old daughter over to her.

'I know that Fleur couldn't have anyone better to look after her than you, Ella,' Tanya acknowledged emotionally. 'After all, you became my mother as well as my sister when Mum and Dad died. I just wish I could have got a job that didn't mean I have to be away, but this six-week contract on this cruise liner pays so well that I just can't afford to give it up! Yes, I know you would support us both,' she continued before Mariella could say anything, 'but that isn't what I want. I want to be as independent as I can be. Anyway,' she told Mariella bitterly, 'supporting Fleur financially should be her father's job and not yours! What I ever saw in that weak, lying rat of a man, I'll never know! My wonderful sexy dream fantasy of a sheikh! Some dream he turned out to be—more of a nightmare.'

Mariella let her vent her feelings, without comment, knowing just how devastated and hurt her half-sister had been when her lover had abandoned her.

'You don't have to do this, Tanya,' she told her gently now. 'I'm earning enough to support us all, and this house is big enough for the three of us.'

'Oh, Mariella, I know that. I know you'd starve

yourself to give to me and Fleur, but that isn't what I want. You've done so much for me since Mum and Dad died. You were only eighteen, after all, three years younger than I am now, when we found out that there wasn't going to be any money! I suppose Dad wanted to give us all so much that he simply didn't think about what would happen if anything happened to him, and with him remortgaging the house because of the stock market crisis.'

Silently the sisters looked at one another.

Both of them had inherited their mother's delicate bone structure and heart-shaped face, along with her strawberry-blonde hair and peach perfect complexion, but where Tanya had inherited her father's height and hazel eyes, Mariella had inherited intensely turquoise eyes from her father, the man who had decided less than a year after her birth that the responsibilities of fatherhood and marriage simply weren't for him and walked out on his wife and baby daughter.

'It's not fair,' Tanya had mock complained to her when she had announced that she was not going to go to university as Mariella had hoped she would, but wanted to pursue a career singing and dancing. 'If I had your eyes, I'd have a ready-made advantage over everyone else whenever I went for a part.'

Although she knew how headstrong and impulsive her half-sister could be, Mariella admired her for what she was doing, even whilst she worried about how she was going to cope with being away from her daughter for six long weeks.

Whatever small differences there might ever have been between them, in their passionate and protective love for baby Fleur they were totally united.

'I'll ring every day,' Tanya promised chokily.

'And I want to know everything she does, Ella… Every tiny little thing. Oh, Ella…I feel so guilty about all of this…I know how you suffered as a little girl because your father wasn't there; because he'd abandoned you and Mum…and I know too how lucky I was to have both Mum and Dad and you there for me, and yet here is my poor little Fleur…'

Holding Fleur in one arm, Mariella hugged her sister tightly with the other.

'The taxi's here,' she warned, before releasing Tanya and tenderly brushing the tears off her face.

'Ella! I've got the most fab commission for you.'

Recognising the voice of her agent, Mariella shifted Fleur's warm weight from one arm to the other, smiling lovingly at her as the baby guzzled happily on her bottle. 'It's racehorses, dozens of them. The client owns his own racing yard out in Zuran. He's a member of the Zuran royal family, and apparently he heard about you via that chap in Kentucky, whose Kentucky Derby winner you painted the other year. Anyway—he wants to fly you out there, all expenses paid, so that you can discuss the project with him, see the beasts *in situ* so to speak!'

Mariella laughed. Kate, with her immaculate designer clothes and equally immaculate all-white apartment, was not an animal lover. 'Ella, what is that noise?' she demanded plaintively.

Mariella laughed. 'It's Fleur. I'm just giving her her bottle. It does sound promising, but right now I'm pretty booked with commissions, and, to be honest, I don't really think that going to Zuran is on. For a start, I'm looking after Fleur for the next six weeks, and—'

'That's no problem—I am sure Prince Sayid

wouldn't mind you taking her with you and February is the perfect time of year to go there; the weather will be wonderful—warm and mild. Ella, you can't turn this one down. Just what I'd earn in commission is making my mouth water,' she admitted frankly.

Ella laughed. 'Ah, I see…'

She had begun painting animal 'portraits' almost by accident. Her painting had been merely a small hobby and her 'pet portraits' done for friends, but her reputation had spread by word of mouth, and eventually she had decided to make it her full-time career.

Now she earned what to her was a very comfortable living from her work, and she knew she would normally have leapt at the chance she was being offered.

'I'd love to go, Kate,' she replied. 'But Fleur is my priority right now…'

'Well, don't turn it down out of hand,' Kate warned her. 'Like I said, there's no reason why Fleur shouldn't go with you. You won't be working on this trip, it's only a mutual look-see. You'd be gone just over a week, and forget any idiotic ideas you might have about potential health hazards to any young baby out there—Zuran is second to none when it comes to being a world-class cosmopolitan city!'

One of the reasons Mariella had originally bought her small three-storey house had been because of the excellent north-facing window on the top floor, which she had turned into her studio. With Fleur contently fed she looked out at the grey early February day. The rain that had been sheeting down all week had turned to a mere drizzle. A walk in the park and some fresh air would do them both good, Mariella decided, putting Fleur down whilst she went to prepare her pram.

It had been her decision to buy the baby a huge old-fashioned 'nanny' style pram.

'You can use the running stroller if you want,' she had informed Tanya firmly. 'But when I walk her it will be in a traditional vehicle and at a traditional pace!'

'Ella, you talk as though you were sixty-eight, not twenty-eight,' Tanya had protested. Perhaps she was a little bit old-fashioned, Mariella conceded as she started to remove the blankets from the running stroller to put in the pram. Her father's desertion and her mother's consequent vulnerability and helplessness had left her with a very strong determination to stand on her own two feet, and an extremely strong disinclination to allow herself to be emotionally vulnerable through loving a man too much as her mother had done.

After all, as Tanya had proved, it was possible to inherit a tendency!

She frowned as her fingers brushed against a balled-up piece of paper as she removed the bedding. It could easily have scratched Fleur's delicate skin. She was on the point of throwing it away, when a line of her sister's handwriting suddenly caught her eye.

The piece of paper was a letter, Mariella recognised, and she could see the name and address on it quite plainly.

'Sheikh Xavier Al Agir, No. 24, Quaffire Beach Road, Zuran City.'

Her heart thudded guiltily as she smoothed out the note and read the first line.

'You have destroyed my life and Fleur's and I shall hate you for ever for that,' she read.

The letter was obviously one Tanya had written but not sent to Fleur's father.

Fleur had always refused to discuss her relationship with him other than to say that he was a very wealthy Middle Eastern man whom she had met whilst working in a nightclub as a singer and dancer.

Privately Mariella had always thought that he had escaped far too lightly from his responsibility to her sister and to his baby…

And now she had discovered he lived in Zuran! Frowning slightly, she carefully folded the note. She had no right to interfere, she knew that, but… Would she be interfering or merely acknowledging the validity of fate? How many, many times over the years had she longed for the opportunity to confront her own father and tell him just what she thought of him, how he had broken her mother's heart and almost destroyed her life?

Her father, like her mother, was now dead, and could never make reparation for what he had done; but Tanya's lover was very much alive, and it would give her a great deal of satisfaction to tell him just what she thought of him!

Blowing Fleur a kiss, she hurried over to the telephone and quickly dialled her agent's number.

'Kate,' she began. 'I've been thinking…about that trip to Zuran…'

'You've changed your mind! Wonderful… You won't regret it Ella, I promise you. I mean, this guy is mega, mega rich, and what he's prepared to pay to have his four-legged friends immortalised in oils…'

Listening to her, Mariella reflected ruefully that on occasion Kate could show a depressing tendency to favour the material over the emotional, but she was an excellent agent!

CHAPTER ONE

ZURAN had to have the cleanest airport in the world, Mariella decided as she retrieved her luggage and headed for the exit area, and Kate had been right about Prince Sayid's willingness to spare no expense to get her to Zuran. In the first-class cabin of their aircraft Fleur had been treated like a little princess!

Arrangements had been made for her to be chauffeur-driven to the Beach Club Resort where she would be staying along with Fleur in their own private bungalow, and, thanks to the prince's influence with the right diplomatic departments, all the necessary arrangements to get Fleur a passport, with Tanya's permission, had also been accomplished at top speed!

Craning her neck, Mariella looked round the busy arrivals area searching for someone carrying a placard bearing her name.

Behind her she was vaguely aware of something going on, not so much because of an increase in the noise level but rather because of the way it suddenly fell away. Alerted by some sixth sense, Mariella turned round, her eyes widening as she watched the way the crowds parted to make way for the small phalanx of white-robed men. Like traditional outriders, they carved a wide path through the crowd to allow the man striding behind them to cross the marble floor unhindered. Taller than the others, he looked neither to the right nor the left so that Mariella's artist's eye was able to observe the patrician arrogance of a profile that could only belong to a man used to being in command.

Instinctively, without being able to substantiate her reaction, Mariella didn't like him. He was too arrogant, too aware of his own importance. So physically and powerfully male, perfect in a way that sent a hundred unwanted sexual messages skittering over her suddenly very sensitive nerve endings. He had drawn level with her, and, whether because she sensed her antagonism or because Mariella had gripped her just a little bit more tightly, Fleur suddenly broke the silence with a small cry.

Instantly the dark head turned in their direction whilst the equally dark eyes burned into Mariella's. Mariella registered his gaze as her body gave a small, tight shudder.

The dark eyes stripped her, not of her clothes, but of her skin, her defences, Mariella recognised shakily, leaving them shredded down to her bones; her soul! But his gaze lingered longest of all on her face. Her eyes, she realised as she returned his remote and disdainful look of contempt with one of smouldering fury.

Fleur made another small sound and immediately his gaze switched from her to the baby and stayed there for a while, before it switched back to her own as though checking something.

Whatever it had been it brought a sneering look of contempt to his mouth that curved it into an even more dangerous line, Mariella noticed as her body responded to his reaction with a slow burn of colour along her cheekbones.

How dared he look at her with such contempt? She didn't care who or what he was! Once she imagined her father must have looked so at her mother before walking out on her, before leaving her to sink into the needy despair and dependence that Mariella remembered so starkly from her childhood, until her stepfather with his love and kindness had come to lift them both out of the dark, mean place her father had left them in.

As swiftly and as silently as they had arrived the small group of men swept through the hall and left. As a production it had been ridiculously overdone and theatrical, Mariella decided as she found the chauffeur patiently waiting for her and allowed herself to be carefully driven along with Fleur in the air-conditioned luxury of the limousine.

The Beach Club Resort was everything a five-star resort should be and more, Mariella acknowledged a couple of hours later when she had finished her exploration of her new surroundings.

The bungalow she had been allocated had two large bedrooms, each with its own bathroom, a small kitchen area, a living room, a private patio complete with whirlpool, but it was the obvious forethought that had gone into equipping the place for a very young baby that most impressed Mariella. A good-sized cot had been provided and placed next to the bed, the bathroom was equipped with what was obviously a brand-new baby bath, baby toiletries had been added to the luxurious range provided for her own use, and in the fridge was a very full selection of top-of-the-range baby foods. However, it was the letter that had been left for her stating that the Beach Club's chef would prepare fresh organic baby food for Fleur on request that really made Mariella feel she could relax.

Having settled Fleur, who fell asleep as easily and comfortably as though she was in her own home,

Mariella checked her watch and then put a call through to her sister. Tanya's cruise liner was on an extended tour of the Caribbean and the Gulf of Mexico.

'Ella, how's Fleur?' Tanya demanded immediately.

'Fast asleep,' Mariella told her. 'She was fine on the flight and got thoroughly spoiled. How are you?'

'Oh…fine… Very busy…we're doing two shows each evening, with no time off, but as I said the money is excellent. Ella, I must go… Give Fleur a big kiss for me.'

A little guiltily, Mariella looked at the now-silent mobile. She hadn't said anything to Tanya about her determination to confront her sister's faithless ex-lover and tell him just what she thought about him! Tanya might have gone willingly to his bed, but Mariella knew she hadn't been lying to her when she had told her that she had believed that he loved her, and that they had a future together.

Mariella struggled to wake up from a confused and disjointed dream in which she was being dragged by her guards to lie trembling at the feet of the man who was now her master. How she hated him. Hated him for the way he stood there towering over her, looking down at her, looking over her so thoroughly that she felt as though his gaze burned her flesh.

He was looking deep into her eyes. His were the colour of the storm-tossed skies and seas of her homeland, a cold, pure grey that chilled her through and through.

'You dare to challenge me?' he was demanding softly as he moved closer to her. Behind her Mariella was conscious of the threatening presence of the guards.

She hated him with every sinew of her body, every pulse of blood from her heart. He left the divan where he had been sitting and came towards her, bending down, extending his hand to her face, but as his fingers gripped her chin Mariella turned her head and bit sharply into the soft pad of flesh below his thumb.

She felt the movement of the air as the guards leapt into action, heard them draw their swords, and her body waited for the welcome kiss of death, but instead the guards were dismissed whilst her tormentor stepped back from her. One bright spot of blood glistened on the intricately inlaid tiled floor.

'You are like a wildcat and as such need to be tamed,' she heard him telling her softly.

She could feel the cleanliness of her hair on her bare skin and froze as he slowly circled her, standing behind her and sliding his hand through her hair and then wrapping it tightly around his fingers, arching her back against his body so that her semi-naked breasts were thrown into taut profile. His free hand reached for the clasp securing her top and her whole body shook with outrage. And then abruptly he released her, turning to face her so that she could see the contempt in his eyes.

Swimming up through the layers of her dream Mariella recognised that his face was one she knew; that his cynical contempt was something she had experienced before...

In the half heartbeat of time between sleeping and waking she realised why. The man in her dream had been the arrogant, hawk-eyed man she had seen earlier at the airport!

Getting out of bed, she went into the bathroom, shaking her head to clear her thoughts, and then, when that tactic did nothing to subdue their dangerous, clinging tentacles of remembered sensuality, she turned on the shower, deliberately setting it at a punishing 'cool,' before stepping into it.

The minute the cool spray hit her overheated skin she shuddered, gritting her teeth as she washed the slick film from her body, and then stepping out of the shower, to wrap herself in a luxuriously thick, soft white towel. In the mirror in front of her she could see the pale, pearlescent gleam of her own skin, and dangerously she knew that if she were merely to close her eyes, behind her closed eyelids she would immediately see her tormentor, tall, cynically watchful, as he mocked her before reaching out to take the towel from her body and claim her.

Infuriated with herself, Mariella rubbed her damp skin roughly with the towel, and then re-set the air-conditioning. In her cot Fleur slept peacefully. Going to the fridge, Mariella removed a bottle of water and opened it. Her hand was shaking so much some of it slopped from the bottle onto the worktop.

Mariella and Fleur had just finished eating a leisurely breakfast on their private patio when a message came chattering through the fax machine. Frowning, Mariella read it. The prince had been called away on some unexpected business and would not now be able to see her for several days. He apologised to Mariella for having to change their arrangements, but asked her to enjoy the facilities of the Beach Club at his expense until his return.

Carefully smoothing sun-protection lotion onto Fleur's happy, wriggling little body, Mariella bent her head to kiss her tummy, acknowledging that this would be an ideal time to seek out Fleur's father. She had his address, after all! So all she needed to do was summon a taxi to take her there!

Kate had been quite correct when she had described Zuran's February weather as perfect, Mariella admitted half an hour later as she carried Fleur out into the warm sunshine. Since she was here on business and not holiday she had packed accordingly, and was wearing a pair of soft white linen trousers and a protective long-sleeved top. When she showed the taxi driver the sheikh's address he smiled and nodded. 'It will take maybe three quarters of an hour,' he told her. 'You have business with the sheikh?' he asked her conversationally.

Having learned already just how friendly people were, Mariella didn't take offence, replying simply tongue in cheek, 'You could say that.'

'He is a famous man. Revered by his tribe. They admire him for the way he has supported their right to live their lives in the traditional way. Although he is an extremely successful businessman it is said that he still prefers to live simply in the desert the way his people always have. He is a very good man.'

Mariella reflected inwardly that the picture the driver had just drawn for her was considerably at odds with the one she had gained from her half-sister.

Tanya had met the man in a nightclub, after all. Mariella had never liked the fact that Tanya worked there—although she had been employed as a singer, it openly advertised the sexual charms of its dancers, and Tanya had freely admitted that the majority of the customers were male.

And, certainly, during the twelve months they had been together, Mariella had never heard Tanya mention any predilection on her sexy sheikh's part to spend quality time in the middle of the desert! In fact, if she was honest, she had gained the impression that he was something of a 'playboy,' to use a perhaps now out-dated word.

It took just under forty minutes for them to reach the impressive white mansion, which the taxi driver assured her was the correct address.

A huge pair of locked wrought-iron gates prevented them from going any farther, but as if by magic an official stepped out of one of the pair of gatehouses that flanked the gates, and approached the car.

As firmly as she could Mariella explained that she wished to see the sheikh.

'I am sorry but he is not available,' the official informed her. 'He is away at the oasis at the moment and not expected back for some time.'

This was a complication Mariella had not been expecting. Fleur had woken up and was starting to grizzle a little.

'If you would care to leave a message?' the official was offering courteously.

Ruefully Mariella acknowledged inwardly that the nature of the message she wanted to give to the sheikh was better delivered in person!

Thanking him, she asked the taxi driver to take her back to the hotel.

'If you want, I can find someone to drive you to this oasis?' he suggested.

'You know where it is?' she questioned him.

He gave a small shrug. 'Sure! But you will need a four-wheel drive vehicle, as the track can be covered with sand.'

'Could I drive there myself?' Mariella asked him.

'It is possible, yes. It would take you two, maybe three hours. You wish me to give you the directions?'

It made more sense to drive to the oasis under her own steam than to go to the expense of paying a driver for the day as well as hiring a vehicle, Mariella decided.

'Please,' she agreed.

Methodically, Mariella checked through everything she had put on one side to pack into the four-wheel drive for her trip into the desert. The Beach Club's information desk staff had assured her that it would be perfectly safe for her to drive into the desert, and had attended to all the necessary formalities for her, including ensuring that a proper baby seat was provided for Fleur.

The trip should take her around three hours—four if she stopped off at the popular oasis resort for lunch as recommended by the Beach Club. But just in case she decided not to, they had provided her with a packed lunch in the form of a picnic hamper.

If it hadn't been for the serious purpose of her trip, she could quite easily have felt she were embarking on an exciting adventure, Mariella thought. Like everything else connected with the Beach Club, the four-wheel drive was immaculately clean and was even provided with its own mobile telephone!

The road into the desert was clearly marked, and turned out to be a well-built, smooth road that was so easy to navigate that Mariella quickly felt confident.

The secluded oasis where apparently the sheikh was staying was located in the Agir mountain range.

The light breeze, which had been just stirring the air when she had left the Beach Club, had increased enough to whip a fine dust of sand over her vehicle and the road itself within an hour of her setting out on her journey. The sand particles were so fine that somehow they actually managed to find their way into the four-wheel drive, despite the fact that Mariella had the doors and windows firmly closed. She had left the main road, now branched out onto a well-marked track across the desert itself.

It was a relief when she reached the Bedouin village marked on her map. It was market day and she had to drive patiently behind a camel train through the village, but fortunately it turned off towards the oasis itself, allowing her to accelerate.

In another half an hour she would stop for some lunch—if she hadn't reached the second oasis, marked on her map, she and Fleur would have their picnic instead.

The height of the sand dunes had left her feeling surprised and awed; they were almost a mountain range in themselves. Fleur was awake and Mariella turned off the radio to play her one of her favourite nursery rhyme tapes, singing along to it.

It was taking her longer than she'd estimated to reach the tourist base at the oasis where she had planned to have lunch—it was almost two o'clock now and she had expected to be there at one. A film of sand dust had turned the sky a brassy red-gold colour, and as she crested a huge sand dune and looked down into the emptiness on the other side of it Mariella began to panic slightly. Surely she should be able to at least see the tourist base oasis from here?

Ruefully she reached for the vehicle's mobile, realising that it might be sensible to ask for help, but to her dismay when she tried to make a call to the number programmed into the phone the only response was a fierce crackling sound. Stopping the vehicle she reached for her own mobile, but it was equally ineffective.

The sky was even more obscured by sand now, the wind hitting the vehicle with such force that it was physically rocking it. As though sensing her disquiet Fleur began to cry. She was hungry and needed changing, Mariella recognised, automatically attending to the baby's needs whilst she tried to decide what she should do.

It was impossible that she could be lost, of course. The vehicle was fitted with a compass and she had been given very detailed and careful instructions, which she had followed to the letter.

So why hadn't she reached the tourist oasis?

Fleur ate her own meal eagerly, but Mariella discovered that she herself had lost her appetite!

And then just as she was beginning to feel truly afraid she saw it! A line of camels swaying out of the dust towards her led by a robed camel driver.

Relieved, Mariella drove towards the camel train. Its leader was gravely polite. She had missed the turning to the oasis, he explained, something that was easily done with such a wind blowing sand across the track. To her alarm he further explained that, because of the sudden deterioration in the weather, all tourists had been urged to return to the city instead of remaining in the desert, but since Mariella had come so far her best course of action now was to press on to her ultimate destination, which he carefully showed her how to do using the vehicle's compass.

Thanking him, she did as he had instructed her, grimly checking and re-checking the compass as she drove up and down what felt like an interminable series of the sand dunes until eventually, in the distance through the sand blowing against her windscreen, she could just about see the looming mass of the mountain range.

It was already four o'clock and the light seemed to be fading, a fact that panicked Mariella into driving a little faster. She had never dreamed that her journey would prove so hazardous and she was very much regretting having set out on it, but now at last its end was in sight.

It took her almost another hour of zigzagging across the sand dunes to reach the rocky thrust of the beginnings of the mountain range. The oasis was situated in a deep ravine, its escarpment so high that Mariella shuddered a little as she drove into its shadows. This was the last kind of place she had expected to appeal to the man who had been her sister's faithless lover.

Would his villa here be as palatial as his home in Zuran? Mariella frowned and checked as the ravine opened out and she saw the oasis ahead of her. Remote and beautiful in its own way, it was very obviously a place of deep solitude, the oasis itself enclosed with a fringing of palms illuminated by the eerie glow of the final rays of the setting sun. Shielding her eyes, Mariella stopped the vehicle to look around. Where was the villa? All she could see was one solitary pavilion tent! A good-sized pavilion, to be sure, but most definitely not a villa! Had she somehow got lost—again?

Fleur had started to cry, a cross, tired, hungry noise that alerted Mariella to the fact that for Fleur's sake if nothing else she needed to stop.

Carefully she drove the vehicle forward over the

treacherously boulder-rutted track, which seemed more like a dry river bed than a roadway! Sand blowing in from the desert was covering the boulders and the thin sparse grass of the oasis.

There was a vehicle parked several yards from the pavilion and Mariella stopped next to it.

A man was emerging from the pavilion, alerted to her arrival by the sound of her vehicle.

As he strode towards her, his robe caught by the strong wind and flattened against his body revealing a torso muscle structure that caused her to suck in her own stomach in sharply dangerous womanly response to its maleness.

And then he turned his head and looked at her, and the earth halted on its axis before swinging perilously in a sickening movement as Mariella recognised him.

It was the man from the airport. The man from her dream!

CHAPTER TWO

HIS hand was on the door handle of the four-wheel drive. Wrenching it open, he demanded angrily, 'Who the devil are you?'

He was looking at her eyes again, with that same look of biting contempt glittering in his own as he raked her with a gritty gaze.

'I'm looking for Sheikh Xavier Al Agir,' Mariella responded, returning his look with one of her own— plus interest!

'What? What do you want with him?'

He was curt to the point of rudeness, but then, given what she had already seen—and dreamed—of him, she wouldn't have expected anything else.

'What I want with him is no business of yours!' she told him angrily.

In her seat Fleur's cries grew louder.

Peering into the vehicle, he demanded in disbelief, 'You've brought a baby out in this?'

The disgust and anger in his voice made her face sting even more than the pieces of sand blown against it by the wind.

'What the hell possessed you? Didn't you hear the weather warning earlier? This area was reported as being strictly out of bounds to tourists because of the threat of sandstorms.'

Hot-faced, Mariella remembered how she had switched off the radio to play Fleur's tapes.

'I'm sorry if I've arrived at an inconvenient time,'

she responded sarcastically to cover her own discomfort, 'but if you could just give me directions for the Oasis Istafan, then—'

'This is the Oasis Istafan,' came back the immediate and cold response.

It was? Then?

'I want to see Sheikh Xavier Al Agir,' Mariella told him again, gathering her composure together. 'I presume he is here?'

'What do you want to see him for?'

Mariella had had enough. 'That is no business of yours,' she said angrily. Inwardly she was worrying how on earth she was going to get back to the city and the comfort of her Beach Club bungalow and what on earth a man as wealthy as the sheikh was reputed to be was doing out here with this...this...this arrogant predator of a man!

'Oh, I think you'll find that anything concerning Xavier is very much my business,' came the gritted reply.

Something—Mariella wasn't sure what—must have alerted her to the truth. But she was too shocked by it to voice it, looking from his eyes to his mouth and then back again as she swallowed—hard—against the tight ball of shock tightening like ice around her heart. 'You...you...can't be the sheikh,' she told him defiantly, but her voice was trembling lightly, betraying her lack of confidence in her own denial.

Was this man her sister's lover...and Fleur's father? What was that sharp, bitter, dangerous feeling settling over her like a black cloud?

'You are the sheikh, aren't you?' she acknowledged bleakly.

A brief, sardonic inclination of his head was his only response but it was enough.

Turning away from him, she reached into the baby carrier and tenderly removed Fleur. Her whole face softened and illuminated with love as she hugged her and then kissed her before looking him straight in the eyes and saying fiercely to him, 'This is Fleur, the baby you have refused to both acknowledge and support.'

She had shocked him, Mariella realised, even though he had concealed his reaction very quickly.

As he stepped back from the vehicle for a second Mariella thought he was going to tell her to leave— and cravenly she wanted to do so! The man, the location, the situation were so not what she had been anticipating and prepared herself for. Each one of them in their different ways shattered not just her preconceptions but also her precious self-containment.

The man—try as she might she could just not envisage him in the club where Tanya had performed. The location made her ache for her painting equipment and brought her artistic senses to quick hunger. And her situation! Oh, no... Definitely no! This man had been her sister's lover, and was Fleur's father—

The shadowy fear that had stalked her adult years suddenly loomed terrifyingly sharply in front of her. She would not be like her mother; she would not ever allow herself to be vulnerable in any way to a man who could only damage her emotionally. The ability to fall in love with the wrong man might be learned, but it was not, to the best of Mariella's knowledge, inherited!

'Get out!'

Get out? With pleasure! Gripping the steering wheel, Mariella reached for the door, slamming it closed and then switching on the ignition at the same time, then she threw the vehicle into a furious spurt of reverse speed.

The tyres spun; sand filled the air. She could hear a thunderous banging on her driver's door as the car refused to budge. Looking out of the window, she saw Xavier looking at her in icy, furious disbelief.

Realising that she was bogged down in the swirling sand, Mariella switched off the engine. If he wanted her to leave he would have to move the vehicle for her, she recognised in angry humiliation.

As the engine died he was yanking the door open, demanding, 'What the hell do you think you are trying to do?'

'You told me to get out!' Mariella reminded him, equally angry.

'I meant get out of the car, not...' As he swore beneath his breath, to her shock he suddenly reached into the vehicle and snapped off her seat belt, grasping her so tightly around her waist that it actually hurt.

As he pulled her free of her seat and swung her to the ground she had a sudden shocking image of the two of them in her dream!

'Let go of me,' she demanded chokily, pushing him away. 'Don't touch me...'

'Don't touch you?'

Now that she was on the ground she realised just how far she had to look up to see the expression in his eyes.

'From what I've heard it isn't often those words leave your lips.'

Instinctively Mariella raised her hand, taking refuge in an act of female rebuttal and retaliation as ancient as the land around her, but immediately he seized her wrist in a punishing grip, his eyes glittering savagely as he curled his fingers tighter. 'Hell cat!' he taunted her mercilessly. 'One attempt to use your claws on me and, I promise you, you will regret it.'

'You can't go anywhere tonight,' he told her bluntly. 'There's a sandstorm forecast that would bury you alive before you could get even halfway back to the city. In your case it would be no loss, but for the sake of the child…'

The child…Fleur!

An agonised sound of distress choked in Mariella's throat. She could not stay here in this wilderness with this…this…savagely dangerous man, but her own common sense was telling her that she had no other option. Already the four-wheel drive was buried almost axle-deep in sand. She could taste it in her mouth, feel it on her skin. Inside the vehicle, Fleur had begun to cry again. Instinctively Mariella turned to go to her, but Xavier was there before her, lifting Fleur out.

The baby looked so tiny held in his arms. Mariella held her breath watching him… He was Fleur's father after all. Surely he must feel something? Some remorse, some guilt…something… True, he did pause to look at her, but the expression on his face was unreadable.

'She has your hair,' he told Mariella, before adding grimly, 'The wind is picking up. We need to get inside the tent. Where are you going?' he demanded as she turned back to the vehicle.

'I want to get Fleur's things,' she told him, tensing as he gave a sharp exclamation of irritation and overruled her.

'Leave them for now. I shall come back for them.'

Mariella couldn't believe how strong the wind had

become! The sand felt like a million tiny particles of glass shredding her skin.

By the time they reached the safety and protection of the pavilion, her leg muscles ached from the effort of fighting her way through the shifting sand.

Once inside the pavilion she realised that it was much larger than she had originally thought. A central area was furnished with rich carpets and low divans. Rugs were thrown over dark wood chests, and on the intricately carved tables stood oil lamps and candles. In their light Mariella could see two draped swags of cloth caught back in a dull gold rope as though they covered the entrance to two other inner rooms.

'Fleur needs something to eat, and a change of clothes,' she announced curtly, 'and I want to ring the Beach Club to tell them what has happened.'

'Use a telephone—in this intensity of sandstorm?' He laughed openly at her. 'You would be lucky to be able to use a landline, never mind a mobile. As for the child…'

'The child!' Mariella checked him bitterly. 'Even knowing the truth you still try to distance yourself from her, don't you? Well, let me tell you something—'

'No, let me tell you something… Any man could have fathered this child! I feel for her that she should have a mother of such low morals, a mother so willing to give herself to any and every man her eye alights on, but let me make it plain to you that I do not intend to be blackmailed into paying for a pleasure that was of so little value, never mind paying for a child who may or may not be the result of it!'

Mariella went white with shock and disbelief, but before she could defend her sister, Fleur started to cry in earnest.

Ignoring Xavier, Mariella soothed her, whispering tenderly. 'It's all right sweetheart, I know you're hungry…' Automatically as she talked to her Mariella stroked her and kissed the top of her head. She was so unbearably precious to her even though she was not her child. Being there at her birth had made Mariella feel as though they shared a very special bond, and awakened a maternal urge inside her she had not previously known she had.

'I don't know what she has to eat, but there is some fruit and milk in the fridge, and a blender,' he informed her.

Fridge? Blender? Mariella's eyes widened. 'You have electricity out here?'

Immediately he gave her a very male sardonic look.

'Not as such. There's a small generator, which provides enough for my needs.' He gave a brief shrug. 'After all, I come out here to work in peace…not to wear a hair shirt! The generator can provide enough warm water for you to bathe the child, although you, I am afraid, will have to share my bathing water.'

He was waiting for her to object, Mariella could see that. He was enjoying tormenting her.

'Since I shall only be here overnight, I dare say I can manage to forgo that particular pleasure,' she told him grittily.

'I shall go to your vehicle and bring the baby's things. You will find the kitchen area through that exit and to your right.'

Mariella had brought some dried baby food with her as well as some tinned food, which she knew would probably suit Fleur's baby digestion rather better than raw fruit, no matter how well blended! Even so, it would do no harm to explore their surroundings.

As she stepped through the opening she found that she was in a narrow corridor, on the right of which was an unexpectedly well equipped although very small kitchen, and, to the left, an immaculately clean chemical lavatory, along with a small shower unit.

The other opening off the main room must lead to a sleeping area, she decided as she walked back.

'What is all this stuff?' she heard Xavier demanding as he walked in with his arms full.

In other circumstances his obvious male lack of awareness of a small baby's needs might have been endearing, but right now...

Ignoring him and still holding Fleur, she opened the cool-bag in which she had placed her foods.

'Yummy, look at this, Fleur,' she murmured to her. 'Banana pudding...our favourite... Yum-yum.'

The look of serious consideration in Fleur's hazel eyes as she looked at her made her smile, and she forgot Xavier for a second as she concentrated on the baby.

'I suppose I shouldn't be surprised that she isn't receiving the nutrition of her mother's own milk,' she heard Xavier announcing critically.

Immediately Mariella swung round, her eyes dark with anger.

'Since her mother had to go back to work that wasn't possible!'

'How virtuous you make it sound, but isn't it the truth that the nature of that work—is anything but? But of course you will deny that, just as you will claim to know who the child's father is.'

'You are totally despicable,' Mariella stopped him. 'Fleur does not deserve to be treated like this. She is an innocent baby...'

'Indeed! At last we are in agreement about something. It is a pity, though, that you did not think of that before you came out here making accusations and claims.'

How could he be so cold? So unfeeling! According to the little Tanya had said about him, she had considered him to be a very emotional and passionate man.

No doubt in bed he was, Mariella found herself acknowledging. Her face suddenly burnt hotly as she recognised the unwanted significance of her private thoughts, and even worse the images they were mentally conjuring up for her; not with her sister as Xavier's partner—but herself!

What was happening to her? She was a cool-blooded woman who analysed, rationalised and resisted any kind of damaging behaviour to herself. And yet here she was...

'Just how long is this sandstorm going to last?' she asked abruptly.

The dark eyebrows rose. 'One day...two...three...'

'Three!' Mariella was aghast. Apart from the fact that Tanya would be beside herself if she could not get in touch with her, what was the prince going to think if he returned and she wasn't there?

'I have to feed and change Fleur.'

Luckily she had brought the baby bath with her as well as the changing mat, and Fleur's pram cum carry-cot, mainly because she had not been quite sure what facilities would be available at the oasis.

'Since it is obvious that you will have to stay the night, it is probably best that you and the child sleep in my... In the sleeping quarters,' Xavier corrected himself. Mariella's mouth went dry.

'And…where will you sleep?' she asked him apprehensively.

'In here, of course. When you have fed and bathed the child I suggest that we both have something to eat. And then—'

'Thank you, but I am perfectly capable of deciding for myself when I eat,' Mariella told him sharply.

She was far more independent, and a good deal more fiery, than he had anticipated, Xavier acknowledged broodingly when Mariella had disappeared with Fleur. And quite definitely not his younger cousin's normal type.

Thinking of Khalid made his mouth tighten a little. He had been both furious and disbelieving when Khalid had telephoned him to announce that he had fallen in love and was thinking of marrying a girl he had met in a dubious nightclub. Khalid had been in love before, but this was the first time he had considered marriage. At twenty-four Khalid was still very immature. When he married, in Xavier's opinion it needed to be someone strong enough to keep him grounded—and wealthy enough not to be marrying him for his money.

His frown deepened. It had been his cynical French grandmother who had warned him when he was very young that the great wealth he had inherited from his father would make him a target for greedy women. When he had been in his teens his grandmother had insisted that he spent time in France meeting the chic daughters of her own distant relatives, girls who in her opinion were deserving of inheriting the 'throne' his grandmother would have to abdicate when Xavier eventually married.

Well-born though they were, those girls had held

very little appeal for him, and, practical though he knew it would be, he found himself even less enamoured of the idea of contracting an arranged marriage.

Because of this he had already decided that it would be Khalid who would ultimately provide the heir to his enormous fortune and, more importantly, take his place as leader of their historically unique tribe. But he hadn't been in any hurry to nudge Khalid in the direction of a suitable bride—until he had learned of his plans *vis-à-vis* the impossible young woman who had forced her way into his private retreat!

He didn't know which of them had angered him the most! Khalid for his weakness in disappearing without leaving any indication of where he had gone, or the woman herself who had boldly followed up her pathetic attempt at blackmailing him via the letter she had sent Xavier, with a visit to his territory, along with the baby she was so determined to claim his cousin had fathered!

Physically he had not been able to see any hint in the child's features that she might be Khalid's; she was as prettily blonde as her mother, and as delicately feminine. The only difference was that, whilst her mother chose to affect those ridiculous, obviously false turquoise-coloured contact lenses, the baby's eyes were a warm hazel.

Like Khalid's?

There was no proof that the child was Khalid's, he reminded himself. And there was no way he was going to allow his cousin to marry her mother, without knowing for sure that Khalid was the father, especially now that he had actually met her. It was a wonder that Khalid had ever fallen so desperately in love with her in the first place!

'She has the grace of a gazelle,' he had written to him. 'The voice of an angel! She is the sweetest and most gentle of women…'

Well, Xavier begged to differ! At least on the two eulogising counts! Had he known when he had seen her at the airport just who she was he would have tried to find some way of having her deported there and then!

Remembering that occasion made him stride over to the opening to the pavilion, pulling back the cover to look outside. As had been forecast the wind was now a howling dervish of destruction, whipping up the sand so that already it was impossible to see even as far as the oasis itself. Which was a pity, because right now he could do with the refreshing swim he took each evening in the cool water of the oasis, rather than using the small shower next to the lavatory.

It both astounded and infuriated him that he could possibly want such a woman—she represented everything he most detested in the female sex: avarice, sexual laxity, selfishness—so far as he was concerned these were faults that could never be outweighed by a beautiful face or a sensual body. And he had to admit that, in that regard, his cousin had shown better taste than he had ever done previously!

Xavier allowed the flap of the tent to drop back in place and secured it. It irked him that Mariella should have the gall to approach him here of all places, where he came to retreat from the sometimes heavy burden of his responsibilities. A thin smile turned down the corners of his mouth. From what Khalid had described of the luxury-loving lifestyle they had shared, he doubted that she would enjoy being here. However little he cared about her discomfort, though there was the child to be considered.

The child! His mouth thinned a little more. Little Fleur was most definitely a complication he had not anticipated!

With Fleur fed, clean and dry, Mariella suddenly discovered just how tired she felt herself.

She had not expected Xavier to be pleased to be confronted with her accusations regarding his treatment of Tanya and Fleur, but the sheer savagery and cruelty with which he had verbally savaged her sister's morals had truly shocked her. This was after all a man who had very eagerly shared Tanya's bed, and who, even worse, had sworn that he loved her and that he wanted her to share a future with him!

In her opinion Tanya and Fleur were better off without him, just as she had been better off without the father who had deserted her!

Now that she had confronted him, though—and witnessed that he was incapable of feeling even the smallest shred of remorse—she longed to be able to get away from him, instead of being forced to remain here with him in the dangerous intimacy of this desert camp where the two of them...

Those ridiculous turquoise eyes looked even more theatrical and unreal in the pale triangle of her small exhausted face, Xavier decided angrily as he watched Mariella walking patiently up and down the living area of the pavilion whilst she rocked Fleur to sleep in her arms.

No doubt Khalid must have seen her a hundred or more times with her delicate skin free of make-up and those haunting, smudged shadows beneath her eyes as he lay over her in the soft shadows of the early morning, waking her with his caresses.

The fierce burst of anger that exploded inside him infuriated him. What was the matter with him? When he broke it down what was she after all? A petite, small-boned woman with a tousled head of strawberry-blonde hair that was probably dyed, coloured contact lenses to obscure the real colour of her eyes, skin the colour of milk and a body that had no doubt known more lovers than it was sensible for any sane-thinking adult to want to own to, especially one as fastidious in such matters as he was.

It would serve her right if he proved to Khalid just exactly what she was by bedding her himself! That would certainly ensure that his feckless cousin, who had abandoned his desk in their company headquarters without telling anyone where he was going or for how long, would, when he decided to return, realise just what a fate he had protected him from!

The child, though was a different matter. If she should indeed prove to be his cousin's, then her place was here in Zuran where she could be brought up to respect herself as a woman should, and to despise the greedy, immoral woman who had given birth to her!

CHAPTER THREE

MARIELLA woke up before Fleur had given her first distressed, hungry cry. She wriggled out from under the cool pure linen bedding to pad barefoot and naked to where she had placed the carry-cot.

Her khaki-coloured soft shape trousers could be re-worn without laundering, but the white cotton tee shirt she had worn beneath her jacket, and her underwear—no way.

Fastidiously wrinkling her nose at the very thought, Mariella had rinsed them out, deciding that even if they had not dried by morning wearing them slightly damp was preferable to putting them back on unwashed!

Picking Fleur up, she carried her back to the bed…Xavier's bed, a huge, low-lying monster of a bed, large enough to accommodate both a man and half his harem without any problem at all!

Sliding back beneath the linen sheets, Mariella stroked Fleur's soft cheek and watched her in the glow of the single lamp she had left on. She could tell from the way the baby sucked eagerly on her finger that she was hungry!

She had seen water in the fridge, and she had Fleur's formula. All she had to do was to brave the leopard's den in order to reach the kitchen!

And in order to do that she needed to find something to wear.

Whilst she was deciding between one of the pile of

soft towels Xavier had presented her with or the sheet itself, Fleur started to cry.

'Hush,' she soothed her gently. 'I know you're hungry, sweetheart...'

Xavier sighed as he heard Fleur crying. It was just gone two in the morning. The divan wasn't exactly the most comfortable thing to sleep on. Outside the wind shrieked like a hyena, testing the strength of the pavilion, but its traditional design had withstood many centuries of desert winds and Xavier had no fears of it being plucked away.

Throwing back the cover from his makeshift bed, he pulled on the soft loose robe and strode towards the kitchen, briskly removing one of the empty bottles Mariella had left in the sterilizer and mixing the formula.

His grandmother—an eccentric woman so far as many people were concerned—had sent him to work in a refugee camp for six months after his final year at school and before he went on to university.

'You know what it is to be proud,' she had told him when he had expressed his disdain for her decision. 'Now you need to learn what it is to be humble.

'Without humility it is impossible to be a great leader of men, Xavier,' she had informed him. 'You owe it to your grandfather's people to have greatness, for without it they will be swamped by this modern world and scattered like seeds in the wind.'

One of his tasks there had been to work in the crèche. For the rest of his life Xavier knew he would remember the emotions he had experienced at the sight of the children's emaciated little bodies.

Snapping the teat on the filled bottle, he headed for the bedroom.

The baby's cries were noticeably louder. Her feckless mother was no doubt sleeping selfishly through them, Xavier decided grimly, ignoring the fact that he himself had already noticed just how devoted Fleur's mother was to her.

Fleur was crying too much and too long to be merely hungry, Mariella thought anxiously as she caught the increasing note of misery in the baby's piercing cry.

To her relief, Fleur seemed to find some comfort as Mariella sat up in the bed and cuddled her against her own body.

'What's wrong, sweetheart?' she whispered to her. 'Are you missing your...?'

She froze as the protective curtain closing off the room swung open, snatching at the sheet to cover herself, her face hot with embarrassment as she glared at Xavier.

'What do you want?' she demanded aggressively.

'So you are awake. I thought—'

Fleur's eyes widened as she saw that he was carrying Fleur's bottle.

'What have you put in there?' Mariella demanded suspiciously, holding Fleur even tighter as he held the bottle out to her.

'Formula,' he told her curtly. 'What did you think was in it...hemlock? You've been reading too many idiotic trashy books!'

As she took the bottle from him and squirted a few drops onto the back of her hand, tasting it, he watched her.

'Satisfied?'

Looking fully at him, Mariella compressed her lips.

'My word,' she heard him breathe in disbelief. You even go to bed in those ridiculous coloured contact lenses! Hasn't anyone ever told you that no one actually has eyes that colour? So if it's your lovers you are hoping to impress and deceive...'

As Fleur seized eagerly on her bottle Mariella froze in outraged fury.

Coloured contact lenses. How dared he?

'Oh, is that a fact?' she breathed. 'Well, for your information, whether you consider it to be ridiculous or not this just happens to be the real colour of my eyes. I am not wearing contact lenses, and as for wanting to impress or deceive a lover—'

Fleur gave a wail of protest as in her agitation Mariella unwittingly removed the teat from her mouth. Apologising to the baby, and comforting her, Mariella breathed in sharply with resentment.

Real? The only thing about her that was real was her outrageous lying! Xavier decided lowering his lashes over his eyes as he discreetly studied the smooth swell of her breasts as her agitated movements dislodged the sheet.

No wonder she had not wanted to feed her child herself. With breasts so perfectly and beautifully formed she would be reluctant to spoil their shape. He could almost see the faint pink shadowing of the areolae of her nipples.

Uncomfortably he shifted his weight from one foot to the other, all too conscious of the effect she was having on him. She was doing it deliberately, he knew that... She was that kind of woman!

When he came here it was to withdraw from the fast-paced city life and concentrate on more cerebral matters, Xavier reminded himself sharply.

The sheet slipped a little farther.

Her flesh was creamy pale, untouched by the sun.

He frowned. Khalid had said specifically that he had taken her to the South of France. Surely there she must have exposed herself, as so many did, to the hot glare of its sun and the ever hotter lustful looks of the men who went there specifically to enjoy the sight of so much young, naked flesh?

Knowing his cousin as he did, he couldn't imagine that Khalid would be attracted to a woman too modest to remove her bikini top!

He, on the other hand, found something profoundly and intensely sensual about the thought of a woman only revealing her bare breasts to her lover, her only lover…

Worriedly Mariella studied Fleur's suddenly flushed face, reaching out to touch her cheek. It burned beneath the coolness of her own fingertips. Her heart jumped with anxiety.

Xavier's stomach muscles clenched as she removed her arm, revealing the full exposed curve of her breast. As he had known it would be, her nipple was rose-pink and so softly delicate that he ached to reach out and touch it, explore its soft tenderness, feel it hardening in eager demand beneath his caress.

In her anxiety for Fleur, Mariella had all but forgotten that he was there, only alerted to his sudden departure by the brief swirl of air eddying the door-hanging as he left.

The minute he had gone Fleur started to cry again and nothing Mariella could do would soothe her.

In the end, terrified that he would reappear at any minute and demand that she silence the baby or else, Mariella got out of the bed and, wrapping the sheet around herself, started to pace the floor, gently rocking Fleur as she did so.

To her relief after about ten minutes Fleur began to fall asleep. Gently carrying her back to her cot she started to lie her down, but the minute she did so the baby began to cry again.

Resolutely Mariella tried again…and again…and again…

Three hours later she finally admitted just how afraid she was. Fleur was crying pitifully now, her cheeks bright red and her whole body hot and sweaty. Mariella's own eyes ached and her arms were cramped with holding her as she walked up and down the bedroom.

Outside the wind still howled demoniacally.

'Oh, poor, poor baby,' Mariella whispered anxiously. Tanya had entrusted her precious child to her. How would she feel if she knew what Mariella had done? How she had brought her to the middle of the desert where there was no doctor and no way of getting to one? What if Fleur had something really seriously wrong with her? What if she had picked up some life-threatening infectious disease? What if…? Sick with anxiety and guilt, Mariella prayed that Fleur would be all right.

In the outer part of the pavilion Xavier could hear the fretful cry of the baby but he dared not go in to find out what was wrong. He could not trust himself to go in and find out what was wrong he admitted grimly.

An hour later, still trying to soothe and comfort Fleur, Mariella felt desperately afraid. It was obvious that Fleur wasn't well. The fear tormenting her could not be ignored any longer. Her hands trembling, Mariella relit all the oil lamps and then carefully undressed Fleur, slowly checking her for any sign of the rash that would confirm her worst fears and indicate that the baby could somehow have contracted meningitis.

Not content with having checked her skin once without finding any sign of a rash, Mariella did so again. When once again she could not find any sign of a rash, she didn't know whether to feel relieved or simply more anxious!

Tenderly wiping the tears from Fleur's hot face, she kissed her. Fleur grabbed hold of her finger and was trying to suck on it. No, not suck, Mariella realised— she was trying to bite on it. Fleur was cutting her first tooth!

All at once relief and recognition filled her. Fleur was teething—that was why she had been so uncomfortable. Mariella could well remember Tanya at the same age, her mother walking up and down with her as she tried to soothe her, explaining to Mariella just how much those sharp, pretty little teeth cutting through tender flesh hurt and upset the baby.

Naturally Mariella had tucked a good supply of paediatric paracetamol suspension into her baby bag before leaving home and, still holding Fleur, she went to get it.

'This will make you feel better, sweetheart,' she crooned, adding lovingly, 'And what a clever girl you are, aren't you, with your lovely new tooth? A very clever girl.'

Within minutes or so of the baby having her medicine, or so it seemed to a now totally exhausted Mariella, she was fast asleep. Patting her flushed face, Mariella smothered a yawn. Tucking Fleur into her cot, she made for her own bed.

Xavier frowned. It was well past daylight. He had showered and eaten his breakfast and switched on the laptop he had brought with him to do some work, but his mind wasn't really on it. Every time he thought about his cousin's mistress he was filled with unwanted and dangerous emotions. There hadn't been a sound from the bedroom in hours. No doubt working in a nightclub she was used to sleeping during the day… And very probably not on her own!

The very thought of the woman sleeping next door in his bed drove him to such an unfamiliar and furious level of hormone-fuelled rage that he could barely contain himself. And he was a man who was secretly proud of the fact that he was known for his fabled self-control!

Khalid should think himself very fortunate indeed that he had prevented him from marrying that turquoise-eyed seductress.

But Khalid did not think himself fortunate! Khalid thought himself very far from fortunate and had, in fact, left his cousin's presence swearing that he would not give up the woman he loved, no, not even if Xavier did try to carry out his threat and disinherit him!

His cousin was quite plainly besotted with the woman, and now that Xavier had met her for himself he was beginning to understand just how dangerous she was.

But not even Khalid's love would be strong enough to withstand the knowledge that she had been his cousin's lover. That she had given herself willingly to him! That the thought of ensnaring an even richer man than Khalid, in Xavier himself, had been enough to have her crawling into his bed.

That knowledge would hurt Khalid, but better that he was hurt quickly and cleanly now than that he spent a lifetime suffering a thousand humiliations at her hands! As he undoubtedly would do!

Surely the silence from the bedroom was unnatural. The woman should be awake by now, if only for the sake of her child!

Irritably Xavier strode towards the bedroom area, and pulled back the hanging.

Mariella was lying on the bed deeply asleep, one arm flung out, her pale skin gleaming in the soft light.

The thick strawberry-blonde hair was softly tousled, a few wisps sticking to her pink-cheeked face, lashes, which surely must be dyed to achieve that density of colour, surrounding the turquoise she insisted on claiming was natural.

In her sleep she sighed and frowned and made a little moue of distress before settling back into sleep.

Unable to drag his gaze from her, Xavier continued to watch her. There was nothing about what he knew of the type of person she was that could appeal to his aesthetic and cultured taste. But physically…

Physically, hormonally, she exerted such a pull over his senses that right now…

He had taken a step towards the bed without even realising it, the ache in his groin immediately a fierce, primal surge of white-hot need. If he took her in his arms and woke her now, would it be Khalid's name he heard on her lips?

That thought alone should have been enough to freeze his arousal to nothing, but instead he was filled with a savage explosion of angry emotion at the thought of any man's name on her lips that wasn't his own!

As he battled with the realisation of just what that

meant, his attention was suddenly distracted by the happy gurgling coming from the cot.

Striding over to it, he stared down at Fleur. Her child. The child another man had given her! A surge of primitive aching pain filled him.

Fleur had kicked off her blankets and was playing with her bare toes, smiling coquettishly up at him.

Xavier sucked in his breath. She was so small, so delicate...so very much like her mother.

Instinctively he bent to pick her up.

Mariella didn't know what woke her from her deep sleep, some ancient female instinct perhaps, she decided shakily as she stared across the room and saw Xavier bending over Fleur.

Gripping the bedclothes, she burst out frantically, 'Don't you dare hurt her.'

'Hurt her?' Tight-lipped, Xavier swung round. 'You dare to say that when she has already been hurt immeasurably simply by being brought into being as the child of a woman who...'

Unable to fully express his feelings, he compressed his mouth.

'I suppose she is used to being left to amuse herself whilst her mother sleeps off the effects of her night's work!'

Mariella could scarcely contain her fury.

'How dare you say such things, after the way you have behaved? You are the most loathsome, the most vile man I have ever met. You are totally lacking in any kind of compassion, or...or responsibility!'

Her eyes really were that colour, Xavier recognised in disbelief as he watched them darken from turquoise to inky blue-green.

Did they turn that colour when she was lost in passion? Was she as passionate in her sexual desire as she was in her anger? Of course she was...he knew that instinctively, just as he knew equally instinctively that if she were his...

'It is nearly eleven o' clock, the child must be hungry,' he told her tersely, infuriated by his own weakness in allowing such thoughts to creep into his head.

Eleven o'clock—how could it be? Mariella wondered guiltily, but a quick glance at her watch showed her that it was.

She couldn't wait to get back to the city and the sooner she and Fleur were on their way back there, the better, she decided as Xavier strode out of the room.

CHAPTER FOUR

MARIELLA frowned as she walked into the empty living area of the pavilion. Where was Xavier?

A laptop hummed quietly on a folding campaign table to one side of the pavilion. Xavier had obviously been working on it.

As she looked round the pavilion with its precious carpets and elegant few pieces of furniture, which she recognised as being expensively antique as well as functional, Mariella tried to imagine her dizzy half-sister in such a setting. Tanya was totally open about the fact that she was a girl who loved the bustle of cities, holidays in expensive, fashionable locations, modern apartments as opposed to traditional houses. Although she adored Fleur, self-indulgence was her by-word, and Mariella was finding it increasingly hard to visualise her sister ever being compatible with a man like Xavier, who she could not imagine truly sharing Tanya's tastes. He was too austere, surely. Too...

Tanya loved him, she reminded herself stubbornly, although she was finding that equally hard to imagine! He was just so totally not Tanya's type! Tanya liked happy-go-lucky, boyish, fun-loving men!

Fleur was sound asleep, and Mariella decided she would go outside to check on what was happening. She could no longer hear the sound of the wind battering against the walls of the pavilion, which hopefully meant that she would be able to make her way back to the city.

As she stepped outside she saw to her relief that the wind had indeed dropped. The air was now totally still and the sky had a dull ochre tinge to it. She could see her four-wheel drive, its sides covered in sand.

On the far side of the oasis, the rock face of the gorge rose steeply, its almost vertical face scarred here and there by the odd ledge.

There was a raw, elemental beauty about this hidden place, Mariella acknowledged, seeing it now with an artist's eye rather than the panicky apprehension of a lost traveller.

A scattering of palm trees fringed the water of the oasis, and beyond them lay a rough area of sparse, spiky grass. The rutted track she had driven down probably was a dried-out river bed, she could see now.

The quality of the stillness and the corresponding silence were almost hypnotic.

A movement on the other side of the oasis caught her eye, her body tensing as she recognised Xavier. He was dressed not in traditional robes, but in jeans and a tee shirt. He seemed to be checking the palm trees, she realised as he paused to inspect one before walking to another. He had obviously not seen her, but instinctively she drew farther back into the shadow cast by the pavilion.

He had turned away from the trees now and was staring across the oasis, shading his eyes as he looked up into the sky.

The storm hadn't weakened the roots of any of the palm trees, Xavier acknowledged. There was no reason why he shouldn't go back to the pavilion and continue with his work. And in fact pretty soon he would have to do so. Right now they were in the eye of the storm, but as soon as it moved on the wind would return with even greater force.

But he couldn't go back inside. Not whilst he was still visualising *her* lying on the bed…his bed…

Angrily he stripped off his tee shirt, quickly followed by the rest of his clothes. And began to wade out into the water.

Mariella couldn't move. Like someone deeply beneath the spell of an outside force she stood, muscles clenched, hardly daring to breathe as she fought to repel the sensation coiling through her, and shivering to each and every single sensitive nerve ending as her gaze absorbed the raw male beauty of Xavier's nudity.

As an artist she was fully aware of the complexities and the beauty of the human form, she had visited Florence and wandered lost in rapt awe as she studied the work of the great masters, but now she recognised she was seeing the work of the greatest Master of all.

Xavier was wading out into the water, the dull glaring sunlight glinting on flesh so warmly and evenly hued that it was immediately obvious that such nudity was normal for him.

As he moved through the water she could see the powerful sinews in his thighs contracting against its pressure. Trying to distract herself she visualised what lay inside that heavy satin male flesh, the bones, the muscles, the tissues, but instead of calming her down, it made her awareness of him increase, her wanton thoughts fiercely pushing aside the pallid academic images she was trying to conjure, in favour of some of their own: like a close-up of that sun-warmed flesh, roped with muscle, hard, sleek, rough with the same fine dark hair she could see so clearly arrowing down the centre of his body.

Only his buttocks were a slightly paler shade than the rest of his skin, taut and man-shaped, packed with the muscles that would drive…

Mariella shuddered violently, feeling as though she herself were sinking into a pool of sensation so deep and dangerous that she had no means of freeing herself from it.

Helplessly she watched as Xavier moved farther into the oasis until all she could see above the water were his head and shoulders. He ducked his whole body beneath the water and she held her breath, expelling it when she saw him break the surface several yards away, cleaving through it with long, powerful over-arm strokes that propelled him at a fierce and silent speed away from her.

She felt sick, shocked, furiously angry, terrifyingly vulnerable, aching from head to toe and most of all, deep down inside the most female part of her body, tormented by a need, a knowledge that ripped apart all her previous beliefs about herself.

She could not possibly want Xavier! But that…that merciless message her body had just given her could not be denied.

It sickened her to think of wanting a man who had hurt her sister so much; a man Tanya still loved so much. Such a feeling was a betrayal of everything within herself she most prided herself on. It was inconceivable that such a thing could be happening, just as it was inconceivable too that she, a woman who took such pride in her ability to mentally control the sexual and emotional side of her nature, could allow herself to feel so…so…

Dragging her gaze away from the oasis, Mariella closed her eyes.

Go on, admit it, she taunted herself mentally. You are so hungry for him that if he came to you now, you would let him do whatever he wanted with you right here and right now. Let him? You would urge him, encourage him, entice him…

Frantically Mariella shook her head, trying to shake away her own tormenting thoughts, the tormenting inner voice that was mocking her so openly.

Blindly she headed back for the pavilion, not seeing the hot breaths of wind tugging warningly at the topmost fronds of the palm trees, and not noticing, either, the bronze ring of light dulling the sun so menacingly.

Once inside the pavilion she hurried to check on Fleur who was still sleeping. She had only been outside for around half an hour, but it felt somehow as though she had passed through a whole time zone and entered another world. A world in which she no longer knew exactly who or what she was.

Quickly she started to get together their things. She didn't want to be here when Xavier came back. She couldn't bear to be here when he came back; she couldn't bear to face him, to be in the same room with him, the same space with him; in fact she wasn't sure right now if she could even bear to be in the same life with him.

She had never imagined that there could be anyone who could make her feel so threatened, so appalled by her own feelings, and so afraid of them. Flushed and sticky, she surveyed her uncharacteristically chaotic packing.

She would put their things in the four-wheel drive first, and then pop Fleur in and then she would drive back to the hotel and not stop until she got there.

Mariella took a deep breath. Once she was there she

would no doubt come to her senses and think of Xavier only as the man who had betrayed her sister, the man who was Fleur's father!

The wind was beginning to bend the palms as Mariella hurried out to the vehicle with their things, but she was oblivious to it as she wrestled with the heavy door and started to load the car.

Xavier saw her as he turned to swim another length. Treading water, he watched in furious disbelief as she struggled with the vehicle's door and then started to push the bulky container she had brought with her inside it.

There! Now all she had to do was go back for Fleur and then they could leave, hopefully whilst Xavier was too busy swimming to notice! And anyway, if he had wanted a swim that badly why couldn't he have worn…well, something? Why had he had to—to flaunt his undeniably supremely male and very, very sexy body in the way he had?

Engrossed in her thoughts, she failed to see Xavier wade out of the water and pull on his tee shirt and jeans without wasting time on anything else, before starting to run towards the pavilion into which she had already disappeared.

'Come on, my beautiful baby,' Mariella crooned lovingly to Fleur as she wrapped her up. 'You and I are going—'

'Nowhere!'

Turning round, white-faced and clutching Fleur protectively to her, Mariella glared at him. The fine cotton tee shirt was plastered to his very obviously still damp body and her skittering gaze slid helplessly downward to rest indiscreetly on the groin of his jeans at the same time as her heart came to rest against her chest wall in a massive breathtaking thud.

He was standing in the exit blocking her way, but infuriatingly, instead of registering this vitally important fact first, her senses seemed to be far too preoccupied with taking a personal inventory of the way he looked clothed and the way he had looked...before!

Reminding herself that she was an adult, mature businesswoman, well used to running her own life and making her own decisions, and not the sad female with her hormones running riot that she was currently doing a good impression of, she drew herself up to her full height and told him determinedly, 'I am taking Fleur back to the city and there is no way you are going to stop me. And anyway, I can't imagine why you would want us to stay after the way you have behaved! The things you have said!'

'Want you to stay? No, I don't!' Xavier confirmed harshly. 'But unfortunately you are going to have to, unless, of course, you want to condemn yourself and the baby to almost certain death.'

Mariella stared at him. What did he mean? Was he trying to threaten her? 'We're leaving,' she repeated, making for the exit, and trying to ignore both the furious thud of her heart and the fact that he was standing in the way.

'Are you mad? You'd be lucky to get above half a dozen miles before being buried in a sand drift. If you thought the wind coming here was bad, well, let me tell you that was nothing compared with what's blowing up out there now!'

Mariella took a deep breath.

'I've just been outside. There is no wind,' she told

him patiently, slowly spacing each word with immense care. 'The storm is over.'

'And you would know, of course, being an expert on desert weather conditions, no doubt. For your information, the reason that there was no wind, as you put it, is because we are, or rather we were in the eye of the storm. And anyone who knows anything about the desert would know that. Couldn't you feel the stillness? Didn't you notice the sand haze in the sky?' The look he shot her could have lit tinder at fifty paces, Mariella recognised shakily.

'You're lying,' she told him stubbornly, determined not to let him get the better of her. 'You just want to keep us here because—'

When she stopped he looked derisively at her.

'Yes. I want to keep you here because what?'

Because you know how dangerously much I want you, a treacherous little voice whispered insidiously inside Mariella's head, and you feel the same way.

Shuddering, she pushed her thoughts back into the realms of reality—and safety.

'You're lying,' she repeated doggedly, eyeing the exit rebelliously.

'Am I?' Moving to one side, he swept back the tent flap so that she could see outside.

The palms were bending so much beneath the strength of the wind that their fronds were brushing the sand.

As she stared in disbelief Mariella could hear the strength of the wind increasing until it whistled eerily around the oasis, physically hurting her ears.

Out of nowhere it whipped up huge spirals of sand, making them dance in front of her. She could hardly see the sun or differentiate any longer between sand and sky.

Disbelievingly she took a step outside and cried out in shock as she was almost lifted off her feet when the wind punched into her. In her arms, Fleur screamed and was immediately removed to the protection of a much stronger and safer pair as Xavier snatched Fleur from her.

The thought of what would have happened to them if they had been caught in the open desert in such conditions drove the colour from Mariella's face.

'Now do you believe me?' Xavier demanded grimly when they were both back inside and he had secured the tent flap.

Reaching out to take Fleur from him, Mariella, whose fingers had inadvertently come into contact with the damp heat of his tee-shirt-clad chest, withdrew her hand so fast she almost lost her balance.

Immediately Xavier gripped her arm to steady her, supporting whilst he did so, so that it looked almost as though he were embracing them both, holding them both safe.

Against all rationality, given what she knew about him, Mariella discovered that her eyes were burning with emotional tears. She should be crying, she acknowledged grimly, for her own stupidity in allowing her emotions to be aroused so much for so little real reason! Pulling back from him, she demanded, 'Just how long is this storm going to last?'

'At least twenty-four hours, perhaps longer. Since the storm is making it impossible to receive any kind of communication signal, it is impossible to know.

Such storms are rare at this time of year, but when they do occur they are both unpredictable and fierce.'

As was Xavier himself, Mariella decided as she took Fleur from him.

CHAPTER FIVE

GETTING up from the bed where she had been lying reading one of the research books she had brought to Zuran with her, Mariella went to check on Fleur.

A brief glance at her watch showed her that it was nearly eight p.m. Fleur was awake but obviously quite content, and happy to oblige when Mariella checked her mouth to look at the small pearly white tooth just beginning to appear. Her face was still a little bit swollen and flushed, but the paracetamol seemed to have eased the pain she had suffered the previous night.

Mariella had retreated to 'her bedroom' late in the afternoon, desperate to escape from the highly charged atmosphere in the main living area.

It had become impossible for her to look at Xavier without imagining him as he had been earlier: naked...male.

He had retrieved the things she had carried out to the four-wheel drive and put them back in the bedroom, and when Mariella had come across a sketch-book and pencils she had forgotten she had brought, along with her book, she had fallen on the book with a surge of relief.

Apart from the fact that she genuinely found the subject interesting, it gave her a perfect excuse to distance herself from Xavier, who had been busily working on his laptop.

On the pretext of Fleur needing a nap she had come

59

into the sleeping quarters and had remained there ever since.

A thorough understanding of anatomy was essential for any painter in her type of field, and she had quickly become totally engrossed in trying to trace the development of the modern-day racehorse from the original Arabian bloodstock.

As Kate had said, the potential commission from the prince was indeed a prestigious one.

Picking up her sketch-book, Mariella started to work. Those incredible muscles that powered every movement… Her pencil flew over the paper, her absorption in what she was doing only broken when Fleur started to demand her attention.

Smiling, she discarded the sketch-book and then frowned sharply as she looked at what she had done, her face burning mortified and disbelieving scarlet.

How on earth had that happened? How on earth had she managed to sketch, not a horse, but a man… Xavier…Xavier, swimming, Xavier standing, Xavier: his body lean and naked, clean-muscled and powerful.

Guiltily, Mariella flipped over the page. Fleur was blowing kisses at her and becoming increasingly vociferous.

Tucking the sketch-pad safely out of sight, Mariella went to her and picked her up, fastening her into her car seat and then carrying her into the kitchen.

'Look at this yummy dinner you're going to have,' Mariella crooned to Fleur as she prepared her food.

It had been her intention to take Fleur back into the bedroom to feed her, but instead Mariella carried her into the living area.

Fleur was Xavier's daughter, after all, and perhaps

they both needed reminding just what that meant, albeit for very different reasons! Perhaps too he ought to be made to see just what he was missing out on by not acknowledging her.

He was working on the laptop when Mariella walked in and put Fleur down in her seat so that she could feed her.

She was a strong, healthy baby with a good appetite, who thankfully no longer seemed to be too bothered by the tooth she had been cutting.

Absorbed in her own enjoyable task, Mariella didn't realise that Xavier had stopped work to turn and study them until some sixth sense warned her that they were being watched.

His abrupt, 'She has your nose,' made Mariella's hand tremble slightly. She and Tanya shared the same shaped nose, which they had both inherited from their mother. Fleur had their nose, but, according to Tanya, her father's deliciously long thick eyelashes.

Mariella could feel her face starting to burn. What was it about a certain type of man that enabled him to behave so uncaringly towards the child he had fathered?

The way Xavier was behaving towards Fleur was so reminiscent of the way her father had behaved towards her! She knew all too well what it was like to grow up feeling rejected and unloved by one's father and she couldn't bear to see that happen to Fleur!

Xavier ought to be made to see that she was at least in part his responsibility instead of being allowed to just walk away from her. The way she felt had nothing whatsoever to do with money, Mariella recognised, and everything to do with emotion.

Fleur had finished her meal and was beginning to

drift off to sleep. Bending down to double check that she was comfortably fastened into her seat, Mariella tenderly kissed her downy cheek, then straightened up and headed for the kitchen to wash out her feeding things.

Left on his own with Fleur, Xavier studied her frowningly. She was far fairer skinned than his cousin and, whilst Xavier could see an unmistakable physical resemblance to Mariella in her, he could see none to Khalid. Fast asleep now, Fleur gave a small quiver.

Immediately Xavier went over to her. Desert nights could be unbelievably cold—she felt warm enough, but perhaps she needed an extra cover?

He could hear Mariella in the kitchen and so he went through into the bedroom area, to get an extra blanket from the carry-cot.

Mariella had tucked her sketch-pad in between the carry-cot and the box of baby equipment, and as Xavier reached for a blanket he saw the sketch-pad, and its very recognisable sketches.

Frowning, he picked it up and studied it.

Having washed Fleur's feeding cup, Mariella walked into the bedroom intending to put it away, coming to an abrupt halt as she saw Xavier bending towards the carry-cot.

'Where is Fleur?' she demanded immediately. 'What—?'

'She's fast asleep where you left her,' Xavier answered her adding, 'From looking at her, it is plain to see her resemblance to you, but as to there being a similarity to her supposed father...'

Mariella had had enough.

'How can you deny your own flesh and blood?' she

demanded bitterly. 'I can't imagine how *any* woman could ever desire you, never mind—'

Before she could say 'Tanya' he had cut her off as he asked with cutting brutality, 'Indeed? Then, what may I ask, are these?'

Mariella felt the breath wheeze from her lungs like air squeezed from a pair of bellows as he held up in front of her her own sketches.

Chagrin, embarrassment, guilt and anger fused into one burning, searing jolt of emotional intensity had her lunging frantically towards him, intent on snatching her betraying sketches from him. But Xavier was withholding them from her, holding them out of her reach with one hand whilst he fended her attempt to repossess them with the other.

Furiously Mariella redoubled her efforts, flinging herself at him, and trying to shake off his hard grip of her wrist as she did so.

'Give those back to me. They are mine,' she insisted breathlessly.

As she tried to reach up for them she overbalanced slightly, her fingers curling into his arm, her fingernails accidentally raising livid weals on his olive skin.

'Why, you little...'

Shocked as much by her own inadvertent action as his reaction to it, Mariella went stiff with disbelief as he suddenly dropped the sketches and grabbed hold of her waist with both hands.

'Other men might have been willing to let you get away with such behaviour, but I most certainly do not intend to!' she could hear Xavier grating at her as he gave her a small, angry shake.

Mariella could feel the edge of the bed behind her as she turned and twisted, frantically trying to break free, but Xavier was refusing to let her go and suddenly she was lying on the bed, with Xavier arching over her, pinning her down.

He was angry with her, Mariella recognised as she stared into the lava-grey heat of his eyes, but her senses were telling her something else as well and a savage little quiver then ran unmistakably through her own body as she realised that something else had nothing whatsoever to do with fear.

Xavier wanted her! Mariella could sense, feel it, breathe it in the sudden tension that filled the air, engulfing, locking them both in a place out of time.

This was fate, Xavier decided recklessly, a golden opportunity given to him to prove to his cousin beyond any shadow of a doubt that this woman was not worthy of his love, but, strangely, as he lowered his mouth to Mariella's it wasn't his duty towards his cousin that was filling his thoughts, driving him with an intense ferocity that a part of him recognised was more dangerous than anything he had previously experienced.

This was wrong, desperately wrong, the very worst kind of betrayal, Mariella acknowledged as her whole body was savaged by a mixture of anguish and hunger.

Xavier's mouth burned hers, its possession every bit as harsh and demanding as she had expected, barely cloaking a hunger that scorched right through her body to her fingertips.

Helplessly her mouth responded to the savage demand of his, her body quivering as his tongue probed her closed lips demanding entry. Somehow, some time she had lifted her hands to his body so that she was gripping his shoulders. To push him away, or to draw him closer?

His teeth tugged ruthlessly at her bottom lip and her

resistance ebbed away, like the inner tears of shame and guilt she was silently crying inside for her inability to resist giving in to flames of her own desire as they licked and darted inside her, burning down her pathetically weak defences. Without knowing how she knew, she knew that this man, this moment was something a part of her had been waiting for, for a very long time. Even the merciless intent of his sensual need was something that a part of her was fiercely responsive to.

Her eyes, magnificent in their emotional intensity, shimmered from turquoise to dark blue-green. Xavier was mesmerised by them, caught in their brilliance. How could such cool colours glow so hotly? But not nearly so hotly as his own body.

Without knowing what she was doing, Mariella raked the taut flesh of his arm—deliberately this time— her body galvanised by deep, urgent shudders as his kiss possessed her mouth, his tongue thrusting into its warm softness.

Mariella tried to deny what she was feeling, pulling frantically away from Xavier, in a desperate attempt to escape and to save them both from the very worst kind of betrayal, but having shared her surrender Xavier refused to let her go, pinning her to the bed with the weight of his body hot and heavy on hers, making her melt, making her ache, making her writhe in helpless supplication and moan into his mouth, a tiny keening sound lost beneath the greater sounds of their bodies moving on the bed. The rustle and rasp of fabric against flesh, of two people both revealing their hunger in the accelerated sound of their breathing, and the frantic thud of their heartbeats.

Xavier's mouth grazed her skin, exploring the curve of her jaw, the soft vulnerability of her throat as she automatically arched her whole body. The hot, fevered feel of his mouth against her flesh made her arch even more, shuddering in agonised pleasure.

Just a few kisses, that was all it was… And yet she felt as possessed by him, as aching for him as though he had touched her far more intimately and for far, far longer. The desire she was feeling was so acute, so very nearly unbearable, that Mariella dared not allow herself to imagine how she was going to feel when he did touch her more intimately. And yet at the same time she knew that if he didn't—

When his hand covered her breast she cried out, unable to stop herself, and felt his responding groan shudder through his body. She could hear herself making small, whimpering sounds of distress as she tugged at his clothes, her own body consumed by a need to be completely bare to his touch, to be open to him…

And yet when he had finally removed them and she was naked, a sense of panic that was wholly primitive and instinctive ripped through her, causing her to go to cover her naked breasts protectively with her own hands. But Xavier was too quick for her, his fingers snapping round her wrists, pinioning her hands either side of her head as he knelt over her.

Mariella felt the heavy thread of her own hungry desire. She just had time to see the molten glitter of Xavier's answering hunger before he looked down at her exposed breasts. A sinful desire slid hotly through her veins, her face burning as she watched him absorbing the taut swell of her breasts as her nipples tightened and darkened, openly inciting the need she could hear and feel in his indrawn breath, even before he lowered his head to her body.

The feeling of him slowly circling first one and then

the other nipple with the moist heat of his tongue, whilst she lay powerless beneath him, should surely have inflamed her angry independence instead of sending such a sheet of white-hot sensuality pouring through her that her belly automatically concaved under its pressure whilst her sex ached and swelled.

Mariella closed her eyes. Behind her closed eyelids she could see him as she had done in the oasis, just as she wanted to see him again now, she recognised as her body began to shudder. Slow, deep, galvanic surges of desire that ripped rhythmically through her, her body moving to the suckle of his mouth against her breast.

She could feel his knee parting her thighs her body already aching for the aroused feel of him, hot, heavy, masculine as he urgently moved against her.

He was losing himself, drowning in the way she was making him feel, his self-control in danger of being burned away to nothing. Just the sight of her swollen breasts, their nipples tight and aroused from his laving of them, made him ache to possess her, to complete and fill her, to complete himself within her.

The moment Xavier released her wrists, Mariella tugged impatiently at his clothes, answering her demanding need for him. Immediately Xavier helped her, guiding her hands over buttons and zips and then flesh itself as she moaned her pleasure against the hot skin of his throat when her fingertips finally tangled with the soft, silky hair she had ached to touch earlier.

His body, packed hard with muscle, was excitingly alien and overpoweringly male. His impatience to be a part of her made her gasp and shudder as he kissed her throat, her shoulder and then her mouth, whilst he wrapped her tightly in his arms so that they were lying intimately, naked body to naked body.

The feel of him pressing against her. Hot and hard, aroused, his movement against her urgently explicit, was more than she could withstand.

Eagerly she coiled herself around him, opening herself to him, crying out as she felt him enter her, each movement powerful and sure, strong and urgent.

Already her own body was responding to his movement, her muscles clinging to him. Sensually stroking him and savouring each thrust, she could feel him strengthening inside her, filling her to completion, picking up the rhythm of her body and carrying...driving them both with it.

'Never mind the child he has given you, has my cousin given you this? Has he made you feel like this when he holds you? When he possesses you? When he loves you? Was *this* how it was between you when you made Fleur together?'

Mariella's whole body stiffened.

'Did you give yourself to him as easily as you did to me? And how many others have there been?'

With a fierce cry, she pulled away from him, her brain barely able to take in what he was saying, her body and emotions in such deep shock that removing herself from him made her feel as though she were physically dying.

The shock of her rejection tore at Xavier's guts. He wanted to drag her back into his arms, where surely she belonged, to roll her into the bed beneath him and to fill her with himself, to make her admit that no other man had ever or could ever give her or share with her what he could. But most of all he wanted to fill her with the life force that would ultimately be his child.

A part of him recognised that there was no more elemental drive than this, to fill a woman's body with one's child in order to drive out her commitment to another man and the child he had already given her. The barbaric intensity of his own emotions shocked him. He had done what he had done for Khalid's sake, to protect him, he reminded himself, and to reinforce that fact he told her, 'It's a little too late for that now! You have already proved to me just what you are, and once Khalid learns how willing you were to give yourself to me he will quickly realise how right I was to counsel him against you.'

He had taken her to bed for that? Because of that? So that he could denounce her to another man?

In the outer room Fleur suddenly started to cry. Dragging on her clothes, Mariella hurried in to her, picking her up and holding her tightly as though just holding her could somehow staunch the huge wound inside her that was haemorrhaging her life force. She was shaking from head to foot with reaction, both from what had happened and from what she had just learned.

Fleur was not Xavier's child! Xavier's cousin was Fleur's father! But Xavier believed that she was Fleur's mother. And because of that he had taken her to bed, out of a cold-hearted, despicable, damnable desire to prove to his cousin that she was a...a wanton who would give herself to any man!

Fate had been doubly kind to her, she told herself staunchly: firstly in ensuring that she had not betrayed her sister, and secondly in giving her incontrovertible proof of just what manner of man Xavier was!

CHAPTER SIX

As SHE stepped inside the welcome familiarity of her Beach Club bungalow, Mariella allowed herself to expel a shaky sigh of relief. Her first since she had left the oasis!

Now that she was safely here, perhaps she could allow herself to put the events of the last forty-eight hours firmly behind her. Lock them away in a very deep sealed drawer marked, 'Forget for ever.'

But how could she forget, how could any human being forget an act as deliberately and cold-bloodedly cruel and damaging as the one Xavier had perpetrated against her?

If she herself had been a different kind of woman she might have taken a grim sense of distorted pleasure in knowing that, for all he might try to deny it, Xavier had physically wanted her. In knowing it and in throwing that knowledge back at him! Instinctively she knew that he would be humiliated by it, and if any man deserved to be humiliated it was Xavier!

Just thinking about him was enough to have Mariella's hands curling into small, passionately angry fists. As her heart drove against her ribs in sledgehammer blows. How could he possibly not have recognised that she would never, ever, ever under any circumstances betray her love, and that if she had been another man's lover nothing he could have done would have tempted her to want him? Hadn't her body itself proclaimed to him the unlikeliness, the impossibility of her being Fleur's mother and any man's intimate lover?

But believing that he had been Tanya's lover hadn't stopped her, had it?

She would carry that shame and guilt with her to her deathbed, Mariella acknowledged.

The message light on the bungalow's communications system was flashing, indicating that she had received several telephone calls, all from the prince's personal assistant, she discovered when she went to check them. Before answering them, the first thing she intended to do now that she was safely back at the hotel was ring her sister and double check that she had not misunderstood Xavier—he was not Tanya's lover or Fleur's father!

And once she had that confirmation safely in her possession, then Xavier would be history!

It took her several attempts to get through to Tanya, who eventually answered the phone sounding breathless and flustered.

'I'm sorry, Ella,' she apologised quickly. 'But things are really hectic here and... Look, I can't really talk right now. Is Fleur okay?'

'Fleur is fine. She's cut her first tooth, but, Tanya, there's something I've got to know,' Mariella told her, firmly overriding her attempts to end the call.

'I must know Fleur's father's name, Tanya. It's desperately important!'

'Why? What's happened? Ella, I can't tell you...'

Hearing the panic in her sister's voice, Mariella took a deep breath. 'All right! But if you won't tell me who he is, Tanya, then please at least tell me that his first name isn't Xavier...'

'Who?' Tanya's outraged shriek almost hurt her eardrums. 'Xavier? You mean that horrid cousin of Khalid's? Of course he isn't Fleur's father. I hate him… He's the one responsible for parting me and Khalid! He sent Khalid away! He doesn't think that I'm good enough for him! Anyway…how do you know about Xavier, Ella? He's an arrogant, overbearing, old-fashioned, moralistic beast, who lives in the Dark Ages! Look, Ella, I've got to go… Love to Fleur and lots of kisses.'

She ended the call before Mariella could stop her, leaving her gripping the receiver tensely.

But at least she had confirmed that Xavier was not Fleur's father.

Determinedly Mariella made herself turn her attention to her messages.

The prince had now returned to Zuran and wanted her to get in touch with his personal assistant.

'Don't worry,' the prince's personal assistant reassured Mariella when she rang him a few minutes later to explain why she had not returned his calls.

'It is just that the prince is hosting a charity breakfast tomorrow morning at the stables and he wanted to invite you as his guest. His Highness is very enthusiastic about his project of having the horses painted, but of course this is something you will be having formal discussions with him about at a later date. The breakfast is a prestigious dressy event, although we do ask all our guests not to wear strong perfumes, as this can affect the horses.'

'It sounds wonderful,' Mariella responded. 'However, there is one small problem. I have brought my four-month-old niece to Zuran with me, as the prince knows. I am looking after her for my sister, and—'

'That is no problem at all,' the PA came back promptly. 'Crèche facilities are being provided with fully trained nannies in attendance. A car will be sent to collect both you and the baby, of course.'

Mariella had previously attended several glitzy society events at the invitation of her clients, including one particularly elegant trip to France for their main race of the season at Longchamps—a gift from a client, which she had repaid with a 'surprise' sketch of his four-year-old daughter on her pony, and, recalling the sophistication and glamour of the outfits worn by the Middle Eastern contingent on that occasion, she suspected that she was going to have to go shopping.

Two hours later, sitting sipping coffee in the exclusive Zuran Designer Shopping Centre, Mariella smiled ruefully to herself as she contemplated her assorted collection of shiny shopping bags.

The largest one bore the name, not of some famous designer, but of an exclusive babywear store. Unable to choose between two equally delicious little outfits for Fleur, Mariella had ended up buying her niece both.

She had been rather less indulgent on her own account, opting only to buy a hat—an outrageously feminine and eye-catching model hat, mind you!—a pair of ridiculously spindly heeled but totally irresistible sandals, which just happened to be the exact shade of turquoise-blue of the silk dress she had decided to wear to the charity breakfast, and a handbag in the same colour, which quite incredibly had the design of a galloping horse picked out on it in sequins and beads.

And best of all she had managed not to think about

Xavier at all...well, almost not at all! And when she had thought about him it had been to reiterate to herself just what a total pig he was, and how lucky she was that all she had done was give in to a now unthinkable and totally out of character, momentary madness, which would never, ever be repeated. After all, there was no danger of her ever allowing herself to become emotionally vulnerable to any man—not with her father's behaviour to remind her of the danger of falling in love—never mind a man who had condemned himself in the way that Xavier had!

Having drunk her coffee, she gathered up her bags and checked that Fleur was strapped securely in her buggy before heading for the taxi rank.

It had been a long day. She had hardly slept the night before, lying awake in Xavier's bed, her thoughts and her emotions churning. And then there had been the long drive back to Zuran this morning after her prayers had been answered and the storm had died away.

True, she had had a brief nap earlier, but now, even though it was barely eight in the evening, she was already yawning.

Xavier paced the floor of the pavilion. He should, he knew, be rejoicing in his solitude and the fact that that woman had gone! And of course he would have no compunction whatsoever in telling Khalid just how easily and quickly she had betrayed the 'love' she had claimed to have for him!

That ache he could feel in his body right now meant nothing and would very quickly be banished!

But what if Khalid refused to listen to him? What if, despite everything he, Xavier, had said to him, he insisted on continuing his relationship with her?

If Fleur was Khalid's child then it was only right that he should provide for her. Xavier tried to imagine how he would feel if Khalid were to set his mistress and their child up in a home in Zuran. How he would feel knowing that Khalid was living with her, sharing that home…sharing her bed?

Angrily he strode outside. Even the damned air inside the tent was poisoned by her perfume—that and the scent of baby powder! He would instruct his staff to dispose of the bedding and replace it with new, just in case her scent might somehow manage to linger and remind him of an incident he now wanted to totally forget!

But even outside he was still haunted by his mental images of her. Her ridiculous turquoise eyes, her creamy pale skin, her delicate bone structure, her extraordinarily passionate response to him that had driven him wild, driven him over the edge of his control to a place he had never been before. The sweet, hot, tight feel of her inside, as though she had never had another lover, never mind a child! No wonder poor, easygoing Khalid had become so ensnared by her!

Fleur was certainly attracting a lot of attention, Mariella reflected tenderly as people turned to look at the baby she was carrying in her arms, oblivious to the fact that it was her own appearance that was attracting second looks from so many members of the fashionably dressed crowd already filling the stable yard.

Her slim silk dress had originally been bought for a friend's wedding, its soft, swirling pattern in colours that ranged from palest aqua right through to turquoise. Over it, to cover her bare arms, Mariella was wearing a toning, velvet-edged, silk-knit cardigan, several shades paler than her hat and shoes.

A member of the prince's staff had been on hand to greet her as she stepped out of the limousine that had been sent to collect her, and to pass her on to a charming young man, who was now taking her to introduce her to the prince.

The purpose-built stables were immaculate, the equine occupants of the stalls arching their long necks and doing a good deal of scene stealing, as though intent on making the point that they were the real stars of the event and not the humans who were invading their territory.

The breakfast was to be served in ornamental pavilioned areas, off which was the crèche, so Mariella had been informed.

Her stomach muscles tightened a little as she saw the group of people up ahead of her. People of consequence and standing, no matter how they were dressed, all possessed that same air of confidence, Mariella acknowledged as the crowd opened up and the man at the centre of it turned to look at her.

'Miss Sutton, this is his Royal Highness,' her young escort introduced her to the prince, her potential client.

'Miss Sutton!' His voice was warm, but Mariella was aware of the sharp, assessing look he gave her.

'Your Highness,' she responded, with a small inclination of her head.

'I have been very impressed with your work, Miss Sutton, although I have to say that, especially in the case of my friend and rival Sir John Feinnes, you have erred on the side of generosity in the stature and muscle you have given his "Oracle".'

A small smile dimpled Mariella's mouth.

'I simply reflect what I see as an artist, Highness,' she told him demurely.

'Indeed. Then wait until you have seen my animals. They are the result of a breeding programme that has taken many years' hard work, and I want them to be painted in a way that pays full tribute to their magnificence.'

And to his own, Mariella decided, but tactfully did not say so.

'My friend Sir John also tells me that you have some very innovative ideas... The finishing touches are currently being put to an exclusive enclosure at our racecourse, which will bear my family name, and it occurs to me that there could be an opportunity there for...' He paused.

Mariella suggested, tongue in cheek, 'Something innovative?'

'Indeed,' he agreed. 'But this is not a time to discuss business. I have invited you here as my guest, so that you can meet some of your subjects informally, so to speak...'

Fleur, who had been staring around in wide-eyed silence, suddenly turned her head and smiled at him.

'You have a beautiful child,' he complimented her.

'She is my niece,' Mariella informed him. 'I am looking after her for my sister. I think my agent did explain.'

'Yes. I am sure she did! I seem to remember that my personal assistant did mention the little one.'

Some new guests were waiting to be presented to him, and Mariella stepped discreetly to one side. In the distance on the racecourse she could see a string of horses being exercised, whilst here in the yard there were grooms and stable hands all wearing khaki shorts or trousers, and tee shirts in one of the prince's three racing colours denoting their status within the hierarchy of the stables.

'If you would care to take the baby to the crèche,' the prince's assistant was asking politely.

Firmly Mariella shook her head. Such was her sense of responsibility towards her niece that she preferred to keep her with her for as long as she could, and, besides, the yard was far too busy for her to be able to do even the briefest of preliminary sketches of the animals. The event was providing her with a wonderful opportunity to do some people watching, though.

Surveying the crowd filling the prince's racing yard, Xavier wondered what on earth he was doing here. This kind of social event was normally something he avoided like the plague! It was much more Khalid's style than his, and if Khalid had not taken leave of absence without warning he would have been the one to attend the event! However, since Xavier was involved in shared business interests with the prince, he had felt that perhaps he should attend the breakfast—especially as it was in aid of a charity that he fully supported.

Several people had already stopped him to talk with him, including various members of the royal family, but he now felt that he had done his duty and was on the point of leaving when he suddenly frowned as he caught sight of a silky flash of turquoise-blue as the crowd in front of him momentarily parted.

Grimly he started to stride towards it.

People were starting to move towards the pavilioned area where the breakfast was about to be served, but Mariella hesitated a little uncertainly, suspecting that it would be a diplomatic move now to take Fleur over to the crèche area rather than into the pavilions. A little uncertainly she glanced round, unsure as to what to do, and hoping that she might see the prince's helpful assistant.

Xavier saw Mariella before she saw him, his eyebrows snapping together in seething fury as he realised his suspicions had been confirmed. It was her! And he had no difficulty in guessing just what she was doing here! Some of the richest men in Zuran were here, and very few of them were unlikely to at least be tempted by the sight of her! From the top of the confection of straw and tulle she was wearing on top of her head to the tip of the dainty little pink-painted toenails revealed by shoes so fragile that he was surprised that she dared risk wearing them, especially when carrying her child, she looked a picture of innocent vulnerability. But of course she was no such thing! And dressing the baby in an outfit obviously chosen to match hers seemed to proclaim their mother and baby status to the world.

Unaware of the fact that Nemesis and all the Furies were about to bear down on her with grim zeal in the shape of a very angry and disapproving male, Mariella shifted Fleur's weight in her arm.

'Very fetching! Trust you to be here, and with the very latest European accessory—I have to tell you, though, that you've misjudged its effect in Zuran!'

'Xavier!' Mariella felt her legs wobble treacherously in her high heels as she stared at him in shock.

'I don't know how you managed to get past the security staff—although I suspect I can guess how!' he told her cynically. 'Kept women and those who sell their favours to the highest bidder are normally kept out of such events.'

Kept women! His condemnation stung not just her pride, but her sense of sisterly protection for Tanya. She knew that if this conversation were to continue, she would have to explain she was not Fleur's mother, but right now she was due in the pavilion for breakfast. She was here on business and she would not jeopardise the commission by having an argument with Xavier in front of the prince! 'I refuse to speak with you if you are going to be so rude,' she said tersely. 'Now, if you'll excuse me, I must go and join the others.' A flash of light to her left made her gasp as she realised a photographer had just caught the two of them on camera!

'Don't think I don't know what you're doing here,' Xavier told her challengingly. 'You know that Khalid is going to come to his senses and realise just what you are, and you're looking for someone to take his place, and finance you.'

'Finance her!' The feathers nestling in the swathes of chiffon on Mariella's hat trembled as she shook with outrage.

'For your information, I do not need anyone to finance me, as you put it. I am completely financially independent.' As she saw his expression Mariella turned on her heel.

Hurrying away from him, she tensed as she suddenly felt a touch on her arm, but when she looked round it was only the prince's assistant.

'The Prince would like you to join his table for breakfast, Miss Sutton.' he told her. 'If I may escort you first to the crèche,' he added tactfully.

Angrily Xavier watched as the crowd swallowed her up. How dared she lie to him and claim to be financially independent, especially when she knew he knew the truth about her?

She was the most scheming and deceitful woman he had ever met, a woman he was a total fool to spare the smallest thought for!

The conversation around the breakfast table was certainly very cosmopolitan, Mariella decided as she listened to two other women discussing the world's best spa resorts, whilst the men debated the various merits of differing bloodstock.

After the breakfast was over and people were beginning to drift away, the prince came over to Mariella.

'My assistant will telephone you to make formal arrangements for us to discuss my commission,' he told her.

'I was wondering if it would be possible for me to visit your new enclosure?' Mariella asked him. 'Or, failing that, perhaps see some plans?'

She had the beginnings of a vague idea which, if the prince approved, would be innovative, but first she needed to see the enclosure to see if it would work.

'Certainly. I shall see that it is arranged.'

As he escorted her outside Mariella saw Xavier standing several yards away, her face beginning to burn as he looked at the prince and then allowed his glance to drift with slow and deliberate insolence over her, assessing her as though…as though she were a piece of…of flesh he was contemplating buying, Mariella recognised.

'Highness!'

'Xavier.' As the two men exchanged greetings Mariella turned to leave, but somehow Xavier had moved and was blocking her way.

'I see that you do not have Fleur with you!'

'No,' Mariella agreed coldly. 'She is in the crèche. I am just on my way to collect her.'

'You know Miss Sutton, Xavier? I hadn't realised. I am about to avail myself of her exceptional services, and she has promised me something extremely innovative.'

Mariella winced as she recognised from his expression just what interpretation Xavier had put on the prince's remarks. Excusing herself, she managed to push her way past Xavier, but to her consternation he only allowed her to take a few steps into the shadows cast by one of the pavilions before catching up with her and taking hold of her arm.

'My word, but you are a witch! The prince is renowned for his devotion to his wife and yet he speaks openly of entering a relationship with you!'

Mariella did not dignify that with an answer. Instead she bared her teeth at him in a savage little smile as she told him sweetly, 'There, you see, you need not have gone to all that trouble to protect your cousin. There is no need for you to go running to him now to tell him all about your sordid and appalling behaviour towards me. After all, once he gets to hear about the fact that the prince is paying for my…expertise…'

'You dare to boast openly about it?' Xavier was gripping her with both hands now, his fingers digging into the vulnerable flesh of her upper arms.

To her own surprise Mariella discovered that winding Xavier up was great fun and she was actually enjoying herself.

'Why shouldn't I?' she taunted him. 'I am proud of the fact that my skills are so recognised and highly thought of, and that I am able to earn a very respectable living for myself by employing them!'

As his fingers bit even harder into her arms she viewed the ominous white line around his mouth with a dangerous sense of reckless euphoria.

'In fact, in some circles I have already made quite a name for myself.'

She had gone too far, Mariella realised as her euphoria was suddenly replaced with apprehension.

'You are proud of being known as a high-class whore? Personally I would have classed you merely as an expensive one!'

Mariella was just about to slap him when he said, 'If you strike me here you could well end up in prison, whereas if I do this...'

She gasped as he bent his head and subjected her to a savagely demanding kiss, arching her whole body back as she fought not to come into contact with his, and lost that fight. In the shadows of the pavilion he used his physical strength to show her what she already knew—that despite his rage and contempt he was physically aroused by her! Just as she was by him?

He released her so abruptly that she almost stumbled. As he turned away from her he reached into his robe and removed a wallet, opening it to throw down some money.

White-faced, Mariella stared at him. Deep down inside herself she knew that she had deliberately incited and goaded him, but not for this.

'Pick it up!' he told her savagely.

Mariella took a deep breath and gathered what was left of her dignity around her. 'Very well,' she agreed calmly. 'I am sure the charity will be grateful for it,

Xavier. I understand it helps to support abandoned children.'

She prayed that he would think the glitter in her eyes was caused by her contempt and not by her tears.

Silently Xavier watched her go. His own behaviour had shocked him but he was too stubbornly proud to admit it—and even more stubbornly determined not to acknowledge what had actually caused it.

How could he admit to jealousy over the favours of such a woman? How could he acknowledge that his own desire to possess her went far, far beyond the physical desire for just her body? He could not and he did not intend to do so!

CHAPTER SEVEN

'A FRIEZE?'

The prince frowned as he looked at Mariella.

It was three days since the charity breakfast, and two since she had visited the new enclosure.

After what had happened with Xavier, the temptation to simply pack her bags and return home had been very strong, but stubbornly she had refused to give in to it.

It wasn't her fault that he had totally misinterpreted things. Well, at least not entirely! And besides... Besides, the commission the prince was offering her had far too much appeal for her as an artist to want to turn it down, never mind what her agent was likely to say!

So instead of worrying about Xavier she had spent the last two days working furiously on the idea she had had for the prince's new enclosure.

'The semi-circular walkway that leads to the enclosure would be perfect for such a project,' she told him. 'I could paint your horses there in a variety of different ways, either in their boxes, or in a string. I have spoken to your trainers and grooms and they have told me that they all have their individual personalities and little quirks, so if I painted them in a string I could include some of these. Solomon in particular, they tell me, does not like anyone else to lead the string, and then Saladin will not leave his box until his groom has removed the cat who is his stable companion. Shazare can't tolerate other horses with white socks, and—'

The prince laughed. 'I can see how well you have done your research, and, yes, I like what you are suggesting. It will be an extremely large project, though.'

Mariella gave a small shrug.

'It will allow me to paint the animals lifesize, certainly.'

'It will need to be done in time for the official opening of the stables.'

'And when will that be?' Mariella asked him.

'In around five months' time,' he told her.

Mariella did a quick mental calculation, and then exhaled in relief. That would give her more than enough time to get the work completed.

'It would take me about a month or two to finish. It has to be your decision, Highness,' she informed him diplomatically.

'Give me a few days to think about it. It is not that I don't like the idea. I do, but in this part of the world, we still put a great deal of store on "face", and therefore, no matter now innovative the idea, if it is not completed on time, then I shall lose face in the eyes of both my allies and my competitors. I certainly have no qualms about your work or your commitment to it, though.'

He needed time to check up on her and her past record of sticking to her contracted time schedules, Mariella knew, but that didn't worry her. She was always extremely efficient about sticking to a completion date once it was agreed.

The nursemaid provided by the prince to look after Fleur whilst she had been working smiled at her as she went to collect the baby.

'She is a very good baby,' the young woman told Mariella approvingly.

Once she was back in the Beach Club bungalow, Mariella tried to ring Tanya to both update her on Fleur's progress and to tell her about her work, but she was only able to reach her sister's message service.

If the prince did give her this commission, then at least she would be earning enough to ensure that Tanya did not have to work away from home. She knew her sister wanted to be independent, but there were Fleur's needs to be considered as well, and besides…

She was going to miss Fleur dreadfully when the time came to hand her back to her mother, Mariella acknowledged. She was just beginning to realise what her determination never to become involved in a permanent relationship was going to mean to her in terms of missing out on motherhood.

A little nervously, Mariella smoothed down the fabric of her skirt. She had arrived at the palace half an hour ago to see the prince, who was going to give her his verdict on whether or not he wanted her to go ahead with the frieze.

A shy nursemaid had already arrived to take Fleur from her, and now Mariella peeped anxiously at her watch. Fleur hadn't slept very well the previous night and Mariella suspected that she was cutting another new tooth.

'Miss Sutton, His Highness will see you now.'

'Ah, Mariella…'

'Highness,' Mariella responded as she was waved onto one of the silk-covered divans set around the walls of the huge audience room.

Almost immediately a servant appeared to offer her

coffee and delicious-looking almond pastries glistening with honey and stuffed with raisins.

'I am pleased to inform you that I have decided to commission you to work on the frieze,' the prince announced. 'The sooner you can complete it, the better—we have lots of other work to do before the official opening.'

Quickly Mariella put down her coffee-cup and then covered it with her hand as she saw that the hovering servant was about to refill it.

Whilst he padded away silently the prince frowned.

'However, there is one matter that is of some concern to me.'

He was still worrying about her ability to get the work finished on time, Mariella guessed, but instead of confirming her suspicions the prince got up and picked up a newspaper from the low table in front of him.

'This is our popular local newspaper,' he told her. 'Its gossip column is a great favourite and widely read.'

As he spoke he was opening the paper.

'There is here a report of our charity breakfast, and, as you will see, a rather intimate photograph of you with Sheikh Xavier Al Agir.'

Mariella's heart bumped against the bottom of her chest, her fingers trembling slightly as she studied the photograph the prince was showing her.

It took her several seconds to recognise that it had been taken when she and Xavier had been quarrelling, because it looked for all the world as though they were indeed engaged in a very intimate conversation, their heads close together, her lips parted, Xavier's head bent towards her, his gaze fixed on her mouth, whilst Fleur, whom she was holding in her arms, beamed happily at him.

Even though she had not eaten any of the pastries, Mariella was beginning to feel sick.

The article accompanying the photograph read:

Who was the young woman who Sheikh Xavier was so intimately engaged in conversation with? The sheikh is known for his strong moral beliefs and his dedication to his role as leader of the Al Agir tribe, and yet he was seen recently at the prince's charity breakfast, engaged in what appeared to be a very private conversation with one specific female guest on two separate occasions! Could it be that the sheikh has finally chosen someone to share his life? And what of the baby the unknown young woman is holding? What is her connection with the sheikh?

'In this country, unlike your own, a young woman alone with a child does cause a certain amount of speculation and disapproval. It is plain from the tone of this article that the reporter believes you and Xavier to be Fleur's parents...' the prince told Mariella, his voice very stern.

'But that is not true, Your Highness. We are not,' Mariella protested immediately. 'Fleur is my niece.'

'Of course. I fully accept what you are saying, but I think for your own sake that some kind of formal response does need to be made to this item. Which is why I have already instructed my staff to get in touch with the paper and to give them the true facts and to explain that Fleur is in fact your niece and that you are in Zuran to work for me. Hopefully that will be an end to the matter!'

*   *   *

Mariella frowned as for the third time in as many hours her sister's mobile was switched onto her message-taking service.

Why wasn't Tanya returning her calls?

Because of the length of time it was going to take her to complete the frieze, it had been decided that, instead of her returning to England as had originally been planned, she and Fleur should remain in Zuran so that she could commence work immediately.

The prince had announced that she would be provided with a small apartment and the use of a car, and Mariella was planning a shopping trip to equip both herself and Fleur for their unexpected extended stay.

Fleur's new tooth had now come through and the baby was back to her normal happy self.

Someone was knocking on the door of the bungalow and Mariella went to open it, expecting to see a member of the Beach Club's staff, but instead to her consternation it was Xavier who was standing outside.

Without waiting for her invitation he strode into the room, slamming the door closed behind him.

'Perhaps you can explain the meaning of *this* to me,' he challenged her sarcastically, throwing down the copy of the newspaper she had been reading earlier, open at the gossip column page.

'I don't have to explain anything to you, Xavier,' Mariella replied as calmly as she could.

'It says here that you are not Fleur's mother.'

'That's right,' she agreed. 'I'm not! I'm her aunt. My sister Tanya is her mother…and the woman who I have had to listen to you denouncing and abusing so slanderously and unfairly! And, for your information, Tanya is not, as you have tried to imply, some…some…

she is a professional singer and dancer, and, whilst you may not consider her good enough for your precious cousin, let me tell you that in my opinion he is the one who isn't good enough for her...not for her and certainly not for Fleur!' All the anger and anguish Mariella had been bottling up inside her was exploding in a surge of furious words.

'Your cousin told Tanya that he loved her and that he was committed to her and then he left her and Fleur! Have you any idea just what that did to Tanya? I was there when Fleur was born, I heard Tanya cry out for the man she loved. It's all so easy for a man, isn't it? If he doesn't want the responsibility of a woman's love or the child they create together, he can just walk away. You don't know what it means to be a child growing up knowing that your father didn't want or love you, and knowing too that your mother could never again be the person she was before her heart was broken. I would never, ever let any man hurt me the way Tanya has been hurt!'

'You wantonly and deliberately let me think that you and Khalid were lovers,' Xavier interrupted her savagely, ignoring her emotional outburst.

'Well, at first I thought you were Fleur's father, so I assumed you knew I wasn't Fleur's mother. But, face it, you wanted to think the worst you could about me, Xavier. You enjoyed thinking it! Revelled in it. I tried to warn you that you were getting it wrong, when you totally misinterpreted those comments by the prince! Remember?'

'Have you any idea just what problems this is causing?' he demanded harshly.

'What I have done?' Mariella gave him a disbeliev-ing look. 'My sister is a modern young woman who lives a modern young woman's life. Her biggest mistake, in my opinion, was to fall in love with your wretched cousin, and yet you have talked about her as though—!' Mariella compressed her lips as she saw the flash of temper darkening his eyes.

'Are you trying to say to me that you too are a modern young woman who lives a modern young woman's life, because if you are I have to tell you—!'

Xavier broke off abruptly, remembering the character references the prince had insisted on him reading when he had stormed into the palace earlier in the afternoon, demanding an immediate audience with him.

Mariella was not only a very highly acclaimed artist, she was also, it seemed, a young woman of the highest moral integrity—in every facet of her life!

'That is none of your business,' Mariella told him angrily.

'To the contrary. It is very much my business!'

Mariella stared at him, her heart thumping.

'Fleur is my cousin's child, which makes her a member of my family. Since you are also of her blood, that also makes you a member of my family. As the head of that family I am, therefore, responsible for both of you. There is no way I can allow you to live here in Zuran alone, or work unchaperoned for the prince. Our family pride and honour would be at risk! It is my responsibility!'

'What?' Mariella looked at him in open angry contempt. 'How can you possibly lay claim to any right to pride or honour? You, a man who was quite prepared to take the mother of his cousin's child to bed, just so that you could enforce your wish to keep them apart? This has got to be some kind of joke! I mean, you…you abuse me verbally, and physically. You insult and denigrate me and…and now you have the gall to turn round and start preaching to me about pride or honour! And as for your so-called sense of responsibility! You don't even begin to understand the meaning of the word, as decent people understand it!'

Mariella could see the tension in his jaw, but she suspected that it was caused by anger rather than any sense of shame.

'The situation has now changed!'

'Changed? Because you have discovered that instead of being, and I quote, your cousin's ''whore'' paid to have sex with men, I am a career woman.'

'I have received a…a communication from Khalid confirming that he is Fleur's father, and because of that—' his mouth tightened '—I have to consider Fleur's position, her future…her reputation!'

'Her reputation!' Mariella gave him a scathing look. 'Fleur is four months old! And anyway, His Highness has already done everything that is necessary to stem any potential gossip.'

'I have been to see His Highness myself to inform him that, whilst you are here in Zuran, you will be living beneath the protection of my roof! Naturally he is in total agreement!'

Mariella couldn't believe her ears.

'Oh, no,' she denied, shaking her head vigorously from side to side. 'No, no, no. No way!'

'Mariella. Please see it as a way for me to make amends by offering you my hospitality. Besides, you have no choice—the prince expects it.'

He meant it, Mariella recognised as she searched his implacable features.

'I shall wait here until you have packed and then we will return to my home. I have arranged for my widowed great-aunt to act as your chaperone for the duration of your stay in Zuran.'

Her chaperone!

'I am twenty-eight years old,' she told him through gritted teeth. 'I do not need a chaperone.'

'You are a single woman living beneath the roof of a single man. There will already be those who will look askance at you having read that article.'

'At me, but not, of course, at you!'

'I am a man, so it is different,' he told her with a dismissively arrogant shrug that made her grind her teeth in female outrage.

Mariella couldn't wait to speak to her sister to tell her what had happened!

Right now, though, Mariella dared not take the risk of defying him! He could, after all, if he so wished, not merely put his threats into action, but also take Fleur from her here and now if he chose to do so!

It took her less than half an hour to pack their things, a task she performed in seething silence whilst Xavier stood in front of the door, his arms folded across his chest, watching her with smoulderingly dangerous eyes.

When she had finished she went to pick Fleur up, but Xavier got there first.

Over Fleur's downy head their gazes clashed and locked, Xavier's a seething molten grey, Mariella's a brilliantly glittering jade.

The limousine waiting for them was every bit as opulent looking as the one the prince had sent for her, although Mariella was surprised to discover that Xavier was driving it himself.

Somehow she had not associated him with a liking for such a luxurious showy vehicle. She had got the impression that his tastes were far, far more austere.

But, as she had discovered, beneath his outwardly cold self-control a molten, hot passion burned, which was all the more devastating for being so tightly chained.

It didn't take them long to reach the villa, but this time the gates were opened as they approached them and they swept in, crunching over a gravel drive flanked by double rows of palm trees.

The villa itself was elegantly proportioned, its design restrained, and Moorish in inspiration, Mariella noticed with unwilling approval as she studied its simple lines with an artist's eye.

A pair of wrought-iron gates gave way to a gravelled walled courtyard, ornamented with a large central stone fountain.

Stopping the car, Xavier got out and came to open her own door. A manservant appeared to deal with her luggage, and a shy young girl whom Xavier introduced to her as Hera, and who, he told her, would be Fleur's nanny. Smiling reassuringly at the nanny he handed Fleur to her before Mariella could stop him.

She certainly held Fleur as though she knew what she was doing, Mariella recognised, but even so! A pang of loss tightened her body as she looked at Fleur being held in another woman's arms.

'Fleur doesn't need a nanny,' she told Xavier quickly. 'I am perfectly capable of looking after her myself.'

'Maybe so, but it is customary here for those who can afford to do so to provide the less well off amongst our people with work. Hera is the eldest child in her family, and her mother has recently been widowed. Are you really willing to deprive her of the opportunity to help to support her siblings, simply because you are afraid of allowing anyone else to become emotionally close to Fleur?'

As he spoke he was ushering her into the semi-darkness of the interior of the villa. Mariella was so shocked and unprepared for his unexpectedly astute comment that she stumbled slightly as her eyes adjusted to the abrupt change from brilliant sunlight to shadowy darkness.

Instantly Xavier reached for her, his hand gripping her waist as he steadied her. Her dizziness must be something to do with that abrupt switch from lightness to dark, Mariella told herself, and so too must her accompanying weakness, turning her into a quivering mass of over-sensitive nerve endings, each one of them reacting to the fact that Xavier was touching her. Confused blurred images filled her head: Xavier, naked as he swam, Xavier leaning over her as he held her down on the bed, Xavier kissing her until she ached for him so badly her need was a physical pain.

Her need? She did not need Xavier. She would never, never need him. Never… She managed to pull herself free of him, her eyes adjusting to the light enough for her to see the cold disapproval with which he was regarding her.

'You must take more care. You are not used to our climate. By the end of this month the temperature will be reaching forty degrees Celsius, and you are very fair-skinned. You must be sure always to drink plenty of water, and that applies to Fleur as well.'

'Thank you. I do know not to allow myself to get dehydrated,' Mariella told him through gritted teeth. 'I am a woman, not a child, and as such I am perfectly capable of looking after myself. After all, I've been doing it for long enough.'

The look he gave her made her feel as though someone had taken hold of her heart and flipped it over inside her chest.

'Yes. It must have been hard for you to lose your mother and your stepfather having already lost your father at such a young age...'

'Lost my father?' Mariella gave him a bitter look. 'I didn't "lose" him. He abandoned my mother because he didn't want the responsibilities of fatherhood. He was never any true father to me, but he broke my mother's heart—'

'My own parents died when I was in my early teens—a tragic accident—but I was lucky enough to have my grandmother to help me through it. However, as we both know, the realisation that one is without parents does tend to breed a certain...independence of spirit, a certain protective defensiveness.' He was frowning, Mariella recognised, picking his words with care as though there was something he was trying to tell her. He broke off as Hera came into the reception hall carrying Fleur.

'If you will go with Hera, she will show you to your quarters. My aunt should arrive shortly.'

He had turned on his heel and was striding away from her, his back ramrod straight in the cool whiteness of his robe, leaving her no alternative other than to follow the timidly smiling young maid.

The villa obviously stretched back from its frontage to a depth she had not suspected, Mariella acknowledged ten minutes later, when she had followed the maid through several enormous reception rooms and

up a flight of stairs, and then along a cloistered walkway through which a deliciously cool breeze had
flowed and from which she had been able to look down
into a totally enclosed private courtyard, complete with
a swimming pool.

'This is the courtyard of Sheikh Xavier,' Hera had
whispered to her, shyly averting her gaze from it and
looking nervous when Mariella had paused to study it.

'Normally it is forbidden for us to be here, as the
women of the household have their own private entrance to their quarters…'

'Let me take Fleur,' Mariella told her, firmly taking
her niece back into her own arms and relishing the
deliciously warm weight of her.

A door at the end of the corridor led to another cloistered walkway, this time with views over an immaculate rose garden.

'This was the special garden of the sheikh's grandparents. His grandmother was French and the roses
were from France. She supervised their planting herself.'

For Mariella the rigid beds and the formality of the
garden immediately summoned up a vivid impression
of a woman who was very proud and correct, a true
martinet. Her grandson obviously took after her!

The women's quarters, when they finally got to
them, proved to be far more appealing than Mariella
had expected. Here again a cloistered walkway opened
onto a private garden, but here the garden was softer,
filled with sweet-smelling flowers and decorated with
a pretty turreted summer house as well as the customary water features.

They comprised several lavishly furnished bedrooms, each with its own equally luxurious bathroom

and dressing room, a dining room, and a salon—Mariella could think of no other word to describe the delicate and ornate antique French furniture and decor of the two rooms, which she suspected must have been designed and equipped for Xavier's French grand-mother.

On the bookshelves flanking the fireplace she could see leather-bound books bearing the names of some of France's most famous writers.

'The sheikh has said that you will wish to have the little one in a room next to your own,' Hera was telling her softly. 'He has made arrangements for everything that she will need to be delivered. I am not sure which room you will wish to use...'

Ignoring the temptation to tell her that she wished to use none of them, and that in fact what she wished to do was to leave the villa with Fleur right now—after all, none of this was Hera's fault and it would be unfair of her to take out her own resentment on the maid—Mariella gave in to her gentle hint and quickly in-spected each of the four bedrooms.

One of them, furnished in the same Louis Fifteenth antiques as the salon, had quite obviously been Xavier's grandmother's and she rejected it immedi-ately. Of the three others, she automatically picked the plainest with its cool-toned walls and simple furniture. It had its own private access to the gardens with a small clear pool only a few feet away and a seat next to it from which to watch the soothing movement of the water.

'This room?'

When Mariella nodded, Hera smiled.

'The sheikh will be pleased. This was his mother's room.'

Xavier's mother's room! It was too late for her to change her mind, Mariella recognised.

'What…what nationality was she?' she asked Hera, immediately wishing she had not done so.

'She was a member of the tribe… The sheikh's father met her when he was travelling with them and fell in love with her…'

Fleur was beginning to make hungry noises, reminding Mariella that it was her niece she should be thinking about and not Xavier's family background.

CHAPTER EIGHT

MARIELLA stared worriedly at her mobile phone. She had just tried for the fourth time since her arrival at the villa to make contact with Tanya, but her sister's mobile was still switched onto messaging mode. She had left a message saying that she was staying at Xavier's villa, and had asked Tanya to contact her at the villa or call her cell phone. Mariella realised to her consternation that it was days since she had actually spoken to Tanya. A little tingle of alarm began to feather down her spine. What if something had happened to her sister? What if she wasn't well or had hurt herself. Or…

Quickly Mariella made up her mind. It took her quite some time to get the telephone number for the entertainments director of her sister's cruise liner, but eventually she managed to get through.

'I'm sorry, who is this speaking, please?' The firm male voice on the other end of the line checked her when Mariella had asked for Tanya, explaining that she had been unable to make contact with her via her mobile.

'I am Tanya's sister,' Mariella explained.

'I see… Well, I have to inform you that Tanya has actually left the ship.'

'Left the ship!' Mariella repeated in disbelief. 'But…where? Why…?'

'I'm sorry. I can't give you any more details. All I can say is that Tanya left of her own accord and without giving us any prior warning.'

From the tone of his voice Mariella could tell that he wasn't very pleased with her sister!

Thanking him for his help, she ended the call, turning to look at Fleur, who was fast asleep in her brand-new bed.

As Hera had already warned her, Xavier had instructed a local baby equipment store to provide a full nursery's worth of brand new things, all of which Mariella had immediately realised were far, far more expensive and exclusive than anything she or Tanya could have afforded.

Tanya! Where was her sister? Why had she left the ship? And why, oh, why wasn't she returning her calls?

It was imperative that she knew what was happening, and, for all her faults, her impulsiveness and hedonism, Tanya genuinely loved Fleur. It was unthinkable to Mariella that she should not make contact with her to check up on her baby.

In Tanya's shoes there was no way she would not have been on the phone every hour of every day... No way she could ever have brought herself to be parted from her baby in the first place, Mariella recognised, but then poor Tanya had had no alternative! Tanya had been determined to pay her own way.

Emotionally, she stood over Fleur looking down at her whilst she slept. Increasingly she ached inside to have a child of her own. When she had made her original vow never to put herself in a position where she could be emotionally hurt by a man, she had not foreseen this kind of complication!

Xavier frowned as he paced the floor of his study. A flood of faxes cluttered his desk, all of them giving him the same information—namely that his cousin had not been seen in any of his usual favourite haunts! Where on earth was Khalid?

Xavier was becoming increasingly suspicious that his cousin had been deliberately vague about Fleur's true paternity. Out of a desire to protect Fleur and her mother, or out of a desire to escape his responsibilities?

Surely Khalid knew him well enough to know that, even if he couldn't approve of or accept Fleur's mother, he would certainly have insisted that proper financial arrangements were made for her and Fleur, and if necessary by Xavier himself? Of course he did, which was no doubt why he had now written to Xavier informing him that he was Fleur's father.

It irked him that he had been so dramatically wrong-footed in assuming that Mariella was Fleur's mother. The security information the prince had revealed to him had made it brutally clear just how wrong he had been about her.

Here was a young woman who had shouldered the responsibility, not just of supporting herself, but of supporting her younger half-sister as well. Not a single shred of information to indicate that Mariella had led anything other than the most morally laudable life could be found! There were no unsavoury corpses mouldering away in the dusty corners of Mariella's life; in fact, the truth was that there were not even any dusty corners! Everyone who had had dealings with her spoke of her in the most glowing and complimentary terms.

And yet somehow he, a man who prided himself on his astuteness and his ability to read a person's true personality, had not been able to see any of this! True, she had deliberately deceived him, but...

But he had behaved towards her in a way that, had

he heard about it coming from another man, he would have had no hesitation in immediately denouncing and condemning him!

There were no excuses he could accept from himself! Not even the increasingly insubstantial one of wanting to protect Khalid.

Wasn't it after all true that the last thing, the last person who had been in his thoughts when he had taken Mariella to bed had been his cousin? Wasn't it also true that he had been driven, possessed...consumed by his own personal physical desire?

He could find no logical excuse or explanation for what he had done. Other than to tell himself that he had been driven by desert madness, and he felt riddled with guilt, especially for the way he had coerced her into staying with him at his villa. He would of course have to apologise formally to Mariella!

A woman who already had proved how strong her sense of duty and responsibility was. A woman with whom a man could know that the children he gave her would be loved and treasured...

He had sworn not to marry, rather than risk the hazards of a marriage that might go wrong, he reminded himself austerely.

Surely, though, it was better to offer Mariella the protection of his name in marriage rather than risk any potential damage to her reputation through gossip?

He had already provided her with sufficient protection in the form of his great-aunt as a chaperone, he reminded himself grimly. If he continued to think as he was doing right now, he might begin to suspect that he actually wanted to marry her! That he actually wanted to take her back into his bed and complete what they had already begun.

Angrily he swung round as the sudden chatter of the fax machine broke into his far too sensually charged thoughts.

'So, here we are, then. Xavier has summoned me to be your chaperone, and I am to accompany you to the palace whilst you paint pictures for His Highness, *non?*'

'Well, not exactly,' Mariella responded wryly. It was impossible for her not to like the vivacious elderly Frenchwoman who was Xavier's great-aunt and who had arrived half an hour earlier, complete with an enormous pile of luggage and her own formidable looking maid.

'I am not actually working at the palace, but at the new enclosure at the racecourse, and, to be honest, I don't agree with Xavier—'

'Agree? But I am afraid that here in Zuran we have to comply with the laws of the land, *chérie,* both actual and moral.' Rolling her eyes dramatically, she continued, 'I know how difficult I found it when I first came to live here. My sister was already married to Xavier's grandfather for several years by then. She was older than me by well over a decade. Since the death of my husband, I live both in Paris and here in Zuran. The child I understand is Khalid's?' she commented, with a disconcerting change of subject. 'He is a charming young man, but unfortunately very weak! He is fortunate that Xavier is so indulgent towards him, but you probably know Xavier does not intend to marry and he intended for Khalid's son to ultimately take over his responsibilities! It is such foolishness...'

'Xavier does not intend to marry?' Mariella questioned her.

'So he claims. The death of his own parents affected him very seriously. He was at a most impressionable age when they perished and of course my sister, his grandmother, was very much a matriarch of the old school. She was determined that he would be brought up to know his responsibilities towards his people and to fulfil them. Now Xavier believes that their needs are more important than his own and that he cannot therefore risk marrying a woman who would not understand and accept his duty and the importance of his role. Such nonsense, but then that is men for you! They like to believe that we are the weaker sex, but we of course know that it is we who are the strong ones!'

'You have great strength, I can see that! You will miss the child when you eventually have to hand her back to her mother,' she added shrewdly.

The speed of her conversation, along with the speed of her perceptiveness, was leaving Mariella feeling slightly dizzy.

'I see that you have chosen not to occupy my late sister's room. Extremely wise of you if I may say so...I could never understand why she insisted on attempting to recreate our parents' Avenue Foche apartment here! But then that was Sophia for you! As an eldest child she was extremely strong-willed, whilst I...' she paused to dimple a rueful smile at Mariella '...am the youngest, and, according to her at least, was extremely spoiled!

'You would not have liked her,' she pronounced, shocking Mariella a little with her outspokenness. 'She would have taken one look at you and immediately started to make plans to make you Xavier's wife. You do not believe me? I assure you that it is true. She would have seen immediately how perfect you would be for him!'

Her, perfect for Xavier? Fiercely squashing the treacherous little sensation tingling through her, Mariella told her quickly, 'I have no intention of ever getting married.'

'You see? Already it is clear just how much you and Xavier have in common! However, I am not my sister. I do not interfere in other people's lives or try to arrange them for them! *Non!* But tell me why is it that you have made up your mind not to marry? In Xavier's case it is plain that it is because of the fear instilled in him by my sister that he will not find a woman to love who will share his dedication to his commitment to preserve the traditional way of life of the tribe. Such nonsense! But Sophia herself is very much to blame. When he was a young and impressionable young man she sent Xavier to France in the hope that he would find a bride amongst the daughters of our own circle. But these girls cannot breathe any air other than that of Paris. The very thought of them doing as Xavier has done every year of his life and travelling through the desert with those members of the tribe who had chosen to adhere to the old way of life would be intolerable to them!

'Xavier needs a wife who will embrace and love the ways of his people with the same passion with which he does himself. A woman who will embrace and love him with even more passion, for, as I am sure you will already know, Xavier is an extremely passionate man.'

Mariella gave her a wary look. What was his great-aunt trying to imply? However, when she looked at her face her expression was rosily innocent and open.

Madame Flavel's comments were, though, arousing both her interest and her curiosity.

Hesitantly she told her, 'You have mentioned the tribe and Xavier's commitment to it, but I do not really know just what…'

'*Non?* It is quite simple really. The tribe into which Xavier's ancestor originally married is unique in its way of life, and it was the life's work of Xavier's grandfather, and would have been of his father had he not died, to preserve the tribe's traditional nomadic existence, but at the same time encourage those members of it who wished to do so to integrate into modern society. To that end, every child born into the tribe has the right to receive a proper education and to follow the career path of their choice, but at the same time each and every member of the tribe must spend some small part of every year travelling the traditional nomadic routes in the traditional way. Some members of the tribe elect to live permanently in such a fashion, and they are highly revered by every other member of the tribe, even those who, as many have, have reached the very peak of their chosen career elsewhere in the world. Within the tribe recognition and admiration are won, not through material or professional attainment, but through preservation of the old ways and traditions.

'Xavier's role as head of the tribe means, though, that he has a dual role to fulfil. He must ensure that he has the business expertise to see that the money left by his grandfather generates sufficient future income to provide financially for the tribe, and yet at the same time he must be able to hold the respect of the tribe by leading it in its ancient traditional ways. Xavier has known all his life that he must fulfil both those roles and he does so willingly, I know, but nevertheless it

will be a very lonely path he has chosen to follow
unless he does find a woman who can understand and
share his life with him.'

Mariella had fallen silent as she listened. There was
a poignancy about what she was hearing that was
touching very deep emotional chords within. The
Xavier his great-aunt was describing to her was a man
of deep and profound feelings and beliefs, a man who,
in other circumstances, she herself could respect and
admire.

'*Madame,* I assure you there is really no need for you
to remain here with me,' Mariella told her chaperone
firmly as she studied the long corridor that was to be
her canvas.

Fleur was lying in her pram playing with her toes
and Mariella had pinned up in front of her, on the easel
she had brought with her, the photographs she had
taken of the prince's horses.

'It is for this purpose that Xavier has summoned me
to his home,' Madame Flavel reminded her.

'You will be bored sitting here watching me work,'
Mariella protested.

'I am never bored. I have my tapestry and my newspaper, and in due course Ali will return to drive us
back to the villa for a small repast and an afternoon
nap.'

There was no way she intended to indulge in afternoon naps, Mariella decided silently as she picked up
her charcoals and started to work.

In her mind she already had a picture of how she
wanted the frieze to look, and within minutes she was
totally engrossed in what she was doing.

The background for the horses, she had now decided,

would not be the racecourse itself, but something that she hoped would prove far more compelling to those who viewed it. The background of a rolling ocean of waves from which the horses were emerging would surely prove irresistible to a people to whom water was so very, very important. Mariella hoped so. His Highness had certainly liked the idea.

It wasn't until her fingers began to ache a little with cramp that she realised how long she had been working. Madame Flavel had fallen asleep in the comfortable chair with its special footstool that Ali had brought for her, her gentle snores keeping Fleur entranced.

Smiling at her niece, Mariella opened the bottle of water she had brought with her and took a drink. Where was Tanya? Why hadn't she got in touch with her?

The door to the corridor opened to admit Hera and Ali.

'Goodness, is it lunchtime already?' Madame Flavel demanded, immediately waking up.

Reluctantly Mariella started to pack up her things. She would much rather have continued with her work than return to the villa, but she was very conscious of Madame Flavel's age and the unfairness of expecting her to remain with her for hours on end.

CHAPTER NINE

BY THE end of the week Mariella was beginning to find her enforced breaks from her work increasingly frustrating.

'It disturbs me that you are so determined not to marry, *chérie*,' Madame Flavel was saying to her as she worked. 'It is perhaps because of an unhappy love affair?'

'You could say that,' Mariella agreed wryly.

'He broke your heart, but you are young, and broken hearts mend…'

'It wasn't my heart he broke, but my mother's,' Mariella corrected her, 'and it never really mended, not even when she met and married my stepfather. You see, she thought when my father told her that he loved her he meant it, but he didn't! She trusted him, depended on him, but he repaid that trust by abandoning us both.'

'Ah, I see. And because of the great hurt your father caused you, you are determined never to trust any man yourself?' Madame Flavel commented shrewdly. 'Not all men are like your father, *chérie*.'

'Maybe not, but it is not a risk I am prepared to take! I never want to be as…as vulnerable as my mother was…never.'

'You say that, but I think you fear that you already are.'

Mariella was glad of Ali's arrival to put an end to what was becoming a very uncomfortable conversation.

* * *

It was two o'clock in the afternoon and Madame Flavel was taking her afternoon nap.

Mariella walked restlessly round the garden. She was itching to get on with the frieze. She paused, frowning slightly. And then, making up her mind, hurried back inside, pausing only to pick up Fleur.

Ali made no comment when she summoned him to tell him that she intended to go back to the enclosure, politely opening the door of the car for her. Stepping outside was like standing in the blast of a hot hair-dryer at full heat.

The car was coolly air-conditioned, but outside the heat shimmered in the air, the light bouncing glaringly off the buildings that lined the road.

Like the car, the enclosure was air-conditioned, and as soon as Ali had escorted her inside and gone Mariella began to work.

A moveable scaffolding had been erected to allow her to work on the upper part of the wall, and she paused every now and again to look down from it to check on Fleur, who was fast asleep. Her throat felt dry and her hand ached, but she refused to allow herself to stop. In her mind's eye she could see the finished animal, nostrils flaring, his mane ruffled by the wind, the sea foaming behind him as he emerged from the curling breakers.

Somewhere on the edge of her awareness she was vaguely conscious of a door opening, and quiet but ominously determined footsteps. Fleur made a small sound, a gurgle of pleasure rather than complaint, which she also registered, her hand moving quickly as she fought to capture the image inside her head. This horse, the proudest and fiercest of them all, would not tolerate any competition from the sea. He would challenge its power, rearing up so that the powerful muscles of his quarters and belly were visible… Fleur was chattering happily to herself in baby talk, and Mariella was beginning to feel almost light-headed with concentration. And then just as she was finishing something a movement, an instinct made her turn her head.

To her shock she saw that Xavier was standing beside Fleur watching her.

'Xavier…'

She took a step forward and then stopped, suddenly realising that she was still on the scaffolding.

'What…what are you doing here?' she demanded belligerently to cover her own intimate and unwanted reaction to him.

'Have you any idea just how much you distressed Cecille by ignoring my instructions?' he demanded tersely.

Mariella looked away from him. She genuinely liked his great-aunt, and hated the thought that she might have upset her.

'I'm sorry if she was upset,' she told him woodenly, her own feelings breaking through her tight control as she gave a small despairing shake of her head.

'I promised His Highness that the frieze would be completed as soon as possible; your aunt is elderly. She likes to spend the afternoon resting, when I need to be here working! Whether you believe this or not, Xavier, I too have a…a reputation to protect.'

'In that case why didn't you simply come to me and explain all of this to me instead of behaving like a child and waiting until my aunt's back was turned?'

Mariella frowned. What he was saying sounded so…so reasonable and sensible she imagined that anyone listening to him would have asked her the same question!

'Your behaviour towards me has hardly encouraged me to…to anticipate your help or co-operation,' she reminded him as she went to climb down from the scaffolding, surreptitiously trying to stretch her aching muscles.

'Although she herself refuses to acknowledge it, my aunt is an elderly lady,' Xavier was continuing, breaking off suddenly to mutter something beneath his breath she couldn't quite catch as he strode forward.

'Be careful,' he warned her sharply. 'You might…'

To her own chagrin, as though his warning had provoked it, the scaffolding suddenly wobbled and she began to slip.

As she gave a small instinctive gasp of shock Xavier grabbed hold of her, supporting her so that she could slide safely to the floor.

Mariella knew that the small near-accident was her own fault and that she had worked for too long in one position, without stopping to exercise her cramped muscles, and her face began to burn as she anticipated Xavier's triumphant justification of his insistence that she was chaperoned, but instead of saying anything he simply continued to hold her, one hand grasping her waist, the other supporting the small of her back, where his fingers spread a dangerously intoxicating heat right through her clothes and into her skin.

Dizzily Mariella closed her eyes, trying to blot out the effect the proximity of him was having on her, but, to her consternation, instead of protecting her all it did was increase her vulnerability as sharply focused mental images of him taunted and tormented her, their ef-

fect on her so intense that she started to shake in reaction to them.

'Mariella? What is it? What's wrong?' she heard
Xavier demanding urgently. 'If you feel unwell…'

Immediately Mariella opened her eyes.

'No. I'm fine,' she began and then stopped, unable
to drag her gaze away from his mouth, where it had
focused itself with hungry, yearning intensity.

She knew from his sudden fixed silence that Xavier
was aware of what she was doing, but the shrill alarm
bells within her own defences, which should have
shaken her into action, were silenced into the merest
whisper by the inner roar of her own aching longing.
No power on earth, let alone that of her own will, could
stem what was happening to her and what she was
feeling, Mariella recognised distantly, as her senses
registered the way Xavier's grip on her body subtly
altered from one of non-sexually protective to one of
powerfully sensual. She could feel the hot burn of his
gaze as it dropped to her own mouth, and a sharp series
of little shivers broke through her. Without even thinking about it she was touching her lips with the tip of
her tongue, as though driven by some deep pre-
programmed instinct to moisten them. She was trembling, her whole body galvanised by tiny sensual rip-
ples of reaction and awareness that made her sway
slightly towards him.

She saw a muscle twitch in his jaw and raised her
hand to touch it with her fingertips, her eyes wide and
helplessly enslaved.

'Mariella!'

She felt him shudder as he drew breath into his
lungs, her body instinctively leaning into his as weakness washed over her.

His mouth touched hers, but not in the way she had remembered it doing before.

She had never known there could be so much sweet tenderness in a kiss, so much slow, explorative warmth, so much carefully suppressed passion just waiting to burn away all her resistance. She wanted to lose herself completely in it…in him.

She gave a small cry of protest as Xavier's ears, keener than hers, picked up the sound of someone entering the gallery, and he pushed her away.

Caught up in the shock of what she had experienced, Mariella watched motionless as Xavier went over to where Ali, his chauffeur, was hovering.

Lifting her hand, she touched her own lips, as though unable to believe what had happened…what she had wanted to happen. She had wanted Xavier to kiss her, still wanted him to kiss her, her body aching for him in a hundred intimate ways that held her in silent shock. She and Xavier were enemies, weren't they?

He was walking back to her and somehow she had to compose herself, to conceal from him what was happening to her.

She felt as though she were drowning in her own panic.

'We must get back to the villa, immediately,' he told her curtly.

Instantly her panic was replaced by anxiety.

'What is it?' she demanded. 'Has something happened to your aunt?'

She started to gather up her things, but he stopped her, instructing her tersely, 'Leave all that.'

He was already picking up Fleur, his body language so evident of a crisis that Mariella forbore to argue. Her stomach was churning sickly. What if something had happened to his great-aunt, perhaps brought on by her own stubborn determination to ignore his dictates? She would never forgive herself!

Falling into step beside him, Mariella almost had to run to keep up with him.

They drove back to the villa in silence, Mariella's anxiety increasing to such a pitch that by the time they finally turned into the courtyard of the villa she felt physically sick.

Giving some sharp order to Ali, in Arabic, Xavier got out of the car, turning to her and telling her equally shortly, 'Come with me.'

Even Fleur seemed to have picked up on his seriousness, and fell silent in his arms, her eyes huge and dark.

Please let Cecille be all right, Mariella prayed silently as the huge double doors to the villa were thrown open with unfamiliar formality and she followed Xavier into its sandalwood-scented coolness.

Without pausing to see if she was following him, Xavier headed for the anteroom that opened out into what Mariella now knew was the formal salon in which he conducted his business meetings.

Unusually two liveried servants were standing to either side of the entrance, their expressionless faces adding both to Mariella's anxiety and the look of stern formality she could see on Xavier's face, giving it and him an air of autocratic arrogance so reminiscent of the first time she had seen him that she automatically shivered a little.

Expecting him to stride into the room ahead of her, Mariella almost bumped into him when he suddenly turned towards her. A little uncertainly she looked at him, unable to conceal her confusion when he reached out his hand to her and beckoned her to his side.

Holding Fleur tightly, she hesitated for a second before going to join him. Wide as the entrance to the salon was, it still apparently necessitated Xavier standing so close to her that she could feel the heat of his body against her own as he gave the servants an abrupt nod.

The doors swung open, the magnificence of the room that lay beyond them dazzling Mariella for a moment, even though she had already peeped into it at Madame Flavel's insistence.

It was everything she had ever imagined such a room should be, its walls hung with richly woven silks, the cool marble floor ornamented with priceless antique rugs. The light from the huge chandeliers, which Madame Flavel had told Mariella had been made to Xavier's grandmother's personal design, dazzled the eyes as it reflected on the room's rich jewel colours and ornate gilding. Luxurious and rich, the decor of the salon had about it an unmistakable air of French elegance.

It was a room designed to awe and impress all those who entered it and to make them aware of the power of the man who owned it.

As her eyes adjusted to the brilliance Mariella realised that two people were standing in front of the room's huge marble fireplace, watching Xavier with obvious apprehension as they clung together.

Disbelievingly Mariella stared at them.

'Tanya,' she whispered, her voice raw with shock as she recognised her sister.

Her sister looked tanned and expensive, Mariella noticed, the skirt and top she was wearing showing off her body. She was wearing her hair in a new, fashionably tousled style, and it glinted with a mix of toning blonde highlights.

She was immaculately made up, her fingernails and toenails shining with polish, but it was the man standing at Tanya's side on whom Mariella focused most of her attention. He was shorter than Xavier and more heavily built, she guessed immediately that he must be Khalid, Xavier's cousin and Fleur's father.

'Khalid,' Xavier acknowledged curtly, with a brief nod in the other man's direction, confirming Mariella's guesswork. 'And this, I assume, must be…'

'My wife,' Khalid interrupted him, holding tightly to Tanya's hand as he continued, 'Tanya and I were married three days ago.'

'Honestly, Mariella, I just couldn't believe it when we docked at Kingston and Khalid came on board. At first I totally refused to have anything to do with him, but he kept on persisting and eventually…'

It was less than twenty-four hours since Mariella had learned that her sister and Khalid were now married, and Tanya was updating her on what had happened as they sat together in the garden of the villa's women's quarters, whilst Fleur gurgled happily in her carrier.

'Why didn't you tell me what was going on when I telephoned you?' Mariella asked her.

Tanya looked self-conscious.

'Well, at first I wasn't sure just what was going to happen—I mean…Khalid was there and he was being very sweet, admitting that he loved me and that he regretted what he had done, but…

'And then you left that message on my cell phone saying you were here with Xavier, and I was worried that you might say something to him and that he would find a way of parting me and Khalid again...'

'Have you any idea how worried about you I've been?' Mariella asked her.

Tanya flushed uncomfortably.

'Well, I had hoped that you'd just think I wasn't returning your calls because I was so busy... It didn't occur to me that you'd ring the entertainments director...'

'Tanya, you didn't ring me to check on Fleur for days. Of course I was worried...'

'Oh, well, I knew she'd be fine with you, and I did listen to your messages. But Khalid... Well, we needed some time to ourselves, and Khalid insisted... Please don't be cross with me, Ella. You've never been in love so you can't understand. When Khalid left me I thought my life was over. I'm not like you. I need to love and be loved. I don't think I'll ever forgive Xavier for what he did.'

'Xavier didn't physically compel Khalid to abandon you and Fleur, Tanya,' Mariella heard herself pointing out to her sister almost sharply.

The look Tanya gave her confirmed her own realisation of what she had done.

'How can you support him, Ella?' Tanya demanded. 'He threatened to stop Khalid's allowance; he would have left me and Fleur to starve,' she added dramatically.

'That's not true, Tanya, and not fair either,' Mariella felt bound to correct her, but she couldn't quite bring herself to tell her sister that it was her own opinion that Khalid was both weak and self-indulgent and that he had selfishly put his own needs before those of his lover and their child. She could see already the begin-

nings of a sulky pout turning down the corners of
Tanya's mouth and her heart sank. She had no wish to
quarrel with her sister, but at the same time she
couldn't help feeling that Tanya wasn't treating her
own behaviour with regard to her maternal responsibilities towards Fleur anywhere near as seriously as she
should have been doing.

'Well, we're married now and there's nothing that
Xavier can do about it! And he knows it!'

Mariella knew that this was not true and that Xavier
could have carried out his threat to stop paying Khalid
his allowance, and also remove him from his sinecure
of a job. However, she also knew from what Madame
Flavel had innocently told her that Xavier had not done
so because of Fleur.

'Oh, and you'll never guess what,' Tanya told her
excitedly. 'I haven't had the opportunity to tell you yet,
but Khalid is insisting on taking me for an extended
honeymoon trip. We're going to take Fleur with us, of
course, and then once we get back I suppose we will
have to make our home here in Zuran, but Khalid has
promised me that we'll get away as often as we can.
He says that we can have our own villa and that I can
choose everything myself! Oh, and look at my engagement ring. Isn't it beautiful?'

'Very,' Mariella agreed cordially as she studied the
huge solitaire flashing on her sister's hand.

'I can't tell you how happy I am, Ella,' Tanya
breathed ecstatically. 'And you have looked after my
darling baby so well for me. I have missed you so
much, my sweet,' Tanya cooed, blowing kisses to her
daughter. 'Your daddy and I can't wait to have you all
to ourselves.'

As she listened to her sister a small shadow crossed

Mariella's face, but she was determined not to spoil Tanya's happiness by letting her see how much she was dreading losing Fleur.

'It all sounds very exciting,' she responded, forcing a smile as she looked up and saw the expectant look on her sister's face.

'When will you be leaving?'

'Tomorrow! Everything's already arranged. Khalid just wanted to come to Zuran to tell Xavier about our marriage, and to collect Fleur, of course…'

'Of course,' Mariella agreed hollowly.

'Ella, I can't thank you enough for looking after Fleur for me. We're both really grateful to you, aren't we, Khalid?'

'Yes, we are,' her new brother-in-law agreed.

Mariella was still holding Fleur, not wanting to physically part with her until she absolutely had to, whilst Tanya said her goodbyes to Madame Flavel and Xavier.

Tanya was still behaving very coolly towards Xavier, only speaking to him when she had to do so.

'Darling, can you take Fleur out to the car?' she instructed Khalid.

Mariella could feel herself stiffening as Khalid went to take the baby from her, and, whether because of that or because as yet Fleur was not used to her father, as he reached for her the little baby suddenly screwed up her face and started to cry.

Immediately Khalid pulled back from her looking flustered and irritable.

'Here, let me take her!'

Xavier quietly removed Fleur from Mariella's arms, before she could object. He smiled down at Fleur and soothed her, whilst she gazed back at him wide-eyed, her tears immediately ceasing.

Out of the corner of her eye Mariella saw that Tanya had started to glower at Xavier, obviously resenting the fact that Fleur was more comfortable with him than with her father, but before she could say anything Khalid was urging her to hurry.

They went out to the car together, Xavier still holding Fleur, Mariella wincing in the blast of hot air.

As soon as she got into the car, Tanya held out her arms to him for Fleur, but to Mariella's surprise, instead of handing Fleur to Tanya, Xavier gave her to Mariella.

Mariella could feel her eyes burning with emotional tears, her throat closing up as her feelings threatened to overwhelm her. It was almost as though Xavier could sense how she felt and wanted to give her one last precious chance to hold Fleur before she had to part with her.

Bending her head, she kissed her niece and then quickly handed her over to her sister.

When the car taking them to the airport finally pulled away, Mariella could only see it through a blur.

'Let's get out of this wind,' she heard Xavier telling her when the car had finally disappeared from sight.

If he was aware of her tears he was discreet enough not to show it, simply ushering her back to the villa without making any other comment.

However, once they were inside, Mariella took a deep breath and made her voice sound as businesslike as she could as she told him, 'I'll make arrangements to leave just as soon as I can arrange somewhere else to stay.'

'What on earth are you talking about?' Xavier demanded sharply. 'Nothing has changed. You are still a single young woman who is a member of my family, and as such your place is still here beneath my roof and my protection! This should be your home whilst you're in Zuran,' Xavier told her.

Mariella opened her mouth to argue with him and then closed it again. It was just because she was feeling so upset about losing Fleur that his statement was giving her this odd sense of heady relief, she told herself defensively. It had nothing to do with…any other reason. Nothing at all!

Mariella was dreaming. She was dreaming that she was all alone in an unfamiliar room, lying on a large bed and crying for Fleur, and then suddenly the door opened and Xavier came in. Walking over to the bed, he sat down beside her and reached out for her hand.

'You are crying for the child,' he told her softly. 'But you must not. I shall give you a child of your own to love. Our child!' As she looked at him he started to touch her, smoothing the covers from her naked body with hands that seemed to know just how to please her. Bending his head, he started to kiss her, a slow, magically tender kiss, which quickly began to burn with the heat of a fierce passion. She could feel her whole body trembling with need and longing! And not just for the child he had promised her, but for Xavier himself!

His hands cupped her breasts, his grey eyes liquid with arousal as he gazed at them, shockingly sensual words of praise falling from his lips as he whispered to her how much he wanted her. He kissed each rosy crest, savouring their shape and sensitivity with his lips and tongue until she was clinging to him, digging her nails into his back as she submitted to her own desire.

Possessively she measured the strong length of his arms with her fingertips, expelling her breath on a shuddering sigh as his tongue rimmed her belly and his hand covered her sex, waiting, aching, wanting. Beneath her hand she could feel him harden as she touched him, torn between wanting to explore him and wanting to feel him deep inside her as he ignited the spark of life that would be their child. But as she reached for him, suddenly he pulled away, abandoning her. Desperately she cried out to him not to leave her, her body chilled and shaking, tears clogging her throat and spilling from her eyes. Abruptly Mariella woke up.

Somehow in her sleep she had pushed away the bed-clothes, which was why she was now shivering in the coolness of the air-conditioning. The tears drying stickily on her face and tightening her skin were surely caused by the fact that she was missing Fleur and not because she had been dreaming about Xavier…about loving him and losing him! She would never allow herself to be that much of a fool! But physically she was affected by him, she could not deny that! Fiercely she tried to tense her body against its own betraying ache of longing. Xavier was a man who, even she had to acknowledge, took his responsibilities and his commitments very seriously. A man whose passions…

Stop it, she warned herself frantically. What was she doing thinking like this? Feeling like this?

Wide awake now, she got out of bed, and was half-way toward Fleur's now empty cot before she realised what she was doing. It was only right that Fleur should be with her parents, but she ached so to be holding her small body. She ached so for a child of her own, she admitted.

Tiredly Mariella flexed the tense, aching muscles in her neck and shoulders as she sat beside the small pool in the women's courtyard. She had worked relentlessly on the frieze over the last two weeks, driven by a compulsion she hadn't been able to ignore, and now knew that she would be able to finish the project well ahead of time.

The prince had arrived to inspect her progress just before she had left and she had seen immediately from his expression just how impressed he was by what she was doing.

'It is magnificent...awe-inspiring,' he had told her enthusiastically. 'A truly heart-gripping vision.'

'I'm glad you like it,' Mariella had responded prosaically, but inwardly she had been elated.

Elated and too exhausted to eat her dinner, she reminded herself ruefully as she reached up to try and massage some relief into her aching neck, tensing as she saw Xavier walking towards her.

'I have just come from seeing His Highness,' he told her. 'He wanted to show me your work. He is most impressed, and rightly so. It is magnificent!'

His uncharacteristic praise stunned Mariella, who stared at him, her turquoise eyes shadowed and wary.

'Has your sister been in touch with you yet to reassure you that Fleur is well?' Xavier continued.

Not trusting herself to speak, Mariella shook her head and then winced as her tense, locked muscles resisted the movement.

Quick to notice her small betraying wince, Xavier

demanded immediately, 'You're in pain. What is it? What's wrong?'

'My muscles are stiff, that's all,' Mariella replied.

'Stiff. Where? Let me see?'

Before she could object he was sitting down next to her, his fingers moving searchingly over her shoulders, expertly finding her locked muscles.

'Keep still,' he said when she instinctively tried to pull away. 'I am not surprised you are in so much pain. You work too hard! Drive yourself too hard. Worry too much about others and allow them to abuse your sense of responsibility towards them!'

Swiftly Mariella turned her head to look at him.

'You are a fine one to accuse me of that!' she couldn't help pointing out.

For a moment they looked at one another in mutual silence. She was learning so much about this man, discovering so many things about him that changed her whole perception of what and who he was.

He couldn't have been more wrong about Mariella, or misjudged her more unfairly, Xavier acknowledged as he looked down into her eyes. Her sister, in contrast, was exactly what he had expected her to be, and typical of his cousin's taste in women. The more cynical side of his nature felt that, not only were they suited to one another, but that they also deserved one another in their mutual selfishness and lack of any true emotional depth.

Mariella, on the other hand… He had never met a woman who took her responsibilities more seriously, or who was more fiercely protective of those she loved. When she committed herself to a man she would commit herself to him heart and soul. When she loved a man, she would love him with depth and passion and her love would be for ever…

'Your sister should have been in touch with you. She must know how much you are missing Fleur,' he told Mariella abruptly.

Mariella tensed, immediately flying to Tanya's defence as she told him fiercely, 'She is Fleur's mother. She doesn't have to consult me about…anything. This holiday will give the three of them an opportunity to bond together as a family. Tanya and Khalid are Fleur's parents and…'

'I miss Fleur too,' Xavier stopped her gruffly, his admission astonishing her. 'And in my opinion she would be much better off here in a secure environment with those who know her best, rather than being dragged to some fashionable resort where she will probably be left in the care of hotel staff whilst her parents spend their time enjoying themselves!'

'You are being unfair,' Mariella protested, and then winced as Xavier started to knead the knots out of her muscles, making it impossible for her to move.

'No. I am being honest,' he corrected her. 'And when Khalid returns you may be sure that I shall be making it very plain to him that Fleur needs a secure family environment!'

Xavier would make a wonderful father, Mariella conceded, and then stiffened as she tried to reject the messages that knowledge was giving her! After all, like her, Xavier had no intentions of ever getting married!

'Your muscles are very badly knotted,' she heard him telling her brusquely as his thumbs started to probe their way over the tight lumps of pain.

It was heaven having the tension massaged from her body, Mariella acknowledged, and no doubt what he was doing would be even more effective if she wasn't trying to tense herself against those dangerous sensations that had nothing whatsoever to do with any kind of work-induced muscle ache, and everything to do with Xavier himself.

The longer he touched her, the harder she was finding it to control her sexual reaction to him.

His thumbs stroked along her spine, causing her to shudder openly in response. Immediately his hands stilled.

'Mariella.'

His voice sounded rough and raw, the sensation of his breath against her skin bringing her out in a rash of sensual goose-bumps. Was she only imagining that she could hear a note of hungry male desire in his voice?

She couldn't trust herself to speak to him, just as she didn't dare to turn round, but suddenly he was turning her, holding her, finding her mouth with his own and kissing her with a silent ferocity that made her tremble from head to toe as her body dissolved in a wash of liquid pleasure that ran through her veins, melting any resistance.

The hands that had so clinically massaged her shoulders were now caressing her flesh beneath her loose top in a way that was anything but clinical! A savage, relentless ache began to torment her body. The warm, perfumed night air of the garden was suddenly replaced by the aroused male scent of Xavier's body and Mariella reacted to it blindly, wrenching her mouth from beneath his and burying her face in the open throat of his robe so that she could breathe it—him— in more deeply, her lips questing for the satin warmth of his skin, her moan of pleasure locked in her throat as she gave her senses their head.

Beneath her lips his flesh felt firm and hot, the muscles of his throat taut, the curve where it met his shoulder tempting her to bite delicately into it. She heard him groan as his hand covered her breast, her nipple swelling eagerly against his palm. She felt the warmth of the night air against her skin as he pushed her simple cotton robe out of the way, her whole body shuddering in agonised pleasure as he cupped her breast and lowered his mouth to her waiting nipple.

The pleasure that surged through her tightened her body into a helpless yearning arc of longing, exposing her slender feminine flesh to his gaze and touch, offering her up to them, Mariella recognised distantly as she shook with hunger for him. Wanting him like this seemed so natural, and right, so inevitable, as though it were something that had been destined to happen.

Lifting her hand, she touched his face, their gazes meeting and locking, silently absorbing one another's need. The look in his eyes made her body leap in eager heat, the sensation of the slightly rough rasp of his jaw against her palm as he turned his face to kiss it filling her with a thousand erotic images of how it was going to feel, to have him caressing even more sensitive and intimate parts of her body. She was, she realised, trembling violently, as Xavier stroked his hands down her back and lifted her against his body so that she could feel its hard arousal. She ached so badly for the feel of him inside her, for the fulfilment of his possession of her, the completion. His mouth was on her breast, her nipple, caressing it in a way that made her cry out for the hot, deep suckle of a more savage pleasure.

In the moonlight Xavier could see the swollen softness of her mouth and her breast, his breath catching in his lungs as his gaze travelled lower, to where the delicate mound of her sex seemed to push temptingly against the fine cotton of her briefs.

The thought of sliding his hand beneath them and holding her, parting the delicately shaped lips and opening up her moist inner self to his touch, his kiss, sent a shudder of hot need clawing through him. In the privacy of this garden he could show her, share with her, give her the pleasure he could see and feel her body was aching for. But here in his garden, in his villa, where she was under his protection, a member of his family…a woman as off limits as any of the carefully guarded daughters of his friends.

His hand was already splaying across her sex, his thumb probing tantalizingly.

Hot shafts of molten quivers darted from the point where Xavier's hand rested so intimately on her to every sensitive nerve ending in her body. Within herself Mariella could feel her own femaleness expanding rhythmically in longing. More than anything else she wanted him there inside her. More than anything else she wanted him…

Her raw sound of shocked protest broke the silence as Xavier suddenly released her.

'I already owe you one apology for my…my inappropriate behaviour towards you,' she heard him telling her curtly. 'Now it seems that I am guilty of repeating that behaviour. It will not…must not happen again!'

As he stood up and turned away from her, Mariella wondered if he was trying to reassure her—or warn her! Her face and then her whole body burned hot with mortified misery.

Her throat was too choked with emotion for her to

be able to say anything, but in any case Xavier was already leaving, walking across the garden to the small, almost hidden doorway that led through into his own quarters, and to which only he had the key.

Was she too destined to be a secret garden to which only he held the key?

Fiercely she resisted the dangerous and unwanted thought. It was simply sex that had driven her…a physical need…a perfectly normal response to her own sexuality. There was nothing emotional about what she had felt. Nothing.

Pacing the floor of his own room, Xavier came to an abrupt decision. Since he couldn't trust himself to be in the same place as Mariella and not want her, then he needed to put a safe distance between them, and the best way for him to do that would be for him to return to his desert oasis.

CHAPTER TEN

'IT IS almost a week since he left and still Xavier remains at the oasis.'

Mariella forced herself to concentrate on her work instead of reacting to Madame Flavel's comments.

The prince had come to see how she was progressing earlier in the week and he had brought his wife and their young family with him. The sight of the four dark-haired and dark-eyed children clustering round their parents had filled her with such a physical ache of longing that she had felt as though her womb had actually physically contracted.

She was desperate to have her own child, Mariella recognised. And not just because she was missing Fleur. Fleur's birth might have detonated her biological clock, setting it ticking away with such frantic urgency, but the longing she felt now was beginning to consume her, eating into her dreams and her emotions.

Now she felt she understood why she had wanted Xavier so much. Her body had recognised him as a perfect potential baby provider! Knowing that had in a way eased a lot of the anxiety she had been feeling; the fear she couldn't bear to admit that she might actually have fallen in love with him. Now, though, she felt secure that her emotional defences had not been breached. Now it was easy for her to admit to herself just how much she had wanted him and how much she still wanted him. She wanted him because she wanted him to give her a child!

It made so much sense! Didn't she remember reading somewhere that a woman naturally and instinctively responded to the ancient way in which nature had programmed her and that was to seek the best genes she could for her child? Quite obviously her body had recognised that Xavier's genes were superlative and her brain fully endorsed her body's recognition.

And this of course was why she was being bombarded by her body and her brain with messages, longings, desires, images that all pointed in the same direction. Xavier's direction! Her maternal urges were quite definitely on red alert!

'Xavier has telephoned to say that he will be remaining at the oasis for another week,' Xavier's great-aunt informed Mariella with a small sigh as they sat down for dinner. 'It must be dull here for you, *chérie* with only your work to occupy you and me for company.'

'Not at all,' Mariella denied.

'*Non?* But you do miss *la petite bébé?*'

Now it was Mariella's turn to sigh.

'Yes, I do,' she admitted.

'Then perhaps you should consider having *enfants* of your own,' Madame Flavel told her. 'I certainly regret the fact that I was not blessed with children. I envied my sister very much in that respect. I have to confess I cannot understand why two people like Xavier and yourself, who anyone can see are born to be parents, should decide so determinedly against marriage.

'You are working very hard on your frieze. It would do you good to have a few days off.'

She *had* been working very hard—but if truth were

told, the frieze was practically finished. But Mariella had been painstakingly refining it to make sure it was absolutely perfect. Could she take a few days off? To do what? Have even more time to miss Fleur and to ache for a child of her own? Even more time to wish passionately that Xavier had not brought an end to their intimacy before they had… If only she had pressed him a little harder, persuaded…seduced him to the point where he had not been able to stop, she considered daringly, then right now she could already be carrying within her the beginnings of her own child!

Restlessly her thoughts started to circle inside her head. Once they had finished eating Madame Flavel retired to her own room, leaving Mariella to walk through their private garden on her own. If only Xavier were here in the villa now, she could go to him. And what? Demand that he take her to bed and impregnate her?

Oh, yes, she could just see him agreeing to that!

Why would she have to demand? She was a woman, wasn't she? And Xavier was a man… He had already shown her that he could be aroused to desire for her…

But he wasn't here, was he? He was at the oasis.

The oasis… Closing her eyes, Mariella allowed herself to picture him there. That night when he had thought that she was Tanya, he had come so close to possessing her. Her whole body was aching for him now, aching with all the ferocity of a child-hungry woman whose womb was empty!

Irritably, Mariella threw down her sketch-pad, chewing on her bottom lip as she glowered at the images she had drawn: babies…all of them possessing Xavier's unmistakable features. She had hardly slept all night, and when she had it had merely been to be tormented by such sensually erotic dreams of Xavier that they had made her cry out in longing for him. It was as though even her dreams, her own subconscious, were reinforcing her desire for Xavier's child.

In fact the only thing about her that was still trying to fight against that wanting was…was what? Fear… Timidity… Did she really want to look back in years to come and face the fact that she had simply not had the courage to reach out for what she wanted?

After all, it wasn't as though she would be doing anything illegal! She had no intention of ever making any kind of claim on Xavier—far from it! She actively wanted to be left to bring up her child completely on her own. All she wanted from him was a simple physical act. All she had to do…   .

All she had to do was to make it impossible for him to resist her! And whilst he was at the oasis he would be completely at her sensual mercy! It was even the right time of the month—she was fertile.

A wildly bold plan was beginning to take shape inside her head, and the first step towards it meant an immediate shopping trip, for certain…necessities! There was a specific shop she remembered from a previous trip to the busy souk in the centre of the city, which specialised in what she wanted!

Slightly pink-cheeked, Mariella studied the fine silk kaftan she was being shown by the salesgirl, so fine that it was completely sheer. Surely the only thing that stopped it from floating away was the weight of the intricate and delicate silver beading and embroidery around the neck and hem and decorating the edges of the long sleeves.

It was a soft shade of turquoise, and designed to be worn—the salesgirl had helpfully explained without so much as batting an elegantly kohled eyelid—over a matching pair of harem trousers. Their cuffs and waistband had been embroidered to match the kaftan itself. It was quite plainly an outfit designed only to be worn in private and for the delectation of one man. The sheerness of the fabric would leave one's breasts totally revealed—and Mariella had not missed the strategically embroidered rosettes, which she doubted would do anything more than merely make a teasing pretence of covering the wearer's nipples—and as for the fact that the harem pants incorporated an embroidered and beaded v-shaped section at the front, which she had an unnerving suspicion would draw attention to rather than protect, any wearer's sex…

'And then, of course, there is this,' the salesgirl told her, showing Mariella a jewelled piece of fabric, which she helpfully explained was self-adhesive so that the wearer could easily fix it to her navel.

Mariella gulped. Her normal sleeping attire when she wore any tended to be sturdily sensible cotton pyjamas.

'Er… No…I don't think…it's quite me,' she heard herself croaking, her courage deserting her. Seducing Xavier was going to be hard enough without giving herself the kind of self-conscious hang-up wearing that kind of outfit would undoubtedly give her!

'I…I was thinking of something more…more European,' she explained ruefully to the salesgirl.

'Ah, yes, of course. There is a shop in the shopping centre run by my cousin which specialises in French underwear. I shall tell you how to find it.'

Mariella sensed that the girl was amused by her self-consciousness, but there was no way she intended to pay a sheikh's ransom for an outfit that would take more courage to wear than going completely naked!

The souk was busy, and she paused on her way back through it to admire the wares on some of the other stalls, especially the rugs.

There was far more to seduction than merely wearing a harem outfit, she tried to comfort herself as she headed for the modern shopping centre. Far, far more. Sight was just one of man's senses, after all.

By the time she finally returned to the villa Mariella felt totally exhausted. She was now the proud owner of a perfume blended especially for her, and a body lotion guaranteed to turn her skin into the softest silk; she had also given in to the temptation to buy herself some new underwear, from the harem outfit seller's cousin, in the shopping mall. French and delicately feminine without making her feel in any way uncomfortable. Low-cut French knickers might not be as openly provocative as beaded harem trousers but they did have the advantage of being perfect to wear underneath her jeans!

It didn't take her very long to pack. All she said to Hera when she summoned her was that she wanted her to hand the note she was giving her to Madame Flavel when she woke up from her afternoon nap.

By that time she should have safely reached the oasis, and her note was simply to calm the older lady's fears and told her only that Mariella had driven out to the oasis because there was something she wanted to discuss with Xavier.

She took a taxi to the four-wheel drive rental office, where the car she had organised earlier by telephone was waiting for her.

This time she made sure she had the radio tuned in to the local weather station, but thankfully no sand-storms were forecast.

Taking a deep breath, she started the car's engine.

With a small oath, Xavier pushed the laptop away and stood up. He had come to the oasis to put a safe dis-tance between himself and Mariella but all his absence from her was doing was making him think about her all the more.

Think about her! He wasn't just thinking about her, was he?

The tribe were currently camped less than thirty miles away and on a sudden impulse he decided to drive over and see them. The solitude of his own com-pany was not proving to be its usual solace. Everywhere he looked around the oasis he could see Mariella. There might be a cultural gap between them, but, like him, she had a very strong sense of respon-sibility, and like him she would not give either her heart or herself easily. Like him, too, once she was committed, that commitment would be for ever. And did she also ache for what they had so nearly had and lie away at night wanting…needing, afraid to admit that those feelings went way, way beyond the merely physical? And if she did, then… Could she love him enough to accept his duty to the tribe, and with it his commitment to his role in life…to accept it and to share it? Dared he lay before her the intensity of his feelings for her? His love? Could he live with himself if his secret fears proved to be correct and his love for her overwhelmed his sense of duty?

Switching off the laptop, he reached for his Jeep keys.

*   *   *

She couldn't ever remember a time when she had felt more nervous, Mariella acknowledged as she urged the four-wheel drive along the familiar boulder-strewn track. Up ahead of her she could see the pavilion and her heart lurched, slamming into her ribs. What if Xavier simply refused to be seduced and rejected her? What if...?

For a moment she was tempted to turn the four-wheel drive round and scuttle back to the city. Quickly she reminded herself of sexual tension stretching between them in the garden of the villa. He had wanted her then, and had admitted as much to her!

She had half expected to see him emerging from the pavilion as he heard her drive up, but there was no sign of him.

Well, at least he wouldn't be able to demand that she turn round and drive straight back, she comforted herself as she parked her vehicle and climbed out, going to the back to remove her things, and then standing nervously staring at the pavilion.

Perhaps if she had timed things so that she had arrived in the dark... Some seductress she was turning out to be, she derided herself as she took a deep breath and walked determinedly towards the chosen fate.

Five minutes later she was standing facing the oasis, unwilling to accept what was patently obvious. Xavier was not here! No Xavier, no four-wheel drive, no seduction, no baby!

A crushing sense of disappointment engulfed her. Where was he? Could he have changed his mind and returned to the city despite informing his great-aunt that he intended to stay on at the oasis? How ironic it would be if by rushing out here so impulsively she had actually denied herself the opportunity of achieving what she wanted!

But then she remembered that his laptop was still inside the pavilion, and surely he would not have left that behind if he had been returning home? So where was he?

The sun was already a dying red ball lying on the horizon. Soon it would be dark. There was no way she was going to risk driving all the way back without the benefit of daylight!

So what exactly was she going to do? Spend yet another evening enduring her rebellious body's clamouring urgency for the fulfilment of its driving need? It had simply never occurred to her that he wouldn't be here!

The pavilion was so intimately a part of him. Dreamily, she trailed her fingertips along the chair he used when working at the laptop. The air actually seemed to hold an echo of his scent, a haunting resonance of his voice, and she felt that, if she closed her eyes and concentrated hard enough, she could almost imagine that he was there... She could certainly picture him behind her tightly closed eyelids. But it wasn't his mental image she wanted so desperately, was it?

She knew she ought to eat, but she simply wasn't hungry. She was thirsty, though.

She went into the kitchen and opened a bottle of water. Fine grains of sand clung to her skin, making it feel gritty. Hardly appropriate for a would-be siren! The long drive in the brilliant glare of the desert sun had left her eyes feeling tired and heavy. Like her body, which felt tired and heavy and empty. A sense of dejection and failure percolated through her.

Slowly, she walked out of the kitchen intending to

return to the living area, but instead found herself being drawn to the 'bedroom.' Standing in the entrance, she looked achingly around it.

A fierce shudder that became an even fiercer primal ache gripped her as she looked at the bed and remembered what had happened there. It was just her biology that was making her feel like this, her fiercely strong maternal desire. That was all, and of course it was only natural that that urge should manifest itself in this hungry desire for the man whose genes it had decided it wanted, she reassured herself as she was confronted with the intensity of her longing for Xavier.

Just thinking about him made her go weak, made her want him there so that she could bury her lips in the warm male flesh of his throat and slide her hands over the hard, strong muscles of his arms and his back, and then down through the soft dark hair that covered his chest and arrowed over his belly to where...

She needed a shower, Mariella decided shakily. A very cool shower!

'Safe travelling, Ashar.' Xavier smiled ruefully as he embraced the senior tribesman whilst the others went about the business of breaking camp ready to begin the long slow journey across the desert.

'You could always come with us,' Ashar responded.

'Not this time.' Xavier shook his head.

All around him he could hear the familiar sounds of the camp, the faint music of the camel bells, the orderly preparations for departure. The tribe would travel through the night hours whilst it was cool, resting the herd during the heat of the day.

Ashar's shrewd brown eyes surveyed him.

Ashar remembered Xavier's grandfather as well as

his father. Alongside his respect for Xavier as his
leader ran a very deep vein of paternal affection for
him.

'Something troubles you—a woman, perhaps? The
tribe would rejoice to see you take a wife to give you
sons to follow in your footsteps as you have followed
in those of your grandfather and your father.'

'If only matters were that simple, Ashar.' Xavier gri-
maced.

'Why should they not be? This woman, you are
afraid perhaps that she will not respect our traditions,
that she will seek to divide your loyalties? If that is so
then she is not the one for you. But knowing you as I
do, Xavier, I cannot believe that there could be a place
in your heart for a woman such as that. You must learn
to trust what is in here,' he told him, touching his own
heart with his hand. 'Instead of believing only what is
in here.' As he touched his hand to his head Xavier hid
a wry smile. Ashar had no idea just how dangerously
out of control his emotions were becoming!

He waited to see the tribe safely on their way before
climbing in his vehicle to drive back to the oasis.

A sharply crescented sickle moon shared the night
sky with the brilliance of the stars. Diamonds studded
onto indigo velvet. For Xavier it was during the night
hours that the desert was at its most awesome, and
mystical, a time when he always felt most in touch with
his heritage. His ancestors had travelled these sands for
many, many generations before him, and it was his
duty, his responsibility to ensure that they did so for
many, many generations to come. And that was not
something he could achieve from behind the walls of
a high-rise air-conditioned office, and certainly not
from the fleshpots of the world as Khalid would no

doubt choose to do. No, he could only maintain and honour the tribe's traditional way of life by being a part of it, by sharing in it, and that was something he was totally committed to doing. He must not deviate from that purpose. But his feelings, his love for Mariella could not be denied, or ignored. The strength of them had initially shocked him, but he had now gone from shock to the grim recognition that it was beyond his power to change or control the way he felt.

He saw Mariella's vehicle as he drove up to the oasis. Parking next to it, he got out and studied it warily. He did not encourage anyone to visit him when he was at the oasis and he was certainly not in the mood for uninvited guests, right now! Where and who was its driver?

Frowning, he headed for the pavilion, not needing to waste any time lighting the lamps to illuminate the darkness, his familiarity with it enough to take him from the entrance to the opening to the bedroom without breaking his stride.

Mariella was lying fast asleep in the middle of the bed, where she had curled up in exhaustion like a small child. The white robe she was wearing was Xavier's and it drowned her slender body. She had lit one of the lamps, which illuminated her face, showing her bone structure and the thick darkness of her silky eyelashes. In the enclosed heat, Xavier could smell the scent of her, and of his own instant reciprocal desire for her.

Xavier's hand tightened convulsively on the cord that fastened the curtain to the bedroom's entrance, whilst his heart tolled in slow, heavy beats. If he had any sense he would pick her up and carry her straight

out to the Jeep and then drive back to the city with her
without stopping!

He let the heavy curtain drop behind him, enclosing
them both in the sensual semi-darkness.

Standing next to the bed, he looked down at
Mariella.

Something, some instinct and awareness, disturbed
Mariella's sleep, making her frown and stir, her eyes
opening.

'Xavier!'

Relief…and longing flooded through her. Automatically
she struggled to sit up, her arms and legs becoming tangled
in the thick folds of Xavier's robe as she did so.

'What are you doing here?' Xavier demanded
harshly.

'Waiting for you,' Mariella told him. 'Waiting to tell
you how much I want you, and how much I hope you
want me.'

She watched as his eyes turned from steel to mercury
and recognised that she had caught him off guard.

'You drove all the way out here to tell me that!'

His voice might be curt and unresponsive, but
Mariella could see the way his jaw tightened as he
turned his head away from her, as well as feel his betraying tension. Tiny body-language signs, that was all
she knew, but instinctively she knew she had an advantage to pursue!

'Not to tell you, Xavier,' she corrected him boldly.
'To show you…like this…'

Standing up, she went to him, letting the robe slide
from her body as she did so. She had never envisaged
that she would ever feel such a pride in her nakedness,

her femaleness, such a sense of power and certainty, an awareness of how much a man's still silence could betray how very, very tightly leashed he was keeping his desire.

She was standing in front of him and he hadn't moved. For a moment she almost lost her courage but then she saw it, the way he clenched his hand and tried to conceal his involuntary reaction.

Quickly she raised herself up on her tiptoes and cupped his face with her hands. Never in a thousand lifetimes could she have behaved like this simply for her own gratification, for the indulgence of her own sexual or emotional feelings, but she was not doing it for them, for herself, she was doing it for the child she so desperately wanted to give life! Silently she looked up into his eyes, her own openly reflecting her desire. Very deliberately she let her gaze drop to his mouth. There was no need for her to manufacture the sharp little quiver of physical reaction that pierced her, tightening her belly.

She brushed her lips against his—slowly, savouring the delicate sensual contact between them, refusing to be put off by his lack of response, drawing from her inner self to focus totally on the pleasure it was giving her to explore the shape and texture of his mouth. Very quickly her senses took over, so that it was desire that led her to stroking his bottom lip with her tongue tip rather than calculation, the same desire that drove her to trace tiny kisses along the shape of his mouth and then draw her tongue lightly along that shape.

Xavier couldn't endure what she was doing to him! Mentally he willed her to stop, but instead she opened her mouth over his and started to kiss him properly! Lost in what she was doing, what she was enjoying,

Mariella took her time, putting her whole self into showing him just how hungry for him she was.

And then sickeningly, she could feel the rejecting hostility of his body, and for a heart-rocking second when he raised his hands she thought he was going to push her away. She suspected that he had thought so too, because suddenly in his eyes she saw both his shock and his raw, burning hunger.

He could never be a man who would be a passive lover, Mariella recognised on a deep shudder of pleasure as his hands imprisoned her and his mouth fought hers for control.

How little he realised that her surrender was really her victory, she rejoiced as his tongue thrust urgently between the lips she had parted for him.

'I can't believe that you've done this,' she heard him saying thickly.

'I had to,' Mariella whispered back. After all, it was the truth. 'I had to be with you, Xavier…like this…as a woman.'

He had released her to look at her, and now he lifted his hand to her face. Instantly Mariella caught hold of his wrist and turned her head to run her tongue tip over his fingertips.

She saw the way his skin stretched over his cheekbones, running hot with colour, his chest lifting and falling as savagely as though he had been deprived of oxygen. His forefinger rubbed over her bottom lip, and when she sucked on it his whole body jerked fiercely.

'I want to see you, Xavier,' she told him softly. 'I want to touch you…taste you…I want. I want you to take me to bed and pleasure me, fill me.'

Taking his hand, she placed it against her naked breast.

'Please,' she whispered. 'Please now, Xavier. Please…'

'This is crazy. You know that, don't you?' she heard him mutter. 'You are not your sister, you do not… I have not… I am not prepared…' His voice had become thick and raw as he bent his head to kiss the exposed curve of her shoulder, her throat, his hands sliding down her back to pull her urgently against him.

'There is nothing for you to worry about,' she told him.

She felt light-headed with the intensity of her own longing—but she only felt like that because she wanted his child, she was quick to reassure herself. That, after all, was what was driving her, motivating her, even if that motivation was manifesting itself in an increasingly urgent need to touch him and be touched by him, to allow herself to luxuriate in the slow and delicious exploration of every bit of his skin, absorbing its heat, its feel, the essence of him through the sensitivity of her own pores. So that her child, their child could be impregnated through her with those memories of his father he would never otherwise be able to have?

Ruthlessly she stifled that thought. Her child would not need a father to be there. He or she only needed a father to provide that life.

What he was doing was reckless to the point of insanity, Xavier knew that, but he also knew that he couldn't resist her, that he had ached for her, yearned for her too long to deny himself the soft, sweet, wanton feel of her in his arms…his bed…

But once he had held her, loved her, he also knew that he would never be able to let her go. Could she accept his way of life…adapt to it? Would she?

She was kissing him with increasing passion, stringing tiny, delicately tormenting little kisses around his throat, her tongue tip carefully exploring the shape of his Adam's apple, her fingers kneading the flesh of his upper arm with unconscious sensuality. Xavier recognised his senses on overload from her deliberately erotic seduction.

Mariella gave a small startled gasp as Xavier suddenly lifted her bodily in his arms, so that her mouth was on a level with his own as he took it in a hotly demanding and intimate kiss.

Helplessly she succumbed to it, feeling the desire he was arousing inside her run through her veins as sweetly as melting honey. He lifted her higher, kissing her throat, his lips moving lower to the valley between her breasts, before trailing with heart-hammering slowness and delicacy to first one eagerly waiting, quivering crest and then the other, and then back again, this time to lap tormentingly at her nipple with his damp tongue tip; the leisurely languorous journey repeated again and again until her whole body was crying out in agonised frustration.

Unable to stand the sensual torment any more, when his lips teased delicately at her nipple she buried her hands in the thick darkness of his hair and held his mouth against her body.

Surely he must feel the fierce rhythms pulsing through her flesh; surely he must know how much she wanted him?

Her hands tugged at his clothes, her voice whispering a soft torrent of aroused female longing that swamped Xavier's defences.

His hands helped hers to quickly remove the layers of clothing that separated them.

When she finally saw the naked gleam of his flesh

in the lamp-lit room, Mariella sucked in her breath on a small sob of shocked pleasure.

In wonder she studied him as tiny but openly visible quivers betrayed her body's excited reaction to him. So compulsively absorbed in gazing at him, she was oblivious to the effect her sensual concentration was having on Xavier himself.

'If you are deliberately trying to torment me and test my self-control by looking at me like that, then I warn you that both it and I have just about reached my limit,' he told her thickly.

'Now! Are you going to come to me and put into action all those dangerously seductive promises your eyes are giving me, or do I have to come to you and make you make good those promises, because, I warn you, if I do have to then I shall be demanding payment with full interest penalties,' he added huskily.

For a moment Mariella couldn't do anything. Xavier was watching her as she had been watching him. Excitement exploded inside her. She took a step towards him and then another, measuring his reaction as best she could, but it wasn't easy given the extent of her own intense arousal.

She was only a breath away from him now, close enough to reach out her finger and draw the tip of it recklessly down his body, teasing the silky body hair.

'You don't know how much I've wanted to do this,' she breathed truthfully.

'No? Well, I certainly know how much I've wanted you to do it,' Xavier responded throatily, 'and how much I've wanted to…'

He gasped and shuddered as her fingertip stroked lower, and suddenly in the space of one single heartbeat she was lying on the bed, with Xavier arching over her.

'Play with fire like that and you'll make us both burn,' he told her, his eyes darkening as he groaned. 'Do you know what seeing that look in your eyes does to me? Do you know how much I've wanted to see just what colour they turn when I touch you like this?'

Mariella hadn't realised just how ready she was for his intimate caress until she felt his hand stroke softly over her quivering belly, his fingers gently touching the swollen mound of her sex, his gaze pinioning hers as he parted the lips of her sex and began to caress her.

Mariella knew that she cried out, she knew too that her body arched to his touch actively seeking it, eagerly opening to it, but it was only a vague, distant knowledge, at the back of her awareness. Her self was concentrated on the mind-exploding battle to accept the intensity of her own feelings.

Frantically she reached for Xavier. Touching him, holding him, wrapping herself around him as she pressed passionate kisses against his skin, willing, aching for him to complete what he had begun.

And when he did enter her, moving into her, filling her moist sheathed muscles, filling her with such a soaring degree of pleasure that they and she clung to him, wanting to wring every infinitesimal sensation of pleasure from him, it was like nothing she had ever imagined feeling, a pleasure beyond any known pleasure, a sensation beyond any experienced sensation, a driven need that shocked her in its wanton compulsion as she urged him to drive deeper, harder, breaching every last barrier of her body until she knew instinctively that he could not and would not withdraw from her without giving her body the satisfaction it now craved.

They moved together, his thrusts carrying them both, delivering a pleasure so intense she could scarcely bear it, crying out against it at the same time as she abandoned herself to it.

She heard his guttural cry of warning and felt her body open up completely to him, the first tiny shudders of her orgasm sensitising her to the pulse of his, to the knowledge that she was receiving from him what she had so much wanted.

Was it that knowledge that made her orgasm so intense, so fierce that she felt almost as though she could not endure so much pleasure?

Long after it should have been over, the aftermath continued to send little shudders of sensation through her, shaking her whole body as she lay locked in Xavier's arms.

She had done it, instinctively she knew it. Her child, of the desert and of a man who was equally compelling, equally dangerous, had been given life.

Reluctantly, Mariella opened her eyes. She could hear a shower running, and her whole body ached with an unfamiliar heaviness.

'So you are awake!'

She stiffened as she saw Xavier coming towards her, his hair damp from his shower, a towel wrapped carelessly round his hips.

Leaning towards her, he bent his head to kiss her. He smelled of soap and clean, fresh skin and her body quivered helplessly in reaction to him.

'Mmm…'

He kissed her again, more lingeringly, his hand stroking down over her bare arm.

The quivers became open shudders of erotic pleasure as he pulled the bedclothes back.

She had got what she wanted, and so surely she shouldn't be feeling like this now that there wasn't any need for her to want him!

The towel was sliding from his hips, quite plainly revealing the fact that he most definitely wanted her.

A sharp and unmistakable thrill of female excitement gripped her muscles.

It was just nature's way of making doubly sure, Mariella told herself hazily as his hand cupped her breast, his thumb and forefinger teasing the already eagerly taut crest of her nipple. That was all, and, since nature wanted to be doubly sure, then obviously she must give in to her urgings. Urgings that were demanding that she experience the pleasure Xavier had given her the night before, and right now...

His hands were on her hips, holding her, lifting her. Already Mariella was anticipating the feel of him inside her, longing for it and for him. Needing him.

'There will be things we shall need to discuss once we return to the city.'

'Mmm...' Mariella agreed, too satiated to lift her head off the pillow as Xavier turned to brush a kiss across her mouth.

She looked so tempting lying there in his bed, her face soft with satisfaction and her eyes heavy with their lovemaking, he acknowledged, ruefully aware of the way in which his senses were still reacting to her.

It would be all too easy to let the desire between

them flare into life again, but there were practicalities that had to be considered.

'Mariella.' The abrupt note in his voice caught her attention. 'Because of my position as leader of our tribe, I have always believed that I do not have the…freedoms of other men. I could never commit myself to a relationship with a woman who might not be able to understand or accept my duties and responsibilities to my people. Nor could I change my way of life, or…'

'Xavier, there's no need for you to say any more,' Mariella checked him swiftly. Her heart was pounding heavily, a sharp, bitter little pain, piercing her even though she was fighting against admitting to it, stubbornly refusing to listen to the message it was trying to give her.

'I would never ask you or any other man to do any such thing! And I can assure you that you need have no fear that I might misconstrue what's happened. I shan't. I am most definitely not looking for any kind of commitment from you.'

Only the commitment of conceiving his child, she admitted inwardly.

'In fact, commitment is the last thing I want.' Assuming a casualness that defied everything she had always inwardly believed in, she gave a small shrug and told him, 'We are both adults. We wanted to have sex. To satisfy a…a physical need… And…now that we have done so, I don't think there is any purpose in us holding a post-mortem, and even less in getting involved in needless discussions about the wherefores of why neither of us want a committed relationship. Truthfully, Xavier, I don't want to marry you any more than you want to marry me! In fact, I shall never marry.' Mariella delivered the words in a strong voice underpinned with determination.

'What?'

Why was Xavier looking at her like that? Where was the relief she had expected—the cool acceptance of her claim that they had come together merely to slake their sexual appetite for one another? Xavier was looking at her with a mingling of barely controlled fury and bitterness.

'What are you saying?' she heard him demanding savagely. 'You are not your sister, Mariella! You are not one of those shallow, surface-living women who think only of themselves; who give in to their need to experience what they want when they want, who go from man to man, bed to bed without...whose whole way of life—' He paused and shook his head.

'You are not like her! You don't even know what you are talking about! Mere physical sex is not something...'

Mariella could see and feel the intensity of his growing anger, and she could also feel her own increasingly disturbing reaction of panic and pain to it, but she refused to allow herself to be intimidated by them.

'I am not going to argue with you, Xavier. I know how I feel, and what I do and don't want from life.'

Well, that was the truth, wasn't it? She did know what she wanted, and she had every hope that last night had given her...

'Do you really expect me to believe that you drove all the way out here just because you wanted sex?'

'Why not?' Mariella shrugged. 'After all, I could hardly have come to your room at the villa, could I?' she pointed out, trying to make herself react as though she were the woman she was trying to be—a woman who thought nothing of indulging her sexual appetite as and when she wanted to do so!

'This was the perfect opportunity!'

Xavier was looking at her as though he would dearly love to make her take back her words, Mariella recognised uneasily. It had to be his male pride that was making him react in such an unexpected manner, she decided. Men were quite happy to use women for sexual pleasure without being emotionally committed to them, but apparently they didn't like it very much when they thought that they were the ones being used.

Her legs began to tremble shakily as she mentally digested his reaction and tried to imagine what he might say—and do if he knew that she hadn't even actually wanted him out of sexual lust, and that the desire that had really driven her had been her own female need to conceive his child!

Somehow instinctively she knew that the reaction she was seeing now would be nothing when compared with what he was likely to do were he ever to discover the truth!

The unexpected shrill sound of his mobile ringing broke into the thick silence stretching tensely between them.

Out of good manners Mariella turned away whilst he answered the call, but she could tell from the sound of his curt replies that it involved some kind of crisis.

Her instincts were confirmed when he ended the call and told her abruptly, 'There is a problem with the tribe—a quarrel between two of the younger men, which needs to be dealt with. I shall have to drive out to do so immediately.'

'That's okay. I can find my own way back to the city,' Mariella assured him.

'This matter isn't closed yet, Mariella,' he told her grimly. 'When I do return to the villa, we shall discuss it further!'

Mariella didn't risk making any response. There wasn't any need, not unless she wanted to provoke a further quarrel. The frieze was finished; there was nothing now to keep her in Zuran, no reason or need for her to stay, and she had already decided that she was going to make immediate plans to return home!

CHAPTER ELEVEN

'ELLA, you have to go! The prince will be mortally offended if you don't and, besides, just think of the potential commissions you could be losing. I mean, I've done some discreet checking on the guest list for this do, and everyone who is everyone in the horse-racing world will be there, plus some of the classiest A-list celebs on the planet! This is going to be the most prestigious event on the racing calendar this year, and here you are announcing that you don't want to go! I mean, why? You already know just how impressed the prince is with your frieze, and this is going to be its big unveiling. If you'd been hired by the National Gallery itself you couldn't have got yourself more publicity for your work!'

Mariella could hear the exasperation in her agent's voice, and ruefully acknowledged inwardly that she could perfectly understand Kate's feelings.

However, Kate did not know that she had two very good reasons for her reluctance to return to Zuran.

Xavier...and... Instinctively she glanced down her own body. At three months, her pregnancy was not really showing as yet. She and the baby were both perfectly healthy, her doctor had assured her, it was just that being so slight she was not as yet showing very much baby bulge.

'Just wait another couple of months and you'll probably be complaining to me that you feel huge,' she had teased Mariella.

Even now sometimes when she woke up in the morning she had to reassure herself that she was not fantasising, and that she actually was pregnant.

Pregnant... With a baby she already desperately wanted and loved. Her baby! Her baby and Xavier's baby, she reminded herself warily.

But Xavier would never need to know! No one looking at her could possibly know!

And if she was not careful she could potentially be in danger of arousing more suspicions by not returning to Zuran for the extravaganza that was to be the opening of the new enclosure and the first public airing of her frieze than by doing so.

Tanya for one would certainly have something to say to her if she didn't go!

And of course it would be a perfect opportunity for her to see Fleur, whom she still missed achingly. Her niece would also always have a very, very special place in her heart!

But against all this, and weighing very heavily on the other side of the scales, was Xavier. Xavier whom disturbingly she had spent far too much time thinking about since her return home! Mystifyingly and totally contrary to her expectations, not even the official knowledge that she had conceived her much-wanted child had brought an end to the little ache of longing and loneliness that now seemed to haunt both her days and her nights. There was surely no logical reason why she should actually physically ache for Xavier now. And there was certainly no reason why increasingly she should feel such a deep and despairing emotional longing for him. Those kinds of feelings belonged to someone who was in love! And she knew far better than to allow herself to do anything as foolish as fall in love!

She had actually begun to question, in her most emotional and anguished moments, whether what she was feeling could in some way be generated by the baby—a longing on his or her part for the father that he or she was never going to know. She had promised herself that her child would never suffer the anguish of being rejected by his or her father, because she had made sure there would be no father there to reject it. She would make sure right from the start that her baby would know that she would provide all the love it could possibly need! She would bring him or her up to feel so loved, so secure, so wanted, that Xavier's absence would have no impact on their lives whatsoever. Unlike her, her child would never suffer the pain of hearing his or her mother talk with such longing and need about the man who had abandoned them both, as she had had to do. Her child would never feel as she had done that somehow he or she was the cause of that father's absence; that, given the real choice, her mother would have preferred not to have had her and kept the love of the man who had quite simply not wanted the responsibility of a child!

'You must go,' Kate was insisting.

'You must come,' Tanya was pleading.

'Okay, okay, I give in,' she told Kate, grinning as her agent paused in mid-argument to look at her in silence, before breaking into a flurry of relieved plans.

'You'll be staying with us, of course,' Tanya was chattering excitedly as she bustled Mariella outside to the waiting limousine. 'I didn't bring Fleur because she's been cutting another new tooth. It's through now, but we had a bit of a bad night with her. I can't wait for the opening. It's going to be the highlight of our social calendar. Khalid has bought me the most fabulous dress. What are you going to wear? If you haven't got anything yet, we could go shopping—'

'No, it's okay, I've already got an outfit,' Mariella stopped her quickly, mentally grateful for the fact that Kate had insisted on taking her on a whirlwind shopping trip, following her decision to attend the opening, so that she could vet the outfit Mariella would be wearing, to make sure it made enough of the right kind of statement! Her small bulge might not show yet when she was dressed, but someone as close to her as her half-sister had always been would be bound to spot the differences in her body in the intimacy of a changing room with her wearing nothing more than her underwear!

Of course she was going to tell Tanya about her baby—ultimately—once she was safely back in England, and all the questions her sister was bound to ask about just who had fathered her coming baby could be answered over the telephone rather than in person! The last thing Mariella wanted to do was to risk betraying herself by a give-away expression.

She knew exactly what she was going to tell Tanya. She had already decided to claim that her child was the result of artificial insemination, the father an unknown sperm donor.

They were speeding along the highway towards the familiar outskirts of the city.

'How far is it to your new villa, Tanya?' Mariella asked her.

She had been receiving a constant stream of emails from her sister full of excitement about the new villa she and Khalid were having built, and which they had recently been due to move into.

'Oh, it's several miles up the coast from Xavier's. I'm really looking forward to moving into it now, but I must admit I'm a bit worried about how Fleur is going to adapt. She adores Hera, and to her Xavier's villa is her home and so—'

'What do you mean you're looking forward to moving in?' Mariella checked her anxiously. 'I thought you already had!'

'Well, yes, we were supposed to, but then all the furniture hasn't arrived yet, and so we're still living with Xavier. His great-aunt is visiting at the moment as well. You made a real hit with her, Ella—not like me. She's always singing your praises and in fact... I...'

Mariella could feel her heart, not just sinking, but literally plunging to the bottom of her ribcage with an almighty thump before it began to bang against her ribs in frantic panic. She wasn't prepared for this, she admitted. She wasn't armed for it, or protected against it.

The villa was ahead of them. It was too late for her to announce that she had changed her mind, or to demand that she be taken to the centre of the city where she could book into a hotel! The car was sweeping in through the gates.

Hazily Mariella noticed that the red geraniums she remembered tumbling from the urns in the outer courtyard had been changed to a rich vibrant pink to match the colour of the flowers of the ornamental vine softening the walls of the courtyard.

'Leave your luggage for Ali,' Tanya instructed her.

Where was the trepidation she should be feeling? Mariella wondered as, completely contrary to any kind of logic, the moment she stepped into the villa she immediately experienced a sense of well being, a sense of welcome familiarity, as though…as though she had come home?

'We'd better go straight in to see Tante Cecille!' Tanya pulled a face. 'I'll never hear the end of it if we don't. She's even told them in the kitchen to bake some madeleines for you!'

Mariella had to bite down hard on her bottom lip to subdue the threatening weakness of her own emotional response. The last thing she wanted or needed right now was to be reminded in any way of the fact that she was so very much alone, so very bereft of family, unlike Xavier, who was not merely part of a large extended family group, but who also actively shared a large part of his life with them.

Treacherously Mariella found herself thinking about how a child might feel growing up in a household with so many caring adults, with aunts, uncles and cousins to play with…

'Ella, I'm so thrilled that you're here,' Tanya was telling her. 'I've really missed you! You're in the same room you had before. Xavier has given us our own suite of rooms whilst we're living here. Khalid says there's no way that he would agree to us living like they used to with separate men and women's quarters, which is just as well because there's no way I would agree to it either!

'I couldn't do what Xavier does and go into the desert with the tribe.' Tanya gave a small shudder. 'The very thought appalls me. All that sand…and heat! And as for the camels! Ugh!' She pulled a distasteful face. 'Luckily Khalid feels exactly the same way! He can't understand why Xavier lets his life be dominated by a few promises his grandfather made, and neither can I.

If Khalid was head of the family things would be very different…'

'Then perhaps it's as well that he isn't,' Mariella responded protectively, before she could stop herself.

She could see the way Tanya was looking at her, and she felt obliged to explain, 'Xavier is the guardian of some irreplaceable traditions, Tanya, and if he abandoned that responsibility a way of life that could never be resurrected could be totally lost…'

'A way of life? Spending weeks living in the desert, and having to do it every year! No, I can't think of anything worse. It might be traditional, but I still wouldn't do it! Well, there's no way it could ever be my way of life, anyway. I mean, can you imagine any woman wanting to live like that? Could you?'

Mariella didn't even have to pause to think about it.

'Not permanently, no, but in order to preserve something so important, and to support the man I loved, to be with him and share a very, very important part of his life, yes, I could and would.' Mariella hesitated, recognising that there was little point in trying to explain to her sister how much such a return to traditions, to the simplicity of such a lifestyle could do to rejuvenate a person in a very special and intensely personal, almost spiritual sense, to bring them back in touch with certain important realities of life. Tanya simply wouldn't understand.

'Yes?' Tanya stared at her. 'You're mad,' she told her, shaking her head. 'Just like Xavier. In fact…Tante Cecille is quite right. You and Xavier are two of a kind.'

Before Mariella could demand an explanation from Tanya of just how and when their similarities had been discussed, they were in the salon.

'Mariella, how lovely to see you again,' Madame
Flavel exclaimed affectionately. Automatically as she
embraced her Mariella held in her stomach, just as she
had done when she and Tanya had hugged earlier. An
automatic reflex, but one that wasn't going to conceal
her growing bump for very much longer, Mariella acknowledged ruefully.

Half an hour later, holding Fleur whilst her niece
beamed happily up at her, Mariella began to feel a little
bit more relaxed. Xavier, after all, would be as keen to
avoid spending time with her as she was with him—
albeit for very different reasons! She might even not
actually see him at all!

Totally involved in making delicious eye contact
with Fleur, Mariella was oblivious to what was going
on in the rest of the room until she heard Madame
Flavel exclaiming happily, 'Ah, there you are, Xavier.'

Xavier! Automatically Mariella spun round, holding
tightly onto Fleur more for her own protection than for
the baby's, she recognised dizzily as she felt her whole
body begin to tremble.

The sensation, the need slicing white-hot through her
threw her into shocked panic. She couldn't be feeling
like this. *Should* not be feeling like this. Should not be
feeling this all-absorbing need to feed hungrily on the
sight of every familiar feature, every slight nuance of
expression, too greedy for them to savour them with
luxurious slowness, aching for them; aching for him so
intensely that the pain was sharply physical.

As the girl she had been before, she had fantasised
naively about that wanting and about him, imagining,
exploring in the privacy of her thoughts the potential

of her secret yearnings for Xavier—she had never guessed where those feelings could lead.

But as she was now sharply aware she was not that girl any more. She was now a woman, a woman looking at the man who had been her lover, knowing just how his flesh lay against his bones, how it felt, how it tasted…how he touched and loved. And as that woman she was overwhelmed by the sheer force of her need to go to him, to be with him, to be part of him. Her knowledge of him, instead of slaking her desire, was actually increasing it, tormenting her with intensely intimate memories. She was no longer seeing him as a powerful distant figure, but as a man…*her* man!

But that wasn't possible. What did that mean about her feelings for Xavier?

'Xavier, I was just telling Ella how alike you and she are,' she heard Tanya commenting.

'Alike?'

Mariella could feel his gaze burning into her as he focused on her.

'In your attitudes to things,' Tanya explained. 'Ella, you really ought to have children of your own,' Tanya added ruefully. 'You are a natural mother.'

'I totally agree with you, Tanya.' Madame Flavel nodded.

Mariella could feel her face and then her whole body burning as they all turned to look at her, but it was Xavier's grim scrutiny that affected her the most as his glance skimmed her body, resting on the baby she was holding in her arms. The unbearable poignancy of knowing that in six months' time she would be holding his child as she was holding Fleur right now made her eyes burn with dangerous tears. What on earth was wrong with her? She was behaving as though…

reacting as though...as though she were a woman in love. Totally, hopelessly, helplessly in love. But she wasn't! She wasn't going to let herself be!

Bleakly Xavier watched as Mariella cuddled Fleur. He had told himself that the discovery that she did not return his feelings would be enough to destroy them. And it should have been! But right now, if they had been alone...

The sickening feeling that had accompanied her unwanted thoughts was refusing to go away, and Mariella began to panic. She had suffered some morning sickness in the early weeks of her pregnancy, but these last few weeks she had felt much better. This nausea, though, wasn't anything to do with what was happening inside her body. No, this nausea was caused by her emotions! And what emotions! They surged powerfully inside her, inducing fear and panic, making her want to turn and run.

Automatically she had turned away from Xavier, unable to trust herself to continue facing him. Tanya had run to greet her husband who had just arrived.

'Ella,' Khalid greeted her warmly. 'We are so pleased that you are here, and I warn you that now that you are we shall not allow you to go easily. Tanya is already making plans to persuade you to move permanently to Zuran. Has she told you?'

Move permanently to Zuran! The shock of his disclosure made Mariella sway visibly, her face paling.

Xavier frowned as he saw her reaction. She looked as though she was about to pass out!

'Khalid, get some water,' Xavier demanded sharply, going immediately to Mariella's side and taking Fleur from her.

Just the feel of his hand touching her bare arm made her shudder with longing, and it seemed to Mariella as though the baby in her womb ached with the same longing that she did, for his touch and for his love.

She was vaguely conscious of being steered towards a chair and instructed to sit down, and then of a glass of water being handed to her.

'There's nothing wrong. I'm perfectly all right,' she protested frantically. The last thing she needed right now was to arouse any kind of suspicions about her health!

'Ella, you do look pale,' Tanya was saying worriedly.

'I'm just a bit tired, that's all,' Mariella insisted.

'You will probably feel better once you have had something to eat. We are going to have an informal family dinner this evening.'

'No,' Mariella refused agitatedly. The last thing she felt able to cope with right now was any more time spent in Xavier's company.

'Tanya, I'm sorry, but I just don't feel up to it. I'm rather tired…the flight…'

'Of course, *petite,* we understand,' Madame Flavel was assuring her soothingly, unintentionally coming to her rescue. 'Don't we, Xavier?' she appealed.

'Perfectly,' Mariella heard Xavier agreeing harshly.

Abruptly Mariella opened her eyes. Her heart was thumping heavily. She had been dreaming about Xavier. She looked at her watch. It was only just gone ten o' clock. The others would probably just be sitting down for their evening meal. Her throat ached and felt raw, tight with the intensity of her emotions.

As she slid her feet out of the bed and padded to the

window to look out into the shadowy garden she shivered in the coolness of the air-conditioning. It was there by the pool that Xavier had massaged her aching shoulders, and she had realised how much she'd wanted him. Because she had wanted his child, not because she loved him.

Her eyes burned dryly with pain. What she was feeling, what she was having to confront now, went way, way beyond the relief of easy tears.

So she was her mother's daughter, after all! She was to suffer the same pain as her mother—a pain she had inflicted on herself! How could she have been so stupid? How could she have been so reckless as to challenge fate? How could she have ignored everything that she knew about herself? Surely somewhere she must have realised that it was impossible for her to give herself to a man with the passionate intensity she had given herself to Xavier and not love him?

All she had wanted was to have a child, she insisted stubbornly. A child? No, what she had wanted was Xavier's child. And that alone should have told her, warned her…

With appalling clarity Mariella suddenly realised what she had done. Not so much to herself but to her child!

One day her child was going to demand to know about its father. When that happened, what answers was she going to be able to give?

Now she could cry. Slow, acid tears of guilt and regret, but it was too late to change things now.

'I'm so sorry,' she whispered, her hands on her stomach. 'Please, please try to forgive me…I love you so much…'

She had stolen the right to choose fatherhood from

Xavier, and she had stolen from her child the right to be fathered…loved.

It was gone midnight when she finally stopped pacing the room and crawled into bed to fall into a shallow, exhausted sleep, riddled with guilt and anguished dreams.

'Well, what do you think? How do I look?' Tanya demanded excitedly as she twirled round in front of Mariella in her new outfit.

'You look fabulous,' Mariella assured her truthfully.

'And so do you,' Tanya told her. Mariella forced a smile.

Her own dress with its simple flowing lines did suit her, but she was far more concerned about how well it concealed her shape than how well she looked in it. In less than half an hour they would be on their way to the gala opening of the prince's new hospitality suite at the racecourse, and Mariella would have given anything not to have to be there!

Tanya, on the other hand, couldn't wait, her excitement more than making up for Mariella's lack of it.

The last three days had been total torture for her. It would have been bad enough simply discovering that she loved Xavier without the additional emotional anguish of having to endure his constant presence. Every time she looked at him the pain grew worse and so did her guilt.

She had hardly been able to eat because of her misery and anxiety, and she couldn't wait to get on the plane that would take her home!

Under different circumstances, although she would have been nervous about the thought of the coming event, it would have been a very different kind of nervousness, caused purely by her anxiety about people's reaction to her work. Right now, she recognised ruefully, she hardly cared what they thought!

'Come on,' Tanya urged her. 'It's time to go.'

Reluctantly, Mariella got up.

She could feel Xavier's gaze burning into her as she walked into the courtyard where he and Khalid were already standing beside the waiting car.

The hot desert wind tugged at the thin silk layers of her full-length dress and immediately Mariella reached anxiously to hold them away from her body.

To her relief Xavier got into the front of the car, but she was still acutely conscious of him as Ali drove them towards the racecourse. Unlike Xavier, Khalid favoured a strong modern male cologne, but she could still smell beneath it the scent of Xavier's skin, and deep down inside her a part of her cried out in anguished pain and longing, aching despairingly for him.

'Poor Ella, you must be so nervous.' Tanya tried to comfort her, sensing her distress, but to Mariella's relief not realising the real cause of it. 'You've hardly eaten a thing since you arrived, and you look so pale.'

'Tanya is right—you do look pale,' Xavier told Mariella grimly several minutes later when they had reached their destination and he had opened the car door for her, leaving her with no alternative but to get out. His hand was beneath her elbow, preventing her from moving away from him. Instinctively Mariella knew that he had been waiting for the opportunity to vent the anger he obviously felt towards her against her. She had seen it in his eyes every time he looked at her, felt it in the tension that crackled between them. 'What's wrong, Mariella? If it isn't food you want, then perhaps it's another appetite you want to have satisfied. Is that it? Are you hungry for sex?' he demanded harshly.

'No,' Mariella denied immediately, trying again to pull away from him. He was making sure that no one else could hear what he was saying to her, she recognised, and making sure too that she could not get away from him.

Had he deliberately waited until now? Chosen this particular time to launch his attack on her, when he knew she couldn't escape from him?

'No?' he taunted her. 'Then why are you trembling so much? Why do you look so hungrily at me when you think I am not aware of you doing so?'

'I am not…I do not,' Mariella replied. She could feel her face starting to burn and her heart beginning to pound.

'You're lying,' Xavier told her softly. 'And don't deny it. Unless you want to provoke me into proving to you that you are! Is that what you want, Mariella?'

'Stop it! Stop doing this to me,' Mariella demanded. She could hear her own voice shaking with emotion and was helplessly aware that it wouldn't be long before her body betrayed her by following suit.

'I spoke to your agent today. She told me that she was sure you'd be thrilled to learn that I want to commission you for a very special project. She certainly was especially when I told her how much I was prepared to pay to secure your exclusive…services.'

Mariella reeled from the shock of his taunting comment.

'Xavier, please,' she begged him fatally, her eyes widening as she saw the look of triumph leaping to life in his eyes.

'Please?' he repeated silkily.

'Xavier, Mariella, come on...' Tanya urged them.

'We're coming. I was just discussing a certain plan with Mariella,' Xavier said smoothly as he guided Mariella toward the throng of people making for the entrance to the suite.

'Well, sister-in-law, I think we can safely say that your frieze is an outstanding success,' Khalid commented, grinning at Mariella. 'Everyone is talking about it and it is very, very impressive!'

Mariella tried to respond enthusiastically, but she felt achingly tired from answering all the questions she had received about the frieze, and, besides, her whole nervous system was still on red alert just in case Xavier should suddenly reappear and continue his cynical verbal torment.

'Khalid and I are going to get something to eat, in a few minutes,' Tanya told her. 'Do you want to come with us?'

Nauseously Mariella shook her head. The last thing she wanted was food. She had been feeling sick all day and her stomach heaved at the very thought.

'Here comes the prince,' Tanya whispered as the royal party appeared.

'Mariella. My congratulations. Everyone is most impressed!'

As she acknowledged his praise Mariella suddenly realised that Xavier was with him. Her feeling of sickness increased, but grimly she refused to submit to it.

'Xavier has just been telling me that he has commissioned you to make a visual record of the everyday life of his people,' the prince was continuing. 'A truly excellent idea!' Smiling at her, he started to move on.

So that was what Xavier had meant! Already dropping her head in deference to the prince, Mariella suddenly raised it, intending to glare at Xavier, but instead she was overcome by a dizzying surge of weakness.

'Ella, what is it? What's wrong?' Tanya demanded anxiously. 'You look as though you're going to faint! Feeling sick…looking like you're going to faint—anyone would think you're pregnant!' Tanya laughed.

As her sister turned away Mariella realised that Xavier was looking straight at her, and she knew immediately from his expression that he had heard Tanya's teasing comment and that somehow he had guessed the truth!

The urge to turn and run was so strong that she suspected if the gallery had not been so crowded she would have done so. But once again Xavier seemed to be able to read her mind because suddenly he was standing beside her.

'Your sister isn't well,' she heard him telling Tanya curtly. 'I'm taking her back to the villa.'

'No,' Mariella protested, but it was too late. Khalid was urging Tanya to go with him to get something to eat, and Xavier was already propelling her towards the exit.

It was impossible for either of them to say anything in the car with Ali driving. 'This way,' Xavier told Mariella grimly once they were back at the villa, stopping her from seeking the sanctuary of her own room as his hand on the small of her back ushered her towards his own suite of rooms.

'You can't do this!' Mariella said shakily. 'I'm a single woman, remember, and—'

'A single woman who is carrying my child!' Xavier

stopped her savagely as he opened the suite door and almost pushed her inside.

Mariella could feel herself starting to tremble. She didn't have the strength for this kind of fight. Not now and probably not ever!

'Xavier, I'm tired. It's been a long day.'

'Why the hell didn't you say something? Or were you hoping that by not eating and by exhausting yourself you could provoke a natural end to it?' he accused, ignoring her plea.

'No,' Mariella denied immediately, horrified. 'No! How dare you say that? I would never...' Tears filled her eyes. 'I wanted this baby,' she told him passionately. 'I...'

Abruptly she stopped, her expression betraying her as she saw the way he was looking at her.

'Would you mind repeating that?' he demanded with dangerous softness.

Nervously Mariella licked her lips.

'Repeat what?' she asked him.

'Don't play games with me Mariella,' he warned her. 'You know perfectly well what I mean. You just said "I wanted this baby"..."wanted," rather than "want," which means...which means that it wasn't just sex you wanted from me, as you claimed, was it?

'What? Nothing to say?' he challenged her bitingly. 'Not even an "it was an accident"?'

Mariella bit down hard on her lower lip.

She wasn't going to demean herself by lying to him!

'You don't have to worry,' she tried to defend herself, her voice wobbling. 'I won't ever make any kind of claims on you, Xavier. I intend to take full responsibility for...for everything. I want to take full responsibility,' she stressed fiercely. 'There's no way I intend to let my baby suffer as I did through having a father who...'

'Your baby?' Xavier stopped her harshly. 'Your baby, Mariella, is my child! My child!'

'No!' Mariella denied immediately. 'This baby has nothing whatsoever to do with you, Xavier. He or she will be completely mine!'

'Nothing to do with me! I don't believe I'm hearing this,' Xavier breathed savagely. 'This baby...my baby has everything to do with me, Mariella. After all, without me he or she just could not exist! I'll make arrangements for us to be married as quickly and as quietly as possible, and then—'

'Married! No!' Mariella refused vehemently, her panic showing in her expression as she confronted him. 'I'm not going to get married, Xavier. Not ever. When my mother married my father, she believed that he loved her, that she could trust him, rely on him...but she couldn't. He left her... He left us both because he didn't want me.'

All the emotions she had been bottling up inside her whooshed out in a despairing stream of agonised denial, even whilst somewhere deep down inside her most guarded private self there was a deep burning pain at the thought of just how very, very much she wanted Xavier's total commitment for her baby and for herself. His total commitment and his enduring love! The pain of her own self-knowledge was virtually unbearable. She ached for him to simply take her in his arms and hold her safe, to keep her safe for ever, and yet at the same time her own self-conditioning was urging her to deny and deride those feelings to protect herself.

'I am not your father, Mariella, and where my child is concerned—' his mouth tightened '—in Zuran it is a father whose rights are paramount. I would be within my legal rights in ensuring that you are not permitted to leave the country with my child—either before or after his or her birth!'

Distraught, Mariella demanded passionately, 'Why are you doing this? Your own aunt told me that you had sworn never to marry or have children; that you didn't want a wife or children.'

'No,' Xavier stopped her curtly. 'It is true that I had decided not to marry, but not because I didn't want... The reason I had chosen not to marry was because I believed I could never find a woman who would love me as a man, with fire and passion and commitment, and that I wouldn't be able to find a woman also who would understand and accept my responsibilities to my people. I didn't think that such a woman could exist!'

'And because she doesn't...because I am carrying your child, you're prepared to marry me instead, is that it? I can't do it, Xavier. I won't, I won't be married, just because of the baby.' Her voice began to wobble betrayingly as her emotions overwhelmed her and to her own humiliation tears flooded her eyes and began to roll down her face. Helplessly Mariella lifted her hands to her face to shield herself, unable to bear Xavier's contemptuous response to her distress. It must be baby hormones that were making her cry like this, making her feel so weak and vulnerable!

'Mariella.'

Mariella froze with shock as she felt the warmth of Xavier's exhaled breath against her skin, as he crossed the space between them and took her in his arms.

'Don't!' His voice was rough with pain. 'I can't bear the thought of knowing that you and my child, the two people I love the most, will be lost to me, but I can't bear either knowing that I have forced you to stay with me against your will. When you came to me in the desert, gave yourself to me…it was as though you had read my mind. Shared my thoughts and my feelings, known how much I had wanted us to be together, and known too that I had been waiting for the right opportunity to approach you and tell you how I felt, but I was conscious of what had happened during your own childhood with your father. I wanted to win your belief in me, your trust of me…before I revealed to you how much I wanted to ask you to share my life! I knew how strong your sense of commitment was, your sense of responsibility, and I knew that the future of my people would rest safely in your hands. I thought that together you and I could…but I was wrong, as you made very clear to me… You didn't love me; you didn't even really want me. You merely wanted someone to father your child.

'I want and need both of you here with me more than I can find the words to tell you, but I cannot bear to see you so distressed. I shall make arrangements for you to return to England if that is what you want, but what I would ask you is that you allow me to play at least some part in my child's life, however small. I shall, of course, make financial provision for both of you…that is not just my duty, but my right! But at least once a year I should like your permission to see my child. To spend time with him or her. If necessary I shall come to your country to do so. And…'

Mariella fought to take in what he was saying. Xavier wanted her. Xavier loved her. In fact he loved her so much that he was prepared to put her needs and wishes above his own!

A new feeling began to whisper softly through her,

a soft warmth that permeated every cell of her body, melting away all the tiny frozen particles of mistrust and pain that had been with her from the very first moment she had known about her father. A feeling so unfamiliar, so heady and euphoric that it made her literally tremble with happiness, and excitement unfurled and grew inside.

Instinctively her hand touched her belly. Could her baby feel what she was feeling? Was he or she right now uncurling and basking in the same glow of happiness that was engulfing her?

Xavier's hand covered hers and that small gesture brought immediate emotional tears to her eyes as she turned to look at him without any attempt to hide her emotions from him.

'I didn't know you loved me,' she whispered.

'You know now,' Xavier responded.

She could see the bleakness in his eyes and the pain. Her body could feel the warmth of his hand even through her own. Gently she pulled her own hand away and leaned into him so that he could feel the growing swell of their child, her gaze monitoring his immediate and intense reaction.

Xavier would never do what her father had done, instinctively she knew that, just as she knew too how much time she had wasted, how much that was so infinitely precious to her she had risked and nearly lost because of her frightened refusal to allow herself to believe that not all men were like her father.

Alongside her bubbling happiness she could feel another emotion she had to struggle to identify. It was freedom, she recognised; freedom from the burden she had been carrying around with her for so long, and it was Xavier who had given her that freedom by giving her his love, by being man enough, strong enough to reveal his vulnerability to her!

She took a deep breath and then held tightly to her courage and even more tightly to Xavier's arm.

'It isn't true what I said,' she told him simply. 'It wasn't just sex. I tried to pretend it was to myself because I was too afraid to admit how I really felt, but I think I knew even before, and then afterwards when I still wanted you...' Her skin turned a warm rose as she saw the way he was looking at her.

'Don't look at me like that,' she protested. 'Not yet, not until I've finished telling you... Otherwise...'

'Still wanted, in the past tense or...' Xavier pressed her huskily.

'Still wanted then,' Mariella informed him primly. 'And still want now,' she added, her own voice suddenly as husky and liquid with emotion as his had been. 'I still want you, Xavier!' she repeated. 'And I don't just want you, I need you as well. Need you and love you,' she finally managed to say, her voice so low that he had to bend his head to catch her shaky admission.

'You love me? But do you trust me, Mariella? Do you believe me when I tell you that I shall never, ever let you down or give you cause to doubt me? Do you believe me when I tell you that you and our child...our children, will always have my love and my commitment?'

Mariella closed her eyes and then opened them again.

'Yes,' she replied firmly, and her melting look of love told him that she meant it!

'Xavier,' she protested unconvincingly as he started to kiss her. 'The others will be coming back.'

'Shall I stop, then?' he asked her, brushing his lips tormentingly against her own.

'Mmm… No…' Mariella responded helplessly, sighing in soft pleasure as his hand covered her breast, his thumb probing the aroused sensitivity of her nipple. Her whole body turned liquid with desire, making her cling eagerly to him.

'Every night I've thought about you like this,' Xavier told her rawly. 'Wanted you…ached for you in my arms. Every night, and every day, and if I'd known that there was the smallest chance that you felt the same I would never have let you go. I warn you, Ella, that now that I do know I will never let you go.'

'I will never want you to,' Mariella responded emotionally. 'Take me to bed, Xavier,' she begged him urgently. 'Take me to bed and show me that this isn't all just a dream…'

She was in his arms and being carried from the salon into his bedroom almost before the words had left her mouth. And even if she had wanted to retract them it would have been impossible for her to do so with Xavier kissing her the way that he was, with all the passion and love, all the commitment she now recognised that she had secretly ached for all along.

EPILOGUE

'WELL, what do you think of your anniversary present?' Mariella asked Xavier lightly, whilst she watched him with a secret anxiety she was trying hard to hide.

She had been working on this special gift for him on and off ever since their marriage, only breaking off for their six-month-old son's birth and the early weeks of his life.

Xavier shook his head, as though he found it hard to comprehend what he was seeing. 'I knew you were working on something, but this...'

The stern note in his voice broke through her self-control, forcing her to reveal how much his approval meant to her. 'You don't like it—?'

'Like it! Mariella.' Reaching for her, Xavier wrapped her tightly in his arms.

'There is nothing, excluding your sweet self and our noisy and demanding young son, that I would value more,' he told her emotionally as he swung her round in his arms so that they could both look at the series of drawings she had spent the early hours of the morning displaying around their private salon to surprise him when he woke up on this, their anniversary morning.

As a wedding present from her new husband Mariella had asked to be allowed to travel in the desert with the tribe. Conscious of her pregnancy, Xavier had initially been reluctant to agree, but Mariella had been insistent. It had been on that journey that she had made the secret preliminary sketches for what was now a visual documentation of the tribe's way of life, a visual documentation that betrayed, not only her fine eye for detail, but also her love for the man whose people she had drawn.

'I do have a gift for you, although I haven't followed Tanya's advice and booked a luxury holiday,' Xavier told her ruefully.

Following the direction of his amused glance, Mariella laughed.

Fleur, who was now walking was sitting on the floor next to her six-month-old cousin, the pair of them deep in some personal exchange, which involved lots of shared giggles and some noisy hand-clapping from Ben.

'Don't you dare do any such thing. There's no way I want to be parted from these two!'

With Tanya and Khalid living around the corner, both the families saw a lot of each other, and the two young cousins could grow up together.

'I may have another present for you,' Mariella announced semi-hesitantly, the way her glance lingered on their son informing Xavier of just what she meant.

'What? We said we'd wait.'

'I know…but this time it's your fault and not mine. Remember your birthday, when you didn't want to wait until…'

'Mmm.' He did a rapid mental calculation. 'So in another seven months, then…'

'I think so… Do you mind?'

'Mind? Me? No way. Do you?'

'I've got my fingers crossed that I'm right,' Mariella admitted. 'Although I'm pretty sure that I am, and if I'm not…' she gave him a flirtatious look '…then I'm sure we can find a way of ensuring that I soon am! Anyway, what about *my* anniversary present? You still haven't told me what it is.'

'Come with me,' Xavier instructed her, bending to pick up their son and hand him to Mariella before lifting Fleur up into his own arms.

'Close your eyes and hold onto me,' Xavier said as he led her out into their own private courtyard, and through it to the new courtyard that had been developed behind it.

Mariella could smell the roses before he allowed her to open her eyes, and once he did so she drew in her breath in delight as she saw the new garden he had been having designed for her as a special surprise.

A softer and far more modern planting plan had been adopted for the new garden than the one favoured by Xavier's grandmother. The design was reminiscent of an English country garden with the flower beds filled with a variety of traditional plants, but it was the wonderful scent of the roses that most caught her attention.

'They're called "Eternity",' Xavier told her softly as she bent her head to touch the velvet-soft petals of the rose closest to her. 'And I promise that I shall love you for eternity, Mariella, and beyond it. My love for you is…eternal!'

Warm tears bathed Mariella's eyes as she smiled at him.

'And mine for you!' she whispered lovingly to him.

Silently, they walked through the garden together, his arm around her drawing her close, her head resting against his shoulder, the children in their arms.

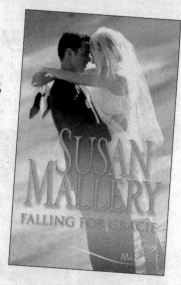

First comes love, then comes marriage...

That was Gracie's plan, anyway, at the ripe old age of fourteen. She loved eighteen-year-old heart throb Riley with a legendary desperation. Even now that she's all grown up, the locals in her sleepy town won't let her forget her youthful crush.

...but it's not as easy as it looks.
And now she's face-to-face with Riley at every turn. The one-time bad boy has come back seeking respectability – but the sparks that fly between them are anything but respectable! Gracie's determined to keep her distance, but when someone sets out to ruin both their reputations, the two discover that first love sometimes is better the second time around.

On sale 1st September 2006

0906/01a V2

MILLS & BOON®

Live the emotion

Modern
romance™

PURCHASED BY THE BILLIONAIRE
by Helen Bianchin

Three years ago, under pressure from her father, Kayla removed bad-boy billionaire Duardo Alvarez's wedding ring. Now circumstance has forced Kayla to ask her ex-husband for help. But Duardo's price is high: marry him again, or he'll walk away…

MASTER OF PLEASURE *by Penny Jordan*

Sasha ran out on millionaire Gabriel Cabrini ten years ago – and he has never forgiven her. Now Sasha is shocked to discover that Gabriel has been named heir to her late husband's wealth. She is completely in his power, and he wants revenge…

THE SULTAN'S VIRGIN BRIDE *by Sarah Morgan*

Sultan Tariq bin Omar-Sharma gets everything he wants – except Farrah Tyndall. Farrah was crushed when she discovered that he wanted her, but only in his bed. Now Tariq needs to marry Farrah to secure a business deal. But having broken her heart, can she love again…?

WANTED: MISTRESS AND MOTHER
by Carol Marinelli

Ruthless barrister Dante Costello hires Matilda Hamilton to help his troubled little girl. Then Dante decides he will offer Matilda the position of mistress – and nothing more… But what Dante thought was lust turns out to be something far greater…

On sale 6th October 2006

Available at WHSmith, Tesco, ASDA, Borders, Eason, Sainsbury's and most bookshops

www.millsandboon.co.uk

MILLS & BOON®
Live the emotion

Modern
romance™

THE RICH MAN'S ROYAL MISTRESS
by Robyn Donald

Princess Melissa Considine is captivated by womanising billionaire Hawke Kennedy. His seduction leads the virginal princess to decide she will let Hawke teach her how to love…and be loved. But Melissa knows that she must put duty before their affair…

AT THE SHEIKH'S COMMAND *by Kate Walker*

Abbie Cavanaugh can obtain her brother's freedom – but only if she marries the Sheikh of Barakhara. The passion between Sheikh Malik and Abbie could mean a marriage of delight… But neither of them knows the other's real identity, and the truth creates a desert storm…

THE SPANIARD'S PREGNANCY PROPOSAL
by Kim Lawrence

Having been burned badly before, Fleur Stewart reckons staying away from Spanish billionaire Antonio Rochas should be no problem. But Antonio is sexy, smouldering, and attracts women like moths to a flame. And he doesn't intend to let Fleur go easily…

AN ITALIAN ENGAGEMENT *by Catherine George*

Max Wingate is broodingly handsome. But his romantic charm won't persuade Abigail Green to fall into his arms. There's something vulnerable about Abby, but Max is driven by desire. He's determined to have her surrender to him, and he'll use any means at his disposal…

On sale 6th October 2006

*Available at WHSmith, Tesco, ASDA, Borders, Eason,
Sainsbury's and most bookshops*

www.millsandboon.co.uk

0906/01b V2

MILLS & BOON®

Live the emotion

Blaze™

RED LETTER NIGHTS
by Alison Kent, Karen Anders and Jeanie London

A red-hot secret love note gets the holidays off to a passionate start for three single girls – Claire, Chloe and Josie – and soon all of them are experiencing all kinds of pleasure in the company of three very sexy men.

POSSESSION by *Tori Carrington*
Dangerous Liaisons, Bk 1

When FBI agent Akela Brooks returns home to New Orleans, she never expects to end up as a hostage of Claude Lafitte – or to enjoy her captivity so much. She immediately knows the sexy Cajun is innocent, but for Akela, that doesn't make him any less dangerous…

MAJOR ATTRACTION by *Julie Miller*

Popular Dr Cyn's latest advice column is sending military men running for cover – except Major Ethan McCormick. But after one sexual encounter with Ethan, she's willing to concede a major attraction – especially when he's *out* of uniform!

ROCK MY WORLD by *Cindi Myers*

A three-day bed-in publicity stunt with the gorgeous Adam Hawkins? Erica Gibson could hardly believe her luck! After the lights go out, Erica breaks all the rules and seduces him. Back at work, they try to forget their nights together, but there's nothing like forbidden passion…

On sale 6th October 2006

Available at WHSmith, Tesco, ASDA, Borders, Eason,
Sainsbury's and most bookshops
www.millsandboon.co.uk